Books by B. V. Larson:

UNDYING MERCENARIES
Steel World
Dust World
Tech World
Machine World
Death World
Home World

STAR FORCE SERIES
Swarm
Extinction
Rebellion
Conquest
Battle Station
Empire
Annihilation
Storm Assault
The Dead Sun
Outcast
Exile
Demon Star

Visit BVLarson.com for more information.

Home World

by
B. V. Larson

ISBN: 9781519006189
BISAC: Fiction / Science Fiction / Military

An excerpt from:
The Galaxy and Our Place in It

2052 AD.

In that blessed year, the Galactics revealed themselves to Humanity. The impact of this singular event can't be overstated. Our entire culture was transformed.

Earth found herself instantly united, a goal sought throughout history. Even better, we weren't just politically merged with every fellow member of our own species, we were simultaneously introduced to countless other life forms. We were called brothers by all of them.

To be sure, there were a few individualists who resisted these changes, but their aberrant thinking was corrected. The survivors embraced the Empire whole-heartedly.

And why shouldn't they? How could any right-minded person deny the superiority of intellect, technology and culture that the Galactics represent? We are like insects at their feet. But far better than most insects, we were able to learn and adapt. Thus far, these traits have kept us from being exterminated.

As a society, we became adults in the year 2052. Before then, we'd been nothing more than wild children—beasts of the field. In return for our whole-hearted allegiance, the Empire bestowed their gifts upon us. These were many and varied, but the most obvious after unification and security were the technological benefits.

After we proved ourselves to be viable members of the Imperial Marketplace by producing mercenary troops, a trade good with sufficient demand in other star systems to warrant exchange, we were allowed to purchase any goods or services that weren't restricted in Province 921.

The first of these services was interstellar shipping. We couldn't build or design ships of our own, of course, as that would compete with the legal holders of such rights in our region of the galaxy. Nor could we serve on ships, as that was the exclusive role of the Skrull.

But we were able to buy passage to other systems in order to deliver our troops to them. There are many archival videos from that first voyage by Legion Victrix, and this author would suggest that all readers touch *here* to view them. The pride, honor and obvious delight of those brave legionnaires should be remembered and emulated.

Using technology we'd only dreamt of, the warp-bubble ships slid through space at unimaginable speeds. Without this technology, the Empire itself could not exist. We used these rented alien ships to gather credits for Earth.

Once Humanity was earning a staple diet of Galactic Credits, we reinvested that hard-won cash into weapons and armor for our troops. Snap-rifles, plasma-belchers and countless other tools of the soldier were soon in abundant supply.

It should be noted here that certain sour individuals have claimed our armament is mere surplus equipment. That it's outdated, previously-used and even obsolete. Snap-rifles, for instance, have been likened to arrowheads made of chipped flint.

How like humanity to bite the very hand that feeds us! This author finds such remarks ungrateful and even scandalous. The Empire is under no obligation to arm our troops. We should take their cast-offs—if we must think of them as such—and use them gratefully to the best effect we can.

The side-benefits of cooperation are obvious in our daily lives. Earth has prospered, bringing countless consumer items to the Home World. Floaters, for instance, are wondrous vehicles that defy gravity. They've become commonplace.

Other alien products have crept into our lives as well. New to the market are sensory suits. They provide an amazing, unique experience, and they're sweeping aside older forms of entertainment.

Nothing but toys and amusements, the critics grumble, but I'd challenge any of them to go back to the days of simple holo-vids downloaded off the public net. They'd be bored and begging to have their sensory units returned to them within hours!

Last of the great gifts of the Galactics, but certainly not the least important, are the revival machines. They're very expensive, yes, but amazingly effective. With this technology, our soldiers are able to live and die over and over again for Mother Earth. Who can argue with immortality?

As to the expense, remember that the savings on retraining and the transport of fresh troops is dramatic and undeniable. Despite their upfront costs, revival machines are a bargain which is why every legion deploys them whenever they take the field.

In summary, it's this author's opinion that the growing dissent on Earth concerning our status within the Empire is the talk of ungrateful traitors. The Empire's many amazing gifts should be reflected upon on a daily basis by everyone who walks this green planet. Do the Nairbs restrict what we can buy? Of course they do, but their restrictions are anything but arbitrary. We should all trust our government and treat our rulers with the utmost respect. After all, they've given us so much.

The Empire and its servants deserve our *praise*, rather than our scorn. Certainly, there are technological gifts that the Galactics haven't shared with us, but we must assume that we've not yet been deemed worthy. We humans might become a danger to ourselves and others if we were allowed unlimited access to all the wonders of the Empire.

It's *right* we have trade restrictions. It's *good* we haven't been allowed to witness the undoubtedly awesome power of the Galactics, a power best reserved for the Core Worlds.

Trust your Empire. Believe in your Empire. And if she should call upon you to die a thousand times in her service, do so without qualm or hesitation.

As the Galactics tell us with regularity: *Service is Strength.*

"What shore knows not our blood?"
– Horace, 39 BC

-1-

After Nagata gave me my twin nano-adhesive gold bars, I became an adjunct. But the bureaucrats shuffling around Central weren't satisfied yet. They wanted to put me through a battery of tests to make sure lowly James McGill was worthy of an officer's commission.

The Hegemony people, or "hogs" as legionnaires from independent legions called them, had a lot of rules. They wanted their rules to be respected, even if a three-star equestrian had already approved the promotion.

In addition to their sheer love of red-tape, I figured there was just a hint of a sneer on their collective lips. They didn't like seeing a grunt work his way up to a commission so fast. They liked the fact that a man from Legion Varus had managed to earn such an honor even less.

Lastly, hogs just plain don't like me, in particular.

"We need to discuss your scores, Veteran McGill," a prim hog named Rossi told me.

"My rank is adjunct," I said.

"Not yet it isn't. Let's go over these results, shall we?"

Rossi wore the uniform of a primus. She was one of those severe types, with her shoulders squared tightly, and her hair cropped down to her scalp on the sides. Her sole concession to femininity consisted of a small pony tail she kept stuffed under

5

her cap most of the time. Today, it had slipped out to touch her neck. I found that intriguing.

"Shall we go over them, McGill?" she asked again.

Pulling my eyes away from her hair, I frowned. Rossi and I stared at one another for about three long seconds. Internally, I thought up and rejected about a half-dozen rude comments I could make.

"All right," I said at last.

"First off," she said, "your latest psych profile has gained my attention. The metrics are alarming, but the worst part is the trend-line. Did you know you're heading down a dark path, McGill?"

"Could you elaborate on that?"

"We're seeing a reduced flight-time—that's what we call it—from a state of calm to a state of rage. This behavioral flaw results in violent outbursts. There's also a marked increase in your propensity to take any criticism as a personal attack. Almost as bad, you've moved into a region of high mendacity."

"A region of high what?"

"You lie a lot."

"Oh…" I said.

Rossi looked at me as if expecting some kind of defensiveness, but she got a blank stare instead.

Taking in a deep breath, she pressed on.

"The truthfulness quotient in your responses to even basic questions has dropped to thirty-seven percent."

"Uh-huh…"

She wasn't done yet. She proceeded to tell me how I lied, and in what situations, and even how long and complicated my lies were.

Thinking about all this, I became alarmed.

"Excuse me," I interrupted when she got to her next complaint, which consisted of accusing me of having too many sexual encounters with a wide variety of women. "Where are you getting all this data?"

"Your psych profile, as I said."

"I don't think so. That was a short test. Sure, you gave me two hours, but I finished it in forty minutes. The data you're prattling on about can't be from that test."

"Of course not. You didn't think our investigation would hinge on a walk-in test, did you? You've been under surveillance for some time."

"Yeah… okay. Drones and all that… but what about your data on how truthful I've been? Who's measuring that?"

"Your tapper is. Your autonomic data is being constantly monitored and fed into the data core here at Central."

I glanced down at my forearm, where my tapper resided. There were a few stray hairs growing out of the fleshy screen—mine always seemed to do that—but otherwise, it looked the same as it always did.

Tappers were parasitical things, that was for sure. Organic computers that were so symbiotic with us that when we died they were revived along with the rest of our bodies. They always came out fully functional again, just like any other essential organ.

My tapper was my friend, my companion. It was like my own arm to me. I didn't like to think it was also spying on me in a new and unacceptable way.

"Are you having dark thoughts about your tapper right now, James?" Primus Rossi asked.

I glanced back up at her.

"Not really," I lied. "I was just wondering how much you guys really know about my personal life. How much you're tracking about all of us."

She nodded. "It is disturbing, but it's for the best. The real answer is that we know everything—and nothing—at the same time."

"What's that mean?"

"What I'm saying is that yes, masses of details are tracked by our tappers. They store measured autonomic impulses going back a decade, and we can use that data to calculate what you were doing on any particular Thursday in May. But we generally don't bother to do so. All of that data stays private—unless we have a reason to delve into it."

I nodded. "So… you're saying we have all the privacy in the world until someone shines a light on us. Then we turn into a bug under a shoe."

"That's about right."

7

Sighing, I thought for a moment about how I could explain myself. The primus had some good points. I *was* a darker-minded individual than I'd been years back, when I'd first stepped into the door of the Mustering Hall and signed up with the only legion that would have me.

"Primus," I began, "how many people have you killed?"

She looked surprised.

"I don't see—"

"It's a simple enough question. Humor me. Count people you shot in training. I'm sure even you Hegemony-types have to participate in live-fire exercises. How many times did you end the life of another human being?"

Rossi hesitated. I could tell I'd gotten her to think. Her lips squirmed for a moment.

"Thinking of a lie?" I asked her. "Your tapper knows you're doing that. The fact will be tracked forever."

"Certainly not," she snapped. "I fail to see the point of your inquiry, but I've killed exactly one person in a live-fire drill."

"Was it up close?"

"No, I did it with a snap-rifle."

"Did you look over the body afterward? Did you see those shocked eyes, wide and staring up at nothing?"

She hesitated again. "I don't see—"

"Never mind," I said. "Don't bother to answer. I can read it in your face—just like your tapper can. You *did* see the face of the man you killed, and I can tell from the way you're reacting that it was a disturbing experience for you."

She shrugged. "All right. You've made your point. I suppose you're going to claim now that killing people for a living changes people. That we can't expect a veteran of numerous conflicts to be a stellar—"

Leaning forward suddenly, I gave her a crazed look. That part came naturally to me. I didn't have to manufacture any of it.

"You're not getting it," I said. "Not quite. My tapper has other data in it. Kills, estimated kills. You know how many times I've looked into the eyes of a human I've murdered? They didn't all come back, either. How many times have you permed another person?"

She shook her head.

"Well, I've done it a number of times. Hundreds—maybe even thousands of times by now."

Rossi was trying not to recoil from me, but I could tell she wanted to shrink back into her seat.

In my mind's eye I could see dead faces. And there were countless more who I'd slain with big equipment at a comfortable distance.

"And if you're including aliens," I continued, laughing ruefully, "let's not even go there. *Millions.* I've killed *millions.* Quite possibly, I'm the biggest murderer living on this planet today—except maybe for Claver."

Claver was an interesting man from my past. He'd started off as a corrupt officer in Legion Germanica and ended up as an independent operator between the stars. As far as I knew, he was the only human trader out there who broke all the rules of the Galactic Empire, and who had thus far gotten away with it. He and I had presided over some serious disasters in the past, and people who got in the way had often lost their lives.

Rossi's eyes flicked down to her computer to verify my words, and when she looked back up again she appeared to be startled.

I smiled grimly. "Does it say I'm a big-time murderer? That I'm telling the truth?"

"The truth, as best you know it."

I nodded and sat back again. "So now you know. I'm different for a reason: I'm a killer. You people made me like this. You, Legion Varus, and several planets-full of hostile aliens. But at the same time, that's exactly why I'm here. Earth needs her best killers now."

Rossi licked her lips. Her expression and her manner had shifted. She sucked in a breath and released it. I noticed how her eyes avoided mine.

"Millions..." she whispered under her breath. "How...?"

"Not everything is in my tapper, Primus. A lot of the best stuff has been deleted."

She glanced at her screens again, then back at me, alarmed all over again. "The data core breach?"

9

I shrugged noncommittally. "Could be. Do you have any more questions for me?"

She thought about it for several long seconds. We sat there in silence, listening to the air-traffic outside the pyramid-like walls of Central.

"No," she said at last. "I don't think I want to know anything else."

"You're right, you don't," I told her. "You really don't."

She stood up and extended her hand. I stood up and shook it.

"Congratulations, Adjunct McGill."

"Thank you, sir."

I slipped on my jacket and my cap. She watched me as I moved toward the door.

"McGill?" she called as I was about to leave.

I turned, eyebrows raised. She looked smaller to me now. The attitude on her face had shifted. She wore a new expression of concern, rather than scorn or severity.

"Sir?"

"Could you try—could you try to kill only aliens from now on?" she asked. "The ones that *need* killing?"

Nodding, I flashed her a smile. "I'll do my damnedest."

"Thanks."

Leaving Primus Rossi behind, I rode the elevator to the ground floor lobby. My ears cracked twice on the way down.

It felt good to be outside again in the crisp November air. Central had been like a prison for the last few days, but I'd finally slid past all the bureaucrats.

They'd taken a hard look under my hood, and they'd promptly slammed it back down again, shuddering.

That was just fine with me.

-2-

As a newly minted officer, my first duty didn't come from my legion superiors. It came from higher up. From Equestrian Nagata, in fact. He was my three-star patron inside Central, and he was the one who'd promoted me—which meant I owed him one. He'd made it clear to me a month ago that I was to keep tabs on his arch-rival, Imperator Turov.

Both Nagata and Turov were Hegemony brass, which should have meant a spacer from Legion Varus couldn't care less. But I had a history with Turov back to the days when she was part of my legion.

Spying on Turov didn't qualify as hardship duty under normal circumstances. I'd come to get along with the woman, in my own way. We'd had a semi-inappropriate relationship, in fact, which afforded me a good excuse to check up on her.

Unfortunately, Turov was at least as smart as Nagata. She knew full well that Nagata wanted me to spy on her. I'd sent her multiple texts on my tapper, and even phoned her a few times, but she'd never bothered to respond.

Frustrated, I prowled around in Central City, uncertain what I should do. I could just go on home. I'd only seen my folks briefly before getting involved in all the cloak-and-dagger politics at the capital. That's what I really wanted to do—but I knew Nagata would be calling on me soon, expecting some kind of report. With nothing to give him, I wasn't ready yet to take a vacation.

Legion life wasn't so bad when you weren't out plundering planets or protecting cargos. In-between missions, due to the long and intensive nature of our work, we were allowed to demobilize and wander the Earth as we chose. We were on call, naturally, expected to report in our full kits within twenty-four hours of a summons. Other than that, we were free men, one and all.

But today, I didn't feel relaxed and free. Instead, I felt like a leashed tiger who hadn't been fed dinner yet.

On a hunch, I headed out to Turov's residence. I'd only been there once before—and things hadn't been entirely cordial between us on that occasion.

After spending a full quarter-hour leaning on her door buzzer, identifying myself repeatedly to the dumb-ass house AI and generally making a pest out of myself, I gave up. I summoned a cab with my tapper and waited irritably for it to show up.

Arms crossed, watching the sparse traffic gliding in the sky over the posh neighborhood Turov lived in, I felt like a failure. Turov wasn't going to let me into her house when she didn't even want to meet me at her office.

Nagata wasn't going to like this turn of events. I was supposed to be his wonder-boy. The man who'd stormed Central, erased the data core, and gotten away with it. How could a few locks and tapper auto-responders get in the way of such a technological dynamo?

The truth was, of course, that I hadn't really done much of the nerd-work when I'd pulled off that stunt. Claver had done the tricky stuff. I'd been dragged along as the muscle, not the brains, of the team.

Finally, after several more minutes, a dark shadow drifted down to settle on the street in front of me. I had to hop back onto the curb because it almost squashed me.

Ready to curse out the air car driver, I popped open the hatch and leaned inside.

My glare melted away. Instead of a pushy driver, I found a young woman at the wheel. She was a hot one, too.

Even more surprising, I knew her very well. It was none other than Imperator Galina Turov.

She was out of uniform—way out. She had one of those skin-tight smart-outfits the college girls all seemed to be wearing this year. The garment was programmed to crawl over her body, revealing various ovals of fine skin at random intervals. As I stared at her, open-mouthed, her navel appeared and vanished again, like a winking eye. It was a very distracting effect.

"Uh…" I said, "Imperator? Are you just arriving home?"

"No, you big idiot. I finally got tired of having you buzz my tapper all damned day long. Don't you know I'm on leave?"

"Yes, of course. I am too."

"So why are you bothering the hell out of me?"

My eyes weren't on hers. Her clothing had shifted from a midnight blue to an acidic greenish-black. Two holes had opened up in the costume, one over each thigh. These spots of bare flesh winked at me like eyes.

"Sorry about that," I said, "I just thought you'd like to see my new bars."

I fingered the gold bars on my shoulders. She eyed them without seeming overly impressed.

"Finally made the officer ranks, did you? What did you have to do for Nagata to get those?"

Frowning, I shrugged. "Nothing much. I just died about a thousand times."

She smiled for the first time.

"No," she said. "That's not it. No one gets rank for dying. You earned it for killing the enemy."

"That too."

She looked me over frankly, running her eyes up and down my person.

"Get in," she said at last. "I'll give you a ride back to Central."

As my cab ride had showed no sign of arriving anytime soon, I did as she asked and the hatch clicked closed.

"How'd you know I was going back to Central?"

She shrugged. "You're gathering information for Nagata, right? Well, now you have at least made contact with the mark."

"Hmmm," I said thoughtfully. "You don't seem too worked up about this situation."

"Why should I be? You're my agent too, remember?"

That did spark an unpleasant reminder in my brain. I'd made a deal with her, months back. I'd said that if she stopped to investigate L-374, I'd work for her instead of Nagata. I was regretting that promise already.

"But I was right," I said, "I led you right to the enemy you were seeking. That's not a favor. You should be happy that I convinced you to stop at that K-class system."

"Going back on your word?" she asked. "I don't like that."

"I didn't say that. I just think—"

"Tell me something about Nagata. What are his plans?"

I hesitated. The truth was I didn't have much insight into what he was up to. But admitting that wasn't going to put her into a forgiving mood.

"You have to know *something*," she insisted. "If you tell me something useful, I'll give you a gem to take back to him. That way, everyone will be happy."

"Okay..." I said. "I know he's planning something big. A full gathering of Earth's fleet. I think we'll be shipping out toward the Cephalopod Kingdom."

She made a careless, flipping motion with her hand. "I know about that. Everyone knows about that. Tell me something that involves him personally."

I wracked my brain, but I didn't come up with much.

"He knows I was in on the hit at Central."

"How?"

"He managed to get camera stills from various body-cams. We wiped the data core, but the individual devices still had a small amount of video they hadn't streamed up to the servers yet."

"Ah..." she said, nodding. "So he knows you were in on it. How the hell did you get out of prison, in that case?"

I shrugged. "Plausible deniability."

"Meaning?"

"I showed him Claver's illusion-box. I changed my face into his, and he freaked out."

She frowned. "Too bad he knows about that. Harder to trick him again. But I suppose you had no choice. Continue."

My mind was a blank. Nagata hadn't told me much more than that. But as was often the case in such situations, my fertile imagination began to fill in the details.

"I think he knows we're in trouble—with the Squids, I mean."

She looked at me, her eyes widening. "They might strike first?"

"They might."

"Damn! Why don't the staff officers trust me? I haven't been briefed on enemy strength or intentions. All they've been going over is some grandiose plan to strike deep into enemy territory as soon as they have enough ships to carry all our legions."

I kept quiet. My hint of Squid preemptive talks was logical, of course, but it was just a rumor. Nagata hadn't said any such thing. Already, I regretted relaying the story to Turov. It had really come from the streets, rather than Central. Who knew? It could be true, or it could be total bullshit.

"All right," she said. "You've been open with me, so I'll give you something to take back to him. He'll be expecting that."

"Okay."

"Tell him that I've been buying expensive things. Very expensive things. He knows how much an Imperator makes—and it's less than he does. I've been spending way beyond my means as a Hegemony officer."

Now that she mentioned it, I realized she was right. The air car, the posh residence, the smart-cloth suit... This stuff hadn't come cheap.

"Where'd you get the money?"

"It's a mystery," she said. "You have no idea. But, you felt you should report it. You'll also need a cover story concerning how you got close to me. How did you trick me into revealing myself to you?"

"Uh...I don't know."

It was about then that I realized we were landing. Confused, I looked outside the canopy in order to figure out where we were. It looked like some kind of wooded area outside the Capital.

While we drifted down like a leaf on the winds, she talked steadily about her displays of wealth. Apparently, she now owned a boat and several vacation homes.

Listening closely so I could report on all this later, I couldn't help but notice that a new teardrop-shaped opening had appeared in her clothes. The opening crept from somewhere—under her arm, I think—then moved across her belly diagonally. It inched along like a caterpillar, and it got bigger as it went, revealing more. By the time it reached her hip and vanished on the far side of her, I'd seen quite a bit of nice territory. My eyes were drawn into an unblinking stare.

"But," I said, "you haven't mentioned the cover story."

She laughed, and the rest of her suit crawled away from her body to reveal her bare flesh. She slithered across the seat into my lap.

Putting my hands on her, I finally caught on. *She* was the cover story. I was supposed to tell Nagata she'd ravaged me in the woods somewhere.

The funny thing was...it would be the God's-honest truth.

Hours later, I finally made it to Nagata's office on the three hundred and thirteenth floor of Central. When there was no answer at the door, I put my hand on the plate, which I knew would identify me to the occupant.

The door stayed cool and frozen for several seconds—then it opened at last.

Inside, I was treated to a sight I hadn't expected.

Nagata was slumped forward over his desk. He was stone dead. The desktop was a computer screen, and it was glowing all around him in a pool of wavering light. I had no doubt it was trying to figure out what the hell kind of command-gesture its master's dead body was performing.

There was someone else in the room as well. He was standing at the bookshelves, calmly thumbing through the books one at a time. At first, I didn't recognize the intruder.

He wore a weird suit. The texture was oddly iridescent, as if the fibers it was woven from were hair-thin wires, rather than cloth. The fabric of it whispered like ripping Velcro when he moved.

"Claver?" I boomed, recognizing the face when he glanced at me.

Three rapid strides brought me close enough to grab him. He lifted arms sheathed in that strange, dark fabric and our hands met. We struggled for a few seconds.

"Nagata wouldn't listen to me," Claver said, grunting with effort. "Maybe you will."

I shoved him bodily against a wall. He fingered a dial on the chest of his strange garment. I slapped his hand away from it.

"Careful boy," he said, "or I'll take you straight to Hell with me."

"Why'd you kill Nagata?"

"I told you. He wouldn't listen. He kept going for weapons and trying to signal his security boys."

"Wouldn't listen to what?"

"They're coming. The squids. Really soon now—but not in the way that anyone thinks."

I frowned. We were both breathing hard, clinched up with our muscles tight. His suit seemed to be too big for him. In fact, he was slipping around inside this loose skin so much I was having a hard time restraining him.

Glancing down, I was surprised to notice his outfit had several extra hanging tubes that flopped on the floor behind the bulbous central body. Two of these tubes were full of human leg—but what were the others for?

With a sudden burst of power, Claver shoved me away from him. He shook his head.

"I give up," he said. "Here I am, playing the good Samaritan to a shit-crowd yet again. You're as big an idiot as you ever were. When the squids come, make sure you remember who tried to warn you."

"You can't get out of here," I told him, "this is Central Command. There are cameras and guards everywhere."

He laughed. "That won't matter. It won't stop me—or the squids, either. Goodbye, dummy."

Before I could grapple him again, he touched the star-shaped dial on his chest, and...that's when things got weird.

The room seemed to *shiver* somehow. It was as if the walls were momentarily blurred, moving very rapidly for several seconds in random tiny jerks. I didn't feel this vibration, but I saw it—at least, I thought I did.

Some of the effect must have been real, because alarms were set off all over the floor. The sirens in the corridor outside began whooping, and yellow flashers began flashing.

18

The clamor made me glance out the open office door. I only turned away from Claver for a split second—but when I turned back again, he was gone.

There was *nothing* where Claver had been standing a moment before. Not even a wisp of smoke. His strange suit had gone with him as well.

Nagata wasn't missing, however. The man's corpse still lay draped over the glimmering desk in a pool of blood.

As Claver enjoyed pointing out, I've never been accused of being a genius. But it didn't take whole lot of brains to realize that I was now in a very compromising position.

I popped back out into the corridor and headed for the nearest elevator. I made it inside and rode the car to the air deck, halfway down the building's incredible height.

Stepping calmly onto the puff-crete landing zone, I walked out into a light blustery rain. There were sirens going off out here, too. Nervous-looking guards approached me.

"Who are you, Legionnaire?" a veteran-ranked hog named Weber demanded. Raindrops ran from his face, but he didn't seem to notice. He just scowled at me.

"I'm an adjunct, that's who I am. I'm headed back to the city after reporting to Equestrian Nagata. Is that good enough for you?"

Weber blinked, but he didn't back down.

"Sorry sir," he said. "We've got a lock-down in progress. You'll have to wait until the all-clear has been sounded."

"No problem," I said. "I'll just hail an air car and—"

"Aren't you listening, sir?" he demanded. "Lock-down! No traffic in or out."

"Got it," I said. Doing a U-turn, I headed back toward the towering main building.

"Sorry sir," Veteran Weber called after me. "I still haven't seen any kind of ID. Is the friend-or-foe transponder on your tapper working?"

I'd disabled it temporarily to make it harder for anyone looking for me to pinpoint my location. I knew, however, it wouldn't do to tell this hog about that.

19

"No, it's not," I said. "There was some kind of electrical discharge up on the three hundred and fifteenth floor. Maybe it took out my tapper."

Weber frowned, looking me over. I gave him my best stern, no-nonsense stare in return. He bought it.

"All right," he said at last, "go on back inside and wait there. We might want to question you later, if you were close to whatever caused—"

The rest of his words I didn't catch as I'd already taken several steps away from him. I gave him a nod over my shoulder and a disinterested wave of the hand.

I could feel eyes on my back, however. They were suspicious, and they had good reason to be. I was lucky no one had recognized me. Not more than a few months earlier I'd been involved in a series of unfortunate events right here at Central. It was the memory of those events, such as the erasure of the data core and several related deaths, that had these hogs so edgy.

I knew full well he was probably working his tapper, doing a data scan on my facial patterns. It was only a matter of time before he found out who I was and that my file was marked on some kind of watch list. Every time I went through security here, even when there was nothing unusual going on, they frisked me and treated me like a fugitive.

To my credit, my smooth exit almost worked. I had time, in fact, to put together a back-up plan. I'd take the stairway down to the garage sub-levels rather than the elevators. That would take time and remove me from most of the security grid. They only had a few drone and AI cameras monitoring that route. In comparison, the elevators were minefields of surveillance equipment.

Once at street level, with any luck this alert would be over, and I'd be able to slip away. If not... well, there were always more drastic options available.

Thundering boots behind me made my heart sink. The veteran was on to me. Heaving a sigh, I turned around with my hand on my weapon.

Weber's eyes were as big around as saucers. He was breathing hard, and he glanced down at my hand on my pistol.

"You must have gotten the message too," he said.

"What message?"

"About floor three-fifteen!"

This was it. They must have discovered Nagata's body. It had been a long shot that I'd be allowed to escape before they found him. I cursed inside, annoyed that I'd been taken so easily.

I realized I was facing a grim choice. I could gun this man down and try to escape, taking comfort in the knowledge they'd revive him soon thereafter. But that would leave me as a fugitive. I would have to be very lucky to stay out of prison.

My rank. That's what changed my mind in the end. I was an adjunct now, an officer. Fooling around killing good men wasn't my job anymore—if it ever had been. This veteran was a hog, sure, but he was only trying to do his job. I could tell by the look on his face I was someone he respected.

What was it Primus Rossi had asked me to do? Only kill the ones that needed killing?

My hand slid away from my pistol.

"What's the problem, Veteran?" I asked. "I haven't heard anything."

"Floor three-fifteen," Weber repeated, stepping right past me and aiming his rifle at the door that led to the stairwell. His partner moved to cover the elevator lobby. "They say the floor is packed with squids, sir. I don't know if I believe it, but I have to take a report like that seriously when it comes from my duty-commander."

"Squids?" I asked, my mind whirling. In my head, I could hear Claver's words before he'd disappeared.

They're coming a lot sooner than you think.

I turned toward the elevator, which had just dinged. I drew my weapon smoothly and joined the other two men. We stared at those elevator doors, waiting for them to slide open.

They seemed to be taking a damnably long time to do so.

21

-4-

When the elevator doors did finally open, I almost blasted the single occupant inside, but I controlled myself as did the two hogs.

It was Primus Rossi. She was clearly in a bad state. The elevator wall behind her was smeared in blood. Her uniform had two black holes in it. Laser-fire, if I had to guess. They'd burned her right through.

Somehow, she was still alive. One white-knuckled hand gripped the railing inside the elevator, and the other was clutching at the holes in her uniform.

She looked up at me, her eyes big and glassy.

"McGill?" she gasped.

"Careful!" I barked at the hogs as they moved to rush to her aid. "Could be a trap. Are you booby-trapped, Primus?"

"What? No… a squid fired on me. I got to the elevator and managed to shut the doors before it could put me down."

She paused to have a coughing fit. I moved into the elevator. Veteran Weber joined me, and we helped her out and laid her gently on the floor. Emergency people had begun to gather, and they went to work on her as soon as they saw her.

I could have told them it was a waste of time. If there's anything I know the look of, it's death. The primus was a goner.

She beckoned me, and I knelt beside her. Her breathing was becoming irregular.

"McGill," she said. "My tapper stopped working up there. They did something—we couldn't get word out. The squid I saw came out of Nagata's office—I don't understand how it got in there."

"Nagata's office? Any sign of Nagata?"

She shook her head slightly. "We have to assume they got him."

"Okay, thanks for the report. I'll lead these men up there and we'll deal with them. You can rest now."

Her white hand shot up and gripped my sleeve.

"No," she said. "There's something else—the data core. I think they damaged it."

Frowning, I looked back down at her. "Why would they do that? Do you think that's why they came?"

Rossi's eyes were closed now. That small pony tail of hers was in full view. It seemed strange to think she'd carefully washed, combed and tucked it up under her hat only this morning.

She shook her head and mumbled something. Then her hand relaxed, letting go of my sleeve. I looked at the medic. He shook his head.

I knew what that meant. She was gone. Blood loss, organ-failure. It didn't really matter. The squids had claimed another victim.

Standing up, I found the two hogs I'd teamed with were looking around uncertainly.

"What are your orders, boys?" I asked.

"Last we heard we were to hold this post. But our tappers don't work now. The net is silent."

Poking at my own arm, I soon confirmed what he was telling me. I walked to the nearest office door and kicked it in. Veteran Weber stopped in the doorway as I walked inside.

Weber watched me in concern. "This is a private office, Adjunct."

"No shit? Well, I need it, and these are extreme circumstances. Central can take the damages out of my next paycheck."

The office was empty, but the desk computer was on. I ran my fingers over it, waking it up. Working on the computer, I was soon frustrated. It wouldn't take my log in.

"You try," I told the veteran.

He did, but with no better luck than I had.

"Primus Rossi said the net was down," I said. "That's why we're not getting any orders. Our command and control is paralyzed, right here at Central."

"Do you think this might be part of a bigger attack?" the veteran asked.

"Could be. Only thing I know for sure is those squids must be repelled."

"Standard operating procedure is to lockdown the building then wait for reinforcements."

"You mean in case of terrorist attack?"

"Yes sir."

I laughed. "We're way past that now. There could be a slaughter going on upstairs, and we're the only ones with guns in this building. You, me, and a few hundred guards."

Veteran Weber looked nervous, but he nodded.

"All right," I said, "I'm going up there. You can stand your post, or you can back me up. Your choice, Weber."

With that, I moved to the elevators. I wasn't surprised when they didn't work. The building still had power, but without an operating network, much of it was malfunctioning.

Not bothering to pause and think about it, I walked to the stairwell and pushed open the doors. There were stairs in there all right. A vast, echoing tower full of them. The stairway itself formed a boxy coil up around an endless central shaft. Natural light blazed through slotted windows on every floor like a dashed line that blurred up out of sight. It had to be a hundred flights up to three-fifteen.

I took the first flight two steps at a time. Then the second flew by.

Hearing footsteps below me, I paused and turned around with my weapon in my hand, peering over the rail.

Veteran Weber and his sidekick were running up behind me.

"You changed your minds?" I asked.

"There's nothing to guard. Most of the building has been evacced now, and the elevators aren't working anyway."

Smiling and giving them a quick nod, I headed up another flight. They were right behind me, huffing.

Somewhere around floor two-thirty, Veteran Weber reached out a hand to pluck at my shoulder. He could hardly breathe.

"Next floor…" he said, "…emergency equipment locker."

"You need an oxygen bottle?" I asked, only half-joking.

These hogs were never in as good of shape as real space-going legionnaires. They rarely saw combat and even those that carried weapons were relatively soft after decades of pointless guard-duty.

He shook his head, gulping down air.

"Lift-disks," he said. "They've got a few in the lockers for evacuating casualties."

"Got it," I said, nodding.

We found the locker and the lift-disks. They were shaped more or less like stretchers. Making our way back to the stairwell landing, we could only lay one out at a time.

"Me first," I said, sprawling on one like a surfboard.

I activated it and began drifting upward. Cranking it up a notch, I got off the ground far enough to ease it over the stairway rails into the vertical shaft. I had to really goose the power to go up instead of down, but it worked.

The lift-disks were a lot like my floater back home. I'd spent many summers gliding weightlessly over the Satilla River, and I felt comfortable guiding the disk up the stairwell.

Looking down, I could tell Veteran Weber and his partner weren't so happy. My years serving the legion off-world had given me a lot of experience with my feet off the ground. These boys looked terrified.

"You'll be fine," I called to them, smiling. "Just don't look down. These things could probably take us all the way to the roof before they run out of power—as long as they have a full charge, that is."

Nodding weakly, they clung to their lift-disks with white-knuckled hands and floated after me.

25

We reached floor three-fifteen about two minutes later. The lift-disks had saved us a lot of time and given us time to catch our breath.

Guns drawn, we circled the door. Veteran Weber's sidekick, a Specialist I'd come to learn was named Jacobs, reached for the handle.

Some kind of instinct kicked in for me. I'm not sure if I heard a click, or my naturally suspicious mind triggered on something else—like the tiny trail of slippery slime on the puff-crete floor.

Reaching out my hand, I pulled Veteran Weber backward toward me. He looked at me in confusion.

Then the bomb went off. Specialist Jacobs flew backward, smashing into Veteran Weber's back. The two of them almost went over the railing.

I still had hold of Weber. Even though the blast had my ears ringing, it hadn't been a big enough one to kill us all. I guess it had been something small and easy to hide.

Despite its relative lack of punch, the tiny charge managed to fire the door handle off and embed it into Jacobs' face.

I saw his blank, disbelieving eyes for a moment as he went over the edge, a piece of metal lodged where his nose used to be.

He fell then, silently, all the way down to the ground floor.

I hauled Veteran Weber back up onto the landing. The door hung open crookedly.

"You still have your weapon?" I asked Weber.

He showed it to me numbly.

"Good," I said. "Keep it ready. These squids are probably commandos. Few in number, but tricky and mean."

White-faced, he let me go first as we stepped into the open passageways of floor three-fifteen.

The first thing I noticed was the darkness. There were no artificial lights operating on the floor that I could see. Not even the emergency glow-runners embedded in the flooring were on. They should be displaying colored arrows to lead people out— but they were all dead.

Here and there along the passageway, which stretched for a hundred meters or more in both directions, were office doors that hung open. Some of these doorways emitted daylight, which allowed us to see a few things.

The passage was smoky, with drifting blue wisps. The acrid smell in the air reminded me of burning insulation—and burnt meat. The squids had obviously been busy, going from office to office, slaughtering anyone they found inside.

Taking a left, we headed toward Nagata's office. We reached it without making contact with the enemy.

Nagata was still dead, still slumped over his computer. That was the only thing about the room that I recognized.

The place had been torn apart. Every book was down from its shelf. Every knick-knack, office equipment item and piece of furniture had been broken, pulled apart and cast down on the floor.

"They were looking for something," Weber said.

"Yeah… just like Claver was," I said.

"Claver?"

"Never mind. Let's keep moving."

We exited Nagata's office and ran smack into a squid.

He'd been waiting there, outside the office. I couldn't explain it any other way.

"Halt!" he said, using a translator app. "Tell me why you're in this office?"

This sort of talk was very like squids. They liked to command people to do things. They'd never been diplomatic about anything to my knowledge. I'd fought them on three different campaigns, and they'd always pissed me off with their poor attitudes.

"Who are you to tell us what to do, squid?" I demanded. "This is our building, our world. We'll give you the orders here."

The squid made a funny, burbling noise.

"You are amusing. I've been tracking you since you entered my security zone. My greatest worry was that my trap would kill you all before I could gather intelligence."

Veteran Weber grew a set about then, and he aimed his rifle at the squid threateningly.

"We've got the drop on you," he said. "Surrender or die!"

"Such bravado," replied the squid. "I like this one. If I wasn't on a time schedule, I'd take it as a slave-pet."

That was enough for Veteran Weber. He shot the squid right between the eyes—only, his gun didn't go off.

"Ah!" said the squid, burbling again. "What is the problem? Could it be your Imperial weapons don't work in my presence? What a pity."

I caught on immediately. They'd hacked our weapons. Imperial technology often had fail-safes built into them. That was supposed to keep us from turning our guns on Galactics. They also had recognition circuits that allowed someone holding something called a "galactic key" to operate them without authorization.

Without much hope, I fired my pistol at the squid. It didn't even click.

"Excellent," the squid said. "Now, if your low-functioning cognitives are capable of comprehending the situation, you know you're my prisoners. You must therefore answer my questions, or I'll apply punishment."

"Low-functioning what?" Veteran Weber asked me.

"I think he called us dummies," I said.

Weber drew his combat knife and assumed a fighting stance. I could have told him that was a loser. Squids stood nearly three meters tall when they arched up, and they had limbs with musculature we couldn't hope to combat without technological help.

I touched his shoulder, indicating he should stand down. The squid had braced itself for the attack and now looked disappointed.

"You control this animal?" he asked me. "Yes, I now clearly see who the master is. Set your hound after me, little master! I wish to punish it."

"Maybe another time, squid," I said. "Listen, we'll cooperate. We'll answer any question you want, if you'll just tell us a few things first."

"Your terms are unacceptable. Full submission is required."

"You'll get that, trust me. All I want to know is why you're here. It all seems pointless. We'll revive our dead. We'll rebuild the damage to the building. Such a waste, attacking us like this and achieving nothing."

"We've achieved a great deal. Your low-quotients simply prevent you from comprehending what has already come to pass."

I shook my head slowly and laughed at him.

"No, I don't think so. I think you're covering up a sick failure. An embarrassment. You realize you've shown us a new technology, an ability to infiltrate the heart of our military headquarters. All that for nothing."

The squid puffed up like a snake. He was angry and prideful. The easiest way to get a snake to strike was to poke it with a stick, and it was working on this guy.

"I shall abuse you for this wanton display of impudence," the squid told me. "Your dead will not be re-printed. Our strike at your commanders has been a permanent and fatal one."

That gave me pause. The squid was claiming he'd permed these people? But how?

"I don't buy it," I said loudly. "You're just bullshitting now, and I know all about that. Strategically, Earth will be far ahead after this screw-up."

"What is your designation, human?"

"Who me? I'm Adjunct James McGill. From Legion Varus."

That appeared to surprise the squid. "McGill? You are the McGill-creature?"

"I just said so. Is your brain malfunctioning? Should I repeat everything I say twice to make sure you get it, dummy?"

Anger came back, replacing his surprise. He took a shuffling step forward, his limbs rasping in his suit.

It was only then that I recognized the outfit he was wearing. It was exactly like the one Claver had been wearing when I saw him in Nagata's office. It was a lot bigger, indicating the garment had smart technology and could resize itself into different configurations, but that raspy material was definitely the same stuff.

So *that's* what all those extra leg-holes in Claver's pants had been for. He'd been wearing an outfit made for a squid.

Slowly, the gears in my head rotated and clicked. The squids must have technology just like Claver's. Maybe he'd even stolen it from them.

They had the power to teleport—or whatever you might want to call it when you rapidly moved your body across vast distances. The technology was startling, and it seemed very useful.

"Standard abuse will be an insufficient punishment," the squid told me. "Your extremities must be removed methodically at the very beginning, but life will not be allowed to leave your husk."

Veteran Weber charged in at that moment. He'd been side-stepping while the squid and I squared-off.

Weber managed to get in one slash which gouged a tentacle. That was impressive—but it was as far as he got. The squid lashed out with a single arm and swept him off his feet. Weber was tossed ass-over-tea-kettle into the hallway beyond.

The distraction had given me just enough time to get in close. I didn't draw my knife, however. I had a different plan.

"Careful!" the squid said, wrapping me in its writhing tentacles. "Don't injure yourself! I must witness a slow, agonizing finish for you."

The squid was grappling my limbs. Very quickly, both my legs and my right arm were pinned.

But my left arm remained free to act.

I didn't draw my knife. I didn't gouge at one of those wet, rolling eyeballs despite the fact I wanted to.

Instead, I reached up to the big star-shaped dial on the squid's suit. I gave it a hard twist, just as I'd seen Claver do.

This didn't make the squid happy. He hurled me away from him.

I slammed into a wall, and the world became a splash of color for an instant. It seemed like I could see the blood flowing inside my own eyes.

The squid was staggering around, burping and farting in his own language. He was struggling with that knob on his suit. Apparently, he didn't like the new setting I'd selected for him.

There was a blur in the air, a ripple in space. Just as Claver had done before him, the squid winked out in the middle of it.

A gleam of residual radiation was all that remained behind where he'd stood a moment before. That and a puddle of black ink.

I hoped that ink-spot meant he'd pissed himself in terror.

Veteran Weber was banged up, but he was still able to hold a weapon. I got him to his feet, and we did a sweep of the floor. There were no more squids to be found.

That was a bit embarrassing. All this time the hog guards had been talking about an army of squids attacking this floor. The fact they'd been bested by a single commando... well, it didn't speak well of their fighting ability.

Just as we reached the last office in line, a full platoon of hogs in body-shell armor finally arrived. They threw flash-bangs at us, and we were almost shot down before they recognized us.

"Hold your fire, you damned trigger-happy hogs!" I shouted at them.

"Identify yourself," demanded the centurion in charge.

"Adjunct James McGill, Legion Varus."

They moved forward in a surge, shoulders hunched, weapons aiming everywhere they looked. Laser dots and flashlights played over every wall and carcass.

"What are you doing up here, McGill?"

"Saving lives and killing squids," I said. "Veteran Weber and I cleared the floor. You might want to check the other levels."

The centurion looked me over unhappily. "I'm the man in charge of this counterinsurgency effort. You and Veteran Weber are away from your posts."

Weber was trying to look small, but I stood firm and snorted.

"You're late to the party, Centurion. We did your job for you. What about the other levels?"

"The attack was limited to this floor."

"What? Well then, why the hell did it take you hogs so long to—"

"Centurion," said an adjunct as she hustled back to us to report. "McGill's right. The floor is clear."

"Body-count?" demanded the Centurion.

"We've got at least forty dead. Aides, senior officers and even a few janitors that were unlucky enough to—"

"I don't care about that. What's the *alien* body-count?"

"Oh…we didn't find any aliens, sir."

The centurion lowered his weapon and turned back around to face off with me again.

"McGill, are you full of shit or what? Was this some kind of prank?"

With a sweep of my arm I referred him to the dead people all over the floor, the kicked in office doors and the general destruction.

"Yeah," I said, "I killed them all. They wouldn't validate my parking."

"You're going down to be debriefed. Veteran Weber, you're going with him. Adjunct, escort these men to the detention center."

I knew the drill. I didn't resist, although I felt like doing so. I had to keep reminding myself that the enemy—the real enemy—had been run off. My only lingering worry was the possibility they'd be back in force.

After about two hours of bullshit, during which I was prodded and interrogated by amateurs, I finally met up with someone who I respected.

None other than Centurion Graves stepped into the room.

"McGill?" he asked when he sighted me. "I might have known. They called me on the emergency channel and demanded I report to Central immediately. They wouldn't say why. You owe me sky-cab fare from Cincinnati, Adjunct."

"Good to see you too, sir," I said. "I'd salute if I could."

He sighed and pulled up a chair next to the stool I was sitting on.

My hands were strapped behind my back, and my neck was tied down to a stainless steel table in front of me. He tilted his head to one side, and he looked me over.

"All your teeth are still there. Why'd they strap your neck down? Did you bite someone?"

I rolled my eyes. "That would be juvenile behavior unfitting of a Varus officer, sir."

Graves nodded. "Right…you bit someone. Where did your shirt go?"

"It's hot in here."

He nodded again.

"Why don't you just tell them what happened?" he asked.

"I have sir, multiple times. Unfortunately, hogs are by nature unimaginative."

"They didn't believe your bullshit… is that it?"

"An offensive mischaracterization. The truth is the truth, sir. I can't help that."

Graves frowned and leaned back in his chair. He seemed unconcerned that I was positioned so I could hardly turn my head enough to look up at his face.

"Tell me the story," he said.

I did so. I repeated my mantra, word for word. All about how I'd come to meet with Nagata and afterward had gone downstairs to the flight deck when the alarm went up. Afterward, I led a search and destroy, clearing the floor of enemy combatants.

Naturally, I left off the part about finding Nagata dead earlier, and the part about discovering Claver going through his office. I also left out why I'd come to report to him in the first place.

Graves didn't miss any of these details.

"Okay…" he said. "I can see why the hogs are upset. They've got a floor covered in dead brass. When the rescue team goes in, they find only you, and one other off-post noncom wandering around. No squids. No electronics showing vids of what happened. No nothing."

"Revive Nagata and ask him about it."

34

"He's been permed. They all have. I think that's part of the reason they're so upset."

That did bother me. Rossi had suggested that would happen, and it apparently had. I'd only just met the woman, and she'd died in my arms for good. Perma-death was a strange thing to contemplate for a man who's lived so many times.

I swiveled my eyes up to look at Graves. "There's ink, sir. The squid pissed himself when I took him out."

He tossed down a computer scroll he'd been nonchalantly perusing while I talked.

"Right, I got that part from your story. The centurion in charge of the sweep mentioned it in this report, and they did find a puddle of liquid that might fit that description."

"There's got to be other evidence of a squid presence though," he said.

"I'm sure there will be."

"We've got their DNA samples," Graves said. "We'll sweep the floor and find every centimeter they touched. The problem is there are no actual cephalopod bodies. How did they escape?"

"First off, there was only one that I saw. The hogs shit themselves and ran from a single commando. As to how he got in and out—"

"Ah of course," Graves interrupted, "the magic teleportation suit. Damn, that's a good one, McGill. I have to admit it, when you lie, you like to go big."

"It's not a lie, and it wasn't magic, either. The squids have tech we don't. Is that so hard to believe?"

Graves lowered his face to my level on the tabletop. He watched my eyes, which were angry. I couldn't hold that back any longer.

"All right," he said. "I'm going to give you a break. I'm going to check your story out personally, rather than dismissing it as total crap from the start."

He stood up and hammered on the door. Guards soon released him.

"Should we untie him, Centurion?" asked one of them.

"Nah," Graves said. "He likes it that way. Don't you, McGill?"

"I think this table has fixed my bad back, sir," I agreed, my chin rubbing against the steel table top as I spoke.

The guards closed the door, shaking their heads.

About an hour later the door opened again, and I snorted awake.

"Don't tell me you fell asleep like that?" said a new voice. It wasn't Graves, it was Imperator Turov this time.

"Varus Legionnaire's sleep with rocks for pillows," I said. "This table is smooth and cool."

She came close to me and ran her hand over my back.

"Sweaty... What kind of mess are you in today, McGill?"

"Graves went to investigate my story. Where'd he go?"

She shrugged and paced around me in a circle. Mostly, I watched her butt as she walked by. I did make the effort to lift my eyes to check out her expression on her third time around, however. She looked thoughtful, rather than pissed off.

"You must have read my report by now, sir," I said. "Do you have any questions?"

She stopped strutting around and lowered her face right into mine.

"Oh yes… plenty of questions. But I have to get you out of here first, so you can answer them."

I almost blew it and claimed I didn't know anything else. But in truth, I was getting tired of having my neck strapped to a table, so I shut up and looked at her.

She nodded knowingly.

"That's what I thought," she said. "Guard!"

About seven minutes later, I was limping along behind the Imperator like a bad dog on a leash. She walked me through a half-dozen checkpoints and glaring hogs. You would have thought I'd shot all their uncles by the way they looked at me.

When we got up to the flight deck at last, I recognized her personal air car. It looked as flashy and expensive as ever.

Climbing stiffly inside, I took a deep breath and eyed her rudely.

"We're heading back to the woods?" I asked hopefully.

She glared back. "Certainly not. You cost me a lot of political capital today. I'm not in the most forgiving mood."

I shrugged and leaned back. I found a bottle of water and upended it, chugging for a good twenty seconds. She grabbed it out of my fingers and put it on her side of the cab, out of my reach.

"All right," she said, "I got you out of there. Now, start talking."

"You've got my story. Everyone does. I took the initiative during an attack, and I repelled the enemy with only two supporting—"

"Cut the bullshit. Talk about the parts of the story you left out. You went up there to meet Nagata. What did he say?"

"Uh..." I said, feeling a half-dozen lies run through my head. I'd almost settled on one when I realized I needed to give her something good. For one thing, she deserved it for helping. For another, she wouldn't buy an easy "nothing to see here" response.

"He didn't say anything," I told her. "He was dead on his desk when I got up there."

She looked at me in alarm. "What? And you didn't sound the alarm? You tried to walk out?"

"I didn't know he was permed at the time. I figured they'd blame it on me."

"Well, you were right about that. They're blaming you for everything. They don't really believe there were any squids. The only witness you have is this Veteran Weber. His story matches yours—almost like you two rehearsed it."

"Or almost like we're telling the truth."

"Okay, let's say I believe you. When you got to Nagata's office, you found him dead, so you panicked."

"I didn't say I panicked."

"What the hell would you call it?"

"A strategic withdrawal."

She chuckled. "Fine. You retreated from the scene of the crime. That does sound like James McGill. Later, you met up with the squid commando, and you managed to kill him single-handedly."

"See? There you go embellishing and misstating the facts. I found the squid, sure, but all I did was get in close and twist the dial on his chest. That must have activated the suit he was wearing, and he was transported somewhere else."

"I should have let them keep you," she said, shaking her head slowly. "Your story is hopeless. No one will believe it without direct evidence."

"Well... I think they might."

"Why?"

"Because that space-jumping squid isn't done yet. He tore up Nagata's office. He was clearly looking for something he didn't find. He'll be back to try again, that's my prediction."

Turov squirmed uncomfortably in her seat. "I don't like not knowing what's going on, McGill. You'd better not be withholding critical information from me."

I thought of Claver immediately. Not just because I was withholding everything I knew about his part in all this, but because of something he'd once told me.

Never give them everything they want to know at once, he'd said, *because if you have more to tell, they'll have to bring you back to life again later to get it.*

It was his idea of an insurance policy. There had to be wisdom in those words, because a lot of powerful people had wanted Claver dead over the years, and he was still very much alive.

-6-

Sure enough, Turov didn't fly me to the woods for another love-making session, which I found disappointing. She didn't take me to her house, either. Instead, she dropped me off at the public sky-train station and flew away.

I'd been ditched, and I was uncertain as to what I should do next. I was pretty sure the boys at Central would want another piece of me if I went back there, so that was out of the question.

In the end, I bought a cheap seat on the sky-train and spent the night with my head lolling onto other passengers. In the early morning, we'd arrived in Georgia Sector.

I took public transport all the way back to my parents place near Waycross. After hugging my folks and lying about how great everything was for their newly christened adjunct, I headed to my shack on the back of their land.

Home sweet home.

Checking the fridge first, I found the milk had gone bad and there were only five beers left. I dumped out the milk, drank all the beers, and crashed.

My dreams were haunted by squids and the dying eyes of Primus Rossi. I hadn't liked the woman at first, but she'd come around to understanding me during the few hours we'd spent on Earth in each other's presence.

I figured what was bothering me about her was that she'd been permed. I wasn't used to that. For sure, people *did* get permed now and again in my business. But to meet someone,

39

forge a connection with them, and then lose them all in one day... that was disturbing.

Something woke me up a few hours after midnight. Maybe I had to piss, or maybe one of my floorboards had creaked.

A figure stood over me. I couldn't see the face, but I recognized the saggy-pants, multi-limbed look of a man standing in a suit made for a squid.

"Claver?" I asked the intruder.

Reflexively, my hand dug in my couch.

Claver lifted a laser pistol and aimed it at my forehead. I could see the red glow of the aiming dot. It played over my skin, catching a few stray hairs and making them shine. The dot was hot enough to make my skin uncomfortable. It was like being too close to a heat lamp.

"What did you tell them about me?" he demanded.

"The hogs?"

"No, you idiot. I'm talking about the squid agent. How does he know I was in Central before he was?"

"Maybe he noticed Nagata was already dead," I suggested. "Or maybe he noticed the item he was looking for was missing."

Claver made an angry noise. "I'm going to burn your eyes out of your sockets, so you don't see anything else."

"Don't you want to know the rest?" I asked him.

All I could see in the red-lit dimness was his snarl. I had that effect on a lot of people.

"You don't know crap," he said. "I'm wasting my time."

"I know you stole a squid jump-suit. And I know how they work."

"How could you...? Doesn't matter," he said. His weapon shifted slightly and he fired it. My wrist stung.

"You shot my tapper?" I hissed.

"Yeah, I have a scrambling field up, and your data back at Central has been erased from the core. I'm afraid this is the end of the line, McGill."

I knew what he was talking about. My tapper tracked my mind hour-by-hour. Using the data core, they could reconstruct my memories as well as my body. But without a backup copy in Central, and with my tapper dead—well, they could bring back my body but not my mind. They wouldn't even bother. I would be permed if I died now.

It was high time I made my move, so I did it. My left hand had been digging in my couch since I'd first realized there was an intruder in my shack.

Now my hand came up with a well-oiled machete in its grip. The blade flashed as I made a lateral cut across my body.

The laser snapped, but Claver must have been rattled. He burned a dime-sized hole right through my couch cushion near my left ear.

The machete caught his wrist, but it was stopped by the squid jump-suit. They were made of woven metal, after all. The edge sparked, and the gun was knocked away.

Although I hadn't managed to sever his wrist, I had managed to break it. Cursing, he scrambled for the gun.

I dove after him, machete raised high.

"Kill me and you'll never know what's in store for Earth!" he shouted.

"You came to the wrong shack, Claver!"

With that, I sank the blade into his face. It was the only part of him that wasn't covered by that tough squid-suit.

Standing over my kill, panting, I immediately began to curse.

He'd performed his little trick on me, I realized. He'd given me a reason to bring him back to life. Even as he drew his last breath, the man had been scheming.

Dragging the carcass to the garage in the dark, I shoved it into the backseat of the family tram.

My dad must have heard something. He came out hesitantly with a shotgun wrapped in tight fingers.

"James?" he asked. "What's going on?"

"Nothing, Dad."

"Don't tell me that. Something's up."

My mind worked fast. Some would say I'm at my best when caught red-handed, and I couldn't deny it.

"Uh... Della called," I said, "I need to borrow the tram. I'll have it back to you soon, okay?"

"Della?" he asked hopefully. "Is this about the trip?"

My dad was talking about a trip we'd been planning—to go see Etta, my daughter. She was my folks' one and only grandchild, and they'd yet to meet her. I felt kind of bad lying about that, but I was in a bad place now.

"Uh-huh," I said, standing squarely between him and the open door of the tram.

"Looks like you hurt yourself," he said, noting the way I held my burned arm.

"Something's wrong with my tapper," I said, "now Dad, if I could just—"

"But if your tapper isn't working, how did Della call you?"

He had me there. I was running out of lies.

"Uh…" I said.

Then he caught sight of the body slumped over in the backseat. He lowered his voice.

"Is that Della?" he asked. "I get it…"

"Sure… she's tired out."

He chuckled and shook his head. "You never quit, do you boy?"

"I try not to, sir."

"Well, okay… Don't ding it up or fill it with hamburger wrappers this time, okay?"

"You got it, Dad. It'll be better than new when I get home again."

Shaking his head with the air of a man who'd heard such promises before—because he had—he turned and headed back toward the house.

I climbed into the tram and tore out of there before anyone investigated further. I saw the lights go on all over the house as I reached the corner. My mom was probably buzzing my busted tapper with a thousand queries. Before she could think to bomb the com-box on the tram, I shut that off, too.

But the part about my tapper being dead was true. It had been burned to scrap. I was relatively free and off the grid.

Humming to myself, I took the tram to the puff-crete expressway, put it into automatic, and laid back to take a nap.

The dead man in the seat behind me didn't bother me a bit. Sure, he stank a little. All the dead do. But that was a smell I was well familiar with.

I recalled something they'd taught us in our early legion history classes. An ancient Roman by the name of Alus Vitellus had once said: *"A dead enemy always smells good."*

Today, I had to agree with old Alus.

-7-

When I woke up, I took stock of my situation. I had Claver's body, and I had a squid jump-suit. The question was, how could I parlay these two items of dubious value into the most points possible with Central?

Normally, I'd have taken the whole mess directly to Nagata. He was my patron saint among the brass. He was also on the very short list of officers who'd believed in me enough to promote me.

But Nagata had apparently been permed. That fact made things tricky from my perspective. I wasn't sure who was left that I could trust.

Sure, I knew Turov and Winslade pretty well, and they had rank. But those two were snakes on the best of days.

No, I didn't trust any officers—not even Graves. The problem with Graves was he was too straight of an officer. He'd probably turn me over to Central, playing it by the book, and possibly get me screwed in an entirely new way in the process.

In the end, I fell back on my enlisted buddies from Legion Varus. They weren't exactly cub scouts, but they knew me, and we'd all trusted one another with our lives in the past.

With a wince, I contacted Carlos from a public com-box in Greenville. I'd decided not to use the tram's com-box because that would be too easy to trace.

"Whatever you're selling, I don't fucking want any of it," he announced when he finally answered.

"Carlos? I need help."

"Who is this?" he demanded.

"Don't screw with me. I'm calling in a favor."

He was quiet for a second.

"You don't have any of those left," he said at last. "In fact, you couldn't buy one with your last credit coin."

Carlos had never been easy to deal with, but he always came through in the end. You just had to know how to get his mind focused on what you wanted.

"I've got something new," I said. "Something alien."

"Alien? Did you screw a squid chick?"

"That's a pretty close guess," I said, "but I'm talking about new technology. Something that's never been seen on Earth before."

He paused again.

"You're in Mid-Atlantic Sector. What the hell are you doing there?"

He'd traced me already. That made me grimace. If people had set up alarms on the net for any contacts I made, they were probably scrambling to this spot right now.

"I don't have much time. Are you interested or not?"

"I notice you're not pulling rank. You're just asking. That means this is as illegal as shit."

"Are you in?" I demanded.

"Promise I get to die? Lots of times?"

"Probably," I admitted.

"You tease… okay, I'm in. Where?"

"Central City. Our favorite bar. Give me ten hours to get there."

The connection closed. He'd shut it down without saying goodbye, which was probably a wise decision.

I drove for another three hours before I made similar calls. The gang all agreed to come meet me. None of them seemed really happy about coming, but they were game. They were always game.

When you live and die with a group of people over and over again, you form a tight bond that's difficult to describe. I mean, hell, my own momma had yet to watch me die, and she'd only presided over my birth once. These people had done both a dozen times each.

Della was the center of my attention, mostly because Kivi and Carlos were an item. She was long of leg and easy on the eyes. I could feel myself being drawn to her, and we'd had a number of flings before. Unfortunately, our get-togethers didn't always end on a happy note.

The key member of the crowd, the one I really wanted to see the most, was Natasha. She showed up late, and the rest of us were a little drunk by then. I'd spilled credits on the bar tab, and they hadn't been shy about taking me up on my generosity.

"Adjunct McGill?"

I spun around and saw Natasha walking up to me. She ignored the greetings of the others. She eyed me seriously.

She had a soft-spoken manner, but she was the smart one in our group. Her cheeks were perfectly shaped, and she had eyes that disappeared when she smiled.

Sadly, she wasn't smiling now.

"Hello girl," I said. "You're a sight for sore eyes."

"Are those bars on your shoulders real?" she asked.

"All gold and nanites, love," I said.

"Don't call me that. Why did you call in your chip? To get us drunk and celebrate your promotion?"

"Nope, I've really got something, just like I said."

The group had quieted somewhat, and they scooted close to listen in. The team was small: just Della, Kivi, Carlos, and Natasha. All the people I trusted most in the world when it came right down to it.

I'd thought about calling Harris, but passed. He was still upset that I'd been promoted over him. Seeing me make adjunct had been his greatest fear, I think, since our first campaign together on Steel World.

Natasha looked over the group. She was the smartest person in the bar, and we all knew it. I needed her if my plan was to have a chance. I think everyone else knew that, too.

"Okay…" she said. "I'm here, so I might as well find out why."

She sat down. I ordered her a booze and tonic, and we huddled up even tighter.

As I laid out my story, they were amused at first. But slowly, the seriousness of the situation began to sink in.

"I *knew* it!" Carlos proclaimed. "I knew the second I saw Central on fire that James McGill had to be involved somehow. I said that, didn't I babe?"

He said this last to Kivi, who nodded. Kivi and Carlos had been romantically involved on-and-off again over the last year or two. They were both shorter than average, but Kivi was voluptuous while Carlos was kind of chunky. If I had to guess, I'd say she was thinking about dumping him again.

"I was just a victim of circumstance," I explained.

Della rolled her eyes. The others looked bemused or disgusted, depending on their personalities.

"But it's true," I said. "I just wandered into Nagata's office and caught Claver red-handed."

"There's no way I'm buying such an obvious line of bullshit McGill," Carlos said.

I was starting to get angry, but Natasha put her hand over mine.

"Think about it," she said. "Who sent you in to meet Nagata at that moment?"

"Uh..." I said, not wanting to say Turov's name. Natasha was jealous of Galina Turov. She was a demon as far as all these people were concerned.

Natasha caught on. Her hand leapt up off of mine like I'd burned it.

"Turov?" she hissed out the name. "You've been seeing that witch again?"

"It's not like that."

"Yeah right, McGill," Carlos hooted.

He was the only one that seemed to think this was all funny. The three women looked pissed off. That might have had something to do with the fact I'd been romantically involved with all of them at one point or another.

"It doesn't matter," I said. "Just listen to the facts. I walked in there to talk to Nagata. He and I have had... discussions, recently. He's the one who personally gave me the gold bars to make me an adjunct. I counted him among the few people in

47

the world I could trust. But when I got to his office, he was dead, and Claver was searching the place."

Natasha nodded slowly.

"Okay," she said, "so Turov sent you in there to catch Claver. That's what you're claiming. Let's assume you're right."

Of course, that wasn't what I was saying at all. But now that I thought about it, it did make a certain kind of sense. The timing did seem oddly precise, after all.

"So," Carlos said, leaning in, "Claver was obviously looking for something he thought Nagata had. Maybe he found it, maybe he didn't. Later on though, another party came looking for the same thing."

"The squid commando, right," I said.

"Just one agent?" Kivi asked. "Why wouldn't the cephalopods send an army?"

Natasha answered that one. "Maybe they only have a few of these suits. Or maybe it takes a lot of power to generate the transportation effect."

"Any theories on how they might be doing that, by the way?" I asked.

She shrugged. "Entanglement theory? A one-man Alcubierre drive system? I don't know. I'd have to see one of these units."

My eyes must have shifted. Della caught that.

"Oh no," she said.

"What?" Carlos demanded.

"He's got one," she said. "That's it, isn't it James? You've got one of these alien jump-suits."

My eyes ran over the group. "Yeah. It's in the tram outside. Keep it down."

"Holy testicles!" Carlos exclaimed.

Natasha's eyes were alight. Her hand, which had leapt from mine like I'd bitten her a few minutes before, slipped back to touch me again.

"I want to see it," she whispered hotly.

I smiled. I had them. I had them all. They were hooked.

The best part was I hadn't even told them about Claver's body yet.

We couldn't very well reveal our discovery in a bar or a parking lot. Della lived close to Central, so we went to her place.

The group had traveled using public transport to make it harder to be traced. I was the only one with a private vehicle on hand.

We piled in, and the complaints began. The girls were upset about having to cram into the back with Claver's body. As experienced legionnaires, they were hardly squeamish, but they could still get disgusted.

"He doesn't smell right," Della complained. "Did you burn his flesh?"

"A little," I admitted.

"I thought you said you killed him with a machete," Carlos pointed out.

"That's right, but I was still pissed off after that. I beamed him in the throat to be sure."

"Have you got his pistol?"

I reached under my seat and handed it over.

"Hmm," Carlos said. "This is illegal."

"So sue me."

"I mean it's unregistered, non-standard, and you don't have the right license to possess this weapon on Earth."

"It's probably a squid weapon. You calling the cops, Carlos?"

"I'll let you off with a warning this time."

When we reached Della's place, we were immediately disappointed.

Her apartment was on the fourth floor. Instead of taking the elevator, she insisted we climb the fire escape. She ran up the ladder like a monkey, and after admiring the view for a second, I sighed and followed her, hauling the corpse with me.

The alleyway where we'd parked had the look of a place that had seen more than one murder before. We covered Claver with a tarp from the little trunk anyway and grunted our way steeply up to the fourth floor.

"No elevator?" Carlos complained as he stepped into the window. "What century is this?"

"There's an elevator," Della said, "but it has cameras. There are no cameras on the fire escape."

"Oh yeah... right."

When we'd gathered in Della's starkly furnished place, we examined the suit. Carlos was the bio, so he was given the job of removing Claver from the suit and examining him. His lip stayed slightly curled during the exam, but he did his job.

"He looks human enough. The squids didn't do anything especially weird to him. According to my med kit he's been breathing off-world air, but that's hardly a surprise."

"This suit was definitely constructed for a cephalopod," Natasha said, her eyes shining. "The fabric matches their known standards, and the configuration matches their anatomy. There's a power unit, a control box and some instrumentation. It's kind of simple, for what it does."

"Yeah," I said, "that's what I thought. It doesn't seem possible that a thing like this could transport itself around the cosmos."

"Maybe there's, like, a squid fortress right under Central," suggested Carlos. "And maybe they're not really coming from their home planet. Maybe they're just popping in from a short distance away and attacking us that way."

"That's actually not a bad theory," I said.

Carlos beamed. He rarely got compliments of any kind, so he had to make the most of it when he did get one.

We fooled around with the suit for several minutes, taking readings, photos and making observations. Della and I stayed quiet throughout most of this time, as the others had more training in bio science and tech than we did.

But along about two hours into the investigation, something happened that changed everything.

"What the hell...?" demanded Carlos. "You touched it, didn't you?"

He pointed at me, accusing me of something.

"Touched what?"

"That button—dial—whatever. You—"

He trailed off, as the suit began to shimmer. The room darkened, and my vision blurred. I knew all too well what that meant.

50

"Get away from it!" I shouted.

But I was too late.

Natasha had always been fascinated with tech. She'd been in trouble for creating artificial life since college, and there'd never been a toy made by an alien intellect she didn't want to dismantle and play with.

Unsurprisingly, she was the last one to remove her hands from the surface of the suit. She wavered when the effect reached its zenith, like everything around us.

When the blurring effect ended the suit was gone... and so was Natasha.

-8-

After we got over our initial shock, we crept closer to the spot—and stared. We must have looked like a pack of monkeys trying to figure out a mouse trap.

"Poor Natasha...why'd it have to be her?" Kivi asked.

"Why her?" Carlos demanded. "Because she had her hands into those sleeves a meter deep. She's always been too curious for her own good."

"You dick," Kivi said. "She's been permed, and you're making jokes?"

"Permed?" Carlos asked.

I glanced at both of them and slowly nodded.

"Yeah," I said. "Kivi's probably right. Natasha might well be permed. If I can't find a way to get her back, that is."

"Why?" Carlos demanded. "They've got the data core working again. We'll just tell them she was vaporized by an experiment gone bad. They'll pop her right back out of a revival machine by morning."

I shook my head. "No. I don't think so. We've got no body. If we show them the vids and sensor data on this suit, they'll know she's been transported somewhere else. No body, no revive. You know the rules."

"That's bullshit..." he muttered weakly.

"We have to get out of here," Kivi said. "This place is no longer safe."

"What do you mean?" I asked.

"The enemy will have this apartment zeroed soon if they don't already. I'm sure they must be able to tell where the suit came from. They'll trace it back to this place."

"What enemy?" I asked.

"James," she said, "you don't think this suit is a secret? You don't think whoever made it will try to come here and make sure we keep quiet?"

"You want to bail out of here now?" Carlos asked Kivi. "What if Natasha comes back? What if she figures out how to get the suit to transport her home again? She might need our help."

"I'll stay," Della said. "I'll watch the place discreetly. If she returns—or something else does—I'll contact you."

"Good idea," I said. "Okay, I think we have no choice now. We have to take this to Graves at least. It's gone beyond anything we can handle."

"Graves will screw us," Carlos said.

"Yeah, probably. But that's the only chance we have of getting Natasha back."

The group grumbled, but we loaded the newly unencumbered corpse of Claver back into his tarp and headed down the fire escape. After sort of forcing Claver to fold in half, we found he now fit neatly into the tiny trunk of my folk's tram. Carlos helped me lean on the lid until it latched, and we piled into the seats. Della stayed behind.

Carlos looked agitated once we began crossing the city toward Central.

"What's wrong?" I asked him.

"I don't know… I mean, I don't know why I have to go put my head on a platter with Graves. I'll never get rank."

"You want to bail out now?" Kivi demanded from the back seat. "You coward."

"What good can I do anyone? I'm a bio. Kivi, you've got the tech data, the recordings. They'll listen to you. McGill, you're an officer. You'll be fine."

"Sure I will. Brass loves shit like this."

We drove on for a time in silence.

"Are you going to let me out on the street, or what?" Carlos asked.

"No," I told him. "I need witnesses. Besides, your face is in the vids. In fact, your hairy butt mooned the camera-stick at one point as I recall."

"Ohhh... damn. Okay, right. I'm screwed. Let's just do this. Somebody break out some handcuffs and shock-rods."

Glumly, we drove up to Central and parked the tram on the street. We got out, but before we could go inside, a dark shape hummed and swooped down on us.

It was an air car. A fancy one. I thought I recognized it, so I waited for the cupola to pop open.

Sure enough, Imperator Turov climbed out. She wasn't alone, either. Primus Winslade got out of the car with her.

"Evening Imperator," I said loudly. "Nice night for a drive."

"Shut up, McGill," she said. "Do you know how long we've been staking out Central looking for your rattle-trap piece of shit tram?"

"I'm sorry if I wasted your valuable time, sir, but I'm wanted inside, and I—"

"No more games, McGill," Winslade said, stepping around with a laser carbine in his hands. "Hand over the suit. We know you have it."

"Damn," I said. "I can't get away with anything in this town. All right, it's in the trunk."

Carlos and Kivi exchanged glances. They looked nervous but ready for anything. Winslade and Turov both outranked us by a multiple of about a thousand each, but they were way off script with this gangster routine. I knew my friends were calculating how far we could go in defending ourselves, if it came down to that.

Even more importantly, I knew my little core group of peers was watching *me*. They'd take their cue on how to behave and run with it. They were loyal that way—they'd follow me off a cliff if I led them to the edge. The funny thing was, they'd probably bite and curse and kick me all the way down to the rocky bottom of said cliff—but they'd follow me, all the same.

Cheerfully, I opened the tram's trunk. Winslade edged around to look. He had the carbine on me the whole time, as if he expected me to pull something. People often treated me with a pathological paranoia I didn't fully understand.

Winslade explored my cargo with the tip of his weapon.

"What the hell...?" he said. "Is that Claver? What'd you do, burn him—?"

That was as far as he got. In his moment of distraction, I slammed the lid of the tram down on his carbine, catching him on the wrist as he'd been prodding the corpse with the gun barrel.

I think I did it too hard. There was a cracking sound, and Winslade began hissing something awful.

"Oh, crap. I'm sorry about—"

"McGill, you difficult piece of—" Turov spat in my ear. She'd moved on me, putting a small flat pistol to my head.

"No way, Imperator," Carlos interrupted from behind her. She turned to see both Carlos and Kivi standing to either side. They both had their service knives out, glittering in the street lights.

"Look," I said, "everyone seems overly tense. Let's call a truce and move to a safe location. If I may point out the obvious, the AI governing the cameras has noticed the excitement and probably dispatched MPs by now."

Turov sneered. "I shouldn't be surprised that I'm looking at a dead body in your trunk instead of a magic squid-suit."

She looked over her shoulder then and cursed. An MP detachment was already approaching. There was no mistaking that quadruple set of blue-white spotlights crawling over the street as they glided toward us.

"Get in my car—all of you," Turov ordered.

"What about him?" Carlos said, indicating the body still inside my open trunk.

I slammed the lid down in response, and we all got into the air car. We launched into the sky with alarming speed. The MP vehicle stopped and did a slow perusal of the site. Fortunately, they were ground-bound and legally prohibited from forcing my trunk open without a warrant.

After a few seconds, one of the cops got out. He flipped us the bird, then printed a ticket and shoved it under the wiper blades.

"Bastard…" I muttered.

My dad hated tickets. At least I hadn't littered the tram's cabin with hamburger wrappers this time.

Satisfied they weren't going to find Claver immediately, Turov veered away and took off toward her place.

We landed on the roof in the pitch black. There weren't even any landing lights on her air car.

"You modified this thing for stealth?" Carlos asked. "That's illegal. Did you know that?"

"Shut up, Specialist," she said. "And Winslade, shut up about your arm. McGill could have killed you—I probably would have."

Winslade pouted, and we all headed upstairs. Turov distributed drinks to everyone, giving nano-sutures and painkillers to Winslade.

While Winslade worked on his arm, Carlos moved to help him. He was a bio, after all. He had the bone set and injected the nanos into the site with a skilled hand.

"Okay," Turov told me. "It's time we laid our cards on the table."

"Yes, I agree."

"What do you know about this project?"

"So it's a project? A defense project? In that case, why's Claver involved?"

She rolled her eyes. "It's a military project, but not one sponsored by our government. The cephalopods have decided to move on us and take over. They will gain control of Earth shortly."

That statement threw us all for a loop. My mouth sagged open.

"You're a traitor?" I demanded. "You're straight-up admitting that to me?"

"Not at all. I'm saving Earth— the only way it can be done."

"Through surrender?"

She made a flapping motion of dismissal with her hand. She strutted around while she talked, but for once I didn't even care to admire her form.

This was big. This was serious. This was treason.

"Listen to me, McGill," she said. "You, out of everyone in Earth's military, should be able to understand. The Cephalopod Kingdom is unbeatable to us. They have three hundred worlds compared to our one."

"But the Empire—"

"The Empire is a toothless old man. Battle fleet 921 has left this province and will never return. We have to fend for ourselves. All I'm suggesting is you keep an open mind while I explain things to you—can you do that?"

"An open mind is an empty mind, my momma always said," I told her.

She rolled her eyes at me.

"Just listen. Earth capitulated to the Empire a century ago. We're doing the same thing this time. We'll become a vassal state to a different set of aliens in order to survive. Does that make sense to you?"

"Uh... sort of. But I don't recall this being brought up as a possibility on the news vids. Nor do I think the governing council has voted it into law."

"I would expect you're right about that," she said. "Often in these situations, the old guard doesn't want to accept new realities. They would prefer to die standing on tradition rather than live under a new set of rules—or rulers, in this case."

For about a minute, I studied my hands and thought hard. Many things were pieced together in my brain during that short time.

Claver and Turov had worked together before. They'd both dealt with aliens illegally as well—but this was *big*. They were talking about a coup. About taking over Earth. I was fuzzy on how they planned to do it, but that was obviously the goal.

Looking back up at Turov, I saw her in an entirely different light. Ever since I'd met the woman, I'd known she was ambitious to a fault. She was a pragmatist, an egotist and God knew what-all else. But still, I wouldn't have quite guessed she was capable of this kind of sweeping scheme. Claver yes,... but Turov? She'd surprised me.

"You trust Claver?" I asked her

"Absolutely not," she said.

"What hold do you have over him then? That man is as slippery as a flea on a snake. You can't deal with him unless you have an angle."

"You've dealt with him quite effectively, it seems to me," Winslade commented in his usual snotty tone.

"Listen, McGill," Turov said. "I need muscle. You're a man of action. You get things done. That's very valuable to me."

I thought hard for another few moments.

"I want Natasha back," I said. "I want a revive for her—immediately after this is over."

Turov's lips spread into a smile.

"Done," she said.

"James, we can't trust her," Kivi said in my ear.

Turov ignored her. She knew she had my attention, so she didn't care what Kivi said.

Turov just kept staring into my eyes, like a cat staring down a mouse.

-9-

The plan was simple. We landed on Central's roof at 4:03 am. Attacks usually came just before dawn for a reason—that's when people were their most bleary-eyed and fuzzy of mind.

We left Winslade with his broken wrist in the air car. Armed only with our service pistols, we escorted Turov to the elevator. There were two guards there. They checked our IDs and let us pass. After all, Turov was brass.

On the way down in the elevator, we didn't even talk. Carlos and Kivi exchanged worried looks, but they weren't saying anything. They had orders from superiors, one of whom was a friend, so they were playing along. They were nervous, sure, just like I was. After all, we were doing something that was bat-shit crazy on the face of it.

But the plan was simplicity itself. The first squid attack on Central had been designed to take out certain key members of the brass with combat experience. Men like Nagata had to go.

The second step was even more sinister. The defense networks were located deep underground, beneath Central. These computers managed communications and planet-wide defenses. If they could be knocked out, our fleets wouldn't stand a chance against the Cephalopod Armada that was closing in on our star system even now.

Turov had explained it to us this way: we'd be saving lives. Possibly, we'd save the life of everyone on Earth. If Earth didn't fight, but capitulated instead, we'd be a valuable vassal state for the squids. We could give them intel on the Empire and provide them with an unusually strong planetary defense force that could be used in the wars that were sure to be in our future.

As we moved deeper and deeper into Central, particularly when we went underground, the guards became less congenial. Turov's rank was no longer enough to sway them.

When a frowning hog veteran finally put his hand up and shook his head, we were stopped dead.

Turov frowned in return, pulling out a computer scroll and consulting it. She shook her head.

"We're not close enough yet. McGill!"

I didn't want to do it. I really didn't. But I saw no other choice. I shot the hog veteran, and then I shot the two men who were lounging in the hallway behind him. None of them even managed to pull their guns out of their holsters.

With shocked looks, they slumped to the floor.

"Excellent," Turov said.

As she used her Galactic Key to bypass the security locks, an alarm went off. Apparently, the system couldn't keep us out, but it was still smart enough to know something had gone very wrong.

"Pick up the pace," Turov ordered, "we've only got about three minutes left."

She began to run down the passage, and we followed at a rapid jog.

"This is bullshit McGill!" Carlos hissed to me. "Let's arrest her and call ourselves heroes."

"We'll be dead heroes," Kivi said. "We've gone too far. They'll perm us after torturing us to death a dozen times."

I didn't answer either one of them. I just kept running after Turov. My reluctant companions trotted after me, not knowing what else to do.

We made it to an empty meeting room just outside the data center. A handful of nerds were there, drinking coffee to stay awake.

We gave them a reason to perk up. Bursting in with our guns out, they scrambled to their feet and ran. Turov shot two in the back, then let the rest go.

"Push the tables out of the way!" she ordered.

We moved the tables to the sides of the room.

"This is where they're coming through. It's the only area big enough and open enough to allow a full squad to jump in at once."

I only half-knew what she was talking about, but I saw the timer on her tapper. There was only one minute to go.

"Pull back to the entrance," I ordered.

"What?" Turov demanded. "What are you talking—"

I grabbed her. First she squeaked, then she raged. "Let go of me, or you'll never see Natasha—"

"Look at your tapper, Imperator."

She did, and her eyes widened. There were only nineteen seconds left.

I backed up into the doorway and stood with her in front of me. I had my pistol at her back.

"I have to open the doors to the data center!" she shouted, lifting the Galactic Key in her hand. "You're screwing this up, McGill!"

I plucked the key from her fingers. "I'll take care of that—thanks. When you revive, Imperator, take credit for everything and play the part of the hero. You do that so very well."

For the rest of her short lifespan, Imperator Turov cursed my name loudly and repetitively.

During that same brief period, the squids began popping in. They seemed disoriented for a few seconds after jumping, and that was all the opportunity we needed. We shot them down one by one.

"Don't wreck the suits," I told Kivi and Carlos. "Keep firing at their heads."

Squids don't die easily, even when you nail one in the brain-pan. Two of them made it to us.

One reached up a long, long tentacle and grabbed Turov. Some might have claimed I shoved her into his grasp, but I'll always maintain that was an optical illusion. She was taken from me by the inexorable strength of that single, worm-like limb.

Dragging her into a clutch, the two squids who had survived thrashed on the floor. They lived long enough to tear her limb from limb. We shot them over and over until they stopped flopping around.

Just like that, the commando attack had been thwarted. Security forces arrived and viewed the scene with horror. Bodies, blood and wisps of vapor filled the room.

"Who the hell are you?" roared a hog centurion.

He put his gun in my face, and we all put our hands up.

"I'm Adjunct James McGill, sir," I said smartly. "Sorry we didn't have time to go through regular channels on this, but we—"

"Did you shoot my guards, Adjunct?"

"Sir, Imperator Turov ordered me to do so in order to help her on this mission."

"Imperator…?"

He looked down then, stunned to see who was lying in pieces at my feet.

"*She* led this action?"

"She's the real hero here, sir. She found out about the squid commando raid and grabbed some commandos of her own to counter it."

He stood up slowly then walked around the room, kicking dead squids. A few of them shivered at his touch, and he jumped back warily.

"What was their plan?" he asked.

I almost blew it then. I almost smiled. But I managed to stay business-like. I had the fish on the hook, and all I had to do was reel him in.

The next half-hour we spent explaining that Turov knew about a squid attack on Central somehow, and how she'd been quick-thinking enough to call up my team and order us to counter it.

I could have turned in Turov, of course. I could have said she was a traitor to all humanity. The real truth was monstrous. She not only wanted Earth to be defeated, she wanted us to serve the squids as fighting slaves.

But there were serious problems with that level of truthfulness. The brass wouldn't be happy with an easy tale of Turov's treachery. They'd want to lump us into the whole thing. Why hadn't we stopped her? Why hadn't we warned Central?

The truth, of course, was that Central wouldn't have acted quickly enough. I knew there was an attack coming, but not exactly where or how it would go down. In order to get Turov to take me to the exact spot I needed to be at the right time to shoot down the squids, I had to play along with her game.

The brass wouldn't have been happy if I told that story. They'd have hung me along with Turov. I was damned if I did, and damned if I didn't. That's why I'd written my own script and played my own tune. Now, all I had to do was get away with it.

We repeated our story on up the chain of command. By the time we were marched up to the VIP offices again, we'd been disarmed and handcuffed.

Most importantly, I'd managed to hold onto the Galactic Key. They'd taken it from me and looked it over, but as it resembled a seashell with no obvious interface capabilities, they'd given it back to me before taking us upstairs.

The hogs were understandably pissed and confused. They took me to a fancy office on the three hundredth floor and let me into the room. Carlos and Kivi were left outside under guard.

"Ah," Winslade said. "I see you finally made it, Adjunct."

My eyes flashed up to meet his in surprise. Winslade had always been able to redefine the word slippery, but even for him, this move was masterful. Somehow, he'd kept himself from being arrested at all.

"Good to see you too, Primus," I said. "You can corroborate my story?"

Winslade's eyes widened then narrowed again. He had no idea what kind of tall tale I'd told the guards.

"To a point," he said noncommittally.

There was only one other person in the room. None other than Tribune Drusus watched the interplay between the two of us. He was the commander of Legion Varus. He outranked Winslade, but Turov outranked him.

The trouble was, Drusus was no pushover. He was almost as good at detecting bullshit as I was at slinging it.

"It's simple enough, sirs," I said to both of them. "I've got nothing to hide. As best I understand it, Turov got wind of a squid commando attack on Central. Apparently, she didn't have enough time to go through channels and explain herself. She brought us along, and we battled the squids downstairs. Fortunately, we stopped them before they achieved their mission goals."

Winslade relaxed a fraction. Apparently, my bullshit matched his—or at least it was close enough.

"Exactly," he said. "It's just as I told you, Tribune. Turov deserves a medal."

Tribune Drusus hadn't said a word throughout this exchange. He'd just been watching the two of us as we went back and forth.

"There's only one problem, gentlemen," he said. "I don't believe a word of this."

I looked dumbfounded. Winslade pretended to be indignant. "Really, Tribune?" he asked in a hurt tone. "I don't think casting aspersions is an appropriate—"

"Stuff a sock in it, Winslade," Drusus said. "Let me give you an alternate scenario: Turov is mixed up in this somehow, I'm willing to buy that. She might even be in contact with the cephalopods."

Winslade made an inarticulate gasping sound, as if scandalized. I kept a flat, dumb-ass expression frozen on my face.

"Yes," Drusus continued, "that's right. I wasn't born yesterday. I know her ambitions are beyond measure. She'd be just the type to learn of an attack and cook up an insane scheme like this to gain status as a heroic figure. The only trouble is, she's no commando herself."

Winslade picked up on his thread of logic with smooth grace. He was still going with outrage.

"Tribune," he said, "jealousy of the Imperator's achievements doesn't flatter you."

Drusus gave him a sour glance, then he turned to me. "That's where you come in, McGill. What are the odds of us finding a room full of death and you standing in the middle of

64

it? You should be ashamed of yourself for getting tied up in this mess. It besmirches all of Legion Varus."

"I'm sorry sir," I said, contriving a rueful look.

Winslade and I were both copping to a lesser charge. Drusus seemed to be buying that Turov wasn't a traitor, but a glory-hound. That was an infinite improvement as we were both tightly tied to her fate.

Drusus dragged in a breath then let it out slowly.

"Now," he said, "if both of you understand you've been reprimanded, it's time we discussed my new orders. I've been put in charge of Earth's defensive network."

With a flair, he took out a double-starred rank insignia—the twin sunbursts of an imperator. Despite everything, I was impressed. He'd gained rank in a big hurry, probably because so many of the top brass were dead.

"Congratulations, sir," I said with feeling. "But what about all the hogs that were in line ahead of you?"

He shrugged. "In times of true peril, even bureaucrats can become desperate enough to face reality. There are very few senior officers on Earth with decades of combat experience. Besides, most of the existing Hegemony brass have been permed."

"Right…" I said, thinking about it. "Only real mercenary legionnaires have been to the stars. With the upper ranks wiped out, the council put you in charge of everything, is that right?"

"Not of everything. The fleet is independent. They're up in orbit now, trying to patrol the system. They're understandably nervous."

"That's a good idea, sir," I said. "I believe the cephalopods intend to attack us."

Winslade tossed me a venomous glance which I pointedly ignored.

"An interesting supposition," Drusus said. "I've come to much the same conclusion. What information do you have about it, McGill?"

"Not much—but I know who does. Claver's body is outside, in the trunk of my tram. If we were to revive him… well, he might know more about this incoming attack than anyone else does."

Playing my trump card, I proceeded to tell him about Claver and his squid jump-suit. Drusus listened intently. During my talk, Winslade moved to slip out the door behind me.

"Where are you going, Primus?" Drusus asked loudly.

"Nowhere, sir! I just thought I might take a moment to use the facilities…"

"You can hold it," Drusus said, "or you can piss down your leg. I don't care which."

Reluctantly, Winslade took his good hand away from the door.

After Drusus was satisfied he had our stories straight in his mind, he let us go. My handcuffs were removed, and I was thrown out of his office.

In the lobby, I found Carlos and Kivi had been dismissed. I figured I could catch up with them later and headed toward the bio-level.

Winslade caught up with me and strode along beside. He seemed upset.

"McGill," he whispered loudly, "I'll get you for this. For all of it."

I glanced at him in surprise. "What's your problem, Primus? I thought you'd be happy."

"Happy? About what?"

"You attempted treason, and you're still not permed, for one thing. Not yet, that is."

He glared at me. We reached the elevator and rode down a few floors in angry silence. I figured he owed me, but somehow he didn't see it that way.

"The damage you've done," he sputtered at last, "I told her not to trust you."

"Damage? The way I see it, I saved the world from squid slavery."

He laughed bitterly. "Saved it? The cephalopods are still coming, you know. They'll show us no mercy now."

"We'll see," I said shrugging. "Better to die on our feet than live on our knees, anyway."

"Noble words to kill your home planet with," he said, then broke off and looked around. The doors opened. "Floor two thirty-one? Why has the elevator stopped here?"

"Because I chose this floor to get off," I said.

Without further comment, I stepped off and left him in the elevator car. I could feel his eyes burning a hole in my back. He was full of anger and suspicion. I knew he might well shoot me in the back. It wouldn't be the first time that had happened.

I heard slapping feet behind me. "Blue level? The bio people? Are you injured?"

I didn't even look at him. "Nope."

The wheels worked in his head.

"Turov? You're here because she's being revived now—that has to be it."

"Only took you two guesses, sir. You're getting better."

He narrowed his rat-like eyes. "I get it, but I'm not sure of your plan. Are you here to kill her or coach her?"

Glancing down at the shorter man, I smirked. "I'm in enough trouble without killing officers. I'd never do that."

"Right..." he snorted. "Let's get our stories aligned this time. I almost had a heart attack when you were talking to Drusus."

"What do you suggest?"

"Don't show yourself right away. Hold back. I'll speak to the Imperator. She'll be more cooperative that way."

Shaking my head, I refused. "No sir. That's the wrong play. I'll greet her. She'll think I'm the one whose story she must align with."

"You're certain she'll overcome her natural anger at seeing your face again?"

"Initially, no. But she'll play along. She's always good at analyzing her situation and making a safe move."

The corridor we were in wasn't like the other levels of Central I'd been on. There were no doors except for the occasional janitor's closet. When we got to the big blue doors of the bio level, we were challenged.

Winslade's rank got us past security. He also seemed to have a blanket clearance for the building. That was probably Turov's doing.

We stepped into the inner sanctum and found it bustling with activity. The bio people were rushing around, carting supplies of raw bone meal and blood plasma from one room to another.

"What's going on?" I asked a specialist with two barrels as big as she was stacked up on a power-cart. "Are you still doing revives from the attack?"

"That's right," she said, looking stressed. "One of our ships must have been hit. The whole crew is queued up for revival."

Winslade and I exchanged worried glances.

She wasn't talking about the attack on Central. She was talking about a battle on-going in space. Apparently, the war we'd all feared had begun.

-10-

Fortunately, the bio people were too freaked out about reviving fleet crewmen to question a couple officers who wanted to see Turov's rebirth. They let us into the waiting area immediately outside the revival center. I calmly strode over to the nearest bio with an admin look to her and leaned in for an earnest word. She nodded and I headed back for my seat.

Nervous as a cat in a bag, Winslade eyed everyone that walked past.

"Do you think they know yet?" he asked me in a whisper.

"Know what?"

His eyes slid to me and then he shook his head. "That we fabricated this whole business of being cephalopod-killing heroes."

"No, no way."

"How can you be so sure?"

I chuckled. "Because I'm still breathing, that's why. Stop worrying so much. We'll be fine. Turov won't blow our cover—at least not until she's sure she can blame everything on us."

After thinking this over, he nodded to himself and sat back in his creaky waiting-room chair.

We didn't have long to wait. The doors flapped open and an efficient-looking bio stepped out, glancing around. Her eyes fixated on me.

"Are you Adjunct McGill?" she asked.

"Yes ma'am."

"Come with me, Adjunct. The Imperator is up and asking for you."

Winslade stood up and followed me, but the bio put her hand on his chest firmly.

"Just McGill, sir," she said. "I'm sorry."

She didn't sound sorry, but I could have been mistaken.

Winslade blustered, pulling rank and all that. But none of that would wash with any bio on their own turf. I could have told him that. They had jurisdiction here, just as they did on any Blue Deck in the fleet.

I left Winslade behind, enjoying how he hopped from foot-to-foot in agitation while he watched me stroll into the revival chamber.

The smell of the place hit me right off. I'd never liked it. It always reminded me of blood, disinfectant and stale piss all mixed together.

Turov was up, but she wasn't quite on her feet yet. She was naked, of course, and dripping with slime. She still had her wet butt on the gurney she'd been delivered on. Her eyes were squinting, and her teeth were clenched. The bio people were trying to towel her off, but she was hissing and slapping them away.

"Imperator," I boomed. "Good to see you're back and ready to lead us to victory!"

"You bastard, McGill," she said. "I'll see you in Hell for this."

"Hah-ha," I chuckled nervously. "A little off-kilter, huh? Maybe you don't remember everything clearly. We saved Earth, sir. We're heroes. The brass is very happy."

She snatched a towel from a bio specialist and rubbed at her eyes with it. "This shit always burns my eyes. Why don't they fix that?"

"It's been a while since you were revived, I guess?"

She glared at me. Suddenly aware of her nakedness, she ripped a nano-cloth suit from the hands of an attending bio and wrapped it around herself. The fabric crawled and inched its way over her body until her bare skin was hidden underneath. It was a shame to see it go.

"I knew you'd be waiting for me to come out," she said. "But how did you get past their security?"

That perked up the bio people. The chief specialist frowned. "He told us you required a briefing the moment you were revived, Imperator. We're sorry if—"

"No," she said, "forget it. It's all right."

She seemed to be regaining her wits and her composure. I was glad, as it had been looking like she was going to blow our entire plot open wide a minute ago.

"Where's that weasel Winslade?" she asked me.

"He's just outside," I said. "Weaseling, as you might expect."

She took two steps then her left knee gave out. Her hand flew out, and I caught her by the wrist.

"Let go of me, you ape!"

"You almost took a nasty fall there, Imperator."

Reluctantly, she let me walk her to the door and out into the waiting area. The bio people hovered around us, but they weren't quite sure what to do. Normally, they were bossy with newly revived troopers. But Turov was so high-ranked she must have scared some respect into them.

One of them pushed a computer scroll at me, and I signed the release. She gave me a nod and an eye-roll. I knew what that meant: they thought Turov was suffering from minor dementia, and they were glad to make her my problem.

When you get revived, sometimes your circuitry doesn't all knit-up right off. I likened it to waking up from a long, deep sleep. You might get up refreshed and bounce out of bed. Or, you might fall out and stumble around, cursing and confused.

Turov seemed to be experiencing the latter type of revival right now. The bio people didn't know that she also had a very good reason to be pissed off at me. They'd explained it away in their heads, and I was just fine with that.

"Imperator!" Winslade gushed, clapping his hands together. "You look even younger and even lovelier than you—"

"Shove it up your ass, Winslade. Get out of my way!"

She walked weakly toward the exit. I was still holding her up by one wrist, but she seemed not to notice. By the time we

71

all made it to the elevators, she was walking normally and slapping at my hands as if I'd been taking liberties.

"Dying sucks," she said in a guttural voice.

"Yes sir," I agreed.

Winslade had the brains to stay quiet. He followed us like a nervous ghost and tried to stand out of her sight. That was a difficult trick in an elevator, but he managed it somehow.

"Give me the sitrep," she said when the door dinged. "Where do we stand?"

"Well…" I said, not quite sure where to begin, "the squid commando raid was successfully repelled. But they seem to have taken a dim view of that reality. They've attacked our fleet. I don't know all the details, but it seems that at least one of our battle-wagons has been destroyed."

Turov looked at me with hatred. "*Now* do you see why I took drastic action? We're at war with a fleet ten times the size of ours. We can't win. It's just a matter of time until they come here and burn Earth to bedrock."

I nodded thoughtfully.

"Could be," I admitted. "I just couldn't stomach the idea of trading the distant Galactics for the squids. They annoy the hell out of me."

She nodded slowly, studying me.

"I miscalculated. I'd thought you were simple, but useful. Instead you've turned out to be uncontrollable—a monster that must be put down."

"I told you," Winslade dared to say, speaking up from behind her.

That was a mistake on his part. Whirling around, she drew my pistol from its holster before I could react and shot him in the chest.

Lunging forward, I grabbed her wrist.

My eyes widened when I saw the pistol wasn't there. She'd dropped it—and caught it with her other hand.

"Good night, McGill," she said.

Then, that ungrateful woman shot me in the face.

-11-

I'm not sure I'd ever gone out like that before, shot in the nose at point-blank range. When I came back to life, I could remember the heat of the beam on my skin, and the brilliance of it hurting my eyes.

Gasping, breathing hard, I felt myself becoming angry before I'd even left the table.

With a growl, I pushed away the orderly. A bio came at me with a hypo full of sedative—but I straight-armed her and sent her sprawling on the floor.

Then a powerful hand grabbed each of my wrists. I struggled, still half-blind. Finally, I stopped to take a breath. I felt winded.

"You listening to us now, Adjunct?" said a familiar, gravelly voice.

Graves... What was Graves doing here in the bio room? I couldn't see his eyes yet, because my own weren't fully operating. But I knew they were steel-gray and pitiless.

"I don't think he came out right in the head, Centurion," said another voice. It was Veteran Harris. "He's crazy. Let's put him down and reroll."

"No time for that. We've got orders."

I was hauled by the two men from the gurney, and a jumpsuit was stretched over my body.

Harris was your classic legionnaire non-com. He was big, black and mean. His idea of a good time was killing recruits for their first time in rigged training exercises.

"Walk, McGill," Graves said.

I did my best, shuffling along. After ten seconds, my feet could leave the ground when I took a step. One minute later we were in the hallway, and I was walking unaided.

"I'd like to catch a shower, sir," I said.

"No go. Events are happening in real-time, McGill."

"What's happening?"

"First of all, we're at war."

I nodded. "I know that much. How's our fleet holding out?"

Harris and Graves exchanged glances.

"Not good. We lost a lot of ships in the first engagement. The boys made a good accounting of themselves, but it wasn't enough. Turns out our puff-crete bathtubs can fight, but we're outnumbered. We've lost thirty ships, and even though they took fifty of the enemy down with them—"

I stopped walking and grabbed his shoulder. "Thirty?"

"You heard me. Half the fleet is gone. The rest broke off. They're beating a long, spiraling retreat around Jupiter."

"What the hell good will that do?"

"We've got a few missile bases at Jupiter, on the moons out there. But more importantly, running will buy us more time down here to prepare for our final stand."

I felt sick, and it wasn't just due to the revive. It was the magnitude of the disaster we faced sinking in. Had I made a gruesome mistake? Had I, in refusing to surrender, ensured the death of my species?

It was one thing to give up my own life. I'd done that more times than I could count. But to let the innocents of Earth be slaughtered by angry squids...

"Where are we going?" I asked.

"All the way down to the command center. Tribune Drusus is now Imperator Drusus. He's in overall command of Earth's defense."

"I knew about that... but why are we going down there? I figured we should form up above ground somewhere—maybe surround Central."

Graves chuckled. "A waste of time. If the squids break through, they'll just throw a hell-burner down here and scatter us all to radioactive dust."

Baffled, I let them take me to the command center. I'd never been inside Central's nerve center. It looked like any Gold Deck on a dreadnought to me—a really big version of Gold Deck.

There were walls of screens and intelligent work tables everywhere. People were gaming out scenarios. I caught maps of the Solar System. On each of them, there seemed to be a mass of red dots pursuing a small cluster of green.

Some of the screens depicted captains reporting in their status. Many of the ships appeared to be damaged and struggling to keep up with the fleet. I shuddered to think what would happen to any ship that couldn't stay ahead of the Cephalopod Armada.

Imperator Drusus looked up when we came near. He signed off on a report and nodded to us.

"Well, if it isn't our destroyer of worlds," he said.

I couldn't tell if he was joking or not, so I went with the best case and smiled back.

"That's me, sir!"

He didn't appreciate my enthusiasm. He tossed his computer scroll onto the table and sighed. Shaking his head, he walked away. Graves and Harris gave me a little push, and I followed him.

We stepped into a private office where Drusus sat with one leg draped over the arm of his chair. He poured himself a drink, but he didn't offer me one.

This was unusual behavior for Drusus. He'd always been confident in my presence, and he'd never slouched in his chair or drank on duty.

We all stood there while he drew a pistol out on to the table and tapped at it with an index finger.

"You know what this is, McGill?"

"Uh... a gun, sir?"

"It's *your* gun, McGill. The gun Turov used to kill you and Winslade.

"Oh, right."

The conversation trailed off. I gave him my best friendly-but-dumb look. He gave me a flat stare in return.

"Not interested in telling us what happened? Nothing worthy of a comment?"

"What? You mean Turov's crazy attack? Well… you shouldn't be too hard on her. After all, she's only died a half-dozen times in Earth's service, sir. Sometimes, a bad death goes to trooper's head. Even an officer can come out with a bad grow or a false residual memory that they can't shake. Once back on Gamma Pavonis, I was revived thinking that my momma—"

"Shut up, McGill."

"Yes, sir."

He tapped at my pistol again. I had to wonder if I was about to die by my own weapon twice in one day. That would be quite a run of bad luck—even by Legion Varus standards.

He sighed and pushed it away at last. "We detected the discharge of a weapon in the elevator. We didn't have audio, but we saw the struggle. Turov put you and Winslade down, taking you both by surprise."

"Yeah… embarrassing. There I was thinking 'don't let her hurt herself' then pop, Winslade was dead. A second later I joined him. She's small, but she's fast."

"I was more interested in her motivations. I knew something was very odd about your story, and the actions your team took here at Central before the cephalopod attack began. But with the survival of Earth in the balance, I didn't have time to figure any of it out. Now that our fleet is leading theirs on a chase, we have a few days to ponder these details."

"I'll do whatever I can to help out."

His eyes flicked up to mine, and I could tell he didn't believe a word I was saying. That's the trouble with having a reputation for hedging the truth. A man has everything he says second-guessed after that.

"Motivations…" he said. "I've been reviewing security vids. Specifically, I played back the appearance of the cephalopod commando team in the conference room at approximately 0400 hours this morning."

I gave him a polite nod and listened with a blank expression.

"At first, everything looked like your story matched. The enemy appeared, you shot them all, and along the way they grabbed Imperator Turov and dismembered her."

"That's the God's-honest-truth, sir. That's how it happened."

"But what interested me more," he went on, "occurred when I backed the video file up to a point a few minutes before the enemy arrived. Do you know what I saw?"

I shifted my weight uncomfortably from one foot to the other. I wanted to scratch, but I managed to ignore the sudden itching I felt.

"Uh... we chased the nerds out of the conference center, as I recall..."

A hard hand slammed into my back.

"You shot them down as they ran, you bastard!" Harris barked.

"Not true!" I said. "Not true at all!"

"McGill's right," Drusus said. "He didn't shoot them. Turov did."

Everyone fell silent. I could feel Harris' hot eyes on my back. He wanted a fresh excuse to kill me. He never passed up such opportunities.

"I had to slow the file down and play it in slo-mo to get the details," Drusus went on. "You held Turov. You allowed the cephalopods to kill her. Was that intentional?"

By now, I was outright squirming. There was nothing I hated more than getting caught by a pack of my own lies.

Drawing myself up to stand tall, I towered over all of them. "Damn right I let them kill her!"

"Is that because she was ordering you to resist them? Ordering you to shoot at your comrades?"

That one threw me for a loop. My mouth sagged open, and I stared in shock. I'd been prepared to admit that I'd gone along with Turov in order to stop her scheme, but to be accused of having cooked up the entire plot myself—that was too much.

"What? No sir. It was her idea. *She* contacted the squids. She had some kind of deal with them, and I stopped it."

"You realize, of course, that she's already accused you of this same crime."

Finally, at long last, I was beginning to catch on. Turov had decided to use Winslade and me as scapegoats. We were the villains in her version of events, and she was the hero. She'd shot us to make her story stronger and then run off to tell it first.

In the meantime, Drusus had been investigating and trying to figure out who was lying. Probably, it hadn't helped my case that I'd insisted on covering the truth until now.

"Get him out of here," Drusus said suddenly. "Chain him to a chair or something outside. I have to think for a while."

Harris and Graves hustled me out and did as they were ordered. Soon, I found myself alone—chained to a steel chair in the waiting room outside Drusus' office.

I've never liked confinement. Stewing for a short while, I finally got angry. With a roar, I managed to bend the steel tubing enough to make the chair, which was bolted to the floor, break free.

Panting, I managed to control myself enough to think. Blood and sweat ran off of me. I walked with the screeching chair dragging behind me by its chain leash. I made it back to the Imperator's office. I tapped on the door. Eventually, Drusus opened it.

He snatched up my pistol and frowned at me.

"Yes?" he asked.

"If I was in league with the enemy commandos, sir," I said gulping air. "Why would I have been the first one shooting them all down?"

His eyes glazed over in thought for a second. Finally, he gave a tired nod.

"Good point... in spite of many other mysteries you're released, Adjunct. Report to Graves. He has an important mission for you."

He tossed me keys, and I unchained myself.

"He does?" I asked.

"Yes," he said, returning my pistol.

I picked the weapon up in confusion. "Uh... am I going to like this mission, sir?"

He shrugged. "It's better than being executed immediately."

"Right…" I said. "Sounds good enough to me."

I left his office in a cheerful mood and went looking for Graves.

-12-

When I found Graves, he was in a training center with Harris. We were up off the ground floor, at about level ninety-something. Here, the experimental weapons systems were often tested by hog officers. At least, that's what they told me.

"This area is restricted, McGill," Graves said when I arrived.

"I know sir, but Drusus sent me here to join your mission."

He stared at me for several seconds. He seemed unhappy.

"Uh… is there a problem, Centurion?" I asked.

"Yes. It's you. Your loyalty has recently come under suspicion. I'm uncertain you're a good choice for this duty."

"Is it hazardous duty, sir?"

"Deadly."

I nodded, completely unsurprised. "And will it involve violent action?"

"Of course."

"Then I'm your man."

He stared for a few seconds longer then finally sighed. "All right. But if I catch you compromising security in any way, I'm putting you down on the spot. Like a rabid dog."

"Understood and agreed, Centurion. There will be no shenanigans, perversions or misconduct-unbecoming of any sort."

He shook his head and walked away, muttering.

Left uncertain as to my status, I followed him as if I belonged at his side. He glanced at me a few times, the way a man might eye a dog turd he wanted to avoid stepping on, but he didn't order me to back off.

"This is our newest team member," he told the small group who had gathered at the back of the chamber. "Don't let his rank fool you—he's not in charge of anything. He's a grunt on this mission, nothing more."

I stood straight and kept a pleasant expression pasted on my face as the group checked me over. I didn't recognize any of them, but I could tell they were hogs—well-built hogs that had obviously spent a lot of time working out, but hogs all the same.

They were tough-looking, but that didn't impress me much. I'd never yet met a hog I couldn't take out before he knew what was coming.

"McGill," Graves said to me, "meet Omega Team. They're Hegemony special forces. Omega Team doesn't exist, formally."

My friendly expression stayed firmly planted on my face, but it was a serious effort of will to keep it there. Among the mercenary legionnaires, Hegemony-types were a bit of a joke. Few of them had ever seen combat or even been off-world. A special forces team made up of hogs from the gym? I wasn't convinced they could be effective at all.

But I managed to nod at them and keep my mouth shut. I was proud of that simple fact.

"Where's the new gear, Centurion?" a hog veteran named Rork asked. He seemed to be in charge.

"It's coming. The techs are still fooling with it. Apparently, there are power problems."

The veteran nodded and stepped back.

"In the meantime," Graves said, "I want everyone suited up in vac gear. We have to assume there will be nothing breathable where you're going."

The hogs hustled to a bank of lockers and began dragging out vac suits. Rork tossed me a suit. He tossed it high, which caused it to flap up over my head and cover my face.

I ripped it away—but I still kept that friendly expression going. I could tell I was going to have to struggle just to keep my attitude on the positive side around these guys. They were unbearably full of themselves.

"Uh… Centurion?" I asked quietly as I pulled the suit on.

"What is it, McGill?"

"What kind of special equipment are we talking about?"

He stared at me for a moment. "You probably know more about it than the rest of us do."

"I don't get it, sir…"

He walked away. Normally, Graves and I had a good relationship. I sensed that I'd blown that by becoming involved in one of Turov's schemes.

Graves moved to talk to a group of bios and techs. He demanded to know where this 'special equipment' was and why it was late.

Harris stepped to my side when Graves was out of earshot. He wore a shitty grin.

"You still haven't figured this out yet, have you?" he asked.

"Nope."

He boomed with laughter. "That makes it all the sweeter! You see, McGill, you and your team of traitors did a lot of damage—"

"We were trying to stop an attack. Hell, we did stop it."

He flapped a hand in my face.

"Yeah, yeah," he said, "I heard all your bullshit. Made me sick then, and it still does today. You dishonored the whole damned legion. Even if you *thought* you were a hero, you should have known better than to pull your special brand of cowboy shit here at Central!"

I gave him a nod. He had a point there.

"Well, anyway…" he said, "I think you're going to get to pay us back for your sins, so I shouldn't be hard on you."

"You going to tell me what's going on or not?" I asked.

"You see that eager-beaver team of hogs puzzling out their vac-suits? They're Omegas. They've been designated the A-team—I'd call them the B-team, but you know… I'm not in charge."

"A-team for what?"

"For the first jump, of course."

My eyes met his and widened. He was delighted.

"You *really* didn't know, did you? You were completely in the dark? I love it!" Harris boomed with laughter. He clapped me on the back. His eyes were wet, he was so happy.

"McGill," he continued, "this couldn't have happened to a more deserving soldier. You're a human guinea pig, boy! The techs are powering up a fusion reactor they have in the basement. They're going to wrap you and the rest of these sorry-assed hogs up in squid-suits. Then, they'll jolt the suits with juice and see what happens."

At long last, I understood what I was in for. This hog team was supposed to try to utilize squid equipment. Only, no one had any idea how to work the suits.

We were going to attempt a jump. Right off, I found the idea fascinating and terrifying at the same time.

To jump into the blue, without a clue as to how the system worked or where you were going... Yes, that did sound like a job for James McGill.

About an hour later, the first suit arrived. The techs walked around it in a swarm. They had it laid out on a gurney like it was a fallen king. The suit had even been folded with loving care.

"Volunteers?" Graves asked the group.

I immediately raised my hand, but Graves waved me down. He pointed over my shoulder.

I turned to see that Veteran Rork from the hog group had raised his hand as well—hell, the whole squad had. Hogs or not, I had to admit they had balls.

"Get the veteran into the suit," Graves said.

The techs rushed Rork like vultures. They pressed his thick legs into two of the numerous leg-holes and the whole outfit squeezed up, resizing itself intelligently.

"Give him some juice," Graves said when they were finished.

"One second," said a tech officer, moving up to put a hand on the control panel. She was cute with small hands and small features.

"Veteran," she said to the hog in the squid-suit, "I thank you for your service."

"Glad to serve," Rork answered with pride.

83

The tech girl nodded. "Okay... as best we can tell, the suit is powered through this port here. But we don't know how much juice to give it. We've fabricated an adapter plug—but it's guesswork."

"I understand," he said stoically.

She nodded and turned to Graves. "Are you sure you want to start off with human trials already? If we took a few more days..."

"The squids will be in orbit in a week," Graves told her. "Stop wasting time."

She licked her lips and turned back to the veteran. She didn't meet his eyes this time.

"This dial here is the only control on the suit. It's not marked, except for these six points. We think it's a timer—or maybe a distance gauge. In either case, it's best that you give it just the slightest nudge to start with. That way, your journey should be short."

"I got it," he said, his face white but determined.

"First, we'll apply power," she said.

She coupled up the adapter. I noticed that the other techs were hanging well back. That concerned me, and it took all my willpower to not step away a few paces with them.

"Dial up the generator!" the tech called over her shoulder.

Her team did as she ordered, and a hum filled the room. The hum grew into a droning sound that set my teeth on edge.

Shouting now as she stepped away, the tech called out to Rork. "Go time, Veteran!"

He nodded, and he put his hand on the dial.

"For Earth and for Omega Team!" he shouted.

The rest of his hog companions cheered and pumped their fists in the air.

The veteran gave the dial a tiny nudge—and a blue-white jolt of energy was instantly released.

I knew right off that something had gone horribly wrong. When I'd seen the suit operate in the past, it had done so with a blurring effect, a quiet warp in the look of the room. This time, it was more like a bolt of lightning had struck.

And that was exactly how the veteran appeared to have been affected. One moment, he'd been standing around

84

cheering for Omega Team, and the next he'd been blasted off his feet.

He slammed the deck with his face, his body quivering and smoking. The bios rushed forward to help, but I could have told them it was pointless. Hell, the poor man's hair was on fire.

He'd been struck dead.

-13-

Graves didn't look horrified. He looked annoyed.

"Is that suit damaged?" he demanded in concern.

"Not that we can tell, sir," said the tech officer.

"Call in the revive," he ordered, then he turned on the tech girl. "Now, what the hell did you do wrong?"

She pushed a stray lock of hair out of her eyes and shook her head. The tech looked upset. Hog techs weren't used to frying people.

"I don't know... I'm so sorry."

"That doesn't cut it, Adjunct."

He turned to me next. The look on his face indicated he thought this was all my fault somehow.

"What did you do, McGill?" he demanded.

"Come on, Centurion," I said. "I stood right here and watched them electrocute that poor hog, same as you did."

He nodded and looked down at the body again. I could tell he was thinking hard.

"Sir?" Harris said. "May I make a suggestion?"

"What is it, Veteran?"

"I think McGill here is the most experienced man present in regards to this alien equipment. Hell, he's fooled around with more alien tech than both of us combined. Maybe he should go next."

I gave Harris an irritated look. He caught that and grinned back. There was almost nothing that man liked better than to see me die. We had a history, and he'd never gotten over the fact he'd lost most of the battles between us.

"It's not a bad idea," Graves said, "but I've got other plans for McGill."

He walked up to Omega Team again. "I need another volunteer."

This time, there was a wave of hesitation. Earlier, they'd all been gung-ho, but behind Graves they could see a scorch mark and a twitching, partially-cooked corpse.

I raised my hand. Harris pointed at me hopefully.

Graves ignored both of us.

"You," he said, pointing toward a big, red-headed guy with blue eyes that were closer together than a ferret's.

The startled man stepped forward. He'd been volunteered—Legion Varus style.

"Try another suit," Graves told the techs. "That one might be damaged or something."

The techs apologetically brought in another suit and helped their next victim into it. He kept up a brave front, but I could tell he was scared.

"This time, dial the power way down," Graves said.

"Got it," said the tech officer. She was shaken, but she'd put back on an air of professionalism.

I watched her work, and I decided she was the most attractive girl in the room. That might seem like a small thing, but I consider myself to be something of an authority on that topic. Call it a hobby.

They hooked up the ginger test subject, and the generator began to hum again.

Ferguson raised his fist, and his team did the same. This time around, their cheer seemed a little ragged. They didn't have the heart to give him a full-throated shout.

Feeling bad for the hog, I filled in, roaring "VARUS!" at him at the top of my lungs.

He looked at me, startled—and then they flipped the switch.

Obediently, the guinea pig tapped at the dial on his chest and cringed—but nothing happened.

"What's wrong now?" Graves boomed.

"Not enough juice," the cute tech said. "The suit didn't activate."

"Try again," he ordered.

She turned to her crew. "Reset it and bump the power up ten percent."

Sweating, the hog in the kill-suit hesitated when he put his hand on the dial the second time. I felt a measured degree of sympathy. I know from experience that it's hard to murder yourself.

"Come on, come on," Graves complained.

The poor guy did it. He nudged the dial—but again, nothing happened.

"Bump the power up again!"

The fourth time finally did the trick. As before, there was a loud snap and a puff of acrid smoke. The hog was broiled alive.

Possibly due to the reduced power levels, this guy didn't die right away. He flopped and puked, skin peeling up like it had been microwaved.

Graves shot him in the head and put his hands on his hips.

"Shit," he muttered. "Next!"

This time, none of the hogs moved. They were white-faced. They looked like they were going to make a run for it.

Stepping forward, I faced Graves.

"Give me my shot, Centurion."

He looked at me suspiciously. "What makes you so anxious to die?"

"I'm not sir," I said. "But I'd like a chance to redeem myself, if only in your eyes."

He narrowed those eyes. "You're going to teleport right out of here, aren't you? Somehow, some way, you know how these suits operate, and you're engineering your escape right in my face."

"I'm not, sir!" I said, and I meant it. "That's the God's-honest truth."

He released a heavy sigh. "All right, what the hell. Suit up Adjunct McGill."

The techs swarmed me. Their hands shook. They were freaked out by now. They'd just killed two men, and they didn't want to do it again.

"Hey," I asked the cute lead tech. "What's your name?"

She glanced at me. Her hair fell into her eyes, and she pushed it back.

"Lisa," she said.

"Lisa? How about this: If I manage to teleport, will you go out with me?"

She snorted in disbelief. "Hold up your arms."

I did as she asked, and she worked on strapping the suit onto my person. I'm a tall man, fully two meters in height, but the suit was still hanging off me like my daddy had let me borrow it. I felt the nano-tech fabric sense my dimensions and cinch up slowly.

"Come on," I said. "You're about to fry my ass. The least you can do is give me some hope."

"Can't do it," she said.

"Come *on*. I'm just talking about dinner in the cantina. A snack, even."

"Soldier, I—"

"We'll all be squid-meat in a week, anyway," I said.

That line got to her. She met my eyes, and we locked stares for a moment.

"All right, sure," she said, "but you have to jump, not fry."

Smiling hugely, I let them power me up. Then I pulled a little trick I'd been planning all along. I took the Galactic Key out of my pocket and applied it to the dial.

It was a long-shot, sure. Maybe the squids had developed this suit on their own. Maybe the Empire's universal hacking device wouldn't work for some other reason. Or maybe—the failures had nothing to do with a security system but were due to any one of a zillion other possible causes.

But I had a shot, so I took it.

After touching the key to the dial, I tapped the dial a tiny, tiny bit. The pressure I applied was so infinitesimal, I hardly felt the contact.

The room wavered. I felt a thrill of exhilaration. This was it. I was about to discover Claver's secret. Maybe, with luck, I'd find Natasha and bring her back. I was glad I had my laser pistol on me. I wasn't fully geared, but sometimes a single armed man in the right place at the right time—

All those thoughts rippled through my mind in a fraction of a second. But then, the shimmer faded.

Staring, I realized I was in the same room, but about twenty meters away from where I'd started. *I'd done it, I'd jumped!*

There were people rushing toward me. I tried to take a step toward them, but my legs wouldn't move. They were confined somehow, as if they were stuck in cement.

Harris was one of the first people to reach me. He didn't look happy or pissed—he looked disgusted.

The others all had the same expression. The tech girl, Lisa, she had her hand over her mouth in outright horror.

I looked down then. At first, I couldn't sort out what I was seeing. It looked like I was sitting on another man's lap maybe—but I was clearly standing.

Then, over a period of several seconds I began to feel faint, and I realized what I was seeing.

I'd teleported into the space another person had been occupying. I'd merged, in fact, with one of the hogs. He'd been sitting on a bench in front of the lockers, watching the experiments from what he must have thought was a safe distance.

But he'd thought wrong. I'd teleported all right—smack dab into him. Our bodies were a single disgusting mass.

The odd sensations I was feeling now made more sense. It wasn't pain, not exactly. But I could feel swelling as our two pools of blood mixed in my veins and his. My heart was still beating, as it was above his body, but since his head was about where my hips were—well, it was pretty upsetting.

My blood vessels were blocked. My guts were intertwined with his skull. My breathing quickly became short, and I fell over, taking us both down.

I couldn't even hit the floor properly. My legs, at about the knee level, had merged with that damnable bench.

Harris' face came into sight, and he peered down at me.

"Freaky," he said. "I have to admit, boy—that took balls. Where are your balls, anyway?"

"Feels like they're locked inside a hog's brain," I replied.

He grinned, and I grinned back weakly.

90

Lisa appeared next. I reached out toward her. She took my hand, her face twisting.

"Hey," I said hoarsely. "I jumped. We got a date, remember?"

She nodded weakly.

"Here," I said, pressing my Galactic Key into her hands. "Give this back to the new James McGill, will you?"

"Okay," she said. "What is it?"

"My lucky sea shell," I lied. "My mama found it for me years back."

Graves pushed his way through the crowd a moment later. He looked me over critically.

"You want me to do the honors, McGill?"

"I thought you'd never ask."

His pistol came up.

I took a breath and held it.

He shot me then, and I died immediately.

Shot twice in the head within less than twenty-four hours. That had to be some kind of a record, even for me.

-14-

The revival process went normally... if coming back from the dead can be called normal.

The first thing I did was hunt down Lisa. I found her in a lab full of weird equipment. A lot of it looked alien-made, and I had no idea what any of her gizmos did.

The tech adjunct seemed startled to see me. She moved to hide whatever was on a table behind her.

"Hey," I said, smiling. "Can you take that break yet?"

"Um..." she said. She had a funny look on her face. "I don't know if I can do it, McGill."

"Call me James. What's the problem?"

She squirmed as if she didn't know how to tell me. Looking around, I caught sight of the thing on the table behind her. It was a squid jump-suit, and it was a bloody mess. Three techs were working on it, scratching off bits of gore.

I caught on immediately. They were scraping away the merged bodies of two legionnaires. It had to be the suit I'd been wearing when I died. I understood as the suit was too valuable to be discarded.

Looking back at Lisa, I could see the strained look in her eyes. This situation was uniquely troubling to her—and to me. How was I going to capture the interest of a girl who'd just had the horrid experience of watching me die, then cleaning my innards out of the suit I'd been wearing at the time?

"Oh," I said in disappointment. "I get it. I understand. Maybe some other time."

Normally, I'd have cajoled her, but after a grim death and my second revive of the day, I was out of gas to chase her any further.

I turned away, dejected. I walked toward the exit and pushed open the door. It had one of those negative air-pressure systems on it, and it sucked a breeze up into my face.

"Wait…" she said. "James?"

Turning back around hopefully, I found she'd followed me. She pressed something into my hand. It was the Galactic Key. I couldn't believe I'd almost forgotten about it.

"Your mother's shell," she said, giving me a strange look.

"Oh yeah, thanks." I shoved the key into my pocket and moved again to leave.

I made it about a dozen steps down the corridor when I heard small, slapping feet behind me. I looked back.

Lisa fell into step beside me. I slowed down so I wouldn't outpace her.

"I thought you were grossed out," I said.

"I was, I was," she admitted. "But then I thought about what you did back there—it was such a sacrifice. So brave. My part seems trivial in comparison. I decided to swallow my reaction and fulfill my promise."

"Great," I said.

I felt like Lady Luck had finally smiled on me—just a little.

"There's just one thing, James," she said.

"Name it."

"We'll need to start off with a strong drink."

My smile broadened into a grin. "That's the best idea I've heard all damned day," I told her.

One thing swiftly led to another. I've found over the years that women decide pretty quickly if they like you or not. They tend to put a man in a box they have designed for him, too. Sometimes, it's a pretty box with a bow on it. That special space is reserved for friends a girl likes to talk to. Sorry bastards who head into it rarely escape their fate.

That box was *never* the one I wanted to be placed into. The trick I always employed was to reject the box right off, without compunction.

Lisa figured out very quickly I wasn't going to be painting my nails with her. I was dangerous, aggressive, teasing. I took her hand even before we reached the end of the corridor and entered an elevator. She shook my touch away and gave me a headshake.

A few minutes later though, by the time we were having our first adult beverage, my hand was again lingering on top of hers.

This girl wasn't like Kivi. She wasn't as lusty and direct. She didn't have that half-crazy desperation that a lot of Legion Varus girls had driving them. I guess that was because she hadn't experienced death over and over again—not yet, anyway.

But there was some of that pressure in her mind today. She was a hog, sure. She was a non-combatant used to doing dry experiments on equipment at Central. But she knew—everyone did—that the grim wars fought among the stars were about to come home to Earth.

Normally, our legions hired out and went purposefully beyond the sky in great ships to seek adventure. That had been our pattern for about a century now. But this time, death and destruction had decided to pay a visit to us instead.

"James," she said huskily after her third drink, "do you really think the cephalopods will come here? Will they break past our fleet?"

Her question startled me. I'd seen the boards in the command room. Our fleets were on the run. They'd already been beaten. There was no question that the enemy was coming here, but she didn't know it.

How widespread was the truth? Graves had mentioned this reality to everyone in the testing room, but maybe they didn't all know how grim the situation really was.

Forcing a smile, I gave her tiny hand a tiny squeeze.

"Maybe we'll stop them in space," I said, "or maybe we won't. Doesn't matter. When they get down here, the legions will finish the job."

"Won't they just bomb us?"

In my opinion, that was exactly what they'd do. But I could tell right away reality wasn't going to make this girl happy.

"Nah," I said confidently. "I know the squids personally. I've fought them and killed them with these hands. They're slavers. They want to conquer us. That's a lot harder to do than blowing up the planet. We'll stop them on the ground."

She nodded and then stared at my hands. "You've *killed* cephalopods?"

"Yep," I said. I thought about telling her I'd offed several just today, but that was supposed to be kept quiet. Apparently, she didn't know about my role in ambushing the squid-jumpers who were trying to take out the data core.

"Tell me about them."

Shrugging, I proceeded to do so. I described their fighting males, and their vicious queens who were much larger. I'd fought and killed quite a few squids, and my stories had her eyes and mouth wide open before I'd gone half-way through the list.

At last, she shook her head and threw up her hands.

"Okay, that's enough," she said. "I had no idea. It sounds like we've been at war with the Cephalopod Kingdom for years. The news vids always omit details."

"It's been a low-level conflict," I said. "We've fought on a dozen worlds. It's an age-old story. Two empires meet and collide. They grind against one another along the edges—but eventually, one side decides it can't live with the other. At that point, it's on!"

I laughed and tossed down my drink. Looking stunned, Lisa did the same.

"I've had enough," she announced. "What do you want to do next?"

There was a funny look on her face. I wasn't sure what she was thinking—but I didn't entirely care, either. I took her question in the way I wanted to.

Together, we left the bar and went up to her apartment just outside Central. The rent here had to be astronomical.

We made love in the dark, and she turned out to be as hot in bed as she was reserved and professional while on duty.

The bed was too small for two—but we didn't care. We fell asleep in a tangle of sheets and limbs.

-15-

In the morning, Lisa and I woke up late. We showered fast and reported back to the testing center with wet hair.

I could tell right off Graves was in an even worse mood than yesterday. When he saw the two of us walk in together he twisted up his lips. He gave me a slow shake of his head.

"Get over here, McGill."

I hustled to his side. "What's up today, sir? Can I please wear the squid suit again? Maybe I could pop myself into one of these walls. Or maybe, I could dial it up *hard* and experience the warmth of old Sol's fusion core."

He stared at me. "How'd you do it?" he asked. "And don't give me any bullshit this time."

I knew what he meant. He wanted to know how I'd managed to control the suit after the other guys had died.

His bad attitude didn't faze me. I felt refreshed and happy. Lisa had given me new hope somehow. She'd been scared yesterday, sure, but she now seemed fresh and ready too.

Glancing over at her as she began testing her equipment again and scolding her underlings, I turned back to Graves and shrugged.

"Well sir," I said, lowering my voice, "if you really want to know, the art of wooing a fine woman isn't easily explained in a single lesson. I'd have to take you under my wing and—"

He made a gargling noise. I wasn't sure if he was choking or laughing. It might have been a little of both.

"I'm not talking about your midnight escapades," he said. "I'm talking about mastering that suit. You jumped. No one else has managed to pull it off."

"Oh... that. Sir, I'm sure that with a few more tries your people—"

Graves extended his arm toward the members of Omega Team. He pointed at them, and I frowned as I looked them over. There were considerably fewer Omegas than there had been yesterday. Those that remained were looking mighty glum.

"Uh... what happened to them?"

"What do you think? While you've been banging my lead tech, I've been frying these poor hog bastards one after another. Seven of them bought it just this morning. It doesn't matter what we do, they all die."

"Electrocution?"

Graves pointed again, this time toward a sizeable region of overlapping scorch marks on the floor.

"So," he said, "how'd *you* do it?"

The idea of telling the truth struck me. This could be the time to come clean with Graves about the Galactic Key. That would be a huge admission, and I would certainly lose the key to the tech crew.

But there's something about the Galactic Key. The sheer power it represents makes a person want to keep it forever.

The choice was a difficult one—but I made it on the spot.

"I don't rightly know, Centurion," I said, scratching my head and looking as baffled as possible. "Maybe these squid suits just don't like the taste of hogs."

"That's what I thought you'd say," Graves answered. He turned toward the ghoulish team of techs. They were just moving to stalk their next victim among the long-faced Omegas.

"Halt those tests!" Graves ordered. "Stand down, people. I'm going to have a little talk with McGill and a few others. Veteran Harris!"

Harris trotted up to him eagerly. He must have had an inkling of what was to follow, because he seemed very excited. "Yes sir?"

"Arrest Adjunct McGill. We're taking him upstairs with us."

Grinning, Harris whipped out handcuffs and clicked them onto my wrists.

"I smell an execution!" he hissed into my ear. He gave me a shove then, and I followed Graves out of the room.

On the way past the techs, I caught Lisa's eye. She looked horrified.

Winking at her, I gave her a broad Georgia grin. "Nothing to worry about, Miss. My tram is double-parked outside, that's all."

She didn't respond. She just gave me a look of confusion, and then we were out in the corridor heading toward the elevators.

"If this is a matter of personal jealousy, sir," I said. "It seems overblown."

"Shut up, McGill. Unless you feel like explaining how you jumped when everyone else was turned to toast, I don't want to hear another word out of you."

"I'm as much in the dark about that as you are, Centurion."

He grunted and we rode up in the elevator in silence. Graves worked his tapper the entire trip, no doubt making arrangements via texting. This made me sweat a little. Graves wasn't a man to be trifled with.

He was, in fact, a ruthless bastard under the best of circumstances. There was no telling how far he'd go when the stakes were high. In this case, the fate of Earth was arguably in the balance.

When we reached our destination floor, I was surprised by how quiet it was. The floor was packed with offices, but the corridors seemed empty.

We entered one of those offices, the only one in the line that was occupied. Turov and Winslade were there. They'd been stripped down and strapped to steel chairs. They were gagged, and they watched us with wary expressions.

There was a third chair in the line. Without being told, I took my seat in that one.

Grinning broadly, Veteran Harris strapped me in.

"Here we all are," Graves said, closing the door. "Winslade, Turov and McGill. Before we begin, does anyone want to say anything?"

"I do!" I said promptly.

"Shut up. I meant one of these two. They've spent a long night in their respective chairs."

Winslade nodded. Graves loosened his gag.

"Where are the others?" he demanded. "Kivi and Carlos were—"

Graves tightened the gag back up again. Winslade made odd slurping sounds while he did so.

"Trying to spread the love, huh?" Graves said. "They're already dead if that makes you any happier. They've been executed for refusing to talk."

That annoyed me. My friends hadn't really known anything about the key or the suits. I'm sure they would have talked if they could have.

"If that's how you're playing it, why didn't you execute me right off?" I demanded.

"Because Drusus wanted to watch you. We figured you might know more than you were letting on. Sure enough, you teleported. That confirmed my suspicions. You three are still in league with the squids somehow."

Turov's eyes slid around, but she didn't indicate she wanted to speak. I could almost see the tiny gears spinning in her scheming brain. She knew I had the key. She'd probably already figured out how I'd ported.

But she also didn't want to give up the key to Graves. Once Central had it, she'd never get it back. So, she kept quiet.

Graves walked in front of us for a second time. He had his pistol in his hand, and I considered confessing. Again, I rejected the idea. I kept quiet and shrugged.

Graves lifted his laser pistol. The aiming dot shined between my eyes. I gave him a smirking wink.

Grunting, he moved to Winslade. The gun brightened. There was a burning smell. Winslade shivered, pissed himself, and died.

"Get that out of here," Graves ordered.

"Maybe we should work them over a little more first, sir," Harris suggested as he dragged the body away. "Real legionaries don't fear a quick death."

"Shut up."

He walked to Turov. He shot her tapper. She hissed and squirmed.

"Imperator," he said. "I'm authorized to execute you to find out what McGill—or any of you—know. You're under investigation for treason. Note that the back-up of your mind has been deleted from the data core. Now that your tapper is disabled, a kill-shot will be permanent. Would you like to say anything?"

She nodded her head angrily. He loosened the gag.

"This is illegal," she panted. "There's been no due process, no court martial, nothing! I demand to see a lawyer!"

Graves shook his head. "Legal mumbo-jumbo has been suspended. All rights have been suspended. The ruling council has authorized the military to do anything necessary to defend Earth. No questions will be asked."

She breathed hard, thinking.

"I know how to operate the dial," she said at last. "Don't nudge it fractionally. It seems analog, but it isn't—it's digital with several billion settings. So many that it only *seems* analog. Cephalopods have tentacles that are more sensitive and precise than our fingers."

Graves looked suspicious. "Are you saying that these controls are far too touchy for humans to control," he pointedly stared at me. "That by trying to improvise and teleport a short distance, we caused our own men to fry—except of course for McGill who was super lucky?"

"You must click it to the second hash-mark on the dial. That will take you to the point of origin. The others are presets, too. Anything else is unknown to me, but you must stick to the preprogrammed destinations to be safest."

"Interesting control interface..." he said. "But why the fireworks? Why do my men keep getting fried?"

"The dial has security built in. You can't just choose a destination at random. You have to choose a valid one."

Graves nodded. "Hmm. So you're basically saying that McGill chose a valid setting by chance?"

"Yes—he must have."

All this was news to me. I wasn't sure if it was bullshit or real. It could be either one with Galina Turov. She was quite possibly the biggest liar on the planet—if you didn't count me.

Graves, however, wasn't convinced.

"I don't buy it," he said.

Without ceremony, he shot her in the head.

-16-

Stunned, I stared at Turov's slumped body. Could she really be permed? An imperator?

Earth had to be going through a serious political upheaval to allow execution in the ranks. I was reminded of many purges of officers in the past world wars. Losing armies tended to do that. I'd never thought I'd bear witness to that kind of day myself.

Graves walked over to me and stood close. "Do I have your undivided attention now, Adjunct?"

"You sure do, sir. Is that why you permed Turov? To get my attention?"

"Not just that. I thought she was lying. I don't like liars. I never have."

"There's no excuse for lying, sir," I agreed heartily. "Especially not under these circumstances."

Graves chuckled. "I'm glad we understand one another."

Then, that prick shot my tapper.

"Same drill, Adjunct," he said. "Don't upset me, or you're permed."

Graves was good, I had to admit that. He had me sweating. Everyone was dead except for me. I was the last member of the commando team that had dared to storm Central.

The tension even seemed to be getting to Harris. He wasn't smiling anymore. He stood with his arms crossed, frowning at both of us.

When caught red-handed, I like to think I'm at my best. When everyone *knows* I'm guilty, my imagination tends to kick into overdrive.

"Centurion," I said. "Turov left out a vital element when she explained how these suits operate. They can be attuned to individuals. Like our smart guns."

He squinted at me. "So... you were attuned somehow?"

"I believe that is what Imperator Turov arranged."

He chewed that over. "So only *you* can jump?"

"Seems like it, since you killed the rest of us. But I highly recommend you have Harris try it a few more times to make sure I'm not lying."

Harris made an unhappy grunting sound, but he didn't say anything intelligible.

"Hmm," Graves said, nodding and scratching. "Your story does fit the events. I wonder why Turov tried to hide that detail..."

"It's hard to fathom the workings of a twisted criminal mind, sir."

He snorted. "You're up for treason as well, McGill."

"A technicality," I said with my best sincerity. "I'm sure that if I can get these suits working for Central, I can secure a pardon."

"Ah!" he said, suddenly brightening. "Finally, you're beginning to bargain. I've been waiting for that."

"Bargaining? I wouldn't call it that. We'll all be heroes if you'll only give me another shot. We'll unlock these suits, and we'll use them to great effect."

"How so?"

Shrugging, I leaned back as if at ease. "Your plan is obvious, Centurion. You want to use these suits to jump aboard the squid ships and attack them with commandos. If that can be achieved, Earth might survive this battle."

"You've divined our plan. How'd you figure it out?"

"Normally, the defense of Earth would be the fleet's responsibility. The fact Legion Varus has been given a major role—well—we're the best infantry that Earth has. The plan seemed obvious to me after I realized that."

103

"You're right that the fleet has failed us. We're just about the only hope Central has left to win this. Can you do it, McGill? *Will* you do it?"

My guesswork had been confirmed. This display of ruthless terror had been designed to force me to help. I was beginning to understand that Graves didn't really want to shoot me. After all, I was literally the only man he'd ever seen who'd been able to get one of these suits to operate at all.

"I'm one hundred and ten percent sure that I can, sir."

He shook his head bemusedly. "Of course... as long as I take off your cuffs."

"That would be a nice start."

He eyed me like a slab of cold meat in a locker for several seconds.

"Okay," he said at last. "I'm going to take another chance on you, Adjunct. I'm going to put you back into that jump-suit. We'll dial it up and select one of the notches, like Turov said. You'll go for the big jump if you go anywhere at all."

"How will I get back if I succeed?" I asked.

Graves shrugged. "If Turov was telling the truth, then one of the other presets should bring you right back here."

I thought that over. There were six presets on the dial. It would be kind of like playing Russian roulette.

But then again, it was the best option I had at the moment.

Smiling, I nodded to them both. "Let's do this!"

They let me out of the chair, but they kept my hands cuffed.

I didn't care. I knew I wasn't going to die for at least another ten minutes. Sometimes, a man has to look on the bright side of life.

When I returned with Harris and Graves to the testing room, the techs and the Omegas stared at me like I was some kind of rabid dog.

Putting on my smile again, I gave Lisa a quick up-down of the eyebrows.

"Hey," I said. "What did I tell you? All a misunderstanding."

Harris removed my cuffs, and I stretched luxuriously.

"Let's get to work," Graves ordered. "Get McGill suited up. Same suit he managed to port in last time."

The tech team approached me warily. They looked like I might bite them. They also looked apologetic.

The first thing they did was call in a few bio people to replace my tapper. That hurt, let me tell you. There was blood on my arm and quite a few less arm hairs in evidence by the time they were done.

A few minutes later, Lisa was strapping me in. I got snugged up with external straps while the material shaped itself around me to fit my human physique.

Lisa wasn't looking me in the eye. I'm no psych major, I but I know that's not a good sign.

"Loved our date last night," I said experimentally.

"Good," she said, still not looking at me.

"Anything wrong?"

She paused and frowned up into my face. "Are you kidding?"

"No. You seem upset."

"I *am* upset," she whispered. Only the other techs could hear us, but they were being cool about it.

"Uh…" I said, chewing it over. "Did I forget to kiss you or something?"

"No, you idiot. You're about to die! I'm going to fry you in about two minutes. That's what's bothering me. I should never have gotten involved."

"Oh… that. Yeah, it could happen."

She stepped back and looked at me. "How can you Varus people be so callous toward death. I mean, even if you do come back—you *still* died."

"You're right about that. But you have to understand, getting electrocuted isn't a bad way to go. Quick, clean. No watching your guts getting torn out and eaten or anything."

I shrugged. She shuddered in return.

"I don't know," she said, going back to working on my straps and plugging me in.

"Don't know what?"

"If I can see you again after this—I mean, if you…"

"If I fry?"

She nodded her head.

Taking in a deep breath, I tried to come up with an angle.

105

"Trust me," I said, giving her a confident smile. "I'm going to be fine."

She smiled finally. It was only a glimmer, a hopeful wan expression, but it was good to see.

"Come on, come on!" Graves boomed. "What's the hold up? Are you two getting married?"

There were a few chuckles from the team. They retreated, and Lisa held up the power switch. She was doing the honors herself this time.

I lifted my hand and gave her the traditional thumbs-up. With the other hand, I touched the Galactic Key to the dial. That's how you do sleight of hand, by the way. When everyone is looking at your face, or your big thumb sticking up in the air—that's the moment your other hand is doing the dirty work. As any magician will tell you, no one will notice if you do your tricks without hesitation and you time it right.

The generator began to hum. I smelled ozone, but I didn't feel fear. What was to come was to come.

I reached my hand up to the dial, but I hesitated.

"Graves?" I called out.

"Dammit. What is it now, McGill?"

"I need a weapon."

"No."

My hand slid away from the dial. "Come on, Centurion."

He grumbled and walked up to me. He had his pistol in his hand, but he wasn't handing it over yet.

"You're going to shoot me with this, aren't you? All this bullshit about teleporting, and all you want is a little public revenge before you go out? Isn't that right?"

"Did you perm my friends, Graves?" I asked.

He stared into my eyes. "No," he said.

"What about Turov?"

"Galina Turov was convicted of treason by an emergency tribunal. Whether she had cooperated or not, she was to be permed."

That part surprised me. I hadn't been sure about her fate. Not until that very moment. I nodded.

"What about Claver?"

"Are you going to frigging jump or what?" he demanded suddenly.

"I'm the only chance you have. Answer a few more questions."

He muttered something then replied in an even voice. "All right. What do you want to know about Claver?"

"Did you revive him? Did you get anything out of him?"

"How could we do that? You gave us a pile of Claver-meat, sure. But you blasted his tapper. Even if we had a back-up of his brain, it would be out of date. Useless in light of recent events. In short, we didn't bother to bring him back."

"Oh... right," I said. "Okay, I'm ready to jump now."

Reaching up and placing my hand on the suit's dial, I held the pistol up with the barrel pointing at the ceiling.

Graves stepped back in alarm. That made me smile.

"I want dinner and a six pack when I get home!" I told them all, brandishing the pistol toward them.

No one replied.

Sealing my faceplate in case I ended up in space somehow, I put my hand on the dial again.

Then, while they all stared, I twisted the metal control disk firmly to the second setting. The one Turov had said would take me to something she'd called *the point of origin...*

Whatever the hell that meant.

-17-

Everything changed. It was like someone had switched out the lights and dropped me into a trapdoor in the floor.

I knew I was moving—but I didn't know how or in which direction. When I'd jumped across a few meters of space the day before and ended up playing Siamese twins with some poor hog, the feeling had been one of instantaneous translocation.

One second I'd been standing on that scorched floor, and the next, I'd been intermingling my molecules with those of my victim.

This time, however, there was a tiny lag in the process. It wasn't much—I'd say less than two seconds. Just enough time to dream a little and wonder about what was happening to me.

The experience was kind of like waking up again after a death, but it went by much faster. You felt like you'd been nonexistent for a time, then suddenly it was over and you felt disoriented but relatively normal.

When the jump ended there was an odd, momentary sense that my body was coming back together. Like an explosion in reverse, or like smoke being sucked back up into the same tiny bottle it had once been trapped within.

Looking around in a daze, I found myself in a dimly lit, unknown place. My body was suspended above the floor somehow, and what little light there was seemed wavering and diffused. My mass soon settled, falling gently down onto my feet.

Turning this way and that, I caught on quickly enough. I was underwater. This made good sense as the cephalopods were aquatic creatures. Water was a natural environment for them.

Still, I hadn't expected this kind of landing site. My suit had been sealed to prevent decompression, not compression.

The water pressure sank in against my body. I felt briefly like I was being crushed. The feeling soon subsided as my suit began to pump in more air to counteract the effect. My ears popped painfully.

Where was I? Reaching out my hand in the murk I touched a polymer globe that apparently surrounded me. It was a smooth, artificial wall. My eyes were still adjusting to the gloom beyond.

Was I trapped inside some kind of glass bubble? Feeling a little panicked, I reached out in every direction. I almost dropped my pistol when I found a curving barrier all around me—there was no way out.

Then I thought of looking upward. There above me was the top of the fishbowl. It took kicking off the bottom and three hard strokes against the weight of my gear to grasp the slimy edge of my cell. I struggled to get my arm over the lip of the enclosure I'd found myself in.

My head broke the surface and I found a small region of air above the water. Panting with exertion, I clung to the rim of the bowl. I looked around slowly, trying to take it all in. My tapper had been repaired by the tech team before they suited me up for death, so I used it and my body-cams to record everything I saw. Hopefully the resolution in the vids would capture some better details than I could with my naked eyes. Maybe someone would find it useful, or at least interesting, in the future.

Where the hell was I? My mind really wanted to know. I can report that even for me, a combat veteran of a dozen major conflicts, teleporting blind into a dark water-filled fish tank was disturbing. I didn't even know what planet I was on—or if this was a planet at all.

I was sure that my immediate environment was artificial, and there hadn't been any squids waiting around for me to show up. Other than that, I didn't know shit.

Up above the rim of the globe I'd arrived in, the air pocket was full of steamy gas not water. By climbing up on top of the lip of the globe I was able to reach up and grab onto a solid strut. There were exposed wires on the ceiling which was quite low. The wires might carry high voltages, and they were only about a meter above my head. I made a special effort not to touch them.

It occurred to me that an advanced aquatic species might find dry air useful, if only as an insulator. Maybe this region was like a crawlspace to them. An area that wasn't trafficked except by technical squids who worked on wiring and the like.

I found grated plank-ways up there, out of the water, like a network of catwalks over a giant aquarium. Sloshing and grunting, I hauled myself up onto the walkway as water rained off my suit back into the massive tank.

After escaping the fish tank, my first instinct was to hide before I was discovered. I crawled toward a dark alcove nearby. When I managed to tuck myself into a storage compartment of loose junk, I breathed hard from exertion and tried to think.

Okay, I thought to myself, *I've done enough here. I could justify this as a mission accomplished.*

Placing my hand on my dial, I paused. I could twist it, but that didn't mean it would work. For one thing, I wasn't hooked to any major power source this time. Even more importantly, I had no idea where the other settings on that dial might take me.

My hand fell away. I figured I might as well look around a while longer before I permed myself. After all, my eyes were just getting used to the low light. Why not take some more vids from up here?

Slinking out of my hiding spot, I froze. There was something moving around under me, in the water. I stared. A shadow swept gracefully by.

It was so *big* and so smooth while swimming. It had to be a squid.

Was I on their home planet? It could be. The environment seemed humid and wet with high pressure in the extreme, like an underwater cavern, but with metal walls. There was gravity and an atmosphere. My tapper had measured out a rich nitrogen-oxygen mixture of gases. Plenty of methane, too. The water was dank and well lived-in.

The squid seemed to be swimming around the globe in circles. I stayed motionless up on my catwalk. Probably, an alarm or a fault detection system had been tripped. When I'd appeared in the globe, I'd been given away. I was glad I'd been able to get out before this squid arrived.

I watched the creature quietly. It circled the globe twice, maybe wondering where I'd gone. Then I watched as it went over instruments and picked up what looked like a cable.

My heart skipped a beat when I saw the connector on that cable. It was a match to the one I had on my suit. It *had* to be a power cable. There were more of them, too, I hadn't noticed before. They were laying on the deck both inside and outside the fishbowl I'd teleported into.

Would coupling with one of these alien cables permit me to teleport home? Or would I just fry, or maybe alert yet more squids? I had no idea.

The insanity of this adventure was beginning to sink in for me. I was in the middle of the enemy, up proverbial shit-creek without anything resembling a paddle. Hell, I didn't even have a raft.

Something grabbed my leg about then.

I've had my leg grabbed by any number of beings, and I consider myself to be something of an authority on the topic, if I do say so myself. This grab was powerful as they went. It was also fast and mean. This combination, plus the way my leg was being constricted with terrific force, clued me to the fact I was in mortal danger right quick.

Aiming down my leg, I fired at the thing grabbing me. A tentacle smoked and withdrew, slapping angrily at the water and the catwalk I was lying on.

There were two dark hulks moving around down there now—I could see them both. They were circling like pissed-off sharks.

Glancing this way and that, I didn't see anywhere to run. Above my head was a tangle of copper and gold wires. Under the catwalk was a soupy pool with at least two angry squids in it.

I couldn't stay where I was, I knew that. It would only be a matter of time before they grappled me and dragged me into the water. Alternatively, they might decide to go get weapons and kill me.

For the first time in my life, I knew what it must have felt like to be a bird caught inside a house full of panicked humans. They were down there, circling and trying to figure out how to rid themselves of an uninvited pest.

Deciding it was now or never, I touched the dial on my chest. Gritting my teeth, I switched it to the first notched position on the list.

Nothing happened. The suit didn't even hiccup. It had to be out of power.

Cursing, I realized there was only one thing left to do. I rolled off the catwalk and splashed into the water. I drifted down in that tiny prison to the center of the globe again.

It was a big gamble, sure, but I'd reasoned something out. There, at the bottom of that small spherical tank, I found a power coupling. Just what I needed for my escape. I rammed it home on my suit, finding that it fit perfectly. At least it was tighter than the jury-rigged job Lisa and her team had cooked up back on Earth.

Squid tentacles slapped against the globe all around me. They made sucking motions and the water churned out there. I waved at them.

"Creature," said a voice in my ear.

Startled, I almost dropped my laser pistol. One of the squids had an instrument in his tentacle. Some kind of translation device? I knew my suit had a radio transceiver, but I hadn't considered the possibility they'd want to talk.

My hand went to the dial on my chest again. I'd already decided where I was going. My plan was simple. I'd switch the dial to the first setting again, and pray it took me home.

What the hell else could I do? If the second setting took you back to your destination, wouldn't the first setting take you to the targeted destination? It only made sense to me—but then, I wasn't a space-squid.

"Stop beast!" the squid said. "Speak with me! I command it!"

The big bastard was bleeding in the water. I could tell it must be the one I'd shot. These guys didn't seem armed, fortunately. If I had to guess, I'd say they were the cephalopod equivalent of our tech team. They were nerds, not fighters. Therefore, they were reluctant to engage with me and fish me out of my bowl with their bare tentacles.

I almost twisted the dial as the suit hummed and charged up. I came very, very close, but I hesitated.

One of my core flaws, besides being a little untruthful at times, was an overdeveloped sense of curiosity. What was it this squid wanted to say?

"What do you want, you damned Squid?" I demanded.

The creature squirmed in the water. "You must obey me. You are my captive. I claim you as is my right. You will be unharmed by me or any of the other members of my squad."

This was classic squid-talk. They were slavers, and they weren't shy about it. They salivated over a good capture. They wanted humans like me to impress their friends as much as anything else. Sometimes, that could be used as a bargaining chip to the advantage of a wily human.

"What if I agree to become your property?" I asked. "What's in it for me?"

"Pride and glory. You will be gifted with the blissful certainty that you're the proud servant of a genius-level intellect. If you behave in an exemplary fashion, I may even breed you to create a marketable line of chattel."

"Sounds pretty good," I said. "Just tell me where I am, and I'll sit and roll over if you want."

"Your remarks alarm me as they indicate a low intelligence factor. My estimation of your value has fallen significantly."

"Yeah, I love you too. Just tell me where this place is? What planet?"

The squid twitched. He turned toward his comrade, who was hanging back a good distance from the tank.

"The beast is a simpleton," the first one said. "All is lost. An imagined fortune has been squandered by fate, all within a span of seconds."

"You going to answer my question or not? I'm beginning to think *you're* the half-wit."

A tentacle slapped at the globe, and I felt it shake. If that limb had hit me, it might have broken my collar bone.

"Impudent creature! I will agree to your bargain now, but only so that I can punish you properly. This vessel is named *Force*, and you are still within the star system of the humans. Now slave, submit yourself to me!"

Solemnly, I twisted the dial to the first notch.

Nothing happened.

The squid began shaking. He gestured toward his companion, who I hadn't been paying much attention to.

There he was, back there, in the murky corner of the chamber about a dozen meters off. He had something grasped in a coil that dangled from his suckers.

With a cold feeling, I recognized the object: it was a power coupling, just like the one I'd attached to my suit.

They'd disconnected the power line that led to the globe, and I was helpless inside their glass cage.

-18-

The second science-squid was swimming languidly toward the glass now, letting that unplugged cable flutter in his grip. He wanted me to see just how truly screwed I was.

What had possessed me to taunt and argue with these squids? Why hadn't I found a power source then twisted the dial and ported out of this trap about two seconds after I'd arrived?

I wasn't sure what the answers to my questions were, but I thought my initial hesitation might have been due to the fact I *still* had no idea where I would jump to if I tried the dial again. Even if I'd been certain, however, I had to admit to myself that I might have teased the squids anyway. It's just in my nature.

"We have a tiny fish on our home planet," the second squid said as he approached and applied a rippling row of purplish suckers to the glass. I could tell he was the one talking because he'd reached over to press one of his many tentacle tips onto an instrument on his belt. The other squid had done the same when he was being translated.

"We like to eat these tiny fish very much," he went on, "but now there are none left in the wild ocean. They reside only in the small glass prisons of collectors and restaurants. You are just such a morsel to us, human."

"So... you're saying that I'm valuable to you guys, is that right?"

"Hmm," said the first squid. "Slow-witted. It asks repeated questions on points that are already obvious. I am beginning to seriously question its resale value."

"Of course it's stupid," said the second squid. "Why else would it have trapped itself in the middle of our lab?"

"You're right. It would be best that we don't allow prospective buyers to speak with the creature. They would certainly demand a price reduction."

Their insulting conversation gave me an idea. I pushed off the floor and thrashed my way up to grab the upper lip of the large bowl again. Grunting, I pulled myself up and over, dropping into the chamber between them.

They both backed away in alarm. I was pleased to see what I thought was a tiny bit of black ink swirling out of the second one.

"Ha!" I laughed. "Don't soil yourself, squid. I'm not attacking. I surrendered, remember?"

"Put your weapon down!" demanded the first squid. He was clearly the braver of the two. "I insist you honor our agreement."

It hurt, but I felt it was necessary to comply. I dropped my laser pistol. A tentacle shot out and snatched the gun away before it reached the bottom of the chamber.

Judging I probably wasn't going to get a better opportunity to make my move, I did it right then. The scaredy-squid had let go of the power-coupling when he raced away, and the boss-squid was busy grabbing my pistol. That meant neither of them were in a good position to stop me.

Bending at the knees and groping, I found the power coupling on the bottom of the chamber. I plugged it into my suit and reached for the dial on my chest. This one was live, I could tell by the way my suit's charging meter lit up.

The boss-squid didn't like that. He lunged, slapping a half-dozen tentacles all over me. It was like being wrapped up in boa-constrictors. Instantly, I found breathing difficult. I coughed and wheezed.

"It's trying to escape!" raged the squid. "Assist me!"

Out of the corner of my eye, I saw his chicken partner grab a sharp instrument. He swam back toward us, wary but determined.

"You are my property, human!" the grabby one said. "You will not evade your fate."

With two tentacles wrapped around my right wrist, I was overpowered. Another tentacle reached for my left, but I was ahead of him there. I had a combat knife out. I cut that tentacle and the squid shivered, filling the water with a billowing dark cloud of ink and blood.

Dropping the knife, I reached for the dial again. I twisted it to the first position.

Everything changed. I was jumping. For a few seconds, I didn't know if I should be happy or sad, but at least I was out of—

Then I felt something squeeze *hard*. Multiple somethings.

I couldn't see the squid who'd apparently come with me, but I could sure as hell feel him. He was trying to crush me. My ribs crackled, and a few of them snapped. I've felt that sensation before, and it had never been a pleasant experience.

I tried to cry out in pain, but I couldn't hear myself. I couldn't hear anything.

This struggle went on for a long time. The jump wasn't just a few seconds long as it had been the last time. It was more like a minute. Along the way, a few things occurred to me.

For one, the Squid who was trying to throttle me seemed to give up. He relaxed and I could breathe again.

The other thing was that I couldn't be going home—it was taking much too long for that.

Eventually, I was *somewhere* again. Somewhere I'd never been before.

A sky of green and white sprang into existence overhead. I was standing on a seashore just outside a very odd-looking building. It was tall and shaped like a beehive made of carven stone.

Since the ocean was green-black and the sky was green-white, I decided right then to name this place Green World.

The next thing I noticed was the state of the squid who'd ridden through space with me. He wasn't in good shape. He'd

117

been broiled, by the look of it. Like fresh calamari, he peeled away from my body, hot and steaming.

It occurred to me then that the teleportation suit had protected me from suffering the same grim fate. That probably explained why it needed to be a suit in the first place, instead of just a power coupling, some wires, and a control dial.

My hand leapt to the dial. Sucking air in gasps, I felt broken ribs rasp against one another in my chest with every breath.

"Screw this place," I said, and I twisted the dial to the third position.

Naturally, nothing happened. I cursed at length and coughed. Was that blood in my mouth? Yes, it was.

Great, I thought. The squid had managed to puncture a lung.

Picking up the laser pistol from the cooked squid, I saw it was damaged as well. I discarded it into the frothing sea and walked up the beach toward the only building in sight.

Wherever this was, I seemed to be on an island of some kind. I took the opportunity to look around, allowing my cameras to create good panning vids of the environment.

When I reached the building, I hesitated. Should I just walk in? What if there were a dozen squids in there, all hungry for supper?

Deciding I didn't have much choice in the matter, I reached out and touched the chunk of rock it had for a door handle.

That's when I saw it—out of the corner of my eye. It was something that looked like a black garden hose sitting on the ground, protruding from the wall of the strange building. I would have never given it a second thought, but I saw there was a coupling attached to this hose. A familiar coupling which I just knew would fit nicely into the plug on my suit.

Before I could stagger to it and give the dice of fate another throw, the door opened. Apparently, my touching the handle had set off some kind of alarm—maybe it was the squid equivalent of a doorbell.

There was a very odd creature in the doorway. It wasn't a squid. Instead, I recognized it as one of the Wur.

The Wur had never been my favorite alien species. They were probably the weirdest I'd yet to encounter, in fact. They were plants with mobility and excellent genetic reproductive control. They could build whatever they wanted from spores like a tree that could decide how to grow a branch in any shape it wished.

What the hell? That was my first thought, and I could tell the Wur was thinking the same thing.

For about a half-second gap, neither of us did anything. Then I lunged toward the power-outlet and the Wur backpedalled into its beehive-house.

Grabbing up what could only be a weapon of some kind, the Wur came after me a second later.

My hands were weak and floppy. Shock from the broken ribs? I didn't know, but I wasn't feeling too good. I was feeling kind of sick, in fact.

Shoving the plug in, I twisted the dial to the sixth setting— not the third, or the fourth—the sixth.

What made me do that? I honestly don't know. Maybe I was tired of trying to figure out this suit and where all these pathways led. Maybe my hand made the choice on its own by twisting too damned hard.

Whatever the case, Green World with its green sky, green ocean and a lumbering monster that shouldn't be there—it was all gone.

I experienced another long jump. I didn't know where I'd end up, but I'd almost lost hope.

This was the moment of despair. A point in a given lifetime where I was about ready to give it all up and accept death. I knew that feeling very well as I'd been on that brink between light and dark more than a few times.

Finally, I was real again. I was whole. I felt breath in my lungs instead of the half-numbness of the void. Like smoke forming again into a solid, I knew I was... somewhere.

I opened my eyes. I'd hardly been aware that I'd had them closed.

For some reason, I thought I'd be back in the lab if I'd found my way to Central. But wherever I was, it wasn't the lab.

The place was strange at first. All bright lights and a crisscrossing web-work of taped lines, wires and tiny nails driven into the floor.

What fresh hell was this? I turned slowly, my side hitching, taking everything in.

Then I saw them: tables stacked up against one wall. I knew where I was in that happy moment. This was the basement under Central. This was the room where the squids had initially jumped. The place where Carlos, Kivi and I shot them down as fast as they'd appeared.

I was home. That information flooded my brain, and it drove everything else out.

Passing into unconsciousness in stages, I collapsed on the floor in what felt like slow-motion. First, my knees hit. I barely felt that. Then my injured side hit, and my busted ribs crackled like dry twigs. An explosion of sickness, rather than pain, swept through me.

Breathing in raspy wheezes, my vision turned white. People were circling around me. They were tech investigators who'd been assigned to figure out how the teleportation trick had worked—how the squids had appeared here in the midst of our holiest of holy basements.

As I wasn't quite out yet, I was aware of people circling and kneeling around me. Someone opened my faceplate and removed my helmet. I coughed, but I couldn't answer their questions coherently.

My vision dimmed. The pain in my side had become dull as had my hearing and thought processes. The last thing I remembered was thinking that the cool concrete under my cheek felt kind of nice. Almost cushy.

People were fussing, but before I could comprehend what they were doing or saying to me, I lost consciousness.

-19-

What happened next seemed to me to be a crying shame. They recycled me.

For some reason, this really pissed me off.

I'd *liked* that last version of James McGill. That fellow had accomplished a lot. He'd slept with a pretty woman. He'd shot a few squids and visited two alien environments. Damn it, even by my standards, the previous version of myself had been a worthy legionnaire.

But none of that mattered to the ghouls we called bio specialists. They took the easiest path they could whenever faced with a difficult problem. They were the sort of people who'd throw out a perfectly good chair because they didn't feel like spending a few extra minutes driving a new screw into it.

"Bullshit…" that was my first word after I came out of the revival machine.

"What's that, Adjunct?" a bio asked me.

"This is all bullshit."

"What's his Apgar score?" she asked her assistant.

"He's a nine—but he's acting belligerent. Should we reroll?"

"Nah, give him another few seconds to come around. We don't have enough time to fool around with this one."

"Get off me," I growled, pushing away orderlies and some fool who was shining a flashlight into my face. That fool turned out to be the bio who'd just given birth to me.

"Adjunct McGill?" she asked angrily. "Do we have a problem?"

"We sure do. I hate dying for nothing, and I hate coming back even more."

"I'd suggest a recycle," the orderly said.

I was really beginning to dislike the guy. With bleary eyes, I swung my legs off the table and tried to spot him. He was a blob, but a blob that would rapidly come into focus as my freshly grown eyes began operating.

Standing up, I got in his face, swaying on my feet. "You just try it, boy!"

They backed off after that. I put on some fresh one-size-fits-all legionnaire blues and staggered out into the hallway. After managing to make it to the elevator, I punched buttons until I made it back to the lab.

When I reached the lab, I was still in a bad mood, and I made a scene.

"Who authorized recycling me?" I demanded loudly from the doorway.

The tech team melted away from me. Unlike the rest, Lisa rushed up and hugged me. I winced reflexively—but then realized my ribs didn't hurt anymore. They'd all been regrown.

Giving her a light squeeze in return, I slid her to one side and walked toward Graves. He was standing over a fresh mess on the floor.

"There you are, McGill," he said. "The bio people just texted me that you'd come out of the oven not five minutes ago, and you're already back for more. It's good to see this kind of dedication in a junior officer."

"Was it you?" I demanded, ignoring everything he said. "Did you have them grind me up and crap me out again?"

He looked at me coldly. "So what if I did? Are you going to whine about it?"

"Just seems unnecessary. I fought so *hard* to get back to Earth. I did amazing things. What was my reward? Execution and a new body."

"You know, we could have left you dead. Getting the treason charge dropped wasn't easy. Would you have been happier with that?"

I might have done something extra stupid right then, but I felt hands on my midsection. Lisa had come close and touched me. She looked up into my face, concerned.

"What's wrong?"

"Your boyfriend is an extremely tall baby," Graves answered. "Listen McGill, we don't have time for ribs to heal. We had to recycle you. The squid fleet is still coming. There was no time."

"He's right, James," Lisa said quietly. "There's no time for recuperation."

Heaving a great sigh, I shook my head and found a place to sit down. "I did so much. I saw so much."

Graves walked closer and stared at me. "Yes, you did. We've been reviewing the recordings you made. I'm quite impressed. Any idea where that second world was located?"

"I was hoping you could tell me."

"We'll figure it out. There's a team of techs somewhere in this building going over every detail of your vids."

"Like the team in the basement?"

"Those people are low-tier. They haven't come up with much yet. The best people we have are working on your suit. The one you jumped in successfully is right here, by the way."

"All right, I guess I have been a baby," I said. "Sorry."

"Apology accepted. However, disorientation is uncommon in a legionnaire with your level of experience. Hmm... Did you feel odd after teleporting?"

I thought about it then nodded my head. "It's like turning to smoke then coming back together again each time."

"Interesting. Maybe teleporting is like dying. Maybe these devices don't actually transport you, but they break you down to code and rebuild you in a new place. Maybe you feel like you died multiple times in rapid succession—because you did."

I looked at Graves in surprise. He appeared thoughtful, which was an abnormal expression for him. He usually just kicked whiners in the butt until they stopped whining.

"Is my slate clean now?" I asked.

"Yeah," he said. "Your rank and status have been restored. I'm going to release Kivi and Carlos, too."

"What?" demanded Harris from several paces away. He'd been listening in, apparently.

"That's 'what *sir*' to you, Harris," I barked.

Harris walked over, glaring. Graves stepped away from us, moving back to the tech group. He began to harangue them as they worked on a set of nine suits on tables. Lisa gave me kiss and trotted after him.

"I can't believe you got yourself out of a well-deserved perming, McGill," Harris told me. "Personally, I can't see it. All you did was pop around and get yourself—"

"Centurion Graves!" I called over Harris' shoulder. "Veteran Harris hereby volunteers for teleport test-duty, sir."

"McGill, I don't care what—" Harris began angrily, but he shut up in a hurry when Graves walked back to the two of us.

Graves looked Harris over. Then he turned to me.

"McGill, you're going to have to jump again, but I'm going to have you lead a team this time. This mission was supposed to go to Omega Team, but you've proven you can do better. I'm not sure any of these hogs could tolerate teleporting if it feels like dying every time."

Stunned, my mouth hung open. This was what I got for playing hero and getting crushed by squids?

"That doesn't seem like much of a reward, sir," I pointed out.

"It isn't. Legionnaires aren't supposed to be looking for perks. We're here to serve and die—as many times as necessary."

Harris chuckled. I gave him a cold glance.

Graves looked at Harris too. He wasn't laughing.

"McGill," Graves said thoughtfully, "you'll need a noncom to help you with your squad, won't you?"

"That's right sir," I said, my mood lifting. "I'll definitely need a vet or two to keep the troops in line. I hereby request that you make it an experienced man. One who takes to dying like a pig takes to mud."

Graves and I both studied Harris.

"Oh now... hold on. Just *hold on* a second, Centurion..." Harris said, staring in alarm at both of us in turn. "You can't be thinking that I'm going to serve under McGill! I'm in Adjunct Leeson's platoon."

Graves awarded us both with one of his rare, deadly smiles.

"Not anymore," he said. Then he clapped Harris on the shoulder, just as Harris had done to me the day before. "Thanks for volunteering, Vet. I've always thought you and McGill were a match made in heaven."

Sullen, but resigned to his fate, Harris fell into line and did what he did best. He marshaled up the team of Legion Varus troops Graves had hand-picked.

The Varus team was top-notch. There wasn't a fresh recruit in the bunch. All of them held at least the rank of specialist. Besides Harris and me, Kivi and Carlos were going. The last familiar face on the team was Veteran Sargon. He was one of the best legionnaires I knew.

"Centurion?" I asked, frowning. "I thought you said nine of us were going. There's only six here."

"That's right," Graves said. "I couldn't ditch the hogs entirely. Sorry about that, but you'll have to take a few of them with you on your next jump."

I waited to meet these lucky souls. The first of them was none other than the red-headed, rat-eyed fellow I'd seen fry several times the day before. He'd never smiled, and I knew why. His name was Ferguson, and I figured he'd earned the right to join us if he wanted to.

The second was a meatball weaponeer named Lund. He had muscles that would have made a bulldog proud. He wasn't smiling either, but he looked like he could handle himself.

The third and final member of the hog delegation was the only surprise in the mix. It was none other than Lisa, the tech Adjunct I'd slept with the night before.

She looked so scared I thought she was going to puke.

"All right," Graves said loudly. "Listen up. We're putting it all on the line this time. McGill here has managed to penetrate the enemy ship known as *Force*. We're going to try to do that again, but with an assault team this time."

Glancing over at Lisa, she shot me a nervous flash of a smile. I could tell she wasn't happy. I raised my hand.

"What is it, Adjunct McGill?" Graves demanded.

I pointed at Lisa. "Why is a non-combatant part of my team?"

"Because she's the best tech we have. If something goes wrong with one of these magic suits, she's the only one who might be able to fix it."

"I've already got Kivi. A commando raid isn't suited for desk-hogs."

Lisa winced as if stung. I knew she didn't like my comments, but I felt I had to protect her—and the rest of my team.

"Adjunct Smith?" Graves said, looking at Lisa. "Do you feel unqualified to perform this mission?"

"No sir," she said.

I heaved a sigh. She'd blown her chance to get out of this alive. There was nothing I could do after that.

"Fine," Graves said. "You'll do. Okay team, I want you rested and back here at 0600 hours. We'll gear everyone with special equipment then, and we should have information on the target ship's layout by that point. The nerds downstairs will be working on it all night long, but I want you fresh and ready to chew nails in the morning. Rest up! That's an order. Dismissed."

After people began to melt away, I walked over to Graves, frowning.

"Centurion? Could I have a word?"

He put up a gauntlet defensively. "My decision is final, McGill. I'm sorry about your girlfriend, but no other tech officer has the knowledge she does about these suits and their operation."

I shook my head. "That's not what I'm talking about. I was wondering what, exactly, our mission is when we get aboard *Force*?"

He blinked twice in surprise. "I would think that would be obvious. You're to eliminate her crew and take control of the ship."

"Is that all? You don't want us to repaint it or nothing?"

He chuckled. "I would think that capturing her will be challenging enough for you."

I thought about it for a second, and then I nodded.

"I guess it will be at that, sir."

-20-

There were questions in my head. How could there not be? I'd thought of a dozen holes in the plan.

What if the enemy killed us all? There would be no more teleport suits to utilize.

Worse, we'd pretty much be permed unless they disregarded Galactic law, which they might if they thought we could save Earth. That was unlikely, however. It wouldn't make any sense. Nine revived legionnaires couldn't do squat to an enemy fleet parked in orbit over our home world. We were only important because we could get to the enemy before they could get to us. We only mattered because of the jump-suits.

I spent the evening with Lisa. She was impressed with me—even more than she had been. I'd popped around the cosmos, killed squids, and returned to tell the tale. I think it was the fact I'd faced the enemy and bested them on their own ground that really turned her on.

"The evidence you brought back..." she said, shaking her head. "I wouldn't have believed it if I hadn't seen it with my own eyes."

"Really?" I asked. My eyes were closed, and I was balancing a beer on my stomach. Love-making usually put me in a sleepy mood, while Lisa seemed to be one of those women who got all energized from the experience.

"It's just incredible," she said, talking fast. "I've accepted that these suits could transport a living being over thousands of kilometers—but light years? I'm amazed. The technology can't be utilizing any kind of light-based transmission of data. It has to be so much more than that."

"Uh-huh," I said.

I heard her sliding closer to me. "What did it feel like, James?"

"Hmm… Like being torn apart and put back together again. Like being vaporized and reconstituted somewhere else."

"That sounds unpleasant."

"It wasn't my favorite way to move around, that's for sure."

She slid away again and replayed my body-cam vids. I didn't look. I didn't want to relive my encounters with squids, green skies or plant monsters.

"Where do you think they got them?" she demanded suddenly.

I snorted awake. "Huh?"

"The suits. They're Imperial-made, you know."

My eyes opened. I regarded her, and she regarded me.

"How do you know that?" I asked.

"It's my job to know the origin of any piece of alien tech when I see it. That dial… did you know each of the control dials has an Imperial stamp on the back? It's only visible when you study them under an electron-microscope."

She had a funny look on her face. She was studying me. That look—it was usually given to me by a woman I was involved with when she suspected me of infidelity. But this time, I figured it had to be something else.

"That small, huh?" I asked.

"Yes. Each stamp is less than a thousand molecules strung together. It's amazing all by itself. But it also indicates these suits come from the Core Systems. They have to."

I nodded thoughtfully.

"Why are you looking at me funny?" I asked.

"I've only seen a few stamps like these, James. None of the devices that have them are legal on Earth. They're Galactic gear. We techs at Central know about them, but we're not supposed to."

Feeling a little uneasy, I sat up in bed. I caught my beer before it could spill and drained it.

129

"Are you supposed to be telling me this?" I asked.

"Not really. But you've already used this forbidden tech. It hardly matters if you know more about it—it might even help."

"How so?"

She slid around in the bed and no longer lounged beside me. She sat up cross-legged and faced me. The look on her face was all business, which I found instantly disappointing in a new girlfriend.

"James... have you seen anything like this before?"

"You mean teleporting suits? Or Galactic tech stamps? No."

She nodded, looking down.

"What about other items? Other devices unknown to Earth? Have you ever encountered any of them?"

Warily, I nodded. "Sometimes—I've been on a lot of planets, you know."

She licked her lips. "Right. How about something that can override security systems?"

Immediately, my mind froze over. That was it. She was on my trail. She knew about the Galactic Key, or at least she suspected I had something like it.

At moments like these, I tended to fall back upon the tried and true. Accordingly, I played dumb.

"I don't know what you mean," I said.

A flash of frustration crossed her features.

"Fine," she said in sudden irritation. "Forget I brought it up."

"Okay."

She got up and began to dress and pack her stuff.

"Aw now, come on," I said. "I've got a twelve-pack left here. Don't make me finish it and sleep alone."

She didn't even look at me.

Hopping out of bed, I put my hands on her shoulders. She shrugged me off.

"What's wrong?" I asked her.

"I don't like being lied to. Especially about something so important."

She took a step toward the door.

"Lisa," I said, "did you ever think I might have my own secrets? And my own reasons for keeping them?"

She hesitated, then whirled around on me. She pointed a finger at me like it was a gun.

"James McGill, you're the one who's not thinking. I know you did something to get your suit to work. Something none of the rest of us could figure out. Tomorrow we're going to port to an enemy ship and try to take it."

"Damn straight," I said. "That's why I'd rather be getting some solid sleep in right now."

She rolled her eyes. Women did that all the time around me.

"First of all, I don't even understand how you could sleep on a night like this before going to battle."

I shrugged. "I just try not to think about it."

"Secondly," she continued, "I *know* you're a lot smarter than you pretend to be, but you're not thinking this time. How are you going to fix all nine of our suits before we port out of here tomorrow?"

A funny look must have swept over my face.

"Oh," I said.

"That's right," she said, coming closer. "Now you get it."

That finger was still up, and it was right in my face. Normally, I would've gotten angry about that, but she'd made a very good point.

Sure, I could touch my key to my own suit and make it work for me—but what about the rest of the team? How would it look if I went around fluffing up everyone's collar and giving them a kiss before we launched? Would that even work?

"We've got a problem," I admitted.

"We sure as hell do," she agreed. "Now, as your senior tech on this mission, I demand that you come clean. Tell me how you did it. Let me save this mission."

My jaw slid side to side as I thought it over. I couldn't come up with a dodge or an easy solution.

So I sighed, and I spilled my guts. My story was brief, but informative. I told her about the Galactic Key, how it worked, and what it could do.

When I was done, her eyes were as big around as a bug's.

"And you've somehow kept this from your officers for *how* long?"

"Years, actually," I said. "But it wasn't like it sounds. For most of that time, the key belonged to Imperator Galina Turov. I was under strict orders not to reveal anything about it. Seeing as how she's been permed now, I figure I'm free to talk."

Lisa began to pace and tap at her arm. I could see her mind was working way too fast. I wondered how I always got mixed up with the smart ones.

"Let me see it," she said, holding out her hand.

Reluctantly, I put the seashell-like thing in her hands. She stared at it.

"*This* is a powerful artifact? I had this in my possession before."

"Yeah. Luckily, they returned it to me after my last recycle. I formally listed it as a 'personal item' a long time ago, and they always give it back. Funny how they never catch on."

"I can't believe..." she said, trailing off. "You told me this was a gift from your mother!"

"Uh... I might have said something like that."

Lisa slapped me lightly for lying and carried the key to the bed. She held it like it was made of glass. In reality, it was pretty tough. It had been through some hard knocks, and it still worked.

"What a glorious find..." she said. "In a way, this is better than the teleport suit."

"Uh... can I have that back now?"

"No, not yet. I must perform a few experiments."

She walked around the room and touched the key to items as I'd explained she could. She hacked her tapper, killed the lights on the entire floor, and unlocked her own apartment door.

"Amazing," she said. "But how are we going to launch the team with it?"

"Well... you're the tech. You could do a final, personal check on every suit. Walk from person to person and unlock their suits. When you're done, we'll launch."

"Such a simple plan—do you think it will work?"

I smiled and caught her around the waist.

"The simplest plans always work best."

Lisa resisted a little, but pretty soon her robe was off again, and I had her in my arms. Her body was warm and all her original excitement and energy seemed to have returned.

She was a techie, after all, and I'd just rocked her world.

-21-

The next morning came all too soon. We were rounded up and suited up. The only good news is they gave us a few new pieces of gear I'd never seen before.

"This tech is the good stuff," Lisa told the team. "Things we've developed here on Earth, but which are illegal as far as the Galactics are concerned. Now that we're facing extinction, Hegemony has authorized the use of everything we've got in the arsenal."

The Galactic Empire operated through a simple but inflexible set of rules. Every star system in the Empire had to have a valid trade good to be eligible for membership. This membership was very desirable—mostly because the only other option was planetary extermination.

From the beginning, Earth's trade good had been mercenary troops. We were allowed to buy weapons and military hardware, but only the kind of gear that the Empire had deemed our fringe civilization was good enough to buy. We couldn't manufacture better weapons or copy alien designs. Aliens held patents on every weapon we could come up with. If we tried to build stuff like that anyway, the penalty would have been species removal.

Galactic Law only had one punishment for any infraction: death. The amount of death was the only variable. In mild cases, an individual death might be enough to atone. More serious infractions required that a family unit, a city, or even a planet had to be removed from the living. In extreme cases, complete extermination of the species was called for.

Because of the danger, Earth had studied alien tech but dared not use it. We'd never had enough credit or trading partners to get everything that was wanted legally, but we'd stolen a few secrets here and there.

Today was different. The Galactics were no longer our biggest problem. They were far away and toothless. There hadn't been so much as a visit from the Nairbs or the Mogwa for years.

As was always the case, when the cat was away, the mice began to play.

"Cinch this up tighter, McGill," Lisa said, hooking yet another gizmo onto my belt.

"What's this thing?" I asked doubtfully.

"It's a tracker. It tracks physical bodies that are in motion."

"Hmm…" I said, less than impressed. "Do I really need a device for that? If I can see them, I can shoot them."

"This is better than your eyes. It sees through walls. It will show you what the enemy is doing, even if they are on the far side of a solid wall."

"Ah…" I said, catching on. "You carry it."

She complained, but she finally did as I asked. I didn't want to be overburdened with gear. Sure, these things were useful, but we were going to be swimming most of the time, and I didn't want to be weighed down.

Graves let me handle the details any way I wanted. He'd put me in charge of the mission. Unless he saw me actively disobeying his orders, he wasn't going to get involved. This mission was *my* baby.

Half an hour after we got to the lab, we were all suited-up and ready to jump. I looked at Lisa, and she met my eyes. She gave me a tiny nod and showed me the Galactic Key. She had it in her palm, ready to go.

"Okay," I said, "we're going to pop through one at a time. Even if you die the second you appear in the glass ball, try your best to fall out of the way. We can't afford to merge up with one another when we arrive."

The team looked a little green when I mentioned "merging up." They'd seen me kill myself and one of the Omegas accidentally by teleporting into the same space he occupied.

"We can assume that a liquid medium like water or air will displace. We've seen that firm solids do not. We don't want any new disasters. The second you get there, move out of the way for the next guy, got it?"

Everyone nodded grimly.

"If you possibly can," I continued, "hustle out of that bubble. Kill any squid you see. We should have surprise on our side, but that's it. The crew will outnumber us and outweigh us. We have to take them down before they know what's happening."

"McGill," Graves said. "What's your order of battle? Who's on point?"

"I'm going first," I said. "After me comes Ferguson, then Carlos."

I continued the list. Every ten seconds, a team member was to jump. Lisa would bring up the tail end of the squad, right after Harris.

We did a final check, and they all looked at me like I was some kind of undertaker. All except for Lisa, that is. She seemed to believe I was a miracle-worker. I only hoped for her sake that my luck would hold out.

Go-time came all too soon. I stepped up to the plate—literally. There was a disk-like plate now on the floor. Maybe Graves had gotten tired of cleaning up the deck itself. Lisa approached and touched the key to my dial and stepped away, nodding.

"Checked. Ready to fly, McGill."

We'd practiced this maneuver in the early morning. She'd gotten good at handling the key and palming it afterward.

Since we didn't know how long the security on the teleport unit would be disabled, I wanted her to send off each trooper personally. She'd come last so that she didn't have to wait around too long, either. Putting my girl at the end of the queue also meant she would have the most cover-fire and therefore the safest entry into hostile territory.

Slamming down my heavy visor and turning on my exo-skeletal gear, I felt I was ready. I had plenty of new toys on my person that the nerds at Central had cooked up but never dared use before in combat. All that nonsense about Galactic Laws and patents was being blissfully ignored by the brass now. Even better, the squid jump-suits had plenty of room inside for us to pack with gear.

"For Legion Varus and Earth!" I shouted over the tactical channel, and the assembled group cheered me.

Mid-cheer, their voices cut out. I'd switched the dial on my chest, selecting the second notch.

Instantly, I was cast into limbo. My body had been torn apart and felt as if it was floating. My consciousness seemed to be spread thin for a moment, then I felt myself coming together again.

About a second and half passed. Suddenly, I was aboard the cephalopod ship *Force* again—unfortunately, I was not alone.

The glass globe was gone. In its place were no less than twelve squids.

My first thought, in the split-second before the fireworks began, was that the enemy had set up an ambush. They'd been waiting here for me to come back, and now they'd formed a firing squad to rip me apart.

But that wasn't the situation. I could tell as I reached for my belt and set off a pulse-bomb that the squids were actually prepping to teleport themselves. Nine combat-squids were there, and they were all heavily armed and wearing jump-suits.

In addition were two technical types who wore normal spacer-gear. They were checking over their equipment. The whole scene reminded me of the one I'd just left behind.

There was no doubt in my mind that this group was heading to Central. Their techs were about to launch a team at us—but we'd beaten them to the punch.

The squids, rather than being trigger-happy and ready to blast me, were taken completely by surprise.

The pulse-bomb was something new. Developed for aquatic combat but never used before by Earth troops to my knowledge, the device created a concussion wave that was designed to rupture every eardrum and organ in the vicinity.

Naturally, I'd been fitted with protective padding and reactive armor designed to mitigate these same affects.

When I set it off, I expected to hear a pop and go on my merry way. That wasn't exactly how it turned out, however. Even with my protective gear, I was stunned. It felt like I'd been slammed in the head with a big rubber mallet—from multiple angles all at once.

When my mind and my vision cleared, I could see the squids had fared worse than I had. Half of them weren't even moving. The rest were flopping around, leaking blood and ink. Their eyeballs had ruptured, and they seemed to be blind and virtually helpless.

My chronometer went off—or maybe it had been going off for a while. I couldn't hear it, I could only feel it vibrating my tapper. Still groggy from the point-blank effects of the pulse-bomb, my first instinct was to silence the alarm...

Somehow, somewhere in my brain, another urgent thought struck through the fog: *get the hell off the launch pad, McGill!*

Numb legs propelled me one step, then as I began the next, my left boot froze. I looked back and down—it was Ferguson. He'd ported in and the tip of his boot had been fused with mine.

At first, I thought we might both be as good as dead. Two idiots trying to fight with a pair of merged feet? That would be hopeless.

"You're not off the pad!" he told me needlessly.

Then he caught sight of the carnage around us in the murky water and freaked out a little. It's one thing to train hard on Earth, and quite another to be surrounded by hulking aliens that are still thrashing.

His gun came up, and he shouted and fired at the twitching carcasses like he was being eaten alive.

My chrono was going off again. I knew what that meant. I drew my knife, a fine blade with a molecularly aligned edge that could cut through damn-well anything, and slashed at our conjoined feet.

The boots came apart. I shoved Ferguson, who went rolling away and landed ass-up on top of a big-daddy squid. He didn't like that. He scrambled around bubbling and cursing.

The chamber shivered again. Another man appeared—Sargon this time.

"What's up, boss?" he asked. "Are these guys all as dead as they look?"

"Step off the pad and check them," I ordered. "Ferguson, grow a pair and help him out."

"You cut me, sir," Ferguson complained. "I'm bleeding. My suit has sub-chambered my boot—it's full of water!"

"So apply some frigging nu-skin to it," Sargon bellowed over his shoulder at him. He was already kicking squids and aiming that automatic plasma-bolt rifle at everything he encountered.

I gripped Ferguson's arm and dragged him to his feet.

"Look at Veteran Sargon," I told him. "You see how his weapon and his pecker are both in the upright and locked position? Get with the program! Check those squids and cover those entrances!"

"Sorry Adjunct," Ferguson said, hustling to do as I'd ordered.

I could see a slight blood-trail wisping up in the water from his boot. That was too damned bad, but he had to pick up the pace, rookie or not.

More of my team kept popping in. After another minute or so, we were fully assembled.

"We have to assume there will be a response," I told them, "we're moving fast and traveling light. If you can't walk, you're squid-chow. Move out!"

My helmet beeped, and Lisa contacted me. "Commander, we've got three incoming on local sonar."

"Which way?"

"The big open portal at the far end of the room. I can't tell if they're armed or not."

Signaling with my hands, I directed Sargon and Ferguson to follow me. I ran in underwater slo-mo to approach the circular door she'd indicated.

"Harris, take your fire-team and cover the other entrance. Keep talking to me, Lisa."

"Seventy meters—this ship is bigger than I thought it was—fifty meters. They're swimming fast!"

I eyed the passage on the far side of the open portal. It teed off to the left and right.

"On my count," I said, "we're going to step through and blast those squids."

I didn't want to give the enemy time to get in close. Sargon and I exchanged glances. It was a risk, sure. I knew that. We had no idea how the enemy were armed or if there were already others out there, waiting to pick us off with rifles.

But it was a calculated risk. We couldn't take this ship if we got pinned down and didn't keep moving.

Taking in a deep breath of rubber-tasting air, I stepped out into the passageway. Ferguson and Sargon were right behind me.

-22-

Three pissed-off squids came at us like they meant business. They were armed with what looked like long-handled forks that had two tines each. The tips of these weapons were quite sharp and occasionally loosed a jolt of electricity that cracked between them.

I knew right away what their game had to be. We were in water, and we had mesh suits on. A hard thrust would arc through our bodies and right down into the metal deck under our boots.

With all our gear on, we weren't able to swim. We were pretty much walking around on the floor of the passage, with just enough gravity to keep us grounded there.

Our new plasma-bolt rifles came in two different varieties. Either type was designed to be fully operational underwater as they essentially released particle radiation in a tight beam. The rifles carried by Ferguson and me were standard-issue, meaning they fired single shots in a semi-automatic fashion. These weapons had slightly longer burn-rates and therefore greater effective range.

Sargon's weapon was different. He had a heavier version with three rotating emitters. With a big pack on his back to power it, he could hose down the enemy with a nearly continuous spray of bolts. Each shot, however, was less powerful and less accurate at range.

Our approach was simple in any case. Sargon took the center, held his weapon at the hip, but held back on firing. At this range in water, it was best for him to wait before unleashing a brilliant display of firepower down the passage.

Ferguson and I stood beside him and laid down purposeful, aimed bursts. We opened up the moment our targets came into view, taking as many early shots as we could. We managed to do the squids some damage, but we didn't stop them.

I could see the squids flinch and recoil in pain, but they kept coming. Our bolts lost punch rapidly when firing through water, and they were such large and vital creatures they kept charging. They didn't have to take too many hits before they reached our line as they were moving at least forty kilometers an hour through the water.

After I'd hit my squid two times and missed a third shot, they were already closing with us. Finally, Sargon's big gun came into play. He tore up the center squid and hosed down the one on the right. Ferguson and I shot the last one to death, backing up and placing careful rounds into it as it slowed and floundered.

Ferguson panted and cursed steadily when it was over, but I didn't admonish him about that. After all, it was his first time taking down a deadly alien charge.

When the fight was over, I clapped Sargon on the back.

"Excellent," I told him. "These guns are better than I'd hoped. Good job holding your fire until they were in close. You turned so much water into superheated steam, we couldn't see squat once you opened up."

"Agreed," Sargon said. "I like how—"

That was as far as he got. A slot in the ceiling opened overhead, and a fork jabbed down. It stabbed into Sargon's shoulder and there was a crackling snap and a flash of light.

He did a little dance before his arms splayed and his back locked into an arch. I could see his eyes through his faceplate—they were wide and unblinking.

Ferguson and I shot that squid at least a dozen times before it gave up the ghost. The entire time, it kept feeding Sargon with a sustained jolt. I think it must have had a particular hate for the man and his weapon. By the time the alien finally slid down out of the ceiling, lifeless, Sargon was well-done. He'd been electrocuted and then some.

Growling, I touched his tapper to mine, but I didn't get a reading. His mental engrams hadn't been transferred yet. Maybe that was a mercy. At least Sargon would never remember this death—assuming we were able to revive him at some point in the future.

I picked up his weapon and checked it out. While I was doing so, Ferguson tried to aim his rifle in every direction at once. He was looking alive now, at least.

"Let me guess," Carlos said as he came out into the passage to check out Sargon's body. "He insulted your mama, didn't he?"

"Nope, I just wanted to try out his cool new gun."

"Figures, you cold bastard."

Ferguson looked at us with eyes as big around as Sargon's bulging orbs. I knew he was probably thinking we were crazy and ghoulish, but we knew he'd understand our mood better after he'd died and come back another twenty times. You had to die a lot before you could see the humor in these situations.

"Harris, what's the sitrep on your side?" I called.

"All quiet, McGill."

"Lisa, what do you have on scope?" I asked.

"Uh…" she said, sounding stressed. "Nothing, really."

"Where do we go? We have to keep moving."

"We don't have a complete map of this vessel," she said. "I don't know where the engine room or the bridge are. Um—I guess we should head toward the ship's prow…?"

I rolled my eyes.

"Your girlfriend is pretty sharp," Carlos commented unhelpfully.

I shoved him away from me. We had a man down, all my hog troops were panicking, and we'd hardly met any resistance yet.

"Follow me," I ordered, and I chose to head in the direction the three squid crewmen with the big forks had come from.

When in doubt, move out. That was my motto. We marched, leaving behind Sargon and his boiled-egg eyeballs for a better day. Sure, we needed his teleport suit, but we didn't have time to strip him down until we secured the vessel.

The crew attacked us as we made our way down that long passage, which I soon realized ran the length of the ship. Judging from the internal dimensions, I figured *Force* was a cruiser-class vessel.

They didn't make an outright charge toward us again. Instead, they ambushed us from the sides so they could get in closer.

They all seemed to have been issued those nasty forks, and they applied them to good effect. When we got to the end of the passageway, they killed the muscular Lund who might have been voted 'least likely to dance out of the way of a stabbing squid fork' and then nailed Kivi to a wall.

She squirmed and cursed up a storm while we pounded her attacker to hamburger with plasma-bolts.

Finally, inking and thrashing to a stop, it settled to the floor. Kivi was still alive somehow, but she wasn't in good shape.

"It only caught the fabric of my suit," she said, panting and sweating. "I think I can walk."

She couldn't, of course. Not a step. Her whole side had been seared. She had to be in agony.

"Uh-huh," I said, lifting my service pistol to her faceplate.

"James McGill, don't you dare!" she said, breathing hard. "You'll never get anything from me the rest of your damned lives!"

Now, you have to understand that Kivi and I had an odd relationship. We hooked up now and then, whenever the mood struck Kivi to do so. That's what made me hesitate.

Unprofessional, I know. But when you live and die with a team over and over again for years, you develop an entirely different set of private rules your inner circle plays by.

While I was frowning and deciding what to do, a plasma bolt went off. I turned to see Carlos standing behind me. He lowered his weapon and shrugged.

"She'll think you did it," he said, giving me a little smile.

That was Carlos for you. A sneakier puke of a man had never been born. He and Kivi had been an item, and he probably didn't like the idea of her and me getting together

144

again in the future—so pop! He'd solved everyone's problem all at once.

"Squad, get clear of this ink. Move out!" I boomed, and they followed.

I could hear Harris at the back of his team, laughing his ass off.

"That was a good one, boy," he told Carlos. "I couldn't have done better myself. Don't try that on me, though."

"But I already did, Vet," Carlos said.

"What?" demanded Harris.

"I offed you back on Tech World," Carlos said, raising his voice. "You just don't remember because your tapper didn't update fast enough. You remember that, don't you, McGill?"

I didn't look back, but I smiled inside the privacy of my helmet.

"Damn straight you did," I lied with perfect conviction. "Twice on Death World, too."

"Oh yeah, forgot about that."

"Are you fucking with me?" Harris demanded angrily. "Cause if you are, Ortiz, I'm—"

"Squids!" Lisa shouted over our talk. "Dead ahead and behind that bulkhead on the left."

"How many?" I demanded, halting the group.

"Looks like all of them," she said after fiddling with her equipment. "I count at least twenty individual contacts."

"Has to be an important chamber," I said. "They're making their stand. Advance!"

I moved forward at a faster clip, but just before we reached the bulkhead, the world spun on me.

The ship had gone into wild motion. We were being thrown around, off our feet. I slammed into walls so hard I feared my helmet would crack, but it didn't.

The water in the passageway sloshed around violently. Everyone left alive in the squad looked like toys in a washing machine.

That's when the squids made their play. They rushed us, in-close and all-out.

The pitched battle I'd been expecting finally began.

145

-23-

Humans are wired to be land-creatures—meaning we like living and walking on a flat surface. When someone throws us into deep water, unless we have special training, we eventually breathe the water and die.

Thus far in this boarding action, we'd managed to keep the squids from using these simple facts of environmental advantage. Their aquatic natures hadn't helped them.

That changed when they spun the ship. To aim properly, a man has to have firm footing. It's a fact of life. Once you're spinning around with your center of gravity shifting violently, you just don't know which way to shoot.

The squids seemed to know this. They came on with a vengeance, seeking to take out every frustration they must have felt about our incursion into their territory.

Before we could do much more than spin around in a hopeless effort to get our feet back on the ground, they were in close and shoving forks in our butts. Snaps and howls came from all around me.

Ferguson was gigged like a bullfrog right in front of me. Two of them rammed home their forks and applied the power. He spazzed and puked—it was an awful way to go.

Giving up on regaining solid footing, my training as a spacer kicked in. I went *with* the spinning chamber, forcing myself to act as if in open space. The key was not to fight the spin, but to use it.

Directing my heavy plasma gun, I squeezed the triggers and didn't let go. The thing spun and spat radiation in a relentless spray of fire. I took out both the squids that were toasting Ferguson, as well as Ferguson himself. I figured I was doing him a favor, really.

Carlos and Harris, for all their harsh talk, had thrown their backs together and were firing in opposite directions. I left them alone and turned toward the front line.

There was a full school of squids pouring out into our ranks now. There was no doubt in my mind—we were going to be overwhelmed.

Gritting my teeth, I did what I thought I had to do—I set off another pulse-bomb right in the middle of my own team.

The results were dramatic. Every human convulsed in shock and pain. But the squids took the worst of it. Their first ranks went into spiraling swims shaking their tentacles and leaking vital fluids. They hadn't all been quite close enough to get the full effect, but at least half of them were out of the fight.

I honestly expected the rest to turn and run. After all, when most creatures are shocked by a devastating attack, they reel back and self-preservation instincts kick-in.

Not so the squids. Just like ants with a kicked-over nest, killing a lot of them only made the rest furious. They came at me with a singular purpose. They lusted for my death.

The first fork caught on my weapon. Maybe the squid was blind, I don't know, but some of its eyes were ruptured and leaking fluids. The jolt stung my hands, nothing more.

In return, I lit him up with point-blank fire. He almost ripped the weapon from my hand in his death throes, but I managed to hold on.

Harris and Carlos were at my side, firing steadily into the massed squids. Several were fouled up by the floating bodies of their comrades. Others stabbed blindly, catching one another with jolts in the aft-tendrils as often as they did a marine.

The fight continued until it petered out to a finish. The last squid died under combined fire from the last four of us—and suddenly, it was over.

Lisa was crying. There were tears running down her face inside her helmet. But she'd done all right. She had a pistol in each hand, having picked up someone else's. Usually techs and bios didn't get put into frontline combat, and they cared more about their gear than they did their guns. Lisa may have changed her mind on that point.

"Where are we?" I asked.

"We're good and royally screwed, that's where," Carlos said.

Harris elbowed him, but I could tell his heart wasn't in it.

"At least that damned spin is slowing down," I commented.

"The ship's stabilizers must have kicked in," Lisa said. "I can feel it, and my instruments indicate the control wires are transmitting to the external jets."

"Any way to hack into that?" I asked.

She shook her head. "Not from here. Get me to engineering or the data center—better yet, get me to the bridge."

I looked around at my team. More than half of my troops were down. I'd talked to Graves about this possible situation. What we didn't want was a total failure. If I thought we were in danger of being wiped out to the last man, I was to find a power source and bring back every teleport suit I could. That way, we could try again. After all, there were still a few days left before the enemy reached Earth orbit.

But I'm an optimist—I didn't want to give up. The crew of *Force* had to have reported this boarding attack. Even if we could get to another of their ships, they'd be ready the next time we hit them. The advantage of surprise would have been lost.

Besides, in my own personal view, we had to gamble to make any of this work. This wasn't the right time to make the safe play. We had to get lucky—*very* lucky—or none of this would make a lick of difference.

"We press on," I said. "Let's see what's at the end of this passage."

All the fun and games had been beaten out of Carlos and Harris by this time. I could see beads of sweat on their faces inside their helmets. They held their rifles to their cheeks, quiet and professional.

We advanced in a tight group until we reached the final portal. Without hesitation, I opened it.

I've been on the bridge of a squid slaver ship before. This ship was different. Instead of being built on a massive scale with vast holds, it was designed for combat.

It wasn't a troopship, it was a gunship. The bridge was accordingly designed along lines that were familiar enough to an experienced spacer. There weren't any seats as floating squids didn't need to sit down. Instead, there were grab rails everywhere. They had instrument panels—but those were all over the place. They covered the floor, the ceiling and every wall with equal frequency.

There were only two squids in there. They both looked surprised. Harris moved to fire his weapon, but I pushed the muzzle up and the beam scarred harmlessly across an access hatch.

"Surrender your ship!" I ordered, activating an external translation device.

"You speak of an impossibility," said the smaller of the two squids.

Aiming with some care, I shot the shit out of him. Then I turned to the larger squid.

"Surrender your ship or die," I said.

At first, he didn't say anything. Then he dropped his electric fork onto the deck. It crackled and spit a few sparks when it touched metal.

"Good," I said, "you're my captive. You must serve me."

The squid's tentacles squirmed for a moment, then it spoke. "I am your slave."

The rest of my troops looked at one another in shock. I didn't have time to explain cephalopod psychology to them— that this enemy only understood master-slave relationships. There were no such things as "equals" in their society.

Naturally, squids preferred to be the masters, but they could accept the opposite role if given no choice. I'd noticed that the upper-crust squids were the most likely to give up like this— they probably liked dying even less than their underlings did.

"What's your name and your previous title?" I demanded in the confident voice of a master.

"I was Storm, and I was the captain of this vessel."

149

"Excellent. You will now be my pilot. You will fly this vessel."

His numerous eyes tracked me. "I will fly this vessel."

"Storm—I return to you your name for the sake of my convenience."

"Of course."

"Are you the only one of your crew left alive on this ship?"

"Yes. That's why I've accepted defeat."

I turned to Lisa. "Confirm that. Send out all your swimming buzzers."

She released a dozen tiny drones. We'd kept them close to hand until now, but it was definitely time to map the entire ship. Lisa watched her tapper as they swam and transmitted back their findings.

"Did you communicate with your fellow cephalopod captains during the assault?" I demanded. "Did you tell them you were under attack and losing your ship?"

His eyes again slid around the room. He looked uncertain.

"Will a poor answer result in punishment?"

"Only a false answer is a poor one."

"Then yes, I did so."

I grinned inside my helmet. The squid probably would have lied to evade a fate he didn't like. I couldn't blame him for that. He was my slave—but that didn't mean I could trust him any farther than a man could trust any prisoner of war in such a situation.

"In that case," I said, "am I correct in assuming your comrades are maneuvering to board this ship and take her back?"

"What else would they be doing?"

"As expected. You shall take *Force* out of formation. Let her fall back so they must slow down to board her. Take no other action. This includes responding to any communication from other ships. Make it appear as if she's lost power."

"Your instructions are confusing... but I will obey."

The squid turned to the controls. When he touched them, my team reacted uneasily.

"We can't trust this monster, McGill," Harris hissed at me. "Are you insane?"

150

"I've been called worse," I told him. "The cephalopod is under no obligation to screw us. Unlike a human prisoner, it's not his duty to sabotage our mission. He's completely self-centered now. He serves only me—or himself if he thinks his odds are better by defying my will."

"Strange," Lisa said, stepping forward a pace and watching Storm work. "He switched sides that fast?"

"Not really. It's kind of like being taken prisoner. Only, in their case, they take that role very seriously."

She nodded and watched him closely.

"Master," Storm said after a time, "we're falling back from the formation—but it will not stop the enemy from assaulting this ship."

"I know that. I'm only trying to buy us some time. Harris, guard our new friend. Lisa, come with me. We're going to gather up every teleport suit we can."

"That's the best idea you've had all day," she said, her eyes alight with excitement.

What was it about techs and technology? They were like drunks in a liquor cabinet every time they found some new gadget to play with.

We hustled back to the room we'd ported into first. Around us, the ship lurched and the pressure of deceleration pushed us back. We had to fight the water and centrifugal force to get to the aft of the ship again.

Gathering the jump-suits turned out to be a time-consuming task. The main problem was that the suits were full of dead squids. We had to peel them off and roll massive bodies away. It was a good thing we were in water. Without buoyancy on our side, I doubted we could have done it.

After shucking the third suit, we had a workable system and even split up—making faster work of the rest.

"Got them all," Lisa reported finally, with clear excitement in her voice. "None of them look damaged."

"Good, I'm calling Harris. We have to rig this ship to blow up then jump home again."

She put a hand on my elbow. With all my armor and gear, I barely felt her touch. But I stopped anyway.

"What's wrong?"

151

"Are you sure we have to ditch this ship?" she asked. "There's so much here. I've been recording everything, and—"

"Get on the pad. Take all the suits with you right now. That's an order."

Her hand slid away from mine. She nodded. "You're right. We have to secure the suits."

While we'd been stripping down squids, Lisa's drones had mapped out most of the ship. We had the data we needed for future strikes.

I gave her all the suits, plugged her into the ship's central power and watched her jump out. Then I moved toward the engine room, which was now displayed on my tapper after we'd shared her maps.

Moving down the long central passage, the ship lurched suddenly.

"Harris?" I called. "What's going on up there?"

"I don't know," he said. "Looks like something's hit us. I can't read these squid instruments—McGill, it's time to get out of here."

I nodded, hearing muffled clangs and screeching sounds of metal-on-metal. The enemy was on the hull.

"No time to rig the engine to blow," I said. "Find any plug and port out."

"Got it—luck, McGill."

Switching directions, I moved to the nearest hatch according to Lisa's maps—yes. It was a gun turret.

"You still there, Harris?" I asked.

There was silence on my chat channel. "Carlos?"

More silence. I was alone on the squid ship. That meant the captain would probably rethink his role and come after me.

The ship lurched again, and I saw sparks in the ceiling. The squids were burning their way through the hull.

I looked around, but I didn't see any of those handy power ports. Behind me, a dark figure appeared in the murky water. It was Storm—he'd changed his mind very quickly.

"I order you to stand down, Storm!" I shouted.

A bubbling sound came back to me. "You are now *my* slave. You're outnumbered. Submit or die."

"Humans make bad slaves," I told him as I climbed into the turret. It was a tight squeeze as it was built for an invertebrate and therefore was perfectly spherical in nature. My spine had to curve painfully, and my bulky suit made it even harder.

"Get out of there!" Storm raged. "I demand you provide me the same courtesy I did you. I demand you become my servant in all things. I demand—"

I never heard his third demand, and I didn't much care to, either. I'd figured out by that time how to operate the triggers in the turret. They were built for someone with multiple hands—but how hard was it to fire a big gun at a range of a few dozen meters?

The turret roared, and my eyes were blinded by the flash. A second squid ship, identical to the one I was on, had latched onto us and hugged up tight—that was a mistake. They should have just stood off and blown us apart.

But that wasn't the squid way. They liked captives. Catching people really turned them on.

The gun turret was amazingly effective. That was probably due to the close range. Fully a quarter of the enemy ship was blown away from the rest of the hull. A brief plume of plasma and radiation bathed me, and it made me smile.

I fired one more time before I died. That shot took out the front nodule where the bridge was.

Then they fired back—or some other squid ship did, I couldn't tell which.

Either way, I died fast. There was a huge grin on my face right to the end.

-24-

Revival was never pleasant, but this time, I came out laughing. Choking on slime, I spat it out, and kept laughing.

"What's so funny, McGill?" asked a familiar voice.

It was Anne Grant, I knew her voice anywhere.

"Anne?" I asked, eyes still glued shut.

"Yeah, it's me. They've been calling more and more Varus people to Central for some reason. You wouldn't know anything about that, would you?"

"Not a thing," I said, knowing the teleport-suits were beyond classified. If she hadn't been briefed, I sure as hell wasn't going to be the one to do it.

They worked on me for a few minutes. When I could see, I stared at her through blurred eyes.

"Why do we always come out of these machines with eyes glued shut like kittens?" I asked her.

"I don't know. Ask the aliens who made it—or the kittens. But you never answered my question. Why did you come out laughing? That's a rare response to a violent death."

I finally caught on. She was doing a psych eval. Whenever a legionnaire behaved oddly after being revived, it was her job to investigate and report it.

In my particular case, I knew she was doubly concerned. I'd once woken up with a screw loose and tried to kill Winslade immediately afterward. Come to think of it, though, that hadn't been such a bad idea...

"I'm fine," I said, then I explained how I'd died fighting squids and gotten two of their ships to blast one another.

She looked at me, stunned. "You were on a squid ship? How in the hell—?"

I'd blown it. The recent revive had caused me to let my guard down. I'd promised myself I'd keep quiet, but then I went right off and blabbed not thirty seconds later. Groping for a dodge, I came up with one.

"Hey," I said. "Don't you owe me a date?"

"No," she said. "That was several James McGills ago."

Anne smiled even as she looked down at my arm and measured my vitals.

"You sure you aren't interested?" I pressed.

"I'm sure—that's over with, James. I'm seeing someone else."

"Who? Winslade?"

She moved to slap me, but I caught her hand. I kept smiling and kissed her fingers.

"James," she said, sighing and looking at me. "You're definitely the man I know. Personality checks out, you're cleared for duty. Graves wants you to report to his office immediately."

"No shower?"

"No shower."

Disappointed, I pulled on my clothes and made it to the doorway. There on the far side was a small, pissed-off tech. Lisa had been waiting for me to be revived. Apparently, she'd seen the whole finger-kissing thing with Anne through the window in the door.

"Hey babe," I said, reaching for her.

She dodged away.

"Don't touch me. Why were you kissing that bio?"

I looked over my shoulder in surprise. "Who? Anne? She's like my mama. She's birthed me twenty times over. My mama only did it once."

Lisa put her hands on her hips and glowered up at me.

I was still a little foggy, but my brain seemed to be wired for moments like this.

"Look," I said squinting at her through burning eyes, "did you notice she tried to slap me the second I came out? I'm not talking about my bottom, either. She was testing my memory, and I gave her some smart-ass answers. Are you that jealous already? We've only been together for a few days."

"Well…" she said doubtfully, "don't paw any more women in front of me, okay?"

"I promise. How long was I dead, anyway?"

"Not long. Just a few hours. Graves ordered your revival to be prioritized."

Figuring that had to be a good sign, I moved quickly upstairs with Lisa at my side. When we reached Graves, he was in a positively good mood. That was rare with the Centurion.

"Hey Graves," I called. "You gonna torture me or blow my face off? Which one, I'm running a pool."

"Neither, McGill. That was excellent work you did up there. How did you manage to destroy two ships?"

I explained and embellished freely. That was one of the finest things about living on after death in combat: you got to make yourself out as a hero every time—as long as you didn't die too early.

He listened with a near-smile. When I was finished, he nodded and clapped me on the shoulder.

"When those ships blew," he said, "I figured anyone who hadn't ported back was a safe bet for ordering a revive—even without the evidence if you know what I mean. As to your story, I almost believe it. But the part about making the squid captain your slave seems a step too far."

"Didn't Harris tell you about that?"

"Harris? He's not been revived yet. He didn't make it out."

Frowning, I thought about that. He'd been ordered to find a plug and port out. Maybe he hadn't made it.

"Don't worry," Graves said. "I've prioritized Harris and Carlos both. They died with you on the cruiser. From Earth, we knew the story when it blew up in tandem with another ship. From here it looked like you'd gotten them to ram into one another. The story about the turret—that's gravy."

"It's true sir, every word," I assured him. But then I had a thought, and I frowned. "Sir? How do I remember all these

156

details? I died out there beyond the reach of the net. The data core here at Central couldn't possibly—"

Graves waved my words away.

"That your tech's work," he said. "The minute you got there, she rigged up a relay transmitter. We didn't want to miss anything, so it was all transmitted back to Earth. Took nearly an hour to get here after the explosion, but I figured it was worth the wait."

I nodded slowly, thinking about it. I was now wondering about the key, too. Lisa had taken it with her when she returned. I had to get it back as soon as possible.

"What really matters is that you got Lisa back with those suits," Graves continued. "We've now got fourteen working jump-suits even after taking a few losses. The trouble is…"

I looked at him expectantly, and his smile faded.

"The trouble is that the enemy ship was destroyed. That lab you popped into was assumed to be a reprogramming point. All the equipment that presumably sets up these suits is gone. This effort might be at an end."

"No sir," I said firmly. "We've got several more missions in us. I'm sure of that much."

My finger indicated the dial on my chest. There were, after all, three more settings. Only three of them had been explored so far.

"I hereby volunteer to take my team on another mission," I said. "We'll hit the island I jumped to last time. There was power there to return, and maybe we'll even find some answers about how this gear works."

He thought that over. "I'm going to have to get approval for that. Give me a few minutes."

I frowned. "A few minutes? I was thinking I'd shower-up and get some sleep."

"No way. That cephalopod fleet is still out there, you realize that don't you? You can shower, but as soon as the rest of your team is on its feet, you're on your way again."

He pointed toward a big chrono on the wall.

"Four hours," he said. "That's all you get."

"Good enough," I said, and I exited the chamber.

Lisa followed me. "We're going out there again?" she asked in concern.

"Yes ma'am. That's what legionnaires do."

"Couldn't someone else do it this time?"

I looked at her. "You've got the key still, don't you? The shell thing?"

"Yes, of course."

Suddenly, I realized what had happened to Harris and Carlos.

"Oh no," I said.

"What?"

"The key opened the security on their suits to jump out there—but the effect must not have lasted. It must be on a reset timer or something."

She looked horrified. "You mean you ordered them to jump back home—and they fried instead?"

Nodding slowly, I considered my thoughtlessness. We'd lost two good suits and two good men.

"We'll have to play it tighter next time," I said. "Good thing they probably don't know what hit them."

"That's all you have to say? Don't you even want to apologize to them, James?"

"Hell no. They'd never let me live it down if they knew I had something to do with it. Besides, the key has to stay a secret."

"Why?"

"Because it's too powerful and very illegal. Just possessing such a device is a Galactic offense. An *extinction-level* offense."

That made her eyes widen. She reached reflexively toward the lump in her pocket.

I knew right where her mind was at that moment. It was very alarming to realize that you were holding an object that would cause the Empire to exterminate your entire species just because it was in your possession.

"Sort of makes drunk-driving seem trivial, doesn't it?" I asked.

She shook her head wonderingly. "I don't know what I see in you."

158

"Hey," I said, reaching for her hand. "I need a shower. You want to keep me company?"

Lisa looked at my hand suspiciously for a full second.

"I'm not going to bite," I told her.

She sighed and followed me to the showers, which were communal in the lower levels of Central. Afterward, we ate dinner—it was dinnertime, I'd learned—and crossed the street to her place.

In her tiny apartment, we made gentle love. It wasn't wild and urgent the way it had been the first few times—when we had the threat of death hanging over us. I guess we were used to that by now. We'd gone out into space together, faced the enemy and defeated him.

Instead, it was pure victory-sex. Sweet and triumphant.

At length our tappers began beeping. We had thirty minutes left before go-time. Dragging on our clothes and heading back to Central, we ended up trotting for the elevators. We made it back just in time for the briefing.

"Nice of you two lovebirds to show up," Graves said sternly. "Are you taking point again, McGill?"

"That's the plan, sir," I said. "Lisa, fix me up."

She came to me solemnly. She had the key in her palm, I could tell by the odd way she was holding her hand. She touched it to the dial on my chest and whispered: "Luck."

"I don't need luck," I said. "I need to make the right choices."

She smiled. "Okay then—don't do anything stupid."

I gave her a nod and checked all my seals. Then I raised my weapon to my shoulder and teleported away.

-25-

The dial on my chest was set for the first notch, the first target of importance. When I'd selected that setting before, I'd gone to the world with the green oceans and the green skies.

The trip was a long one. At least this time, I didn't have a squid cracking my ribs as he burned to death outside my suit.

Those long trips… they were soul-wrenching. I knew I wasn't myself. I knew I wasn't in the state of existence that I'd been familiar with all my life. Did that mean I was alive or dead? Is this what being dead felt like?

I didn't know, but I knew I felt lonely. Logically, the rest of my team was jumping too, all popping into nothingness behind me while I was reconstructed on another world. It was weird to think they were out here in the void with me, impossible to contact or sense.

Before I got used to the whole thing, I arrived. I stumbled and gasped. Taking a few half-steps, I moved up the beach. I didn't feel like merging my foot up with the next guy again.

Ferguson arrived second. He took a step and tripped, falling flat on his face.

"Get up!" I shouted. "Move out! The next one is coming in seconds."

He scrambled, throwing sand everywhere. He looked scared, and I didn't blame him for that. He'd experienced a merge-up, if only with my boot.

I helped lift him to his feet, and we took cover behind some boulders. We were supposed to make sure the entire squad had arrived before we moved inland.

Sargon was next. He was a pro. He stepped up the beach, his weapon ready to fire. He smiled at me.

"Good trip, Sargon?" I asked.

"A little long," he said, "but there was nothing to it, Adjunct. I almost fell asleep."

Ferguson snorted and shook his head. Even so, he made an effort to stop breathing hard and tried to act like we did. The trick was to stay alert and keep scanning the environment without looking like you were going to piss your pants. Ferguson pretty much managed it, and I began to have hopes for the hog.

"You ever think of joining a real legion, Ferguson?" I asked him.

"What? You mean like Victrix or something?"

"Exactly. A legion that fights. A legion that goes into space."

"Well sir..." he said, "it seems to me that I don't have to now. Hegemony is fighting for Earth every day."

He had a point, and I nodded.

"Good answer. You're right. We're all on the line now. Us out here and everyone back home. You're all right, Ferguson."

"Thank you, sir."

He nodded toward the port-in spot, and I turned to look. Three more of my team had arrived. They stumbled away from the landing zone and took up defensive positions around it.

I clapped my gauntlets together loudly. "Harris, get these people off the beach. Lead A-team. Take up firing positions on that rock formation. From there, you'll be able to cover the beehive structure and our LZ at the same time."

He gave me a glance that said he didn't feel like taking point, but he didn't say anything. He knew dodging or arguing would only get him a kick in the pants.

"You heard the man, move out!" he shouted at his people.

Ferguson, Sargon and a couple of others hustled up the beach. I waited around as the softies in the group began to arrive. Carlos, Kivi and Lisa rounded out the team.

161

When we were all accounted for, we moved up to join Harris.

"Anything?" I asked him.

"Zippo sir. This place looks abandoned."

"Take your team around to the back of the building. The rest of you take cover here."

Harris gave me another of those "thanks asshole" looks and led his group to the far side of the building. He took the long way around, circling at least a hundred meters toward the shoreline. I didn't care as long as he got the job done.

Before he made it, the Wur came out. The massive door opened, and what passed for a head section on a Wur creature slid out to greet us. It had orange, snake-like fronds for sensory organs, and these were all alert and squirming independently.

I don't know who panicked. Right off, I suspected one of the hogs. They were still new to the whole 'meet-the-new-alien' thing, after all.

A plasma bolt flashed and struck the alien in the middle of those inquisitive fronds. At least the hog could shoot straight. I had to give him credit for that.

The Wur didn't drop. Instead, it tucked itself back into the doorway, its head region smoking, and slammed the door shut.

"That's great," I said, "who did that? Who fired without orders?"

"I did, sir," said one of the hogs. It was the bench-guy, the one I'd merged up with days back. He looked ashamed.

"Right..." I said. "Bio? Put this man on my do-not-revive list, will you?"

"Got it, sir," Carlos said promptly. "He's as good as permed."

"Excellent."

"But... but sir," sputtered the hog.

"Next time, hold your frigging fire until you're ordered to fire, unless you're attacked! Understand?"

"Yes sir! Sorry sir!"

He was white-faced. Behind his back, Carlos flashed me a grin. Kivi thought it was funny, too. Only Lisa seemed disturbed. The Varus people knew I was joking, but she didn't.

162

"Okay, now that we've managed to turn an easy kill into a barricaded, pre-warned enemy, who's going to volunteer to open the door for me?"

No one so much as moved, except for Carlos. He was pointing at the scared hog with his thumb.

"We have a volunteer," I said. "Get going, hog!"

"Me sir? But—"

"You heard the man, get your ass up to the door!" Carlos shouted. "Don't worry, the Wur always kill people fast—unless they're in a chewing mood, that is. Then it takes a while."

"How do you know what that thing is?" the hog asked. "Or what it does?"

Carlos laughed.

"Carlos knows," Kivi said, "because he's been eaten by one before."

The man looked alarmed. I thought he might wet his pants and bolt, but since we were on an alien planet, and he didn't have the juice in his suit for another port, he had no choice.

He walked up to the door like a little kid visiting his first haunted house on Halloween. Without more than a second's hesitation, he tried the door. It didn't budge.

"It's locked, I think, Adjunct," he said over his shoulder.

"Well, no shit," I said. "Get it open!"

He tried to open it more forcefully. The handle was simple. It looked like a lumpy, porous chunk of rock. He grunted and strained, but it didn't budge. Turning back to us, he threw his hands up in the air, defeated.

In that instant, the door popped open about a half-meter. A long, gray-skinned arm reached out. It had seven, multi-jointed stick-like fingers. I remembered that look well from the time when the Wur had boarded our ship in the L-347 system.

The large hand grabbed the hog and snatched him away. It was all over in a second.

"Sir!" Sargon roared. "Permission to blast that door down!"

"Wait!" Lisa shouted, running to my side. "McGill," she said. "There's sure to be valuable intel inside that building."

"A man's getting killed in there right now, tech," I told her.

"Yes, but we can revive him."

I frowned and tried to listen. I couldn't hear the hog screaming anymore. Either his radio had been broken or the walls of the building were causing interference.

Internally, I felt a little bad. I hadn't meant for the hog to have another bad death. Hell, I'd teleported my small intestines into his head just a few days back. He really didn't deserve this kind of treatment his first day out in the field.

"Sargon," I shouted, "take down that door for me. But try not to burn out the whole place. Our tech here wants to go gadget-hunting."

"Roger that," Sargon said.

Less than a second later, he lit up the door. It began to melt and transformed into black slag. Smoke poured off, and the building above the door caught fire.

Lisa threw up her hands and slapped her helmet in frustration. "You guys are wrecking the whole place!"

"That *is* what we do best," I said.

After a six-second burn, the door was a smoking hole. Sargon hadn't done a surgical job, but at least he didn't follow-up by lobbing any grenades into the interior. Lisa didn't seem to realize she was lucky on that score.

"Okay," I said. "Did you see any other entrances around to the back, Harris?"

"Nothing sir. Just more weird growths. There do appear to be some power outlets."

"Stay away from those for now," I ordered sternly. "We're busting in. Harris, you have the ball."

"Thanks, sir," he said sarcastically.

He hustled up to one side of the building, and his team assaulted the door. It felt odd, watching other men do my dirty work. I was used to being at the front of the line when it came time to be tossed into the furnace. Sending other men into the flames seemed wrong somehow.

When I heard hoarse screaming from the interior, I signaled my back-up team.

"Non-combatants, hang back. Combat team, follow me."

We kicked down the rest of the door, which was still smoking and orangey-hot. Inside we found the Wur, dead on the floor.

164

The screaming was coming from the hog we'd sent in first. Miraculously, he was still alive—but his limbs had been ripped right off his body.

Apparently, the Wur hadn't known quite how to kill an armored human. It had decided to pluck off arms and legs. Harris' team must have gotten there before the Wur had a chance to remove the man's last appendage—his head.

Harris already had his pistol out, but I waved him aside. I knelt beside the trooper, who was in shock but still aware. That was due to the miraculous efforts of the modern combat kit he wore beneath the jump suit. He was being pumped full of drugs, and wire tourniquets were being applied to the missing limbs so he didn't bleed out.

"What's your name, soldier?" I asked him. His nametag was missing, having been ripped away in the fight.

"Johan, sir... but... I can't remember my last name."

"That's all right. You'll wake up in the morning, and this will all have been a bad dream."

"Really?"

I forced a smile. "Really."

Then, I shot him in the head.

-26-

Some might think I was a right-bastard at that moment. But really, shooting Johan was a mercy. Taking him home and trying to get the bio people to patch him up was hopeless. They'd have recycled old Johan immediately, laughing at me for having bothered to drag him all the way back to Central.

I stood up when it was over and looked around.

"Are we clear?" I asked Harris.

"As far as I can tell," he said. "I do think there's something strange about this particular Wur, though."

"How's that?"

"He's got some kind of leash or tether attached to him."

I examined the ropy, fibrous line that reached to the mid-section of the creature. It *did* look strange. Calling in Carlos, Kivi and Lisa, we searched the rest of the place.

We didn't find much else. There was quite a bit of electrical equipment, a bizarre-looking generator, and a few vats of nasty-looking fluid.

"Stay away from the liquids," Carlos urged. "Highly caustic."

He offered up a smoking gauntlet as proof.

"Carlos, quit screwing with the tech stuff," I told him. "Tell me what the deal is with this hose attaching the Wur to the floor."

He examined the situation closely.

"I don't know…" he said. "I wish Natasha was here."

That gave me a pang. I hadn't had much time to worry about Natasha, but I still wanted her back. I'd half hoped to find some scrap of her body here. If I could prove she was dead, they'd authorize a revive back at Central.

Pushing those thoughts away, I gave my head a shake. "All right, what do we have?"

"This equipment is advanced," Kivi said. "Biological stuff like we saw back on Death World."

"Lisa?"

She shook her head. "I can't understand most of it, but there's definitely a power-generator involved. It works chemically, like a battery. Organic chemistry for sure."

"Hmm..." I said. "Why the hell would this place be on the list of stops for every squid with a teleportation suit? That's what I don't get."

"Hey, I think I found it," Carlos said.

He was on his knees in the center of the room. I stepped quickly to his side.

"What do you have, Specialist?"

"The tether goes here—but it doesn't stop. It goes into the floor itself. There's got to be something under this floor. Something the Wur was attached to."

Less than overwhelmed with his discovery, I grunted.

"So what? Maybe this hose fed the Wur or kept him chained here. This whole trip was a waste of time."

"I don't think so," Lisa said. "There has to be something important about this place. We just have to figure out what it is."

Now, people might not be surprised to learn that I've never been fond of mysteries. I like shooting things. I like chasing women. But puzzles? No thanks, I always pass them by in disgust.

Feeling that sense of disgust now, I headed for the door. I almost made it, too, before Lisa called me back.

"I've found something else," she said. "Have a look at this, James."

Crowding my way to her, I saw she'd located what looked like a rubber plug. But it was too big to be a plug.

"What's that?" I asked. "Some kind of drain?"

167

"Help me pull it out."

"Okay—helmets back on, everyone."

As the atmosphere on this strange water-world was breathable, some of my troops had opened their faceplates. They quickly slammed them shut again.

I gave the plug a mighty heave, and it popped loose. Beneath the plug was a black hole. We shined our lights into the darkness and saw a distant bottom.

"Some kind of cave?" I asked.

"I hate caves," Carlos said.

Normally, I'd have sent him in on point, but he was our bio now, not a grunt. I scanned the group and my eyes landed on Harris.

"Vet, take two men down and recon this hole."

He eyed me in resignation.

"Thanks for this opportunity, sir," he said.

"You're welcome, smart ass."

Harris dropped down first, howling a little as he fell. I think the drop was farther than he'd thought. Landing with a splash, he struggled to his feet and aimed his weapon in random directions.

"Get down here, Sargon!" he shouted up. "The water's fine!"

Sargon jumped in next, then Ferguson. We watched them for a minute or so as they searched around and called the all clear.

"Nothing down here but some kind of big-ass cactus," Harris said as I jumped down to join the others.

"Big-ass what?"

"See? Over there."

Sargon and I both advanced, raising our weapons. Looming at the far end of the cavern was indeed what resembled a giant, barrel-cactus.

Sargon and I knew right off that it wasn't a cactus. It wasn't a normal desert-dwelling plant. Oh, it had spines all right. They were each a meter long, easy. And it had a gushy center, too. But that center wasn't full of fleshy vegetable matter, it contained a brain of sorts.

"A Nexus," I said, staring. "A brain plant."

Sargon sighted on the dead center of the monster, which was a good ten meters high and five wide. Shaped like a pale green cylinder, I might have wondered how it could survive down here. But I'd already spotted ultraviolet radiation sources. It was being fed and cared for like a hothouse orchid.

"Hold off, Sargon," I said. "We've got this thing trapped. Without minions, they've never been dangerous."

"What's the deal?" Harris demanded, gawking at the monster.

"This is a Wur leader," I told him. "A brain-plant. They're all plants, but only a few varieties are capable of much thought. Oddly, the one with the mind can't move. The simpler plants *can* move. Such a strange race."

"Wur? They're the ones that permed your parents, right?"

"Well, they tried. My parents left the ceremony early back on Earth."

For some reason, this struck Harris as extremely funny.

"I can see it now," he laughed. "They ran out on you the second they dropped you off, didn't they?"

Annoyed, I didn't answer him. Instead, I circled around the giant cactus and eyed it from various angles.

"Remember," I told him, "we pretty much permed their entire planet."

"Right… There can't be any lost love between our two species. McGill, as your senior veteran, I hereby recommend that you burn down this lump of spines right now."

"Suggestion noted and filed, Harris. But I'm going to try to talk to it instead. I watched Claver do it once. This could be a diplomatic coup if I could pull off the same trick."

He snorted, but he didn't argue. I took Carlos, Kivi and Lisa closer to the plant.

Like the last one I'd encountered in a hole on Death World, this beast was squatting in a pool of muck. They must like it that way—all slimy and wet around the roots.

We found tubers, and I tried not to damage them. When we got close, I asked Lisa to transfer the program Claver had been running on L-374 to my tapper. It was a translation app that allowed our species to converse with the Wur.

She hesitated. "That's classified and untested, McGill."

169

"Yeah, well, what difference does it make? Earth has about seventy-two hours before doomsday. You think we should hold onto every secret until the bitter end?"

Reluctantly, she let me have the program. It had come from Claver's tapper originally. The Lord only knew where he'd gotten it from.

With Kivi's help, I followed the procedure. Me and this building-sized cactus had to mingle, one-on-one. It was a mind-meld of sorts, but involved getting abused a bit by one of the weird tubers around its base. There were many fine filaments which lengthened from the tuber and penetrated the flesh of my forearm—sticking like tiny spines. I felt calmer immediately after they were stuck deep into me, and I watched my tapper. My pulse dropped to the mellow zone on the bio-readout.

Claver had told me it got you kind of high when you melded with the plant. The toxins involved in exchanging body fluids had side effects.

When I was linked up to the plant, I did feel strange. It was like I was dreaming—or on hallucinogens.

"All right cactus," I said, "let's talk. What are you doing here on this world?"

"What creature dares to question a Nexus?" it answered.

"I do. I'm an Earthman. You've talked to one of my kind before, his name is Claver."

"The creature you speak of is a thief. A villain. A devil-of-the-flesh."

"That's him," I said, chuckling.

"What message do you carry to me from the Claver-creature?" the plant asked.

At that point, I almost blew it. I almost told the green blob that I had no message from Claver. I almost admitted, in fact, that I wasn't Claver's friend or errand-boy at all.

But then I got hold of myself. Despite my floating state of mind, I managed to come up with a lie instead.

"You've got it wrong," I told the plant. "Claver works for me. He is my servant."

The needles around me shook and rattled. The plant seemed pissed off.

"The Claver-creature has manipulated me. Its words have no substance."

"What did Claver tell you?"

"That it was the master of Earth. That it could arrange any deal with Earth. That it spoke on behalf of its entire species."

This information honestly didn't surprise me at all. If there was anyone in the universe that I acknowledged as my master when it came to the fine art of telling a whopper, it was Claver.

"I see," I said. "Don't you worry about a thing. I'll punish Claver for his misbehavior next time we meet."

"What of the deals I've made with him in good faith? What of our arrangements?"

"Hmm," I said. "Give me a hint. What are these deals about?"

The spines shook again.

"More lies! Claver is a monster! You should put it down and never let its roots regrow. How can Claver's master submit if it doesn't even know about our treaty? How can Earth be expected to lie supine while the cephalopod fleets conquer her? Much time has been wasted."

"Ah..." I said, catching on. "So, that was the plan. You Wur control the cephalopods. It's *you* who are trying to conquer Earth, not the squids on their own. I get it."

"Your pathetic comprehension does not gratify me. I'd heard reports of resistance, but I'd dared to hope they were overstated. Too much time has been lost. The end grows near for your species. Without an arrangement, you must be put down."

"Now hold on," I said. "We can come to a real, binding arrangement. We're here, aren't we? We're talking."

My nerves tingled, and I smelled something like tangerines. Part of my chemical melding with the Nexus included some awareness of its private thought processes. The plant didn't seem to be listening to me any longer. I had the sense it was sending communications to somewhere else.

"Another of your kind is known to me," the plant said. *"I've tasted this flavor of thought before. There was one of your species here. I dissected her and consumed her with my roots. The same fate shall befall you, creature."*

171

Those words—or thoughts—penetrated the haze in my mind. Who could it be talking about? There was only one missing female human I could think of that might possibly be out here on an unexplored world: Natasha.

To test the plant's memories, I thought of her. I envisioned her soft skin and soft voice.

"Is that who you're talking about, cactus?" I demanded.

"I believe so. She squatted right where you are now when I melded with her. She succumbed to my toxins—as you will shortly. She wanted to talk at great length."

I felt a little sick from the plant's biochemistry, but I wasn't dying yet. Natasha might have taken something like this too far. If she made it down here and talked to this plant, she'd probably get excited and commune with it all day long.

"What about our deal?" I demanded, hating the plant now. "Give me an answer."

"Your answer is 'no' and there is no more time to discuss it. The fleet must be instructed. My servant above is not responding to my will. What has happened to it?"

Rousing myself with a great effort, I got to my feet and swayed in a semi-trance. I lifted a finger and shook it at the plant.

"What are you trying to tell your servant?" I demanded.

"To relay my orders to the fleet, of course. Earth must be cleansed. Holding back the cephalopod ships is now pointless. Your race is feral, and—"

It went on like that, but I was no longer listening. I staggered away, and the tuber that had stuck in my arm decoupled. It was no longer mixing our blood and linking our nervous systems.

My team gathered around me, and I realized after a moment they were propping me up. I was barely able to stand.

Pushing them away one at a time, I fell to my knees in the muck. I felt around down there, and I touched a human arm.

My heart beat faster. It was Natasha's body. It had to be. I'd found her at last, dead and forgotten on this muddy planet.

I almost shouted and called for Carlos, our bio. But I held back. I was upset, but I'd gotten the inkling of an idea concerning Natasha.

Getting to my feet again, I struggled to Sargon. I put my hand on his armored shoulder, and I pointed with my other hand at the bulging cactus behind me. My lips curled in anger.

"Sargon," I said, "would you please blow that thing's big green brain out?"

His frown transformed into a grin. He shouldered his weapon and sighted.

"What took you so long to figure that one out, McGill?" he asked.

He blew a hole the size of a hubcap right through the nexus plant's rind. The mushy goop that flowed out, steaming and sticky, fouled the water around us.

Kivi and Lisa, who'd been poking around at the roots, retreated making sounds of disgust. They never did find Natasha's remains.

-27-

Soon after destroying the nexus plant, we jumped back to Earth. My first thought was to report Natasha's death, but I didn't do it. I'd had a better idea by then. These teleport suits... they had serious possibilities.

When I made my report to Graves, he was less than happy.

"We'd better take this upstairs immediately," he said.

Without another word, he turned and marched toward the elevators. I followed him. Harris fell in behind us, and I glanced over my shoulder at him. I didn't like the look on his face. I could tell he was hoping he'd get the chance to arrest me again. It almost made me wish I'd gotten him killed somehow on Green World for sheer spite.

Imperator Drusus didn't become violently angry after I made my report, however. He brooded instead. When he'd thought it over to his own satisfaction, he unfolded his bony elbows and turned to question me once again.

"So," he said, "you made contact with the enemy's supreme commander—as far as we know."

"I guess that's right, sir."

"And your immediate response to the situation was to blow its brains out?"

"Well... now hold on, Imperator."

Harris had his grin back. His hand slid to the pistol on his hip. He could smell an execution faster than a dog smelled shit.

"Hold on?" Drusus asked sternly. "You didn't hold on when dealing with my counterpart."

174

"That thing told me that the cephalopod fleet was here to conquer Earth," I said. "It said that Claver had made a deal with the Wur, promising them we'd throw the fight."

"Yes, that's what you just described to me minutes ago."

"Well?" I demanded. "Think about it. Wouldn't you rather have the squids try a ground invasion? That's *way* easier to stop than having their fleet come here with orders to bomb us out."

Drusus looked thoughtful. "You think an invasion is better than a bombing?"

"Yes, I surely do. Invasions take time, and we need more time to figure out how to win this."

He nodded slowly.

"It was my fault," he said at last. "I'm the one who put such a critical mission into the hands of an amateur. A man known for fits of drastic action."

"Sir, if I'd tried to negotiate further with the nexus plant, it would have simply ignored me. I know these aliens. It's their way or the highway. I knew the brain-plant would signal its fleet the first chance it got. We'd be facing bombs right now instead of an upcoming invasion."

Drusus stared off into space for a time as if deep in thought. Finally, he met my eyes again.

"The situation has changed in your absence, McGill. The enemy has already begun their invasion."

"I don't understand," I said, looking at both the officers.

Graves just shrugged and Drusus didn't meet my eyes.

"But..." I began, "I thought the Cephalopod Armada was between Jupiter and Mars, chasing our fleet out in the dark somewhere."

"They caught the last of our fleet and destroyed it during the night," Drusus explained. "But instead of driving straight to Earth, they paused at the asteroid belt. We've been preparing to do battle with them, gearing up our fortifications on Luna and other orbital platforms. But they've continued to hang back, out of range."

"Why?"

Drusus tapped at his desktop. A diagram appeared, but instead of depicting local space, it showed Earth.

"They've set up a beachhead in northern New York Sector," he said. "in a forested region known as the Adirondack Mountains."

"What the hell...?" I asked, looking at the map.

Harris and Graves crowded around me, staring at the map.

"No frigging way!" Harris blurted in a sudden outburst. "McGill? How the hell did you manage to get Earth invaded? Oh.... sorry sirs."

"It's quite all right," Drusus said grimly. "Your astonishment is shared by all of us. McGill appears to have caused this move by the enemy. They apparently have technology beyond simple teleportation suits. They've set up some kind of... station. A gateway. A connection point between Earth and their invasion forces."

My jaw hung low. "How's that even possible?"

Drusus shrugged. "Did you honestly think that Earth has been exposed to the most advanced technology in the known universe? We've only seen cast-off trinkets from the Galactics—hand-me-downs the Mogwa and their ilk don't want anymore. But these squids have a much larger Kingdom to back them up. They're under no restrictions as to what kind of tech they can develop and deploy."

"It makes sense," Graves said, speaking up for the first time. "If they can teleport, how much harder could it be to set up a connection between two points in space and move freely between them? But what I don't understand is how they built the station here on Earth to receive their troops."

"So..." I said as we stared at the map. An irregularly-shaped region glowed red in the center. "They built a beachhead under our noses? When did all this happen?"

"As far as we can tell, it's been ongoing for over a week. Part of the plan was to take out Central first. But when that failed, they stopped coming here. They switched tactics and launched a ground campaign. As far as we can tell, they brought down their gateway equipment in bits and pieces to install it in the forest. When they were ready, they marched through with a larger force and began infiltrating the surrounding country side."

"Are we talking about squid troops?" I asked. "Are cephalopods really overrunning upstate New York?"

Drusus shook his head. He tapped at the region, and it zoomed in sickeningly. We were soon looking up-close at snowy fields shadowed with a thick forest.

When the zooming image slowed and transformed from a blur to a clear picture, I saw what I'd never expected to see again. A group of nine very large humanoids came marching out from under the pines.

They wore black, and they carried muskets. Huge sabers were strapped to their armored backs.

"Heavy troopers?" I asked incredulously. "Like the ones we beat back on Dust World? I can't believe it."

"That's not all—watch," Drusus said.

After another few moments, while the square of nine litter-mates stood shoulder to shoulder in perfect formation, the trees shook. They parted like tall weeds pushed aside by a strong man.

Shoving through them, a massive figure stepped into view. It was a monster, a full six meters in height. It carried a heavy energy projector, and a glittering shield of force wrapped around its body like a glassy nimbus.

It was a true giant bred from human slaves stolen from Dust World. I'd fought its kind before—and they didn't go down easily.

The sight of the giant floored me. I couldn't believe it. I'd seen these beings before, years ago, but I'd never thought I'd run into them again.

"They use humans as breeding stock," I said. "They've always used us for slaves. To them, we're chattel. These creatures have been bred to serve as ground troops."

"That's right," Drusus said. "That's why the cephalopods are so determined to take Earth. They see us as a good source of raw material."

Stunned, I kept staring at the vid feeds. More and more heavy troops were marching out of the forest now. Teams of nine litter-mates overran a local automated farm as we watched.

Of the few people there, the humans that cowered were captured while those that resisted were killed. They even destroyed the farming robots they ran into. They seemed not to know the difference between harmless automated servants and dangerous enemies.

"Della told me about this," I said. "The squids used to periodically send ships to Dust World to pick up fresh slaves. They needed new basic stock. From our bodies they bred these abominations. They should all be destroyed. Why don't we just nuke the whole sector?"

Drusus shrugged. "We tried that at the start, but they've got excellent tech. Our aircraft are immediately shot down. Missiles as well. In addition, they have a large dome over the region. It moves with them—they can't be taken out en masse."

Finally, at long last, I caught on.

"Uh…" I said. "Are you saying we have to fight them on the ground, sir?"

"That's exactly what I'm saying. We have to stop this invasion the old-fashioned way."

I hooted loudly, and they all three jumped.

"That's the best damned news I've heard in a week, Imperator! Harris, get out the standards. Legion Varus is marching to battle in the open field!"

Harris looked nowhere near as excited as I was.

Drusus actually chuckled at my comments.

"I admire your spirit, McGill," he said, "but you're still our most experienced man on the teleport team. I was thinking of using your particular talents again—but in a more refined way."

"Damn," I muttered, crestfallen. The idea of facing a squid army in the open field was both terrifying and exhilarating at the same time.

I'd really been looking forward to it.

-28-

When I heard the details of Drusus' plan, I was even less excited than I'd been at first.

"Let me get this straight," I said to Graves when we'd been dismissed from the Imperator's office. "I'm supposed to jump to all the locations on the dial? Alone?"

"That's pretty much it."

Harris, who'd somehow snuck into the meeting with us, chuckled evilly.

I didn't even glance at him.

"That doesn't work for me," I told Graves. "I want a partner."

"Ah," he said, "I was expecting this. You want that little tech to come along, don't you?"

Shaking my head, I lifted a long arm and directed a finger at Harris. "No sir. I need a fighter. The best sidekick a man could hope for. Senior Veteran Harris."

Graves glanced at Harris who appeared to be in shock. Then he looked back at me and crossed his arms.

"State your reasoning, Adjunct."

"Wait one damned second!" Harris complained. "Are you seriously listening to him, Centurion? He's just out to screw me over for laughing. McGill's the most vindictive, cold-hearted, son-of-a—"

"That's enough, Harris. McGill usually has a good reason for even his oddest requests. Let's hear it, McGill."

"Well sir, it goes like this: two of us are harder to take out fast than one. If we go, the point man will engage any threat. He'll probably die, but the other man can port in right after him, see what's going on, and port back out again."

"Who's going to be that point man?" Harris demanded angrily.

"You're way out of line, Harris," Graves warned him.

Harris backed off and sulked a few paces away, giving me the stink-eye all the while. I didn't react. I pretended I didn't even notice him.

"What about it, sir?" I asked.

"Hmm," Graves said. "It *would* mean risking two suits instead of one, but the exploration should go faster."

"Much faster," I said, without being sure why it would go any faster at all.

Graves nodded. "Correct me if I'm wrong, McGill, as I put flesh on the bones of your idea. Your theory is to have two men jump, with the intention of having one of the two come back almost immediately, if they run into trouble. The first returning scout could then tell us if there was a problem and give us basic information on the environment."

"That's exactly right, sir," I lied.

Naturally, I had no such elaborate plans. But if I'm anything, I'm an opportunist. When I hear a good idea, I steal it immediately.

He looked thoughtful. "If neither man comes back, we'll know that destination is deadly. But, barring an extreme threat on the other side, we'd have twice the eyes and manpower to secure intel."

"It's a win-win," I agreed.

"I *do* like that…" Graves continued.

"Seriously?" Harris demanded, his voice cracking high. He was unable to contain himself any longer. "What's to like about this plan, Centurion? He's just trying to get out of the jump. He'll send me, then when I don't come back, he'll say 'hey wait a minute, we can't risk another suit!' and my ass will be permed, just like that."

Graves glanced at him then turned back to me.

"What about such a scenario?" he said to me.

Shaking my head, I still avoided Harris' eye.

"That's not going to happen. I'm going out there with Harris. We'll go ten seconds apart, just like before. If no one comes back in five minutes... well... consider us lost and crank up the revival machines."

Graves nodded, thinking it over further.

"I like it. Good, creative mission-planning. Sometimes, thinking outside the box is a good thing, McGill."

"That's what I always told my teachers back in school—for all the good it did me."

Graves left, chuckling quietly.

When he was gone, Harris pulled out his combat knife. I took a step back and tensed up, ready for an attack. It would be nothing unusual for him to take a shot at me. We'd been fighting out our differences with lethal aggression since we'd met.

"Attacking an officer, Harris?" I asked. "That's grounds for serious punishment."

He shook his head angrily and put the blade up to his own neck.

"No sir! I'm just speeding up the process by slashing my own throat right away. I'm not porting out with you again. I'm not playing second banana on another suicide mission."

"Seriously?" I asked. "Is it too cold in the pool to find your own balls?"

He glowered in hate. "Respectfully, Adjunct—fuck you! I'm not afraid of nothing!"

"Excellent," I said, turning away and heading for the door. "Cut yourself or not, Harris. If you do, I'll have you revived. Then I'll take the expense out of your next paycheck. Either way, you're going with me on the next jump."

"Shit..." Harris said, defeated.

I tossed him a glance over my shoulder. "Don't worry. If we get into trouble, we'll fight like the dogs we are: back-to-back, just like in the old days."

Letting out a sigh that sounded like it came from the depths of his soul, he put away his knife and walked after me toward the lab. He truly had the defeated air of a man marching toward the gas chamber.

Less than thirty minutes later, we were suited-up and good-to-go. Lisa did the final check, just like last time. Graves watched us closely.

Lisa tapped Harris' dial, and then he twisted it to a fresh notch and jumped away. She stepped to me next.

She looked worried. She touched the Galactic Key to my dial, and I put my hand on hers. She slipped the key into my palm, but it looked like we were having a moment, saying goodbye.

To cover, I snaked a kiss while she was in range. She made a small tsking sound and backed away. Graves shook his head, and several others rolled their eyes.

Grinning, I slammed my helmet closed, pocketed the key, and ported out.

The jump was a short one. Just the blink of an eye. That part surprised me—how close could this destination be?

The answer came after a very brief change of scenery. When I jumped back into reality, my impression was that I was still on Earth.

It was a cold, northern place. A wilderness. There were pines overhead, blocking out most of the sunlight. A recent snow had thickly caked the pine limbs and much of the forest floor.

Nearby stood a half-dozen hulking figures. They wore fluttering black cloaks and held massive swords in their hands.

I was standing in the midst of a group of enemy heavy troopers. Fortunately, they were distracted. Several of them were walking away with something.

That something was Harris. He was held up over their heads, with all three of their swords thrust into his back. Sprouting from his guts were the sword tips, gleaming silver and splashed with fresh red blood.

Without really thinking about it, I knew I'd ported into an ambush. These hulking soldiers had been standing here, on guard, waiting for someone to pop into existence in their midst. The moment Harris had done so, they'd butchered him.

He was still alive. I could see his right hand twitching and reaching feebly for the dial on his chest. He seemed unable to reach it.

Fortunately, the spectacle of Harris lifted high like a gigged frog had everyone's attention diverted.

My instinct was to try to jump home, but I didn't. Not right off.

There were nine of these huge men. Any of them would stand three meters in height if they were to stand up straight, but they generally hunched over. Slope-shouldered, they were as massive as they were tall—but I knew from experience they weren't invincible.

Running in the opposite direction, away from where they were carrying Harris, I shot the first heavy trooper I met in the ankle.

The odd grin on his face faded, and he toppled with a grunt as his leg could no longer hold his vast weight. I vaulted over him and ran into the forest.

Now, you have to know a few things about litter-mates in order to understand what happened next. For them, killing Harris and holding him up like a trophy was all good fun-and-games. But seeing one of their brothers go down, well, that was unacceptable.

They quickly lost what small minds they had and charged after me. They dropped Harris to flop in some snowy ferns and thundered after me.

I could hear them grunt and crash through the forest and the snow. It sounded a lot like getting chased by a small herd of horses.

My next move had to be timed precisely—and I didn't have much time to pull it off.

Popping out a plasma grenade, I twisted the detonator and waited a few seconds, all the while hearing them get closer, then I dropped it in the snow.

They never even noticed. They were so intent on catching me and tearing me limb from limb, that a small object in the snow at their feet wasn't worth their attention.

The grenade went off, and resulting explosion was a weird one. In water, the gravity-based weapons tended to have the strange effect of grabbing up splinters of liquid and casting them in every direction like shrapnel.

In snow—well—that was just frozen water. The effects were dramatic. Tiny crystalline particles exploded in every direction, shredding the closest three and wounding three more.

Two were left uninjured. As shooting one of their brothers had pissed them off, well, blowing down two-thirds of the family drove the last of them totally berserk.

There was no way to outrun them any farther. I turned at bay and raised my rifle.

It was smashed from my hands. The power of that blow was almost enough to shatter my wrists.

Fortunately, I was armored, but that wasn't enough to stop weapons driven with the force these apes had behind them. I only had one chance to kill them before they could kill me.

Pulling a move I'd seen Harris do with a knife, and which had always impressed me, I threw my small blade into the face of the second brother in line.

His eyes were huge. His mouth was open, blowing like a smith's bellows with foaming spittle clinging to the corners of his fat lips.

It was right into that open mouth that I neatly flipped my combat dagger. It flicked end over end once and sank into the soft upper palate. I can only assume it severed the spinal cord or hit the base of his brain. Either way, he went down hard, sending up a shower of snow.

The last brother raised his sword up again. He was in no less of a raging state.

I rushed in under the blade and when he swung it down, I grabbed his wrist and added my weight to his mighty blow, pulling him forward and off-balance.

These heavy troopers must not have been trained in basic Judo. The monster did a face-plant in the snow, but he sprang up again a moment later, roaring.

By that time, I had my laser pistol out. Two quick shots into his face took out both eyes.

He didn't die right away. Roaring and wheezing, he followed me around slashing and thunking his sword into tree trunks blindly. Hot blood sprayed everywhere, melting the snow into pink, icy slush.

Doing my best to make a get-away, I ran off into the forest again. I was down to my pistol, but I circled around to where Harris lay on the ground.

That had been my goal all along. I didn't want to lose another teleport suit.

Strangely enough, Harris was still alive. He had horrible wounds, but his combat kit inside the squid suit had pumped him with drugs and clamped off arterial bleeding. He probably wouldn't last long—but he'd made it this far.

"You're still here?" he rasped.

"I came back for you."

His next word came out after a lot of wheezing.

"Liar," he said.

"I'm sending you back," I said, "but I want my suit cameras to get a little bit of intel. This has to be the enemy camp on Earth, and we're right in the middle of it."

Harris lay back in the snow, each breath a struggle. "Take your... fucking... time..."

Laughing, I checked his suit's power-levels. As I'd expected, there was still enough juice in the suit to make it home. The jump was a very short one.

I twisted his dial, and he vanished.

I trotted down a nearby path, one that had obviously been used by the giants. Huge footprints had crushed down a wide trail in the snow exposing the dark mud underneath.

There, through the trees... What was that?

Wavering lights washed over me, bluish and silver—if that made any sense. Could a light be so bright that it looked not white, but reflective? I didn't know, but that was the impression I got.

Near the end of the trail, I found a massive clearing. Trees had been felled for a kilometer around. In the midst of this space, which had been churned to black slush, were thousands of heavy troopers. And in their midst was a huge alien machine that was producing the silver light effect.

The machine resembled an archway. It was constructed not of metal, but of something that looked more like stone. The middle of it was a maelstrom of distortion and twisting light.

Ripples of altered space traveled silently away from it in every direction.

There was a ramp that led up to the alien artifact, and it was thronged with more and more heavy troopers. Out of the void in the middle, they marched in a continuous mass, one group of nine brothers following the last.

There was one other figure, however, that caught my eye. He was singular and smaller than all the rest. He stood at the base of the archway, tending to it.

He'd once been known as "Old Silver" due to his extreme age as a mercenary without dying. I'd fixed that, and now he was just known as Claver.

A bullet snapped and splintered into a tree near my head. I realized I'd been spotted.

Without further hesitation, I twisted the dial on my chest and teleported home.

-29-

When I made it back to the lab, I staggered into the middle of a group of concerned faces. I leaned tiredly on the hands that came up to support me.

"Wounded, McGill?" Graves asked in an uncompromising tone.

I looked at him. "I'm not sure," I admitted.

"Medic!" Graves shouted over his shoulder.

Carlos rushed up and began looking me over.

"I'm sorry man," he said quietly as he worked. "If I find a bad injury—I'm sorry."

Nodding, I didn't complain. I knew what he meant. We were in desperate straits. He was hinting I'd have to accept a recycle if I'd been disabled. By the time I healed up from anything serious, this war was likely to be over.

Carlos read my tapper and ran instruments over my body.

"No breaks, no organ failure..." Carlos pronounced at last. "He looks like he got banged around pretty good. Contusions and trauma, but I think he'll be okay."

"That wrist is swollen," Graves said critically. "Can you hold a rifle with that arm, McGill?"

My wrist did hurt, but I straightened my spine and reached out to clasp Graves' hand. I grabbed his gauntlet and squeezed real hard. I grinned while I did it, too.

Graves let his face twitch, but otherwise he didn't show any discomfort from my grip.

"All right," he said. "You're good to go."

"Where's Harris?" I asked, looking around. I spotted a crumpled form on the floor nearby. The ghoulish techs were already stripping the teleport suit off him.

"Don't even look at that," Graves said. "That's not Harris. Not anymore. He's downstairs on blue deck inside a revival machine. He's a seed now, being spun up like cotton candy on stick."

Nodding, I understood the situation. Graves had finished Harris after seeing how badly hurt he was.

"I'm ready to make my report now, sir," I said.

Graves beckoned me to follow him to his office. I did so, and he watched the vids I'd forwarded to his tapper. My body-cam recordings showed all the action.

Graves grunted and frowned as he watched them. I did my best to put a good face on things, but the mission-time had been so short there wasn't much I could do in the way of bullshitting. All he had to do was watch the action unfolding on his arm. He didn't need a summary.

He lowered his arm and looked thoughtful.

"Body-cams don't lie," he said. "You fought like demon, McGill."

"Thank you, sir."

"You also went off-script. Way the fuck off."

"Well sir, there's always a certain amount of leeway in judgment calls that are being made on the spot by the commander in the field. I don't think—"

"That's right," he said. "You didn't think. You should have ported out the second you saw Harris was down. That was the whole goddamned plan. *Your* goddamned plan, I might add."

"Yeah… well… yeah, I know. But I saw an opportunity."

"To do what? Lose two teleport suits and a lot of time? To get yourself killed along with Harris?"

"To gain valuable intel on what the enemy is doing on Earth. They're right here on our home world, Centurion. Doesn't that interest anyone? I took a risk because I wanted to know what they were up to, and I think I brought that information back to Central."

We glared at one another for a few seconds. To my surprise, Graves lowered his eyes first.

"All right," he said. "You did okay. I'm just worried. I feel like I should chew you out because you took a risk, but that's short-sighted. If I'd wanted a mission commander who didn't take risks, I should have sent someone else."

This almost floored me. Graves rarely admitted he was wrong about anything. In fact, I couldn't recall a time when he *had* made a mistake. His judgment was legendary. You couldn't get closer to a full blown apology from him.

"I'm sending this up to Drusus right now," he continued. "Don't be surprised if he contacts you personally for details."

"All right," I said, standing up. "Am I dismissed?"

"Yeah," he said. "Take two hours off. Get something to eat. I'm sending you two out again as soon as Harris is on his feet and his head is clear."

"Uh..." I said, not relishing another trip with Harris.

"You wanted him, McGill," Graves said sharply. "You practically demanded that he go along. Now, you get to live with that."

"Right... thank you, Centurion."

Leaving the office, I grumbled all the way down the hall to the elevator. When I reached the mess hall floor, I tiredly slumped on a bench and ate a tray of food.

The truth was I felt sore and exhausted. I'd been more than banged around. You don't fight a squad of half-ton ogres without taking your licks, trickery or no.

Carlos' report concerning my state of health had been incomplete. I probably had a concussion, and I could still feel blood trickling down into my left boot.

After a quick meal, I made it down to blue deck. I looked up Anne Grant on my tapper and beeped her. She came out and gave me a wan smile.

"A visit?" she asked, eyeing me warily. "This isn't another attempt to land a date, is it, James?"

"Should it be?"

"No," she said firmly.

I shook my head in disappointment. Then I sat down heavily and clawed at my left boot. "Could you help me get this off?" I asked.

189

Concerned, she did so. She gasped and fussed over what she found. I never even looked at it. But she did her job, getting out a portable flesh-printer and injecting me with a random variety of medications.

"I don't understand," she said as she worked. "There are perfectly good bios assigned to your special ops team. Why didn't they catch this and fix it for you upstairs?"

I caught her eye and shook my head. She understood right away.

"Oh…" she said sarcastically. "It's like that, is it? You're not supposed to be hurt? They wouldn't recycle you instead of letting you have a few days off, would they?"

Huffing with laughter, I threw my hands up. I was feeling better. Whatever she'd shot into my leg had gone to my head. I felt a little lighter inside and out.

"With the mood Graves is in, he'd recycle me for a stubbed toe."

"Okay then," she said, wrapping me up carefully and slipping on my boot. "You'll have to hide this. Take two of these antibiotic tabs with every meal and—"

Before she'd completed her sentence, I'd popped them into my mouth and began chewing. They were bitter, and I made a face.

She stood up and put her hands on her hips. "Has there ever been a simple order you didn't modify or simply ignore?"

"Probably not," I admitted. "I didn't want to forget later, that's all."

"What's happening later?"

"Nothing."

She frowned and finished putting away her gear. "Later, hmm? What's her first name?"

"What? Oh—no, it's not like that. I'm heading out again in another hour. Don't even have time for a shower. Unless you're asking…?"

"I said no, James—take away that hand before I do."

I noticed then that my hand had absently slipped onto her knee. It seemed so natural there that I was reluctant to remove it. Anne and I had enjoyed some sweet times a few years back.

"We had some good times," I said wistfully.

She looked at me in concern. "You're in a strange mood. Are things that bad?"

"Nah," I said, definitely feeling the pain meds. "Everything's fine. We'll kill all these aliens and have a picnic by next week. You up for it?"

Our last date had been a picnic. It had gone disastrously, and she'd announced our breakup on the spot.

She eyed me with a mix of growing concern and curiosity.

"It's bad, isn't it? Worse than anyone is letting on. The news—they say there are aliens on Earth now. Up north of here."

"Crazy talk," I said and sloppily jabbed a finger toward her. "You give me a week, and I'll fix everything."

She nodded slowly. "You do that, James, and you can have your picnic. I don't even care if you bring another girl along."

Snapping out of it, my eyebrows shot up in amazement. Now, there was an offer a man didn't get every day! I knew she'd back out when the time came, but it was the thought that counted. Especially when it came from a straight-shooter like Anne.

Smiling, I heaved myself up and gave her a light kiss on the top of her head.

"You have my promise, lady!" I boomed loudly enough to cause a few bio people to turn and stare at us. "I'll make good, just you wait and see!"

Stomping back out into the long, echoing passages of Central, I left her watching me.

In my heart of hearts, I truly hoped I could keep that boastful promise.

Harris looked as angry as a wet tomcat when I met up with him in the lab. His arms were crossed, and his hair was still matted together with the slime of a fresh revive. He'd always hated dying even more than your average soldier.

"Hey," I boomed at him, "there you are, Vet. I thought you'd gone off to take a nap somewhere."

He glanced at me in hate, flipped me the bird under his elbow then went back to glaring at Graves. I could tell he was mostly angry with the Centurion.

191

It was just one of those things. Your body didn't want to die. Your every instinct went against it. A legionnaire who survived all the way back to camp didn't want to meet up with a quick finish after all that suffering.

I understood his mood, and I'd been there before. But this was go-time.

Clapping my hand on his shoulder, I spoke into his ear.

"Look," I said, "you have to shake it off. We're in this. We're good and screwed. We're probably as good as dead twice more and permed by Sunday—but we're in it deep now."

His eyes slid to meet mine.

"Why'd you do it?" he demanded. "No bullshit. Why'd you insist that I come along on these suicide missions with you?"

"What?" I demanded. "Are you still stewing about that? I told you, Vet, you're the best. You're the man I want at my side when the shit goes bad—and you have to admit, it's been pretty bad already."

He still looked suspicious. That's the trouble with knowing a man too damned long. He got wise to your best moves—eventually.

"That's crap, isn't it? This whole thing about two men going in and one jumping back—that was shit, right?"

"Come on, Harris," I said, looking down.

It was a critical mistake, and I knew it the second I did it. Damn. Normally, I'm a consummate liar. I know all the rules. You never ask forgiveness or show any remorse. You never look down, either. The whole stack of cards will come down if you do. Always.

"Damn you!" he shouted, stabbing a finger at me. "Damn you to Hell, McGill! You brought me along just for spite. I knew it, I totally fucking knew it!"

He did a little walk then, circling around and throwing his arms in the air wildly.

Graves finally took notice. He'd been going over things with the techs. He walked up to the two of us and eyed us in annoyance.

"Pull it together, you two. I don't care if you're ready to duel or get married. I need you in those suits and ready to jump in three minutes. Do I have your attention, Harris?"

"Yeah, yeah. I got the drill, Centurion, but I might as well shoot myself right now as jump into the unknown with this redneck frigger."

"McGill, would you like to request a replacement for Veteran Harris?" Graves asked me.

That shocked both of us. It was unusual for Graves to ask a question like that.

I looked around the group. There were a few hogs in the room. Ferguson was there, but he didn't look happy. I don't think I'd seen a smile on his face since he died the first time.

"Well, if Harris is going to wet his pants..." My arm rose up to point at Ferguson. "How about—"

But I didn't get the words out. Harris had stepped close and pushed my hand back down. I winced, as my wrist was still sore.

"No way!" he said. "No-how! I'm going. I'm suiting up. Can't a man bitch a little after a bad death? I'm going."

That's when I remembered there was one thing Harris hated more than dying: public humiliation. He'd rather die than have everyone in the legion think he was chicken.

Without another word, I lowered my hand and shut up. I'd rather have Harris than Ferguson, anyway.

It occurred to me as we prepped that Centurion Graves knew his men, and he was working us to get the best possible performance. I had to hand it to him.

For his part, Ferguson looked relieved. He tried to hide it, but I could tell.

"Point man, front and center!" Graves shouted.

Harris stepped up to the plate, standing resignedly like a man waiting for the gallows. I'd handed off the key to Lisa again, and she performed her rituals when his jump-suit was fully charged.

Harris raised his rifle to his cheek and put his finger on the trigger.

"I'm killing the first freak I see this time," he muttered half to himself. "I'm blowing them away before they blink. So help me..."

He vanished in a glimmer of unnatural light.

"McGill!"

Forcing a grin, I stepped up, and Lisa performed her magic. I had the key in my palm by the end of it.

Graves seemed to notice something this time. He cocked his head, and opened his mouth.

Maybe he'd been about to ask a question. Maybe he'd been about to ask what the hell Lisa had just passed to me—but I'd never know which, because I gave the suit's dial a hard twist and ported out at that instant.

-30-

The fourth setting on the dial took to me to a place I'd never expected it would.

The port was fast—very fast. There wasn't anything like a second's flight time. One moment I was in the lab at Central, and the next I was standing in what looked like a household library.

There were books everywhere around me—thousands of them. I recognized the books and the room. I'd been here before.

It was Galina Turov's library.

Now, you have to understand that Galina Turov had never been a big reader. But she was a show-off. These books were here to be seen, not read.

I knew that because I'd visited her here from time to time. The only reading that got done was accidental. We'd often made love in the library—on the leather ottoman right next to the big, old fashioned globe that was the centerpiece of the room. She'd called the globe her "focal point" whatever the hell that meant.

What concerned me more than the books, the globe, or even the fat ottoman I'd enjoyed coupling on from time to time, was the bloody mess on the floor.

Harris had been true to his word. He'd ported in and shot the first freak he'd seen. That freak happened to be Claver, who was also wearing a teleport suit.

195

Unfortunately for Harris, Claver had apparently used better aim. The Veteran's eyes were frozen open, his mouth was slack, and his bloody tongue lolled on a thick carpet of amber shag.

Claver was still alive. He was on his back, breathing with difficulty. A sucking wound in his chest bubbled and whistled. He'd been lung-shot.

My weapon was at my cheek in an instant. Claver tried to lift his, but he wasn't fast enough.

"Drop it, Claver," I ordered. "There are seven more porting in behind me. You haven't got a chance."

He wheezed out a coughing laugh. "You're a weak liar, McGill. I've been watching you, tracking you... I knew you'd come here next. I knew you'd come alone or with one side-kick. Harris was fast, I had to give him that. He came in ready to fight. I must have relaxed over the hours, waiting..."

He leaned over to spit blood, dropping the gun as he spoke. I kicked it away. I kept mine aimed at his head. I didn't trust Claver at all. Anyone who did was a fool.

"You knew I'd come?" I asked.

"Of course. I saw you at the gateway—or at least, the security vids of you after you'd escaped. It was hard to make out your face from the drone cams, but when I realized someone had trashed a whole squad of litter-mates, I knew it had to be you. You're more like one of those idiot berserkers than a normal human."

"Thanks," I said. "Now, what did you want to talk about?"

He looked at me in surprise. "Talk?"

I shrugged. "You didn't set up this ambush just to kill me, did you? What's the point? They'd just make a copy. You must want to talk."

He nodded slowly. "I guess that's true. I wanted to talk. Too bad I'm bleeding out on this nice carpet."

"Talk fast," I suggested.

"I'm feeling a little woozy. It's hard to think straight."

He coughed dramatically.

Rolling my eyes, I pulled a medkit out of my pouch and tossed it at him. He winced when it bounced off his chest, but he caught it and applied the unit to his wound. The kit squirmed and unfurled, patching the hole. He soon stopped bleeding, and his collapsed lung began to function, at least partially.

"Drugs?" he asked hopefully.

"Give me something first."

"Like what?"

"Like why you're here."

There was a moment of hesitation. I could see it, plain as day. As a fellow master of the false word, I recognized the signs of a man making up a story. Either he didn't want to tell me what was really on his mind, or he was shaping an edited version in his mind.

I kicked him. Right in the side.

"Talk, damn you!" I shouted. "Why are you here? Why are you helping the enemy take Earth? What pay could possibly be worth selling out your entire species?"

"Pay?" he snorted. "Selling out? Are you mad? That's not what this is. I'm trying to *save* Earth. I have been all along. If it hadn't been for one mentally-challenged ape running around pissing off the cephalopods and derailing plans, I'd have managed it by now."

Frowning, I kicked him again. Fresh blood spotted from under the patch on his chest, and the patch irritably squirmed to a new position to staunch the flow.

"Stop doing that!" he rasped. "I'm hurt, and I'm the good guy, whether you believe it or not."

"Oh, I believe you think that," I said. "Turov explained it all. You wanted us to become the slaves of the squids, who are in turn the slaves of the Wur. Isn't that right?"

"So what?"

"Maybe I have a different point of view. Maybe I want freedom for Earth."

"Impossible. We've got three star systems, McGill. Two of them are barely inhabited. The Mogwa rule us now. Why are they any better than the Cephalopod Kingdom or the Wur?"

"They protect us and give us trading rights," I said, repeating words I'd had drilled into my skull since grade school.

197

He gave a tired, raspy laugh. "Really? Protection? Where are their fleets? They've all gone to the Core Worlds, fighting their own battles for supremacy. Trading rights? Try trading restrictions. Their rules are meant to keep us down forever."

My mouth worked, but I didn't speak. He'd said what I'd already been thinking: what everyone on Earth had been thinking all along, I guess.

"That's right," he said. "Even a gorilla like you can comprehend the brutal screwing the Galactics have been giving us since day one. I honestly think the cephalopods aren't as bad. Sure, they'd treat us like second class citizens. But we could trade with anyone we like. And we'd be allowed to legally build a fleet of our own. They'd insist upon that."

I felt myself being swayed. It was hard to believe, but Claver was doing the impossible. Lying on the floor at my feet, he was getting me to believe that surrendering to the squids and their plant masters would be a good idea.

The whole thing was crazy right on the face of it. How could this man convince me of such an abomination?'

If the squids did manage to invade Earth and take Central, would my home world surrender? Would they fear the endless armies marching out of the gateway—and possibly a dozen more gateways? Would that fleet of theirs, lingering out of reach, persuade them to believe that resistance was futile?

The more I thought about it, the more I began to realize it *could* happen. After all, our rulers had surrendered to the Mogwa. Why not the squids this time around?

"I can see it in your eyes," Claver said, in the tone of a sorcerer from times gone by, "you know the truth of my words. Now I need you to help me, McGill. I need you to get me onto my feet. I have to talk to Drusus and whoever is in charge above him. I'll come unarmed. You don't have to—"

That was as far as he got, because I put my gun to his head.

"You almost had me," I said, "but I'm a stubborn man. I'm going to try it my way, first."

Before he could protest, I shot him in the head. His skull popped nicely, and I took a deep breath.

How to proceed? I was almost due for porting back. But I had work to do first.

Stripping Claver and Harris, I took the two teleport suits and stashed them. Then I got out my Galactic Key and touched it to my monitoring system.

The modern legion body-cams didn't let the wearer tamper with them. A good tech could do it, but not without leaving traces of their illegal activity.

Fortunately, the AI chip that ran the system was an alien trade good. That meant I could hack it with my key. I did so, and after screwing with the unfamiliar interface, I managed to delete most of the video.

My whole talk with Claver was erased. I didn't want his venomous words to go up the line to any of the other clowns back at Central.

When I was finished, I took fresh video of the room and the dead bodies.

"Looks like they killed each other," I said aloud for the benefit of the cameras. "Too bad, but we netted one new suit out of the bargain."

When I was satisfied with my on-camera performance, I ported back to the lab.

-31-

"McGill!" Graves roared at me when I got back. "Where's Harris?"

I gave him an apologetic shrug.

"Damn you, man! Did you shoot him and leave him behind in some alien hole?"

"It didn't go quite like that, sir," I said.

Pissed off, he marched over to me. "You lost me another teleport suit, didn't you?"

I gave him a slight smile then, and I held up an extra suit in each hand. His frown deepened.

"Where'd the extra one come from?" he demanded.

"It's Claver's."

That got his full attention. "You found that traitor out in space somewhere?"

"Sort of... but he's not out in space. He's not all that far away from here, actually. We might want to discuss the details in private."

Graves was on his guard now. His eyes narrowed, and he studied me with crossed arms.

"I'm smelling a fresh patch of Georgia horseshit, McGill. Come with me."

"What's the trouble? I brought back an extra suit. Sure, I lost Harris again, but—"

"That's twice in a row!" he interrupted. "I don't believe in coincidences, McGill, especially not when you're involved. What kind of game are you playing?"

He'd already headed for the door, and everyone around us watched as I handed the suits to the techs and followed him.

Lisa didn't look like she believed me, either. She dropped her eyes after they briefly met mine.

I had to trot to catch Graves at the elevator.

"What's with you two?" he asked me when we were riding upward again.

"Well," I began slowly, "I guess I'm kind of sweet on her. We bonded over some hard missions. Teleporting around sounds like fun, sure, but in reality—"

"No, dammit! I'm not talking about the girl. I'm talking about you and Harris. You two should be a functioning team by now. Why the hell can't you get along? You're always getting one another killed over some absurd disagreement."

I shrugged. "Harris and I don't always see eye-to-eye, that's true," I admitted. "But it's all in good fun. We're not what I would call enemies."

"Good fun, huh?" Graves snorted. "I'd hate to see you working with an actual enemy. Now, are you going to tell me exactly where you left Harris' body?"

"He's dead on the floor of Turov's library."

"Turov's *what*?"

I explained what had happened in detail, but naturally, I gave him an edited version of events. In my story there was no mention of the Galactic Key, and I also left out much of what Claver had told me.

"So…" Graves said thoughtfully, "he was waiting in ambush for you. That makes some kind of sense. He must know where all these dial positions go. He logically concluded you would try the next one and tried to meet you there."

"It didn't work out for him. Harris popped in on him in full-blown paranoia-mode. They shot each other, and I cleaned up the mess, gaining two suits in the bargain."

"Correction: you scored one additional suit and one corpse."

"That's nothing a quick revive won't fix."

Graves sighed as we arrived on the appropriate floor and marched down toward Drusus' office. There were staffers running around everywhere. Everyone seemed like they were in an awful hurry.

"What's going on?" I asked a few adjuncts that skittered by, but they made no comprehensible response.

"It's the army up north," Graves explained. "They're moving. We've thrown up a front to contain them—but it isn't working out."

"Why not?"

He shook his head. "I don't know everything, but I'm certain their ground troops have tech that we don't."

I thought about the teleport suits and nodded. That couldn't be the only critical piece of gear they had. The trouble with the Empire was that, in a military sense, it'd been stagnant for centuries. All their trade restrictions had served to keep the peace, but they also made us weaker when we came up against a new, serious threat. These squids simply didn't play by any rules passed down from the Core Systems.

Drusus was meeting with a command team when we stepped into his office. Once three staff officers left, giving us a curious glance, he beckoned for us to enter and shut the door.

"Good afternoon, gentlemen," he said. "I'll get right to the point. I'm pulling the plug on your experimental operation."

Graves and I both gawked at him.

"But sir," I said, "we've visited nearly every known preset destination on the dial. We learned valuable intel about the enemy camp, and—"

He waved my words away as if they stank.

"I know all that, McGill. But it doesn't really matter anymore. These teleport destinations are too limited in scope—we can't go wherever we want to. I'd hoped we could use them to stop their fleet, but now that their invasion forces are here on Earth, I need every experienced combat unit I've got in this sector to defend Central."

"Are things going that bad so soon, Imperator?" Graves asked.

"They're headed that way. We started off with a bombing campaign that went nowhere. They have anti-air tech that can shoot down a centimeter-long drone when it's more than a hundred meters off the ground."

With a feeling of growing unease, I watched as Drusus manipulated a map display. Northern New York Sector was a densely forested region. What population had lived up there before the coming of the Galactics had been burned out a century ago. The history was they'd been rebels who hadn't wanted to surrender, and most of them had died in the end.

In the wilderness they'd left behind, a new threat had arisen. The squids had seen fit to fill the rough country with their countless minions.

"I've been there, sir," I said as he laid out the scene. "Right there, in the middle of all that."

He looked at me. "Yes, I know. I reviewed the video. That's the primary reason why you're here, McGill. I want you to help Graves with a special mission."

"What's that, sir?"

"We're going to need a man to go into those woods again. Someone must jump into the middle of enemy territory and blow up that gateway."

I stared at him in shock. "Just like that?"

"Just like that. This is the first opportunity I've seen to make real effective use of this newfound technology. Think about it: they can shoot down our missiles. Their shields are keeping us from penetrating their core camp, but they can't stop a teleporter from getting in close and doing serious damage."

"An excellent plan, Imperator," Graves said. "I applaud direct action. If we can destroy that gateway, they'll get no more reinforcements from home."

"We think they're coming from their fleet, actually, but we could be wrong. McGill has shown us that these devices have a great deal of range. They could be coming from their own planets."

"Amazing to think—" Graves began, but I threw up a hand.

"Now, hold on a minute," I said. "If I go in and drop a bomb, how am I getting back?"

They glanced at one another and then down at the desktop. Drusus cleared his throat.

"Oh, so it's like that, is it?" I asked. "Killing two birds with one bomb? No more teleporting, no more McGill."

203

"We'll revive you back here the moment we see the mushroom cloud," Drusus said. "It will be the quickest and cleanest death in your long and storied career, Adjunct."

They were asking me to commit suicide. My mind was having a hard time wrapping around the idea.

"That place was set up to ambush anyone porting in there," I said. "It'll be doubly guarded now, after my successful attack and escape."

"Yes, we've come to the same conclusions," Drusus said. "That's why the suit will be automated. There will be a magnetic detonator. The moment the teleportation is complete and the on-board software realizes your position has significantly shifted, it will go off—even if you're struck dead the moment you arrive."

"How encouraging," I said. "You guys have thought of everything."

"McGill, I know this is a lot to ask," Drusus said. "But think of what a success might mean. No more gateway means no more reinforcements from the stars. We can contain them and mop them up as soon as reserve units from Europe get here."

"Okay, okay," I said, thinking hard. "But why do you have to send a man at all? Why not just send the bomb in a suit?"

Drusus glanced at Graves and nodded.

"We already tried that," Graves said. "It didn't work. The suit doesn't seem to want to teleport at all without an occupant. We don't really know how this technology works, remember, McGill. We're like monkeys with a gun. We've managed to pop off a few shots, but something complicated like reloading or breaking it down…"

"I get it," I said, thinking fast.

I'd forgotten that the suit wouldn't work because no one had touched the key to it. That thought made me plain sick. All my clever work to keep the key a secret was blowing up in my face—literally.

But I could hardly tell them about the key now. To do so would admit I'd hidden critical information from my superiors. Worse, they would realize instantly that the key was something that could get our entire species erased by the Galactics if they figured out we had it. My life wouldn't be worth a penny with spit on it if they knew the truth.

Sighing, I spoke words I'd never thought I'd utter.

"Sirs... I'd like to willingly volunteer for this assignment."

They both looked suspicious.

"Is this some kind of elaborate dodge, McGill?" Graves asked.

"Nonsense," Drusus said. "Let the man have his honor, Graves. You've always been too hard on him. He gets things done—unconventionally—but he gets them done."

Graves glanced over at Drusus and fell silent. He knew me better than Drusus did. He was like the father of an ornery teen who had to endure the scorn of other parents.

"It's just not right the way he treats me," I said. "All I want to do is help. Hell, I'm volunteering for a suicide mission here."

Graves gave me a sour look, and I enjoyed it.

"The gesture is indeed appreciated," Drusus said. "We were thinking of ordering you to do it anyway—but this unexpected offer is more than welcome."

That was about the size of it. I'd figured they hadn't brought me up here and filled me in on a top secret assignment just to satisfy my personal curiosity. When you're screwed, you might as well smile about, I always say.

To make a long story short, it was less than an hour later when they had me dressed up in that eight-armed monkey-suit again.

Lisa was avoiding my eyes. She stepped up to me, and she tapped on my wrist.

I didn't get it right off—but then I did. She wanted the key she knew I was holding onto.

I gave it to her, and she did the honors. She gave me a kiss and said: "You're good to go, James."

Then she retreated rapidly. I stared after her shapely form, feeling a little better. If you can make a girl shed a tear when she says good-bye, the odds are you're in for some good times when you get back.

Of course, I wouldn't be coming back. Not exactly. It wouldn't be the same James McGill.

Thinking that made my heart pound. No matter how many times I died then lived again, I never seemed to get used to it. The cycle didn't bother Graves much, that was obvious. But it still gave me a chill.

"McGill!" Graves complained. "Pick up the damned bomb!"

Startled, I quit staring at Lisa and stooped to lift a large metal capsule. It was heavy, and there were LEDs counting down on top of it.

The bomb was smooth to the touch. When I reached for the dial on my chest disaster almost struck. It slipped, and I performed a bit of juggling. I almost dropped the thing before I got it under control again.

Everyone in the place gasped and threw up their hands—as if that would have done them any good. Their reaction cracked me up.

Laughing, I spoke a few final words.

"I liked this version of myself," I said. "All of you should take pity on the poor bastard who comes out of that machine downstairs afterward. It'll be his turn to play me, and I don't envy him one bit."

Everyone looked at me like they didn't know what to say. It was one thing to watch a man you knew leaving on a suicide mission—but this was different. They knew that I would come back—at least, some kind of copy of me.

Graves saluted finally, breaking the awkward silence that followed, and I threw him one back. That made me feel better. At least there was one man present who understood sacrifice.

With a grim smile, I activated my suit and jumped into the blue.

-32-

My body came back together in a different place, but I was still on the same planet. I had time to take a look around before anything happened.

That simple fact surprised me. I'd kind of expected the bomb to obliterate old James McGill more or less instantly—but it didn't.

My surroundings looked dramatically different than they had the first time I'd been in this primordial forest. Instead of being surrounded by nine hulking troops with slack faces and massive weapons, I found myself in the middle of seven parabolic dishes, all of which were aiming directly at me. The dishes were shiny metal, and they gave off a faint blue radiance. To me, they looked like a firing-squad built of old-fashioned microwave antennas.

The significance of the fact these things were all aiming in my direction wasn't lost on me. They'd been set up here purposefully to surprise whoever dared to port in. That *couldn't* be good.

It was about then that I looked down at the bomb I was holding up against my chest like a metal watermelon. It had changed shape. It was now no longer a perfectly smooth steel egg. Something had ruptured one side.

Frowning, I tried to turn it around to look at the crack with orange light seeping out—but I couldn't budge the thing.

It was a very weird sensation. An object that I'd been carrying a moment before was now immobile. I gently let go—and it hung there in the air.

Walking around it slowly, I looked at the far side. Sure enough, there was a crack in the side of it. That had to be right between where my hands had gripped it.

I looked at my gloves, and found one of them had been scorched black, but that was the only visible effect.

"Pretty cool tech, huh McGill?" a familiar voice asked.

I spun around, reaching for my pistol. Claver laughed at that.

"That won't work—not inside the stasis field. It's set up to catch high-speed motion and freeze it. The second your little gift package began to explode, the field rendered it harmless. It was taken out of phase. At least, that's what the techs call it."

My eyes swung around. The forest seemed empty, except for the stasis projectors. Then I saw him—A deeper chunk of shadow beneath a tree.

I let my eyes slide off him and continue roving about so he wouldn't know I'd spotted him.

"Ah, McGill," he said wistfully. "You're such a predictable sort. Honestly, I'm surprised your team of vandals didn't come up with this bombing strategy earlier. My only question is: why send a man to do a robot's job?"

"They couldn't get the suit to port without a victim inside," I explained.

"Really? Are the techs at Central that far behind? I'm embarrassed on behalf of my entire species."

I had my pistol out now. Instead of aiming it at the figure I thought was Claver, I aimed it at the nearest parabolic projector.

"What happens if I shoot this thing?"

"You can't. It will detect and stop the motion before the bolt strikes. It can stop a small nuke, don't you think it can stop a power bolt?"

Deciding to try it anyway, I shot the projector—or rather, I tried to. The bolt came out about a dozen centimeters before it stopped. It hung in the air, sizzling like a frozen arc of electricity.

"I'm impressed," I said, and I tried to put my gun away. It wouldn't budge. Like the bomb, it was stuck fast.

Claver clucked his tongue. "How can you play the simpleton every time? The bolt is still largely inside the gun— which means the entire weapon is frozen. The burning plasma is inside it, welding it into place."

"Weird," I admitted, letting go of my gun. It hung there in space beside the bomb. "Isn't this a lot of work to go to just to talk to me?" I asked the dark trees.

"That's not my purpose, it's a side effect. Right after your last visit here, we set up the stasis field and moved the gateway to a safe location. Truthfully, I've been bored here, waiting. It took longer for you to make this ham-handed move that I'd thought it would."

"Why are you telling me all this?" I asked.

"Because you won't remember any of it anyway. If you do catch one last revive before Central falls, your memories of this place will have been lost. These shields block all your suit's transmissions, you know."

"Right…" I said. "Well then, we might as well talk openly. What the hell are you up to, Claver? Can you possibly believe the squids will honor whatever deal you've cut with them once they have Earth?"

"McGill, McGill," he said, making tsking sounds. "Haven't you learned anything from me? Lord knows I've tried to enlighten that dim brain of yours countless times. Let me explain it as one might to a small child…"

"Thanks."

"You're welcome. The key, you see, is to never give the mark everything they want. These squids are like any predator, they're always hungry for more. The trick is to never run out of snacks in your pocket."

I frowned in confusion, but I nodded like I understood him. While he kept talking, I took a very slow step toward the nearest projector. He didn't seem to notice or care.

"You aren't getting any of this, are you?" he sneered. "I'm wasting my time."

"Oh no," I said, "I get it. You want to gloat. That's why you haven't killed me yet."

"Ah, so you *do* understand. Very good... where was I?"

"You were about to tell me where the last position on the teleport dial goes."

He chuckled. "Why not? The last—hey now, what are you up to?"

"Nothing," I said, but I had slowly, gently, wrapped my big arms around the nearest of the projectors. Grunting with fantastic effort, I tried to turn it.

The projector was on a stalk, and the stalk had been bolted to a platform. But the metal didn't seem to be anything abnormally strong. It might have been aluminum or some similar alloy.

The shadow under the trees stepped forward and became Claver. He had a pistol.

"McGill, you ape! Let go of that projector or I'll be forced to kill you."

"That's why I came here, you dumb-ass," I told him, grunting and straining with effort.

He shot at me then, as I hunched over the metal stalk. My back popped—but it was just my straining bones, not an injury. The bolt had been frozen in space, just like the other one.

"Ha!" I boomed as I heaved with renewed effort. "This field can come in pretty handy. Where'd you find it?"

Growling, Claver marched down toward me. He had a knife in his hand.

"What are you going to do with that, Claver?" I demanded. "Don't come too close, or you'll find it sticking out of your guts."

He stopped, breathing hard. He looked around in concern.

The projector in my hands had shifted a little. It was now out of kilter. Maybe just a centimeter, but when something depends on a series of concentric fields working in harmony, that can be more than enough.

Already, the bolt I'd fired earlier was wobbling in space. It was flickering like live fire, crackling and shining with uneven light.

"It won't do you any good," Claver said. "See you in hell, McGill."

"I'll give my regards to your mama," I told him.

210

He ported out. I realized I was standing alone in the forest. The bolt he'd fired was sizzling less than a meter from my back.

Then, I thought to look at the bomb.

It was the damnedest thing I've ever seen. The bomb was going off—but in slow-motion. The side had ruptured and come away from the rest. Two other regions, the rounded tips of the watermelon-shaped device, were now exploding as well. They were releasing fantastic forces, but at a tiny fraction of normal speed.

How long would it be before the bomb consumed me and presumably the projectors? Less than a minute, I'd wager. Maybe a lot less, if the reaction sped up as it escaped the field.

It was then and only then, that I went off-script. I knew I shouldn't do it, but I let self-preservation take over.

I reached up to my chest, and I twisted the dial to go home.

Imagine my surprise when nothing happened.

"Damn... not enough power."

I wasn't sure why the suit didn't work this time. The jump was a short one. But it did occur to me that the stasis field was probably stopping it. Reaching down, I fumbled under the projectors. There had to be a power-source—something I could plug into.

When I found it, a big grin split my face. I shoved a power lead home and... well... all hell broke loose.

The projectors lost their grip on the world very quickly. The power I'd taken from them had probably disrupted whatever tenuous balance they had left.

The first thing that I noticed during the next tiny slice of time was the sensation of teleporting. The wavering light, the ripping apart and coming back together, it was all there.

In the brief instant I was teleporting, I couldn't believe what a series of lucky strikes I'd had. Sure, none of it meant much to anyone else since they could have made a new James McGill in half an hour. But I appreciated the gesture from Lady Luck.

First off, I'd managed to get the suit to work with a cannibalized power-supply. Second, the effect beat the bomb, and I wasn't blown up. Third, the key had been applied about five minutes ago and left behind with Lisa. Apparently, the security was still disabled.

Such a series of fortunate events. It was almost like someone was watching over me this time.

Back at the LZ in Central, I pitched forward on my face. It was only then that I felt a searing pain in my back.

"McGill?" Graves asked, rushing to my side. "What went wrong?"

"I've been shot," I said, reaching to claw at my back.

"I don't mean that!" he shouted. "What happened to the bomb? We've had observers watching for several minutes, and they've seen nothing. We assumed that you'd screwed up somehow. Now you show up here with a smoking hole in your back. Let's hear your best excuse!"

I was through listening to him. Gasping for breath over the pain in my back, which was from catching the tail end of Claver's unfrozen power bolt, I worked my tapper while I lay on the floor.

"What are you—oh..." Graves said.

His hands seized my tapper and his searching eyes ran over the vid that was playing there.

"The forest is gone," Graves said. "The whole region went up." Then he looked at me again. "How did you hack into that vid? That's a priority feed from the front lines."

I shrugged. "Some of my best friends are techs."

"Right," he said, releasing my arm, "your new girlfriend. All right, you performed your mission successfully. Now get your ass off that floor."

Painfully, I did as he ordered. My hand went to my back, and my lips curled away from my teeth.

"Permission to hit blue deck, sir?" I asked.

"Granted. But you'd better have the decency to recycle yourself this time if you're disabled. You're supposed to have died today, anyway."

"You're all heart, Centurion."

I gave him a copy of my tapper recordings and left. I didn't feel like making any flashy reports. They could watch my body-cam feed if they wanted to know what had happened.

-33-

The next thing I knew, I was waking up in a hospital bed. For a second, I thought they'd gone and recycled me without permission.

But then I saw Lisa's worried face, and I smiled. No one worries much over a fresh grow.

"Is my back fixed up?" I asked her.

"Anne was here a minute ago. She said she patched you up, but that you might be stiff and sore for a while. She said you can't let on, or they'll recycle you. Is that true? Is Legion Varus that callous with their heroes?"

I laughed painfully. "Nah. They treat us like kings. I'll have dancing women, free booze, and all the candy I can eat tonight in the barracks."

She finally smiled and shook her pretty head. "Doesn't anything get you down?"

"Sure, but not dying. Takes a lot more than that. What's happening? What day is it?"

"It's night—the night after you came back. The enemy is on the move."

I frowned at that. "What do you mean? I thought they were pretty much wiped out."

Her face fell. "No, not entirely. Command thinks you got some of them, and they're sure you destroyed a lot of their shields. But that just got them moving. They're marching now instead of waiting to gather more strength."

213

"Hmm," I said. "Maybe Claver was lying about moving the gateway. Maybe they couldn't do that so quickly. It was pretty big. If they're coming for Central—well, that's an act of desperation. Our legions will take the battlefield and wipe them out!"

She smiled and kissed me, and I enjoyed the kiss. But inside, I was worried. The real battle had started. Not everyone knew it, but this was going to be decisive. It was going to be a battle for Earth herself.

Earth had a pretty good-sized military. Our fleet had been knocked out, but we had plenty of ground forces. Most of them were hogs, but they could learn to fight quickly enough.

The professional legions were our only troops with real experience, and there were a lot of them. Over the past few weeks I'd seen people from Victrix, Germanica, Iron Eagles and Solstice. They were all gathering here to protect the capital.

The trouble was I'd seen the enemy using tech I knew we couldn't handle. From teleport suits to gateways, stasis field projectors and more, I knew we were outclassed. It was going to be like the Zulus fighting the British—and that hadn't worked out well for the Zulus.

"McGill?" Graves asked from the doorway. He'd just stepped in without knocking. "I've been buzzing your tapper for over an hour. You missed the first briefing—get your ass out of that bed."

"Yes sir," I said, heaving myself to my feet. The fresh nu-skin on my back ripped with the sudden movement. I winced, but forced myself to stand tall. "Ready to move out, Centurion!"

He eyed me critically then looked at Lisa. "Say goodbye. We're headed to the front."

"What?" I asked in surprise. "What front?"

"The legions are assembling. The primary Hegemony forces are already out there, but Central wants us to advance. We'll play the part of skirmishers, slowing down the enemy as the main battle force assembles."

"That's Drusus' idea? The man's all heart."

214

Graves glanced at Lisa again then frowned at me. "Meet me upstairs in five."

He left then, and I encircled Lisa with my long arms. She squeaked, but then melted against me. We made out, and I pulled her onto the hospital bed.

"What are you doing? You only have five minutes."

"That's plenty of time," I said.

She was all knuckles and elbows for a few moments, but then she melted. She complained someone else might walk in, but we did it anyway, right there on those thin, hospital sheets. Both of us knew it might be our last chance on this Earth to make love of any kind.

Afterward, she tried to give back the Galactic Key, but I pushed it away. She stared at it in awe.

"Are you sure?"

"It's not forever—I hope. But how are you going to send anyone else teleporting without it?"

"Okay," she said.

We kissed goodbye, and I trotted out of the place. The whole way up in the elevators to the briefing room I cursed about how slow things were going.

When I finally burst into the briefing, every other officer in the unit was already there. They glanced at me, rolled their eyes, and went back to discussing tactics.

"The region the bomb strike destroyed was in the north," Graves said, adjusting his tabletop tactical display to show a blasted zone. "As you can see, that section of New York Sector was flattened almost up to the old Canadian border.

In the south, however, the land remained undamaged. The enemy used some kind of ablation effect, which dampened the bomb and reduced its yield."

"Reduced?" Adjunct Leeson huffed. "That's crazy. You must have flattened twenty thousand square kilometers of trees as it was. At least a tenth of the Adirondack mountains was scorched!"

"Yes, but the original yield of the bomb was around a gigaton. We think their shielding and some kind of stasis effect kept the weapon from operating properly."

"A gigaton?" I asked, feeling a little sick for some reason. To think I'd been carrying that much explosive power against my chest in one tiny egg… it was downright freaky. "Centurion, I didn't think any kind of nuke could contain that kind of power in such a small package."

Graves eyed me in irritation. "No one ever said the bomb was nuclear. At least, it wasn't fission or fusion."

To my mind, that didn't leave a lot ground. Could he be talking about anti-matter? Or something even more exotic? Whatever it was, it didn't make me feel any better to know I'd been carrying it.

"All of northern New York Sector was supposed to have gone up," Graves said, "all the way down to Albany."

"What?" Leeson demanded before I could. "That's crazy. A lot of folks would have died."

"Acceptable losses," Graves said without any change in attitude. "This invasion is a cancer, gentlemen. When you burn out cancer, you don't fool around. Besides, the region is largely uninhabited."

I'd begun to catch on. Back in the early days after the Annexation, there had been certain people who'd fought against the government's decision to surrender to aliens. Some of those people had gathered up in the old forests in that region and built camps there. They'd been beaten, but not without taking quite a few of the original Hegemony troops with them.

The survivors, described in every textbook as arch-villians, had stayed in the area and eked out a difficult existence as pariahs on Earth. The rest of the population had abandoned the area and it had become mostly wilderness again.

As a kid, I'd been taught to hate those rebels. Now, I felt I understood them. Maybe they'd even had the right idea from the start, a century back.

The idea that Claver had decided to set up camp in this spot seemed less and less like a coincidence. Maybe he thought he could find some rebels to join his army. Or maybe he'd just seen it as the only wilderness close enough to Central to make a good hidden start for his campaign.

Even more suspicious to my mind was the use of an overpowering secret super-bomb on the region. I could just hear the Ruling Council approving that option for Central. They must have grinned while they signed off on it. What a stroke of luck to get rid of two problems with one big bomb.

"The squids were moving their forces south before the bomb-strike went off," Graves continued. "They're now in the southern region of the Adirondacks. The area is heavily forested and rugged with glacially formed mountains."

"You know what?" Leeson said, speaking up again. "That's tough country. I used to go hunting up there, back in the day. The Mohawks owned it, centuries back."

"What's a Mohawk?" Graves demanded.

"Some kind of primitive native American," Leeson explained. "They gave people trouble and had to be rooted out of the area—same as the rebels. Now we've got an army of genetic freaks up there that the squids have dropped on us. History repeats itself."

"I don't think you know what the hell you're talking about," Graves said. "Shut up."

Leeson grumbled, but he *did* shut up.

Graves looked around as if he expected more interruptions. When none were forthcoming, he continued.

"The Hogs are already in the area, forming up outside Albany. We're going to be their skirmishers and give them the time they need to dig in."

"You mean we get to play cannon fodder!" Leeson said.

He was right, of course, but he earned himself a meaningful glare from Graves. I was glad that it wasn't me who was getting that kind of look this time. I'd done enough dying lately.

"We're going to be advancing in the center," Graves said, "along with Solstice and the Iron Eagles. Germanica and Victrix will take up the left flank, while—"

"Hold on, sir!" I interrupted. "Did you say we'd be *advancing?*"

"How the frig do you think we're going to defeat this enemy, McGill? We're going to advance into the southern Adirondacks and engage the invaders."

I was stunned. All along, I'd been thinking the plan was to set up ambushes in the trees—Hit and run, booby-traps and the like. But to march into that army and go toe-to-toe with giants? That sounded pretty crazy to me.

"Uh…" I began, but Graves shut me down.

"All right, listen," he said. "I know this isn't going to be a popular battle plan, but we have our orders. We're accustomed to operating as an independently commanded legion, but that's not how this is going to go. We're part of an army now—Earth's army."

"Who's in charge?" Leeson demanded. "This new plan doesn't sound like Imperator Drusus' style to me."

"It's not," Graves admitted. He ran his eyes over each of us. "They revived Nagata somehow. Most of the rest of the hog brass was permed—but someone found his backup. He's calling the shots currently."

I frowned at that news. I knew Nagata pretty well. Suiciding his troops in an important battle—that didn't sound like him. He wasn't a terribly experienced commander, but he wasn't insane.

"Sir?" I said. "I know Nagata. Maybe I could go upstairs and—"

"Absolutely not. We're being flown out to the front right after this briefing is over. Our light cohorts are already in the air. The lifters are working non-stop."

The briefing continued, but I didn't bother to listen to the rest of it. I'd escaped death in those mountains just a few hours ago, and now it looked like I was going to get a fresh shot at dying out there.

-34-

In a way, it felt good to be harnessed up and packed like meat in a can alongside my buddies. It was like going home. The sounds of the lifter, the roar and whoosh, the bitching and whooping, it all brought back memories.

I've died so many times on alien soil that I've lost count over the years. But I'd only died a handful of times on Earth. It'd never been in a pitched battle, either. Usually, I'd been ambushed by some kind of bureaucrat. This time, it would be very different.

On my right sat Carlos. He'd put on a few pounds somehow—but that would melt off the first time he died in the field and caught a revive. They called it a "legionnaire's diet" and there were even rumors that if you got fat enough, Graves would recycle you just to make sure you could keep up when the unit went out for a jog.

Right now, Carlos was arguing with Kivi, who sat on my left. She wasn't in the best mood—but then she rarely was. She'd found out that Carlos had put her down, not me, when she'd been injured on our previous mission.

That was just fine with me, but their bickering was beginning to get on my nerves.

"You know," I said to Kivi, interrupting the two of them as they argued across my chest, "my grandma always told me never to get into a fight with a pig."

"What?" Carlos demanded. "What are you saying, McGill?"

"Don't you want to know why?" I asked Kivi, not even looking at Carlos.

Kivi was grinning.

"Yes," she said. "Tell me why I should avoid fighting with this pig, McGill."

"Because you'll both get dirty, but the pig will like it!"

Kivi laughed. Carlos looked at me for a full second, deadpan. Then he shook his head slowly. "McGill, you've got to be the biggest fucking hayseed left alive on planet Earth. Seriously…"

"You want to hear another pig joke?" I asked him.

"No, I really don't."

That worked. The two of them finally shut the hell up. I felt like a true leader of soldiers in that moment. Not only were they finally quiet, one of them had even laughed at my joke.

The lifter began to shudder and make a singing sound. Servos whined and groaned—the landing gear was being deployed. All our tappers lit up, and we were ordered to button-up our suits and prep for a hot LZ.

"Okay," I shouted up and down the line. "1st Squad hugs my ass, 2nd squad hugs Harris' ass. Break for cover the second we're on the dirt and that ramp goes down."

Carlos looked worried. "Is it going to be that bad?" he asked.

"Look on the bright side," I told him. "You could use a little slimming down, anyway."

I could tell that he wanted to punch me, but he didn't. Being an officer had its moments.

When we came down in a swirling cloud of dust and torn-up weeds, the ramp dropped fast. There was nothing gentle about it. Someone had just cut the cord and *SLAM!* It went down.

"On your feet!" roared Harris.

I felt the urge to obey, although I was in command now. I hadn't quite adjusted to the idea I was his superior officer. I don't think he had, either.

There were two units ahead of us in line. They trotted off at a good clip. I didn't hear any incoming fire, but I knew from Graves that they expected resistance at any moment.

We rushed off the ship and into a clearing. The area around us was heavily forested and there were rolling mountains in every direction. The land looked like it had been wadded up and let go so that there were wrinkles everywhere.

Intermixed with trees were plenty of big, gray granite outcroppings. The region had been carved up by glaciers thousands of years back, and the wounds were still showing on the landscape.

"Platoon leaders," Graves said on command chat, "we've got strange reports. People are being attacked by some kind of effect when they land and scramble. Get away from the lifter. It'll be taking off the second we're all on the ground."

Frowning, I hustled toward my assigned position. Graves, or maybe the primus above him, had marked waypoint positions that showed up inside my helmet. To my eyes, a pyramid-shaped pile of granite with a scraggly tree on top had a green arrow on it.

The effect wasn't enabled for every helmet, just squad leaders. It was distracting and could make it hard to aim. To increase combat effectiveness, it was a burden only Harris and I had to deal with.

Off about a hundred meters to my left, Harris had his group moving at a dead run. I decided he was doing things right and picked up the pace as well. My people ran after me like a pack of dogs.

All around the field, groups were spreading out and taking positions. Most weren't moving fast, however, and only half of the cohort had disembarked before things went wrong.

At first, I didn't get it at all.

"What the hell is that?" Leeson demanded. "What's wrong with you, boy?"

His platoon was bringing up the rear of our unit, and he wasn't running. He led his men at a trot, looking this way and that for danger. I couldn't blame him, but I'd been tipped off by Harris. When it came to staying alive—or even outright weaselry—I always adopted Harris' more experienced approach over Leeson's.

I couldn't really see what Leeson was complaining about. Sure, there was a sort of gray cloud around his troops. It was a dust-devil-like thing. I listened for more details, but Leeson had dropped out of the command channel. I assumed he was talking to his people on the tactical line.

Breathing hard, I reached the rocks we were assigned to. Everyone hugged the big rock and looked around in every direction.

Looking back at Leeson's crew, I saw they'd stopped advancing. I zoomed in with my helmet's assistive optics to take a closer look.

"What's going on with Leeson, Vet?" I asked Harris.

"I don't know, sir. I think they ran into a nest of bees or something."

He was right, that's what it looked like. I tuned into Leeson's platoon channel to see if I could help.

What I heard was chilling. His people were screaming incoherently. There wasn't any speech at all, as far as I could tell.

"Harris," I said, catching on at last, "those aren't bees. They're nanites."

"Oh shit," Harris said with feeling.

Years back on Dust World, we'd fought with squids who'd come in a big slave ship. They'd had some exotic weapons, one of which was clouds of what looked like metal shavings lying on the decks of their ship. When a trooper got too close to one of the swarms, it would rise up and begin eating glass, metal, plastics and flesh.

My eyes dropped to the ground. I saw something I hadn't noticed before. The clearing we'd landed in wasn't a clearing—not exactly. There had been trees here recently. You could see depressions and mounds of mulched wood on the ground everywhere. The nanites had been seeded here, and they'd eaten the trees, forming a perfect trap.

Without further hesitation, I switched to the cohort-wide command channel. As a lowly adjunct, I had the authorization to do so, but I wasn't really expected to say anything. I was expected to listen in, and possibly make a report, if I'd been ordered to. There was nothing a pack of centurions liked less than a junior officer mouthing off on their private line.

But I did it anyway.

222

"Cohort," I said, "this is Adjunct McGill reporting. We've got nanites. I repeat, we've got nanite swarms out here! This clearing is not natural—it's a trap!"

That was all I said. I didn't tell them what to do, I just reported and shut up.

"This is Primus Winslade," our glorious leader said, finally speaking up. "I'm afraid those that have disembarked are on their own. The lifter crew is scrambling. Graves is in command of the survivors."

My jaw dropped as I watched the lifter pull up into the sky again. There were still troops on the ramp, marching down as it took off. The poor men flipped and tumbled down to their deaths in the clearing. Nanite swarms rose up to eat them as they crawled around in the dirt. The tiny machines weren't picky. They liked the taste of troops and armor, dead or alive.

"McGill," Graves said on tactical, "I've lost Leeson's platoon. I'm moving to your position if you think it's safe. What's your status?"

"We're good, sir, for now. The nanites don't seem to be climbers. We're on top of a rock formation, and we're staying here."

"Excellent," he said, then switched over to broadcast mode. Every man on the field could hear him—provided they weren't screaming too loudly, or their eardrums hadn't been popped by hungry bits of metal. "People, I want you to break formation and get to high ground. Preferably, you need to stand on top of the nearest rock pile."

The reaction across the field was dramatic. Several hundred troops ran like rabbits in every direction. Soon, they were panting in huddled groups on top of granite outcroppings.

A few more died, having already been dusted with the deadly metal. While they screeched and roared, they were rolled by their comrades off the rocks and down onto the ground, where they thrashed until they bled out.

"Okay," Graves said calmly, "what's the survivor count? What do I have left?"

After a few minutes, we accounted for ourselves. Several platoons were intact, like mine, but most of them had taken casualties and about half had been wiped out entirely. We'd lost three hundred out of a thousand, and five hundred more had fled in the lifter.

Graves reorganized us into two functional units of a hundred each. He put me in his unit as a personal sidekick. I wasn't sure if that was because he happened to be hugging the same rock I was, or if he thought I'd done well so far. Either way, I felt good about it.

"All right," he said once he'd finished getting us organized. "We're sitting ducks on these rocks if enemy troops show up, and we have to assume they're on the way. We have to get into the trees. Obviously, the nanite swarms aren't in the forest itself, so we should be relatively safe there."

So far, I followed him perfectly. But the next bit left me scratching my head.

"Unfortunately," he continued, "the only way I can think of to get us out of this situation is to run for it. My plan is to use some bait first, however. I'll ask for a volunteer from each platoon. The volunteer will run for the forest and attract the swarms. The rest of us will race past him and, with luck a fair number will make it to the tree line."

He looked around with gray, passionless eyes. "You," he said, pointing to Carlos, "you're my volunteer."

"What?" he demanded. "I'm your bio. Your medic."

"Do you see any wounded? They either stay clean or they die. I don't need a bio, I need bait. Besides, you look slow on your feet."

"Shit…" Carlos said. He looked like he was going to puke.

"Wait a minute," Kivi said suddenly. She was frowning deeply. "I might have a better plan."

"It's got to be fast, whatever it is," Graves said.

"I can improvise an EMP device. Give me some copper wire and a metal rod, preferably of iron."

We hustled to help her out. There were half eaten legionnaires with their discarded kits all over the field. We cannibalized equipment as fast as we could.

Kivi was a tech, and she was a decent one. The job of techs in our legions was to solve any kind of science, communications or engineering-related problem. A need for such skills often arose while doing battle on alien worlds.

Working feverishly, she wound the copper wire that we pulled out of suit power-systems around a rod of iron—which was really part of a discarded snap rifle. Then she hooked up a small flash capacitor to the ends of her coiled wire. Wearing rubber gloves and carrying a battery to charge her capacitor, she looked at us.

"The EMP field will disable my suit, and my tapper," she said, "but I've got a portable computer I can set aside, out of range, and I'll take off my helmet."

"Why waste a suit?" Graves asked. "Just go out there naked."

She frowned at him. "An unnecessary waste of time," she said, "stripping down will only—"

"You're wrong," Graves said. "Strip down. That way the only thing you'll damage is your own tapper. You're going to have to switch suits anyway after you wreck it, and it will make you move more slowly."

Thinking about it, everybody knew Graves was right. If her suit's exoskeletal system seized up, it would be difficult for her to move at all. We were in armor, after all.

Hissing in annoyance, she ripped off her clothes. Carlos reached out to give her a hand, but he was instantly slapped away.

At last, she stood there in her golden-tanned skin, looking pissed off but determined.

We watched, impressed, as she sprinted lightly out into the field. She hadn't gone twenty steps before the air around her started to give off little reflective glints.

"Blast them, Kivi!" I shouted.

Carlos stood excitedly nearby. "She has great boobs, doesn't she? I can hardly believe she's mine."

"Yours?" I scoffed. "Only when she's in a charitable mood."

"Either way, this has to be the best day of my life. A girl decided to save me, and she had to get naked to do it. I'm so happy!"

I chuckled. Carlos hadn't changed much over the years. I think it was due to the effects of revivals. You knew more, but your brain was still in a youthful state because with each

225

regrow, it came back structured as it had been the first time your information was copied into the system. Some people, particularly senior officers, liked to let themselves age a little more so they didn't look and act like hormone-saturated twenty-somethings forever.

Kivi held out her copper-coil wand and set it off. There wasn't any flash as I was expecting. The pulse was really a powerful magnetic effect. It was brief, but highly damaging to sensitive electronics.

I couldn't imagine a more sensitive kind of electronic device than a nanite. They were tiny and delicate. They were difficult to fight because they were so small and there were so many of them. But an EMP didn't have any problem with that. It simply flashed them all dead for about two or three meters around each time she charged the capacitor and set it off.

To speed things up, we made more of the wands and prepped them as she found new swarms and got them churned up. When we'd cleared a pretty good path to the tree line, Graves ordered us to advance immediately.

"Don't I even get to put my clothes back on?" demanded Kivi. Her legs ran with blood and sweat from her efforts.

Graves chuckled. "McGill, grab her suit and drag it to the forest with us. Let's get out of here."

Running hard, we made it to the forest without losing another trooper.

Graves turned to Kivi. "That was good work. It took too damned long—but it was a job well done. They told me I was crazy to recommend you for tech school, but I don't regret it."

"That's right," Carlos said, "pigs *can* fly."

"You would know," she replied.

After that, they messed with one another while she put her suit back on. I'd always found their relationship odd and a bit immature—but who was I to talk?

-35-

The next hour was a slog. We marched in the gloom of the endless forest, avoiding every clearing like it was diseased—which it probably was.

In the second hour, the gloom got seemingly deeper with every step. Night was falling. All along we'd only seen the sun in golden flashes through the treetops, but once it was gone entirely, we really missed it.

It didn't help matters that I had some of the biggest complainers in the legion marching behind me.

"Hey, McGill," Carlos asked, huffing more than he should have as we climbed another ridge. "So this is what a skirmish-line looks like? This is scouting? How are we doing? Is Winslade going to get another early promo for abandoning us in the middle of this shit-fest?"

"I'm sure he will, Specialist," I said.

"I don't even understand how that weasel is still alive. I mean, we were both executed, Kivi and I. How could he—"

"He was executed too," I said, "and Turov was permed."

"What? Really? No shit?"

"No shit—now shut up."

As usual, those words didn't work on Carlos. He was immune to them. He was like a dog who didn't even know his own name, much less how to do tricks.

"That's unbelievable," he mused. "I mean, it's totally cool that the witch is dead—but unbelievable. She should never have lasted this long. I thought she had some kind of frigging guardian angel on her shoulder, overlooking her wonderful rear-end like it was made of gold."

"That is what it seemed like," I admitted, "but her angel didn't get her out of being arrested for straight-out mutiny. Now, she's gone."

"Wow… actual justice from Central. I can't freaking believe it."

"McGill," Kivi asked. "If Turov was blamed and shot, what happened with Winslade? Why is he back on active duty?"

"Why not?" I asked. "We're here aren't we?"

She thought that one over. "You don't think that this assignment—I mean, putting us on the front lines like this—that that had anything to do with our actions. Do you?"

I chuckled. "Whatever gave you that idea? No one in Central thinks like that. They're not mean or petty or vengeful."

She snorted. "Okay. We screwed up, and the legion is paying for it. But you still haven't explained why Winslade is breathing again."

"He's slippery, that's why," I said. "Winslade and I were of the same opinion: we were just following orders."

Carlos coughed.

"That's it!" he said. "I've got your message at last! Listen Kivi, Imperator Turov *ordered* us to attack Central. We were just being good, obedient soldiers."

"It would be the first time in your life," she said.

"That hurts. That really hurts."

They went on like that for a while. They kept asking for details about how events had gone with Turov, but I just shrugged.

Soon, they fell to talking among themselves. They were theorizing that I had some kind of hold over Drusus. It wasn't anything that complicated, of course, but I let them think what they wanted.

Every good officer worked on making his own reputation as impressive as possible, and in my opinion a big part of that was keeping an air of mystery going to muddle important events. These two had big mouths. I knew they'd talk about whatever I told them, and soon the entire legion would be passing it around.

The next soldier that came up to talk to me was a surprise. It was none other than Della, who I hadn't seen in days.

"Hello," she said, falling into step beside me.

"Hey!" I exclaimed, reaching out a big arm to give her a hug.

She resisted at first, but then she softened and let me do it. She'd never been the type to enjoy displays of affection. Sex with her had always been fast and furious, but if you wanted to cuddle or anything like that, you were barking up the wrong tree.

"I survived the nanites," she said. "Most of my unit didn't, and we were folded into Adjunct Toro's platoon. She seems like a fool to me."

"Nah," I said. "Toro is all right. Half her platoon survived the nanites, after all."

She looked around at my group. "You haven't taken a single loss yet. And your tech, Kivi, she got us off those rocks without anyone else being devoured."

"Yeah, I've got a good team."

She had a plan in her head. I could see it working up there. She was the kind of girl that always had a plan. Finally, she came out with it.

"Graves would probably put me into your group if you lost someone," she said, looking around at my platoon again.

"Yeah, he probably—hey!" I said, catching on at last.

There was a look in her eye, a look I'd seen before. The woman could be a cold-blooded murderer when she wanted to be.

"None of that, now," I told her. "Don't you go and get any of my people killed. If you do, I'll ask Graves to put you into someone else's platoon."

"On what grounds?"

"I'll tell him you've been sexually harassing me."

She made a rude sound of dismissal. "As if anyone would believe that."

"I'm feeling harassed already."

She stepped away from me and marched nearby, sulking.

"Ah come on," I said. "I was joking,"

"But I wasn't. I'd like to join your team."

"I know."

She looked at me again.

"Are we ever going to see our daughter again, James?" she asked me suddenly, unexpectedly. "It's been years for me. Maybe I shouldn't have left her. I've been thinking about that. It's very distracting."

"You can stop worrying about it," I said. "I've got it all covered. We'll see her soon. We'll end this, and then we'll find the time. Wars don't last forever. Only legionnaires do."

My line of crap seemed to give her some comfort. We marched together for about two dozen more steps before I turned to say something else to her—but she was gone.

That's how life had always been with Della. She was part she-wolf and part ghost. I could only imagine how our daughter Etta would turn out when she grew up.

We marched into the trees until we reached some point on the compass that had been preselected by people back at Central. I could see it on my HUD, a beam of light was superimposed upon the forest, lancing down between the dark tree trunks and pulsing there. The rest of my team couldn't see it, which was probably just as well.

"Okay," I told them, "this is it. Spread out and take cover. Kivi, get the pig robots up here to dig foxholes."

"This is *what?*" demanded Carlos.

"This is as far as we're supposed to drive into the forest until we receive further orders."

He made disgusted sounds and moved off to set up camp. We were deep in hostile territory, but other than nanites, we'd yet to meet up with any resistance from the enemy. I felt this couldn't last long.

According to the maps I'd studied back at Central, Varus was at the center of three legions that had pressed ahead of the main army. Our task was to probe and locate the enemy lines. The fact that we hadn't met up with them yet wasn't a bad thing in my opinion.

I was sure there would be plenty of battles to be had when we did find the enemy.

-36-

Sometime after midnight, my tapper woke me up. There were alarms going off all around the camp alerting the troops.

We automatically closed our faceplates and steamed up the inside of them. It got *cold* up here in these mountains at night.

"What's up?" I asked on team chat.

"I don't know," Sargon said. "I was on watch, but I didn't see anything."

Using infrared, we scanned the environment. There didn't appear to be much other than a few bugs and a lot of cold trees.

"Adjuncts," Graves said on command chat, "I've got word from Central. They've detected large troop movements in our area via satellite. We're to stay in our holes and not engage. Repeat, stay fixed in your positions. If you must move, stay on your bellies. Stop all transmissions, too. I want radio silence and audio silence until dawn."

Under normal circumstances, our suits were automatically linked up via a local stealth network, a system that intelligently transmitted our voices as code that was designed to look like background radiation and general RF. The idea was that even if an enemy did detect us, we'd look like nothing important and certainly nothing dangerous on their scanners.

The trouble with tech like that was that it depended on the relative capabilities of the enemy, who I knew were pretty advanced. The safest bet, therefore, was to shut down the entire system when in close proximity.

After relaying Graves' orders about the shut down, I switched off our com-link system. Unless someone flagged an emergency, it wouldn't allow them to transmit again.

For the next thirty minutes or so, we waited in our holes. Unlike most of my men, I used this time to sleep. It wasn't a full-on sleep, but what I liked to call a "paranoid sleep." A state from which I could be easily awakened.

Something went wrong about ten minutes after I began dreaming. I dreamt a young woman was crawling to me, worming her way across the dark ground from her foxhole to mine. She was buck-naked in my dream, and her bare hips glistened with frost...

Startling awake, I reached for my rifle. Whoever it was, it wasn't a naked girl. I could tell by the shape that it wasn't a girl at all.

A gloved hand reached out and pushed my gun down. That was a mistake. I reversed my weapon on reflex and bashed the face in front of me with the butt of my rifle.

"Oh fuck—McGill! I think you broke my nose!"

It was Carlos. He was bleeding and cursing like a drunk after a fight.

"Shut up!" I ordered him in a harsh whisper.

Reaching out with both hands, I dragged him into my foxhole with me. He kept making hissing sounds of pain.

"Sorry," I whispered, "you woke me up."

"Woke you up?" he demanded in a low voice. "How could you be sleeping? They only told us we were about to be overrun a few minutes ago."

"Not everyone pisses themselves when they hear bad news."

He heaved a deep breath and rubbed ointments on his face. Nuskin, pain-relievers and the like went to work, sealing his nose and filling the air with a chemical scent.

"I hate this stuff," he grumbled. "And you're a dick, by the way."

"Specialist?" I demanded. "What the hell are you doing away from your post?"

"I came to tell you that Hoskins is gone."

"What?"

"You remember Hoskins, the new guy they just bumped up from the light cohorts?"

"I know who the hell he is, what do you mean he's missing?"

"He was in the hole next to me, and I wormed over to him so I could bum some extra rations. He's new, so I figured he was probably too nervous to eat."

"Uh-huh. Did you find him dead or something?"

"No, he's just gone. I asked the lookouts, but they hadn't seen him. I even checked around in case he was taking a leak— nothing. No one has seen him, so I crawled here to make my report. You're my commander, by the way."

"Yeah, yeah. Okay, get back to your post. I'll kick this up to Graves—wait, on second thought, I want you to worm your way over to Graves' hole. If he doesn't kill you, you can tell him all about it."

Grumbling, Carlos crawled away. My foxhole was in the middle of a rough circle that was inhabited by my platoon. We were downhill from the rest of the troops, on the edge of the group.

For a few minutes, I looked around with night goggles. It was just like Carlos said. Dead quiet. If Hoskins had vanished under these circumstances, then...

Suddenly, I was struck with an idea.

"Della," I whispered. "Damn you, girl!"

The more I thought about it, the more I became fixated on the possibility. Hadn't she just said she was thinking about getting into my platoon? It would be just like her to do it this way, even after I'd told her not to.

My relationship with the girl was beyond weird. We might kill one another or make love, on any given night of the year. Sometimes, we went for broke and did both.

She was a Dust Worlder and had her own way of thinking. She wasn't like girls from Earth. She was tough, stubborn and only half-civilized, in my opinion. That made her fun but troublesome. Sometimes you had to take the good with the bad.

Muttering curses, I got out of my hole and wormed my way across the landscape toward her platoon. They were uphill about a hundred meters from our position.

233

Instead of locating Toro's group, however, I crawled to Kivi's spot and tapped her on the helmet until she popped up with a knife in her hand.

"It's me," I said.

"The answer is 'no' McGill," she said hotly.

"What? Oh… no, no, that's not why I'm here."

"The answer is still 'no.'"

"Yeah, okay, I got that. Have you seen Della, or Hoskins?"

I quickly explained the situation. She was concerned.

"I understand why you're asking about Hoskins, but why did you mention Della?"

"Because she might have something to do with his disappearance."

"Ah," she said, laughing quietly. "I didn't know about that. The girl is active, isn't she?"

She had completely missed the point, but I didn't think it was worth explaining it to her. She and Della had a past, and telling her that the girl might be working to kill off one of our platoon just so she could get closer to me wasn't going to fix anything.

"Have you got any buzzers on you?" I asked.

"Always. But they use radio, and they fly. Deploying them would be against orders."

"Yeah, I know. Can you reprogram a few to crawl only and run them around the area? It will take them longer, but hopefully we'll get some stealthy intel. Put them on full-automatic, and when they come back we'll see what they got us."

"I can do that," she said, and she went to work.

She'd had her tapper repaired by now, and she connected it to a bigger computer in her ruck. After about five minutes, she launched six little crawlers. They were about the size of big beetles and they scuttled off in every direction.

"They'll find something," she said, "I have great faith in them."

We waited about nine minutes until the first one returned. The vids in its tiny memory would normally have been transmitted back as a live feed, but she'd made sure to disable that option.

Together, we watched her tapper display the boring data. Set to locate movement and organics, the drone displayed a few mouse turds, an owl fly-by and lots of sticks.

The rest of the drones came back about one every minute after the first. We checked them all. It wasn't until we viewed the vids from the last one that we got the shock of the night.

"Is that what I think it is?" gasped Kivi.

"Yeah," I said. "It's a slaver."

A huge form loomed. It looked like a very tall, very thin man. It sort of *was* a man, but one that had been genetically altered to serve a special purpose. I hadn't seen one of these freaks since Dust World, and I wasn't happy to see one now.

Despite being easily four meters tall, he moved with unnatural stealth. His huge, splayed nose quivered. I knew firsthand he could follow a scent like a bloodhound and didn't really need much light to get around in a forest.

What really caught our attention was his net, however. He had a prize inside. A human form. Whoever he'd caught and slung over his back, the poor guy wasn't moving.

"Hoskins," I said.

"Yes, I think we found him. But that slaver isn't done yet. He's looking for fresh game."

I nodded, unsure as to how to proceed. "I think I'm going to contact Graves," I said at last.

"You can't. He ordered you not to."

"They know we're here anyway, Kivi," I said.

"Then send me as a courier."

I looked at her, thinking about it, but then I had a better idea. I tapped her bag of tricks.

"Get out another drone. Have it run to Graves' position and tell him."

"What if he smashes it?"

"Send more than one!"

She got to work on it, and after about a minute, she released the buzzers. They ran off into the leaves, rustling and clicking like mice in a barn.

About two minutes later, my radio beeped, and Graves' voice came into my ears.

"What took you so long to notice one of your team was captured, Adjunct?" he demanded.

"You told me not to break radio silence, sir. That slows everything down."

"Hmm," he grunted, "all right. Let's wake everybody up. We can't let that slaver get home. He'll pinpoint us to his commanders. McGill—move your team to his position and take him down."

"On it, sir!" I said, happy to be doing something again.

I stood up, signaling my platoon to do the same. Around me, the ground heaved up and troops popped out of their holes. It was like watching a mass of armed gophers all waking up at once.

As it turned out, it was the worst possible move we could make.

-37-

By hiding in the cold ground, we'd made ourselves blind to the approaching enemy. As best I could figure, they'd been waiting for us to make any move that indicated we were aware of their presence.

We didn't even get to form up or advance into the drifting night mists. Instead, the forces that had encircled us attacked in unison.

First there were flickering shadows. I didn't know what they were. They looked like ripples in the air. But I knew these weird disturbances weren't supposed to be there.

"Something's coming!" I shouted in the clear. "Weapons up, fire if you see a target!"

"What are you seeing, McGill?" Graves demanded in my headset.

I ignored him, breathing hard and looking everywhere at once. The natural sounds of wildlife had stopped.

Then I saw the mysterious effect again. It was like a ripple, something that crossed my line of sight in front of me. I switched off my night vision—that both helped and hurt. I saw a dark hulking shape, but I couldn't see much else. It was too dark under the trees in the cold, crisp night air.

Taking a chance, I unloaded a burst with my assault rifle. Plasma bolts lit up the scene, splashing fire over the trees and making that electrical cracking sound these guns were famous for.

Even in the light of my plasma bolts, I couldn't see the enemy, but one of my shots must have struck home. The leaves on the forest floor burst up like a fountain. Something was down—something we couldn't see. It was snorting and hissing and making an awful fuss.

"What's there?" Sargon demanded. "Adjunct, I can't see my target—"

He got about that far before a massive spear thrust out of the dark and skewered him. He was lifted up into the air on the tip of the weapon.

Punching through a weaponeer's heavy armor and making a shish-kabob out of him was no mean feat. I was impressed and stunned. Sargon had been taken out, just like that.

I was even more stunned when his weapon discharged. He was carrying an old fashioned belcher, and he'd had the foresight to crank it open to a wide-angled beam. At point-blank range, it was hard to miss. He swept the region of empty space in front of him, and the invisible target lit up like a torch.

It was then that I finally understood what we were up against. The shape was unmistakable. It was tall and thin with powerful, dangling arms. The creature was visible inside the center of that gush of fire.

"Slavers!" I shouted. "We've got slavers in the camp, and they're invisible. They must have some kind of camo tech."

"I caught that, McGill," Graves said, "have you got the situation under control?"

All around me, troopers were being engaged by these gigantic ghostly figures. It was the general instinct of every legionnaire to slide back into his hole and seek cover.

The trouble was, we couldn't hide from invisible opponents. They stepped right up and plucked us out of our holes. Kivi was dragged from the ground and lifted high. Screeching, she was held aloft by one foot. She twisted around, howling and trying to get a shot.

I hosed the region of space I thought must have a slaver in it with plasma bolts. Some of them struck home, and Kivi stopped flying away. The air shivered, and I got the sense that—

Swish, a huge object came out of nowhere. I snapped my head to the left, and something big slid past my face. The slaver had thrown his spear at me. Its razor-sharp tip sliced open my cheek to the bone. Growling and feeling blood run down my neck, I fired more bursts until the monster went down.

All around, similar struggles were taking place. A few of the enemy used paralyzation nets, but not many. Maybe they didn't like to use a weapon that would so clearly show where they were.

I lost six legionnaires before suddenly, it all stopped. Panting, I moved to Kivi and dragged her back to a hole. She couldn't walk on her ankle as the slaver had twisted it badly when he'd picked her up.

"McGill," she breathed, "they're the same ones we fought back on Dust World. How are they invisible?"

"The squids must have taught their dogs new tricks," I said. "Looks like they pulled back, though. We killed at least five."

"I still can't see them. Not even their bodies."

"You should switch off your night vision for a second. You can see at least an outline then."

She did so, and she was amazed. "I can see the bodies—a little. They must have designed these stealth systems to fool our night vision."

"Tit for tat, when it comes to tech."

"Hey, your face is bleeding."

"Only a little."

"Liar," she grunted, calling for Carlos.

He made his way over to us and made hissing noises as he worked on my cheek. Soon, the bleeding stopped. All the while he dabbed and sprayed, Kivi and I stared with slowly rotating heads, looking for any sign of another attack.

"I'm totally paranoid," Kivi said, "these things came out of nowhere. My drone saw the one that grabbed Hoskins, but none of the others. I wonder why?"

"Maybe the effect is of short duration," I suggested. "They can stealth, but maybe not all night long. The one you saw with your drone was probably recharging his gear."

"Could be."

Graves showed up with a relief squad about then.

"Don't shoot me," he said. "I'm your commander."

Kivi lowered her weapon with obvious reluctance. She and Carlos hadn't been all that keen on Graves after he'd questioned and shot them a week ago.

Graves walked into the middle of our encampment and surveyed the damage. He took vids with his tapper of each dead slaver. With Kivi's help, he switched off their camo units and had her analyze one as she hopped around.

He had with him a large satchel. He must have gotten it off one of the pig-robots. He never opened it, but he kept it with him everywhere he went.

"Kivi," he said, "are you fit for duty?"

She looked at him with big eyes. "It's just a sprain," she said quickly. "I'll man my foxhole well enough, and I'll be able to march in the morning."

He nodded slowly. "Good. I'll count you as one more effective for now."

Next, he came to me. He eyed my bloody cheek speculatively. "McGill? Are *you* fit to serve?"

"Fit as a fiddle, Centurion," my words were slightly slurred by the searing pain of my injury, but I managed to be convincing enough. "I'm just taking a break. You want to admire my new scar?"

He climbed into my foxhole next to me and put his satchel on the bottom. His hand rested on it, never letting go.

"No, I don't want to admire your scar," he said. "Give me your analysis of this situation."

I gave him the quick version of what had happened and our theories concerning the enemy capacity to stealth. He watched the forest just like we did, with constant wariness.

At last, he stood up and sighed. "We'll have to move to a new position."

"Why, sir?" I asked.

"Because they've zeroed us. They'll be back with reinforcements."

"That's probably true..." I said. "But if it is, moving won't help. These slavers are master trackers. They have noses like bloodhounds. They'll just run us down someplace else."

240

"What do you suggest then, Adjunct?"

"Why, isn't that obvious?" I asked. "We should call for help and hunker down right here until it comes. We'll kill every freak that wanders into range. If we're still alive by morning, maybe Central will see fit to send a lifter out to pick us up."

Graves sighed. "Your plan sucks," he said. "But it's probably the best one we have. I'll report our situation to Central. You man this post. Don't retreat—that's an order."

"I wouldn't think of it, Centurion."

About an hour and a half later, the enemy came again. This time they didn't send just trackers, and the new troops weren't bothering with their stealth gear.

A great number of litter-mates struggled up the rise toward our ridge. Each square marched behind a rippling tracker. They proceeded with what seemed like stoic calm.

I knew that was an illusion. The litter-mates always started battle like a dance, with slow, precise movements. They didn't go ape until you'd killed a few of them.

Deciding I'd watched for long enough, I grabbed hold of Sargon's belcher. It was like a plasma carbine, but it was much bigger and fired a single powerful bolt rather than a spray of lighter death.

I'd been a weaponeer for years before I'd become an officer. Balancing the long weapon carefully, I sighted on the center man in a full squad of nine litter-mates.

His head vanished in a blast of heat and radiation. With a howl, the rest of the group broke and charged up the hill toward us. Two more carefully aimed blasts put down some of them, but even with supporting small-arms fire from my platoon, we couldn't stop the last few from reaching our lines.

Kivi was one of the unlucky ones. She was ripped out of her hole and hacked to death by a huge littermate who howled furiously until he was shot down by what had to be a hundred rounds or more.

"Break the next square!" I ordered. "Everyone concentrate your fire on a single group until they're all down. Then, we'll go to the next. Don't forget to mark the slavers and take them out too."

Up and down the ridge, squares of heavy troopers were battling other entrenched platoons. Flashes of light and noise filled the night. In each firefight, the combat went our way until the enemy got close.

At point-blank, they fired their muskets, blowing fist-sized holes into us smaller humans. Ripping us out of our holes, they hacked away limbs and beat men's bodies against nearby trees in heated fury. In every case, the berserkers had to be shot dozens of times before they fell.

The whole fight was surreal. I'd always found these heavy troopers to be a terrifying enemy. They were human—but they weren't. Genetically altered, they were like Neanderthals to us. Their mentality and vitality was quite different from our own.

After what had to be half an hour of continuous struggle, the battle finally ended. The air was thick with smoke and the cries of the wounded. Here and there, an officer walked among his troops with a bio behind, choosing who lived and who died.

Carlos came to me and tapped my shoulder.

"It's time," he said.

I wanted to say: "time for what?" but I knew better.

Heaving myself up with a grunt, I walked among my own wounded. The worst of them I sent to the revival machines. Some begged to be sent, others begged me to give them a chance.

Like most junior officers, I probably let too many live. In the end, I only put down a few.

Graves came along sometime later. He carried that satchel with him still. I glanced at it questioningly, but he didn't explain anything.

"Why's Kivi still breathing?" he asked me.

"Because she's the only tech I've got left. Her buzzers are crawling through the brush a kilometer out, sending back valuable reports."

Graves shook his head. "You're soft," he said. "A recycle would be merciful and more effective. But, she's your responsibility. You can carry her yourself if we have to move out in a hurry."

"I will, dammit!" I called after him as he left.

He dismissively waved back at me without even looking.

Kivi crawled to my foxhole and sagged down into it with me. There was sweat running down her face, and her ankle looked worse than before.

"I had to run on it," she explained. "Only a dozen steps—but it's broken now."

I didn't even look at her. I just stared out into the forest. "You think they'll come again?"

"If another of their units finds us, then yes, they will," she said. "Why didn't you put me down?"

"You begging for it?"

"No."

"Okay, then. Don't make a fool out of me. When they come again, warn me then fight to the death."

She nodded and sucked in trembling breaths.

Finally, just before dawn, Kivi woke me up. She slapped at my cheek, where my wound stung like fire.

I came awake with a growling intake of air and coughed.

"There's something out there. Something big," she said.

"They're all big."

She nodded and stared out into the forest.

Smoldering trees gave off wisps of smoke. The battle scene stank sharply with a dozen interlaced odors. The pitch-black land was turning gray as the sun came up. I tried my night vision then switched it off again.

"There," she said, looking at her tapper. "Downslope, at four o'clock."

I climbed up and placed my belcher on top of a dead hulk that had once been an armored heavy trooper. All around me, in the other holes, men were stirring. There were only about a dozen survivors in my platoon. None of us wanted to fight again, but we were still game.

"I see them," I said. "They don't seem to know we're here."

A column was marching by. They were heavy troopers, a fresh company of them. There had to be ten squads or more with nine monsters apiece.

Carefully sliding back down into the hole again, Kivi and I exchanged glances.

243

"Text the platoon," I whispered. "Tell them to hold their fire and play dead."

She did, and we waited.

The next few minutes were some of the hardest I'd ever endured. Knowing that death stalked nearby was somehow worse than fighting for my life. It was the anticipation of it. We were waiting for the unknown.

After about five minutes, the column seemed to be gone. I heaved a breath.

"McGill!" Kivi said. "Look at this!"

She'd been retrieving several of her buzzers as they crawled back to her with fresh vids. She showed me her tapper. On her dirty forearm I saw a half-dozen companies marching by in different spots in the forest.

"We're in the middle of them!" she almost sobbed.

"But they don't seem to know we're here."

"Yes, it must be a different formation, moving south. They're heading down to meet the hog troops in the open, maybe."

"It doesn't matter what they're doing, they're all over us."

She looked at me in fear and pain. "What are you going to do, James?" she asked.

I could tell right off she was worried I was going to do something crazy. The thought *had* occurred to me. Why not just pop off a few shots into the next company that came near? We'd ambush them and take out a lot of unsuspecting troops.

Sure, we'd be slaughtered after that. Someone would order all the nearby companies to converge on our little bivouac, and they'd wipe us out. But if we started it, we might take more with us than if we just waited around until another company stumbled onto us.

"I'm going to find Graves and report," I said.

"Don't leave me here in this hole!"

"Kivi, dammit," I said. "If you die, you die. I'll see you next time around."

She blinked back what might have been tears, but then she bit her lip and nodded.

Moving in a crouch, I searched until I found Graves up the hill and off a ways.

"McGill?" he asked, eyeing me critically. "Why are you away from your post?"

"I didn't want to broadcast this in the clear," I said. Then I showed him what Kivi had seen with her buzzers.

He watched for several seconds in silence. Finally, he sighed and struggled to his feet. He opened up his satchel methodically. It seemed to have an awful lot of locks on it.

I watched in confusion. "What are your orders, sir?" I asked.

"Help me with this."

I stood up, looking around. I thought I could see a metallic flicker from armor and blades down near the bottom of the hill. The sun was coming up now, filtering through the trees. That worried me, because if I could see them, they must be able to see me.

"Sir, we should stay low," I said.

"The time for that is over, McGill. We're right where we're supposed to be."

From the satchel, he drew out a parabolic dish. It was a satellite uplink. I'd seen them plenty of times in the past.

I watched in concern as he hooked it up and flipped on the power.

"Sir," I said, "the enemy is sure to detect this transmission."

"I know that. Shut up and turn that amp on."

I did as he ordered. Sweating now and peering downslope at the enemy, I almost didn't notice when he brought the next object out of the satchel.

Staring in shock, I couldn't believe it.

"A bomb, sir?" I demanded. "That's the same type of casing you had me carry from Central."

"Exactly," he said as he looped wire around his wrist. "I only wish the payload was as big. This is only a fusion firecracker."

My jaw sagged.

"What was all this about?" I demanded. "Wait... no, don't tell me! Varus was sent out here to die, is that it? This was the frigging plan all along?"

"What are you griping about?" Graves asked. "Really, McGill, you need to get a clue. Why else would the brass send us this deep into enemy territory alone? I thought our mission was obvious. We're here for one reason and one reason only—to help finish the job you botched yourself the first time."

Before I could even say: "This is *bullshit*, Centurion!" He thumbed the top of the bomb casing.

There wasn't a timer on it—nothing. We were all blown to hell and back in that instant.

The mushroom cloud carrying my atoms went up in the sky and hit the force domes above, spreading out. The particles were as fine as grit, and they carried the remains of me, Kivi, and thousands of enemy troops all mixed together.

-38-

When I came back to life, I was still pissed off.

"He's a good grow, get him off the table," said a female voice. She had to be the bio presiding over my rebirth.

I felt arms gripping mine, and I was hauled to my feet. Standing there swaying, my eyes full of snot, or whatever it was, my mind sought to grasp the situation fully.

"This is bullshit," I mumbled.

"Adjunct, you're assigned to rally point ten. Your platoon will join you there shortly. We're just getting started on them. Move out."

An orderly tried to push my arms into the sleeves of a uniform. That was a mistake. I caught his groping hand and broke one of his fingers. It snapped like a dry twig.

"What the hell! You crazy bastard! I'm calling this a bad grow!"

"Shut up or I'll kill you," I told him. I sounded like a mean drunk at closing time, but I didn't care.

All I could think about was the fight in the forest. We'd been bomb-carriers, nothing more. We'd been expected to drive as deeply into the enemy lines as we could and die hard. That didn't sit right with me.

"Doesn't matter if he's a bad grow," the bio in charge said. She sounded bored. "He's good enough to hold a weapon. No regrows—no matter what."

The orderly gave me a wide berth after that. Staggering away from the revival machine, I realized it was at the bottom of a hastily constructed bunker. A dirt-encrusted ramp formed the only exit. It was laced with puff-crete webbing for strength, but it was pretty primitive. I walked up the ramp and stumbled out into the open.

Cold air. That did me good. It was night—but it shouldn't be, because I'd died at dawn. How long had I been in limbo?

Tugging at the straps and tabs, I coaxed my uniform into cinching up and adhering to my body. I was soon suited-up but unarmed.

I tried to use the mapping function on my tapper, but it wasn't working. Just then, a squad marched by. I could tell by the Crossed Swords emblem on their shoulders they were Victrix pukes.

"Hey Victrix," I called to their veteran. "I'm fresh off the table. Where can I get a weapon?"

"Head to your rally point, Varus," he said. "They'll outfit you there."

He didn't say this disrespectfully. In fact, most of the inter-legion rivalry seemed to have died down now that the independent legions were fighting on Earth along a united front. The only group we all still held in contempt were the hogs. Anyone else was respectable—even Varus.

A few hundred steps of wandering around allowed me to find the nearest rally point. A big Roman numeral IV flapped on a pennant. Moving at a shambling trot, I followed the line for several kilometers more until I reached rally point ten.

Fortunately, the terrain was reasonably flat. It was abandoned farmland, just north of Albany. Here and there I spotted farming drones, still tending to soil that was empty and barren.

A low fog hugged the ground, making it difficult to see how big our formation was, but I got the feeling that there were many thousands of troops on the field with me. When I walked into rally point ten, I was surprised to discover it didn't contain just my unit or my cohort. The whole damned legion was being revived and sent here, where they were busy trying to sort themselves out.

After a full hour of bumping into people, I scored a heavy kit including a breastplate and plasma-bolt rifle.

We were part of a heavy cohort, and that meant we'd be marching in the second rank behind the light units. Looking at the size of the field, I found myself wishing I was still part of an auxiliary cohort of cavalry. A dragon would be nice to ride in today.

Just like the bio had said, I was the first one in my platoon to reach my destination. Soon the next member showed up. It was Kivi, and she looked upset.

"What happened?" she asked me. "How did we all die? One second, I was sighting on a column of enemy troops, and the next I was waking up on a gurney."

"Uh…" I said, unwilling to admit the truth. "I think the enemy dropped a big shell on us. They took us all out at once, as far as I can tell."

"Yeah…" she said, rubbing her face. "That makes some sense. Such a waste. What's the plan now?"

"I'm not sure, really. We're the first people out of the oven. We've got a bunker, at least."

I showed her our unit's meager shelter.

"This is for the whole unit?" she complained. "The floor is dirt, and it's not big enough. We'll never fit in here."

"We'll sleep in shifts—if we have time to sleep at all before we take the field."

She stopped complaining and looked at me. There was a funny glint in her eye.

"What?" I asked. "What are you thinking about?"

"I wanted to thank you for not killing me," she said after a pause. "I was scared. That's stupid, I know. Still, it was a nice gesture."

Shrugging, I wasn't sure what to say. "All we were doing was sitting in a hole. You could still hold a rifle. There was no reason to retire you."

"Maybe not, but I know Graves would have done it."

I nodded. We both knew she was right.

She stepped closer to me, and she smiled.

"Where are the rest of the troops?" she asked. "Are we really the first ones out?"

"As far as I can tell. The commanding officer is revived first then the specialists. You're senior, except for Sargon. I guess they put the tech at the top of the list. I'm surprised Harris isn't here yet, though."

She looked around the chamber. Outside, we could hear the constant din of shouting, tramping feet and the grinding of heavy machinery.

"Do you think we have enough time?" she asked in a husky whisper. "I mean... before the next revival finds this hole in the ground?"

I stared at her for a second. I'm slow on the uptake sometimes, but I was finally catching on.

"Sure we do," I said, grinning. "But... hey, you can't tell Lisa or Della, okay?"

"No problem. Don't tell Carlos."

"You got it."

We jumped on one another without further preliminaries. I don't know what it is about dying and coming back to life that makes a person horny, but it's an undeniable truth of modern military life. We lived hard, we died fast, and we screwed like rabbits in-between.

Kivi was well-known for hook-ups. She was one of the worst offenders in the whole unit—outdone only by yours truly.

About eleven minutes later, we were just finishing up. A head popped into the doorway and heavy boots tramped down the ramp into the bunker's interior.

As smoothly as I could, I sprang off Kivi and tried to pull my kit together. I was only half-successful. Straps dangled and crawled in the air, seeking one another like baby snakes.

"McGill?" Harris said, looking from me to Kivi then back again. "Shit, boy! Don't you ever give it a rest?"

"I rest up whenever I'm dead, Vet," I said.

He shook his head and let out a long sigh. "Well, I'll wait upstairs then, Adjunct."

I gave Kivi a final, soulful kiss and walked up the ramp after Harris.

"Do you know anything about the front?" I asked him.

"I know we got screwed-over properly out in the forest. That bomb killed a good number of the enemy, but it killed the last of our cohort, too. I only hope it was enough to slow them down."

"Anything on comparative forces? Numbers?"

He shook his head. "Hell, it took me half an hour just to find this place. My tapper is giving me nothing. It won't even map to this rally point like it's supposed to."

"It was the same for me."

He eyed me sidelong. "But you managed to find yourself a bunkmate fast enough."

I shrugged. "Well, I don't like to brag, but—"

"Brag? Oh no, not you!"

We shared a rare moment of laughter. I was glad. He was my veteran, and I needed him to back me up in battle. If he was itching to plant a knife in my spine, this war was going to be that much harder. I felt glad to know he'd be watching my back instead of stabbing it.

That made me think for a bit. What had Harris in a better mood? He'd clearly let go of his anger about having died twice during our teleport missions. I could only come up with one good reason: this time, we'd *both* bought the farm. I figured maybe he didn't mind dying so much if his rival suffered, too.

That line of reasoning seemed odd to me, but I felt it was true. Shrugging, I decided it didn't matter. If he was happy again, well, so was I.

-39-

It took all night for the rest of the unit to show up. By the time the last of them came wandering down to our bunker, I was wishing they'd taken longer to find the place. By that time Kivi was looking good to me all over again.

The problem of sharing close quarters with the women you're pursuing romantically soon reared its ugly head. Or in this case, her pretty head.

"James?" Della asked me.

"Huh?" I grunted, startled. I'd been staring at Kivi while she did aerobics and prepped her kit. "Oh, hi Della. Good to see you're back."

Her eyes slid from me, to Kivi, then back again. "How long was I gone?"

"It was about two days for all of us. It's going to be dawn in a few hours. We're reserving the bunker itself for folks who are fresh out of revival. Maybe you should get some sleep."

"I'm not tired," she said. "I heard you were the first one in the unit who caught a revive. Is that true?"

"Well, yeah. I guess it is."

"Who was second?"

I tried not to squirm. "I don't know—Harris, I think..."

"Not Kivi?"

"Oh... maybe... yes, come to think of it. Kivi did beat him back here by a few minutes."

She nodded as if confirming a dark suspicion. For some reason, I found this annoying.

"I wanted to ask you something, too," I said. "Back in the forest, I noticed Hoskins was missing. Then, a little while later—"

"Yes," she said.

"Yes what?"

"Yes, I did it."

That threw me off for a minute. As good at lying as I was, she was at least as good at admitting alarming truths.

"You *murdered* Hoskins? Dammit, girl. I told you I didn't—"

"You misunderstand," she said. "I didn't kill him. I led him to where I thought he might be killed. That's not the same thing at all."

"Yes it damned-well is! But how'd you do it, anyway?"

She shrugged. "I noticed a slaver near our camp. He didn't seem dangerous. He was merely scouting as I was. That gave me an idea."

"That's downright dirty. You flashed some skin and led poor Hoskins out into the woods, didn't you? You led him right to that slaver."

She seemed to be guilt-free. "It was easily done. Men of Earth are servants to their genitals, much more so than the men of my homeworld. Your people aren't wary enough about such traps."

I blew air loudly through my lips. "That's low, Della. You did all that just to get a spot in my platoon? Well, maybe I should give you one now. Would that make you happy?"

She glanced at me, then at Kivi. "I'm not sure it would."

I waved a hand in Kivi's general direction. "Forget about her. She was just having a bit of fun. Now, let's talk about what your problem is. Why are you so dead-set on getting into my platoon again?"

"I will tell you, if you confirm my transfer with Graves first."

I thought about that. Damn, this girl was almost as good at getting what she wanted as I was. In the end, I decided to ask for her transfer. If I didn't, she might cause more trouble. Besides that, I was curious as to her motivations.

"All right," I said. "You're in."

"That was easy."

"Yeah, well… Graves owes me."

She looked at me thoughtfully for a moment.

"For blowing us all up?" she asked.

"That—and plenty of other things."

"Okay. Then I'll tell you my thoughts."

Suddenly, her eyes dropped, and she looked shy.

"I think you and I should try to form a family unit—for Etta's sake."

That floored me. I'd have been willing to buy almost anything that came out of her mouth, but that one…

"Where'd you get this idea?" I demanded.

"The concept shouldn't be new to you. Your mother mentions it constantly. She says such relationships are notably superior for offspring. Is she wrong?"

I wasn't sure what to say. "No… I don't think she is. But listen, what would the nature of this relationship be?"

"You mean, would this involve sex?"

"Uh… among other things, yes."

She looked away again, shyly. "You don't seem like the kind of man who could be satisfied with a single partner. That's been the biggest barrier to our bond in the past."

"What?" I demanded, outraged. "In my opinion, our problems start with how you flit in and out of my life at will, and the fact that you try to—often succeed at—killing me about once every damned year."

She cocked her head and gazed up at me.

"Well then," she said, "if I could amend my ways, do you think you could amend yours?"

That was a good question. I frowned for a bit before answering.

"I don't know," I admitted.

Instantly angry, she turned away to leave. She didn't say anything, she just walked away. She was a silent rager. She didn't give a man any speeches, she liked to leave you standing there like a fool.

"Hey," I said, reaching after her and touching her arm. "Hold on. This is all kind of sudden. We're in the middle of a

254

war, for God's sake. Besides, I've never even met Etta in person."

"If you met her, do you think you could decide?"

"Yeah," I said with a certainty I didn't feel. "I think I could."

She gave me a flickering smile. Then she lifted a finger, and my eyes followed it. She pointed at Kivi, who was giving Carlos a rubdown. They were both grinning.

"Your latest conquest has moved on."

"I don't care."

She smiled more fully. "Good," she said, and left me in a muddled pool of thoughts.

"McGill? Leeson? Toro? Get over here," Graves called out to his officers a few minutes later.

"On my way, Centurion!" I said over command chat. I was still trying to sort out my feelings, and I wasn't having much luck with it. I welcomed the distraction.

Following my tapper's directions, I soon found a command bunker. Inside, Graves met with the rest of the officers in the cohort.

The space was cramped, with the centurions at the battle-planning table, and the adjuncts seated farther away.

"Here's the basic plan," Graves said. "We've been listening to the Primus and the various tribunes argue about it all day long. We're going to meet the enemy head-on."

Everyone listened closely, but there were a few groans at this opening statement. No one wanted to go toe-to-toe with the giants again so soon.

"That's right," he said, "we're going to fight on open land. We thought about falling back to Central in the south or maybe even fighting in Albany. But neither city has been fully evacuated. Using nukes would cost us a lot of collateral damage."

Millions would be permed. That's what he was talking about. The seriousness of our mission began to sink in. My hand rose, almost before I realized I was raising it.

"A question already? What is it, McGill?"

"Sir, didn't our bomb in the forest work? Didn't it at least slow them down?"

255

"It was relatively ineffective. The initial blast took out several thousand of the enemy, but they have shields which dampen radiation and fallout. The dust that came down was disintegrated on those shields. The radiation didn't spread. It was the same for other units that managed to penetrate their lines and set off their tactical charges."

I frowned. It was hard to think of a lack of radioactive fallout on Earth as a "failure", but that's what he was saying.

"We'd hoped to create a deadly hot-zone that would halt or at least slow their advance. We failed to do so. They're now pouring down from the mountains into the open land south of the Adirondacks and advancing on our position."

"What's the count of the enemy?" Leeson asked loudly.

"At least three million. That's not counting the auxiliaries like their—"

He kept talking, but we'd started buzzing among ourselves.

"Quiet!" he boomed. "Are you guys through crying? Did anyone say defending Mother Earth from invaders was going to be easy? We're going to stand here on this patch of dirt, and we're going to stop this enemy. Right here. They go no farther."

Adjunct Toro licked her lips, and she raised her hand reluctantly. "Sir? We've got less than a million men. How can we stop such superior numbers?"

"We've got better firepower," Graves said calmly. "Sure, our nukes aren't doing much, and with their overhead shielding there won't be any airpower to help, but if we can hold out for a week, the Euro Block will bring in reinforcements."

The meeting went on like that, but I didn't listen much. All I could hear in my head was a single number: *three million*.

In my mind, we'd already lost.

-40-

When the battle loomed at last, it promised to be the biggest one I'd ever seen. Hell, with the possible exception of the Tech World Rebellion, it was bound to be the biggest land battle in human history.

Millions of enemy soldiers were on a collision course. Immense battles had happened before on Earth, but they hadn't occurred in such a concentrated area. That was one thing that was different about this conflict, I guess. The gateway had brought the enemy from the stars and deposited them all into a relative pinpoint.

Back on their home planet, I could well imagine hundreds of thousands of troopers marching nonstop into that gateway for weeks. Moments later, each soldier had marched out onto Earth's green fields on the other side. Through that single aperture, one planet had emptied itself onto another's soil. Invasions using starships were old hat.

The fact they'd arrived at a single point necessarily concentrated them, but there was another thing that seemed to differ in this struggle from past wars. That was the nature of our enemy: they weren't entirely human.

They were similar enough in DNA and appearance, but their minds weren't like ours. It was as if we'd met up with an army of Cro-Magnons or some other primitive form of human. I was sure we'd have felt this sense of "otherness" about our ancient predecessors too.

Their heavy troopers, in particular, didn't think like normal people. For one thing, they didn't run from battle. Human wars normally ended when one side surrendered or when they simply ran away. These guys wouldn't do that. They'd come on and on—attacking until the last soldier couldn't lift a weapon.

Our plans, therefore, had taken this knowledge of the enemy into account. We'd set up bait for them, and we'd set up traps behind the bait.

"All right, McGill," Graves' voice droned in my ear. "Our heavy cohort is the killer. The light infantry is the bait. When the recruits bring in an enemy force, we'll focus so much firepower on them they'll melt. That's where you come in."

I nodded, only half-listening. I'd heard the plan for hours. I didn't really need to be told how things were *supposed* to go. I was busy thinking of other elements we hadn't discussed.

Graves stopped after a while. "Why are you staring into space?" he demanded.

"I'm not, sir," I said. "I'm staring at the enemy. I'm picturing how they're going to look when they march into this valley."

Graves followed my gaze. "It's simple enough," he said. "Why can't you just listen to my orders?"

"I already did that," I told him, "but I don't know if the enemy has your plans in mind."

Grumbling, Graves walked away. "Just see that you hold this line. Kill every trooper you spot before they reach your trenches."

I tossed him a salute and sat back down. Harris came over to sit beside me.

"This is bullshit," he said with feeling. "We're going to get mowed."

"I'm okay with that," I said.

"Oh really? You don't mind dying? Is that what you're telling me?"

I glanced at him, and I nodded.

"Yeah," I said, "that's what I'm saying. What worries me are the people in the cities behind us. They've only got one life to live."

Harris stood up, hawked and spat. "Don't worry about them. They've been told to drop to their knees and surrender. The slavers will capture them if they do, but they'll live."

That made me frown. He left, moving up to the higher ground where I'd stationed him. I kept staring at the future battlefield. I didn't like the idea of millions of our citizenry being enslaved.

I stood up and surveyed our defenses, which consisted of pillboxes made of puff-crete on top of berms of earth. It's all we'd had time to build, besides rows of deep trenches full of troops.

Inside each pillbox was an 88, a type of light artillery piece designed to destroy large infantry formations. These guns looked squatty and had bulbous noses on the front projector. The tripod of legs had a distinctly insectile appearance. Alien-built, the 88s always reminded me of beetles with nozzles, but they were deadly at mid-range against soft targets.

Out in front of the main trenches were automated turrets. These had been set up by our techs at regular intervals. They were programmed to wait until the first of the enemy marched past them, at which point they would spring up and spray the advancing troops with fire at close range.

There were other weapons, but there was very little in the way of heavy machinery. We didn't have many battle tanks on Earth anymore, not like they did in the old days. Our legions had been developed to face planetary insurrections, and therefore they'd been built to travel light. We equipped to be transported off-world for service among the stars. Tanks were too heavy to transport to other star systems efficiently.

The closest thing we had to fighting machines was the dragon cavalry. Unfortunately, I hadn't seen a unit of the marching machines all day long. I hoped they'd arrive before it was too late.

"What do you think our chances are?" Della asked me.

She'd moved up to my side as silently as a ghost, just like she always did.

"I don't know," I said. "You've fought the squids more than we have. What other tricks do they have up their sleeves?"

She shook her head. "They'll have something, but I can't be sure what it will be. The cephalopods only hunted us for slaves and sport, remember? This time will be different. This battle will be huge."

I nodded slowly. "What about nanite weapons?" I asked her. "Your people were supposed to produce them to help us."

"We did manufacture nanites. Trillions of them, and they're helping your industry. How did you think Earth managed to loft a sizable fleet of ships in such short order? All our nanites were used for construction proposes."

"You mean you Dust Worlders never produced nanites for battle? You produced them just for building stuff?"

"That's right. It's what Central demanded."

I sighed. I'd dearly love to have an extra techno-surprise for this enemy, but it looked like we were the ones in for all the surprises.

Right before the battle started, it fell quiet. We were all lined up inside our trenches with Sargon tucked into his pillbox to my right, and me down in the dirt listening to my headset.

My HUD displayed warning graphics before I heard a Graves' voice tell everyone to "ready up" for action. The battle was on. It was finally happening.

Like a thousand other officers, I scrambled to my feet and stood on top of a short ladder. Using my helmet with the optical zoom maxed, I surveyed the rolling land.

There wasn't much to see. In the distance, a little haze hung to the North. Behind that was a carpet of trees then the edge of the mountains.

"Do you see them, McGill?" Carlos asked anxiously.

"Not optically yet," I said, "but my helmet is lighting up. Someone in the command chain is marking red arrows. We've got an enemy contact out there, about two kilometers northeast."

"Two kilometers? That's close. Where are our rabbits?"

The light cohort that was associated with our defensive position on the line had been dubbed "rabbits"—and that wasn't a good thing to be. Their job was to pepper the heavy troopers with their snap-rifles. If they could peck away as a group and kill one, that squad would go ape and attack.

The plan was simple. It resembled the one I'd used against this enemy in the past, only on a grander scale. The light troops were trying to piss off thousands of the enemy at once and lead them into our kill zone.

"I see a green arrow now," I said, "about a kilometer out. That's the light troops. They should be springing this trap any minute."

"How hard can it be?" Carlos demanded. "All they have to do is a kill a few of these morons, and—"

"Something's coming in now on command-chat. Shut up."

"Cohort," Primus Winslade buzzed in my ear, "you're about to get the opportunity to earn your pay. The enemy is taking the bait. Ready up, you should have targets at extreme range in the next fifteen minutes."

When Primus Winslade got things wrong, he always did it in a big way. One would think that an advancing force could cross a kilometer in fifteen minutes. That sounded about right. But he hadn't taken into account the speed of this enemy.

Few on planet Earth had faced the litter-mates before. They kind of reminded me of swamp-gators back home. They usually moved slowly, but they could charge like demons when they wanted to.

"The light troops are running!" I shouted. "Sargon, anything yet?"

"No sir!"

"Harris, how about your group?"

I'd taken Harris and placed him at the highest point we had on our patch of dirt. It wasn't much, just about a three meter rise, but it was enough to see farther than the rest of us. I'd put half my force up there with sniper rifles to help out the rabbits when the time came.

"I'm seeing something," Harris said. "I'm seeing muzzle flashes. That windbreak of trees and outbuildings is in the way."

We were positioned such that a farmhouse and its barns and sheds stood between us and the action. I hadn't wanted that kind of setup, but when a trench line was being dug across hundreds of kilometers of open ground, not every adjunct got to be choosy.

261

The red arrows and the green arrows were pretty much lined up on the other side of the farm now.

"Watch those buildings," I said. "It looks like the rabbits are in retreat. They're heading into the farm."

"What the frig...?" Harris complained. "That's not the plan. They're supposed to hustle back to our line, not seek cover."

I didn't argue with him, but I didn't feel I could second guess their commander. The unit of light troops who had their asses in the breeze out there had my sympathies. It was their call to make.

"Unit, listen up," Graves said suddenly, talking to all of us on tactical chat. "The enemy is reportedly advancing too fast. They're overtaking the rabbits. McGill, can you put some fire down on that farm if you have to?"

"Yeah, we're in range," I said, "but it won't be accurate fire."

"That's all right. If you see the enemy, open up."

"But sir, the rabbits will be in-between—"

"McGill," Graves said patiently, "I know the tactical situation better than you do. You have the highest ground in the unit, and you're closest to the farm buildings. If I order you to level that farm, I want you to do it without a moment's hesitation or backtalk. Clear?"

"Clear, Centurion."

Heaving a sigh, I watched things unfold with a sense of growing unease. There were millions of these invaders coming, and things weren't even going right in the first few minutes.

The situation became clearer very quickly. Tiny figures, magnified in my helmet's optics, came into view. They were running for their lives from the barn and the house—running all over the place. It looked like a panic.

"Kivi," I said quickly, "have you got a buzzer feed from that far out?"

"I could send in a few. I've been using them to patrol closer to our line."

"Send them in."

We waited, watching more troops flee. Suddenly, the barn erupted into flames. Something big had hit it.

About a second later a boom reverberated from the farm. The barn had gone up. We saw fire and black smoke roll into the sky.

"McGill?" Graves asked. "You didn't go crazy and blast that building, did you?"

"I wish I did, sir," I said, "but that was almost certainly enemy fire."

"Roger that. Hang on."

We watched helplessly as the rabbits raced toward us. I didn't bother to do a count, but there was nowhere near a full unit of them on their feet.

"There they are!" Harris boomed. "Enemy sighted! Permission to fire?"

I hadn't seen anything of the enemy yet, but Harris was higher up than I was.

"Lay down fire, Vet," I ordered. "Get those heavies off the rabbits if you can."

Above me, snap-rifles began to crack. I watched tensely.

"Kivi," I called, "where are your buzzers?"

"That farm is at their extreme range, but I'm getting some feed now."

"Pipe it to me."

An aerial view filled my helmet. It made me dizzy for a second. The buzzers were flying around overtop the battle, aiming their cameras down into the action.

Heavy troopers were flooding the farm. They'd already run down and gutted a dozen of the rabbits. The men fought back, but they were no match for the crazed, armored giants.

"Are you getting their attention up there, Harris?" I demanded.

"Negatory, sir. We killed a few, but they still seem to be blaming the rabbits for their troubles."

My teeth bared themselves in frustration.

"Centurion Graves?" I called. "I've got buzzer feed."

"Pass it to me."

I did as he asked, giving him the uplink. He cursed and fumed.

"Dammit! Light Centurion Carrington must have screwed up. He was supposed to shoot and run, not engage them all."

263

"Well, it looks like they caught him."

"Yeah… McGill, take out the farm."

"Excuse me, sir? There are at least fifty of them still alive out there—"

"I think we talked about this already, Adjunct."

"Roger, sir. Sargon, burn down that farm!"

"It's about friggin' time!" he shouted, and a gout of heat rushed by my head.

The weaponeer was like a surgeon with the 88. He cut the buildings down like a man running a hot knife through butter. Within seconds, every structure had toppled and flames were everywhere.

That, at long last, got the attention of the heavy troopers.

-41-

They started from nearly a kilometer off, but they didn't seem to care. They charged us.

I'd experienced the thrill of having raving giants charge me more than once in the past, and I didn't relish the feeling.

"Choose your targets!" I roared. "Mark them—but no firing until they come into optimal range. We've got plenty of time."

My troopers shouldered their weapons and sighted carefully. I'm sure every heartbeat on the line was pounding, I knew mine was.

Above us, Harris' squad was snapping away, taking out one of the enemy now and then. But they weren't stopping. Only complete annihilation would accomplish that.

When they were about five hundred meters out, we started putting plasma bolts downrange. The rifle fire snapped and sang all along the trench line. A strange, ozone-like odor rose up and tickled my nose.

Getting into the fight, I sighted and fired. Three bursts sent an enemy trooper spinning, but he didn't go down. A few other beams slammed into him from my supporting troops, and he finally pitched onto his face.

When they got to about three hundred meters out, I gave Sargon the nod. I wanted them to get into the perfect kill-spot before they felt the power of the 88. The big gun hummed—and the enemy was burned to ash.

Hundreds died. Some of our own rabbits went down too, if the truth be told. They'd run for so long and so hard to escape their pursuers, but they'd gotten into the stream of fire. I heard Sargon curse at them, screaming for them to get out of the way.

They couldn't hear him, naturally. He knew his job. He couldn't let the enemy get to our lines just to save a few recruits who were fleeing in panic. So, they were all burned down together along with the fields, the fences, the trees and the heavy troopers from another world.

The trouble with the 88s was control. They were alien-made and quite effective, but they were far from a precision instrument. They were more like flame-throwers that could reach out hundreds of meters to melt steel.

Once you started to release a sweeping gush of energy with an 88, there was no turning back. You could either stop firing and go into the cool-down cycle, or you could keep mowing until you cut a full swathe.

Sargon was a pro. He never gave any of them a break. They went down, and they didn't get back up.

Less than a hundred made it past the kill-zone. They were close to our trenches now, and many were smoking and seared—but they kept coming.

I recalled seeing one of the heavies, eyes burned to white bulbs, staggering in our direction with his mouth wide open. I shot him until he fell.

A few automated turrets activated, taking out the rest of them. Sweating and a little sick, we slumped down into our trench and drank water.

A few people cheered, but not many. We'd won the day, but it hadn't been fun. In fact, it had been the opposite of fun times.

"How many do you think we killed?" Carlos asked me.

I waved at Kivi. "You got an automated count?" I asked.

"Yes, but only for the ones that got past the farm. It was about nine hundred."

Carlos whistled. "Any of the light troops out there alive?"

"I haven't seen one yet," she admitted.

Carlos heaved himself to his feet.

"Now it's my turn to have all the fun," he said, and he joined the other bio people who were heading out into the field.

They were to identify the dead and help the wounded—if they found any.

"The math wasn't good." I said to Kivi, who was still flying her buzzers around, "We lost hundreds of light troops from what I can see. For what? To kill twice as many heavy troopers? Sure, we can revive them all over the next couple of days, but—"

"McGill," Kivi said urgently. "There are more coming."

I scrambled up and studied the field. I couldn't see much through the smoke. I was about to have Kivi kick up her report to Graves, but he beat us to it.

"Unit," he said, "this isn't over. That first bunch was just the knock on the door. A major force is marching on our position right now."

"Listen up!" I shouted, overriding the chatter that erupted. "Everyone back to your station. Bio team, drag in whatever you find and withdraw from the field."

If there was one thing you didn't have to tell Carlos twice, it was to retreat. He hustled back to our lines with a snap-rifle in one hand, and a smoking boot with a few centimeters of charred leg sticking out in the other.

"It was all I could find," he said, panting. "I've DNA-identified just one casualty. He'll get his revive pronto—lucky bastard."

"Stay low, team," I said, eyeing the ground between us and the demolished farm. "Harris, can you see anything through all that smoke?"

"Flashes of metal. There are a few red arrows the recon boys must have marked with buzzers."

"Got that. Fire when you get a clear target. Get them charging as soon as you can."

"Roger that."

When I sank back into the trench, Della came close and eyed me.

"You're provoking them," she said.

"Of course I am. That's the plan."

Her lips compressed, but she kept quiet.

"What is it?" I asked her.

"Maybe you should hold back a little. I know the litter-mates. They'll tend to rush the point of the line that upsets them first. If you aren't first…"

Thinking that over, I felt conflicted. *Someone* had to be first. Della was telling me it didn't have to be me. I could understand that, but I—

"I got one!" shouted Harris. "I sure-as-shit got one!"

I realized then I'd heard the snap and whine of their rifles—set for maximum range. Apparently, he'd gotten lucky.

But the rest of us hadn't.

The land soon boiled with armored shapes. This time, they came by the thousands.

"Hold your fire!" I shouted. "Let them get into the kill-zone!"

To their credit, none of my troops with assault rifles fired so much as a single bolt.

Out on the long, long line of troops that represented Legion Varus in all her strength, similar battles were playing out. I took the time to survey the battle at a higher level while I waited for the enemy to reach us.

Legion Varus was doing rather well, I could see that. We were in the center again—lucky us—but the mid-flanks to either side of us were full of hog troops.

Now, I'll be the first to say that hogs are people too. They live, die, and have mamas at home crying while they do it. But that doesn't mean they really know how to fight.

They were combat-trained—sort of. Back on Earth, the non-space-going legions had gotten softer over the years. With only a smattering of officers and veteran troops who retired into their ranks from outfits like Varus, most of them had never seen real combat outside of some live-fire exercises and net vids.

In comparison, the mercenary legions were made up of troops that had more hard combat experience than any humans in Earth's long and storied history. When we died for our planet, we weren't left to rot in peace. Instead, we were churned out to fight and die again and again.

That process, extended over decades, tended to harden a man more than anything else could. We weren't nice people—we were killers.

Because of all this, I worried about our flanks. It was quite possible that Legion Varus would hold her spot on the line while the hogs at our shoulders broke.

Sargon waited until he could see the charging enemy before he opened up with the 88. That was good because this time there were about ten times more of the bastards. They went down as before, but one or two cuts with the big gun weren't enough.

Any normal army of humans would have reeled from the initial shock. Imagine seeing the thousand guys ahead of you burned to ash. Normal folks would turn and run, and I wouldn't blame them.

But not these crazies. They just kept on coming. They waded into the ash heaps and kicked up a cloud of gray dust that obscured everything.

I could hear them as they got closer to our lines. They were howling. Not roaring or screaming—howling. It was a long, undulating sound. It didn't seem like that sound could come from a human throat.

"Kivi," I said, "trip your automated drone turrets."

"But they aren't in position yet."

"Do it."

She tapped in the override command, and a chattering began. It sounded kind of like big sprinklers, but louder than that.

The press of bodies rushing forward and their ferocity was such that they paid little notice to the turrets at their feet. The only hint, other than that characteristic chattering sound, was the flashing in their midst.

"Line, open up!" I shouted.

As before, everyone in the platoon shouldered a plasma rifle and began to unload into the mass of the enemy. We could hardly miss. They grunted, and some thumped down into the filth, flopping and being trampled.

"Harris," I shouted, "we need your guns. Drop your sniper weapons and provide supporting fire."

Harris' team complied almost immediately. Sargon's gun was doing another buzzing sweep at the same time.

I began to think—to hope, really—that we were going to stop them all. That for a second time, not a single heavy trooper would get to our lines.

An enemy musket boomed. Then another. They were right on top of us. Sargon howled. Carlos didn't need to be told what to do. He rushed up the ladder to the weaponeer, his medkit flapping on his back.

Then we were in close, face-to-face. The nature of the combat changed. It was hard to see the big picture. We just kind of went into automatic, turning this way and that, fighting, killing, surviving and patching up our wounded if possible.

Bodies crashed into our trenches. They walked right over our heads and kind of pitched down into our holes. Maybe they didn't know we were there. Maybe they were blinded or so injured they were barely able to walk.

It didn't matter. We struggled with those that fell among us, hand-to-hand. Harris saved the day then, advancing without orders. He came to loom over my trench with his squad. They hosed down the enemy in the trench, killing them with point-blank, concentrated bursts.

Soon, only the surviving humans crawled out. I coughed and hacked with the rest of them. Carlos came to me, lifting me up and dragging me to the second-line trench.

"Get me up," I said.

"You're hurt, McGill."

"Doesn't matter. They'll send another wave soon."

"That's not our problem. Sargon's dead. Kivi's dead. Half your platoon is gone."

Heaving ragged breaths, I shoved him away and got up. I had a hole in my side, I could feel it.

"Put some skin on this," I said, gritting my teeth.

Shaking his head, he did as I ordered and backed off. I stumbled to where Harris was giving orders.

"Veteran!" I shouted. "Who told you to pull out?"

He frowned at me.

"You're still alive, McGill? I thought I shot you my damned self."

"You must have missed," I told him with a tired grin. "Now, answer my question."

He came close and put an arm over my shoulder. "Graves has ordered us to pull out. The whole cohort is moving back from the front. They're rotating another cohort from the reserves to stand in this hellhole."

"Seriously?" I asked. "This is over?"

"Hell no, not by a long shot," he said, clapping me on the back. "But we did good! We held the line. We held while others broke!"

I could tell he was truly happy about that. I mustered a nod of approval.

Within an hour, we'd been pulled off the front lines entirely. Walking as straight as I could, I marched with my platoon to the rear of the army.

In camp, I found a bunk somewhere with a water bottle and a package of insta-rations on it. I drained the water dry and tried to open the rations packaging. The plastic seemed too difficult for my fumbling fingers—why did they always make these things so damnably hard to get into?

With that final thought, my fingers slipped away from the bag, and I allowed myself to topple over and pass out.

-42-

Waking up in serious pain was a good thing for a legionnaire. It meant you weren't dead yet.

Groaning awake, I forced myself to get up and shake it off. I rose from my bunk and took careful steps to go have a look outside. Rain dribbled down my face.

"McGill," Carlos said from behind me. "You've got an infection. I can't clear it—but I can ignore it. If you want to feel better, you've got to go to the med center."

Forcing down some coffee and a little food, I nodded. "Yeah, I figured. I can't fight like this."

I dragged myself to the bio tents with trepidation. Everyone knew where a trip to that part of the camp might lead. They were mandated to make judgment calls on the wounded. If you were too far gone, well, they just pushed you over the edge and made a new copy. For that reason, troopers often hid serious injuries until it was too late or their real status became obvious.

Deciding I wasn't going to play the chicken this time, I marched down into their bunkers and signed in. They looked at me with pitiless eyes. I had to wonder just how many soldiers they'd already put down today.

When I was finally seen about an hour later, I was pretty annoyed.

"You guys can't just run a wand over my ass and say yes or no, can you?" I demanded to know. "Making a man wait an hour in pain for the verdict—well, that's plain torture."

The bio was a centurion. Since I was an officer, I'd drawn an officer as my doctor. She gave me a cold stare.

"Are you volunteering for a recycle, soldier? That would speed things along."

"No, dammit. I'm complaining about how long this is taking."

Shaking her head, she kept running instruments over me. She didn't move one fraction of an iota faster as she did it, either.

Without warning, she jabbed me in the arm with something sharp. I felt a surge of liquid pumping. It was a sick feeling.

My hand immediately grabbed her wrist, pinning it. I'd been killed by bio people before.

"What's that you're pumping into me?"

"Adjunct, you're on thin ice," she said, shaking me off. "You're assaulting a superior."

"Not if you're assaulting me first."

She pursed her lips tightly. "If it was lethal, you'd be in a fetal ball by now, dying on the floor. It's an antibiotic with some surgical nanites. They'll patch up the hole in your guts. You must have caught a few pieces of shrapnel out there. You've got a standard case of peritonitis."

"Oh..." I said, taking a deep breath. "And you're really curing me? Seriously?"

"We lost thousands on the line today. Under normal circumstances, a recycle might be in order, but today we're tight on resources. We need you to fight. We're patching up anyone who can be returned to the front as quickly as possible."

"I see. Sounds like you're doing your jobs for once. I like the change."

After several more long minutes of harsh, cold fingers and tests, she pronounced me fit for duty. I climbed painfully off the table, and she cleaned her hands.

"What's it like out there," she asked suddenly, "on the lines? How are we doing?"

"Varus held," I said. "Others didn't. They've driven wedges into our trench lines and broken it in places. But so far,

273

they haven't managed to push all the way through and overrun us."

She nodded as if she'd heard much the same all day. "The higher-ups are worried, you know. I patched a primus today. She said the enemy has come close to breaking us a few times already. She said, so far they've only sent probing attacks against us. Small forces to test our strength."

"Small forces?" I asked, both alarmed and amused. "Didn't seem that small when I was up there. We must have killed two thousand of the enemy in a few hours."

"Yeah," she said, "but when you have millions, a few thousand *is* small."

She had me there. I looked her over with new eyes. To tell the truth, she was a fine- looking woman. She was tired and scared, and I liked her better when she wasn't all business. I began to entertain thoughts of a date—but then she was called away to another ward, and my chances were blown.

Shrugging and straightening my kit, I left the med center. It was still raining outside. But the rain had turned cold like it was almost snow.

When I got to our unit's assigned bunker, I found Graves waiting for me. He looked me over with a calculating eye.

"You're the same McGill," he declared.

"That's right," I said, "but now I'm full of piss, vinegar and drugs. Ready to fight, sir!"

"Good. Get back to your platoon. They'll need some morale-boosting."

"Why's that?"

"Haven't you heard? The hogs on our left flank were broken. The regular troops there couldn't take it. I swear, if you kill any more than half of a hog line, it will break every time. I told the primus that, but he didn't seem to care."

Frowning, I looked out toward the front. The signs and sounds of battle were out there, of course. All night long, the sky had lit up in flashes. It was as if lightning strikes were landing all over. The sounds of heavy artillery and beamed energy never seemed to let up.

"Out west?" I said. "I thought they were hitting us harder in the east."

"They're hitting us hard everywhere. They only waited a few hours after that first push to mount another, stronger attack. The hog commanders are shitting themselves. They aren't used to fighting and dying on a line."

"What are your orders, centurion?"

"We're moving out in twenty. We'll catch a low-flying transport and drop off at the breach point. We have to push them back."

"I'm on it," I said, and I trotted to my team.

They were all lounging and complaining. I started right in, kicking ass and shouting. Harris leapt to his feet and joined me, taking revenge on any trooper that looked like he was slacking.

Harris was funny that way. He might plot my death one day but then help me do my job on the front lines the next. As unprofessional as he could be in private matters, he was always supportive when he was doing his job.

Soon, a small transport showed up. It was a skimmer, a vehicle that only flew in atmosphere. The back of it was almost flat, but it had a thin railing and some wimpy looking straps to hold onto.

Our unit and two others piled aboard. The lifter took off with sickening speed. It slewed around, and we hung on for dear life.

The front was very far from our base camp. Less than ten kilometers zoomed by, and we were out in the open. Smoke hung everywhere, barely masking the scent of death.

We reached our LZ and landed in a blast of mud, wind and incoming fire. Right off, I could tell the enemy assault was different. The enemy wasn't made up of simple heavy troopers rushing our lines like angry ants. Instead, there was what we called "star-fall" artillery. These weapons sent bolts of energy in glimmering arcs that moved at a surprisingly low speed to splash down in our midst. This kind of artillery seemed to be immune to the various fields that protect both sides from missiles and aerial assaults.

These star-falls looked like crashing meteors in slow-motion. They rose high before falling to the ground again, smashing everything they landed on. The ground was fused into glass and radioactivity levels spiked, setting off warning buzzers in our helmets.

We were dumped by the transport onto the ground quickly. The pilot seemed to be in an all-fired hurry to get back to the reserve points and load up fresh troops.

"Hustle up!" shouted Graves to the entire unit.

In one minute flat we were all sorted out and trotting behind Graves through the mud and broken trenches. We spread out into a skirmish line and advanced as fast as we dared.

"Listen up," he said, "because I'm only explaining things once. The enemy has already pushed past this spot in the line. We're going to patch that spot, therefore pocketing their advance behind us. We can't allow fresh support troops to take this ground and hold it. We're to keep the enemy at bay from both sides until the regulars come in and crush the troops that broke the line."

I wanted to say something. So help me, I really did, but this time, some angel from above caused Leeson to beat me to it.

"Centurion?" he asked. "Are you saying what I *think* you're saying? That we're going to be smack-dab in the middle of thousands of enemy troops?"

"Your powers of interpretation are amazing, Leeson," Graves said with unaccustomed sarcasm. "There's a hole in this line, and we're going to fill it. Get over it."

"Fucking loser hogs..." I heard Leeson mutter before he cut his transmitter.

I could echo the sentiment. We'd held our spot on the line. We'd done our jobs. As a fitting reward, we'd been called in to clean up someone else's mess.

-43-

When you're in the middle of a battle involving a million troops, it doesn't *look* like a million-man battle. Sure, there might be more smoke and booming on the horizon than there usually was, but you don't care much about that. You only care about that one rifle bolt that jumps up and bites you in the ass. The rest of it... well, that's somebody else's problem.

That said, we were really in the shit this time around. There was mud, death, smoke and dribbling rain everywhere. We crunched over the burnt carcasses of the fallen, both ours and theirs, for over an hour before we met up with anything other than yesterday's destruction.

"Keep moving!" Graves ordered. "Steady pace, don't get too winded, now. Victrix is on the far side. A cohort of their heavies is coming to link up with us."

I strained my eyes and my helmet's optics to look for them but saw nothing. Somewhere out there in the cold, gory slop, our comrades were on the way. I'd never much liked Victrix guys, but today I was willing to kiss the first one I laid eyes on.

"Movement spotted!" Leeson shouted over the unit channel. "Look south!"

A big red arrow darted down on my HUD, and I realized Leeson must have added it. I'd been so busy staring due east, hoping to see a Victrix banner that I hadn't bothered to turn my head.

But there they were, at least a thousand of the enemy, advancing in a ragged line.

We saw heavy troopers moving slowly with many gaps in their squares. Some were dragging their legs, weapons and even their bloody fingers in the mud. They looked as haggard and beaten as we did—but they also looked determined.

"Don't fire on them!" Graves ordered. "It's not our mission to enrage and engage. Let's kick up the pace!"

We went from a trot to a steady running pace. That would exhaust us in time, even with our exoskeletal suits aiding our legs. As an armored cohort, we had gear that wasn't meant to be carried through mud at a frantic pace. But we hustled and covered some ground anyway.

The heavy troopers halted, and for a second, I thought they were just going to watch us all slide by. But then, a row of much bigger figures loomed up behind them. These were real giants.

Cephalopod-bred giants were taller than slavers and several meters taller than the heavy troopers, who were extremely large to begin with. Their bare skins were unarmored except for a grungy tunic, but they each had a blurry field of energy protecting them. A large pack rode on each broad back, and I had to assume the pack held the generator for their artillery-sized weapons and their personal shielding.

Like the heavy troopers, the giants didn't fire on us. It was odd, but nothing I hadn't seen before. These specially bred humans the cephalopods sent to war had never seemed overly bright, and they rarely took the initiative. I figured their orders came from squid officers, and they didn't do crap without orders.

If you shot one, of course, they had standing orders to attack. But we weren't doing that. We were running along right in front of them trying to get past them to link up with Victrix.

Had that fact confused this banged-up horde of invaders, or were they just thinking things over in those slow, vicious minds of theirs? I didn't know, but I was running pretty fast now. The entire unit was way beyond a trot, and complaints had ceased all along the line. The only thing I heard from anyone was panting breath.

Stopping his run, Carlos bent to put hands on his knees.

"What's that over there?" he demanded, sucking air. "McGill, is that one of your beloved squids?"

As the rain slowed, he pointed, and I looked. There, on the hillock, was a squid commander. He stood on the highest ground he could find. His troops were assembling on all sides of him, forming a line.

Like a crystal bolt of lightning, I knew what was going on. Squids *liked* order. They liked things to line up in a neat little row before they acted. That's what this officer was doing. He was gathering his full strength around him before directing them to advance and destroy us.

"Graves?" I called over command chat. "I see their commander. Permission to take him out?"

"Permission denied," Graves snapped back. "I know you can't get enough blood and guts, McGill, but they'll just blitz immediately."

"Yeah, but they're going to anyway. Better to do it without a leader and without their full strength facing us."

"Again, permission denied!"

Grumbling, I stopped transmitting. Kivi trotted up next to me. Her short legs were really pumping, but she was carrying less weight, allowing her to keep up. I fell in and we advanced at a fast trot.

"You should do it anyway, McGill," she said between breaths. "We're as good as dead anyway. They outnumber us ten to one."

I glanced at her, shaking my head. "You shouldn't be listening in on command chat, Specialist."

"*You* always did it when you were a non-com."

"Yeah, but that was different—people expected that kind of crap from me."

She made a rude sound with her lips and slackened her pace, falling back into line behind me.

The truth was, her words weighed on my soul. The old James McGill, the young guy that couldn't get enough of the stockade and public whippings, he would have gone and done it. But I was older, wiser and more serious now—not to mention an officer. The new McGill could control his frequent urges to disobey orders... most of the time.

279

"That's it!" Graves shouted. "See that fortification dead ahead? That's the redoubt. We'll make our stand there."

Out of the mists, a dark hulk materialized. It had walls, mostly earthworks with puff-crete beams holding it together. The top of the walls had big bites taken out, blasted holes with craters behind them.

"We ran six kilometers for this?" Carlos complained. "Looks like a frigging death trap."

Right about then, the commanding squid officer must have realized we were going to be harder to kill inside that wrecked fort than we were right now, running around in the mud. A strange, warbling cry went up, and hundreds of muskets fired.

Explosive pellets like small grenades flew into our midst and popped all around us. Kivi spun around with a cry and did a facer in the mud. Without thinking about it, I stopped, took two steps back and hauled her onto her feet again.

"Let me die," she said, "just let me die."

"How bad are you hurt?" I asked. "I need a tech."

"I don't know."

Deciding we could figure it out later, I pretty much dragged her by the scruff up a rise and toward the nearest breach in the walls. Carlos ran up to help, and we each grabbed an arm. Together, we hauled her butt into the fort.

For just a second, when we stumbled into the muddy interior, I thought we were well and truly screwed.

There were troops already there. My mind saw invaders— but then my vision cleared. It was a unit of Victrix soldiers. They looked like they had yet to suffer a scratch.

"About time you got here, Varus," their Centurion said.

Her name was Olsen, and she was dark-eyed, dirty-faced and just plain mean-looking. Right off, I found myself disliking her, and it was plain as day she felt the same way about me.

"Where's the rest of your cohort?" I demanded. "I thought we were linking up with some real strength from Victrix."

Olsen narrowed her already narrow eyes.

"They're out there," she said, waving vaguely to the west. "Behind us. Victrix has stopped at every strongpoint and fortification, manning them. We were sent on ahead to meet you."

I nodded, understanding at last. They probably didn't like Olsen back at HQ, either. They'd marched her to the end of the line hoping she wouldn't make it back.

It occurred to me then that Graves wasn't popular with the brass, either. That meant there was a good chance Primus Winslade or some other rat back home had put up his name to spearhead the very tip of Varus' advance from the east.

The enemy fire on the fort died down as they'd given up on stopping us from escaping them. But they were still out there, taking up good positions for a siege.

"This whole thing seems under-manned," I told Olsen. "There should be five times this many troops here."

Olsen shrugged. She was totally disinterested in my opinions.

"That's not our call to make," she said. "Where's your commander, Adjunct?"

I looked around but saw nothing of Graves. His name was on my list in my helmet display, but I didn't see him in person. After a few calls that weren't answered, I stared out through the breach behind me. Could he be out there somewhere? Beyond the ragged walls I saw nothing but dark rain and occasional musket-fire.

Then I rechecked my HUD. Graves' name was now blinking red. He'd probably died in the mud outside the fort.

The full weight of the situation sank in, and I turned back to the Victrix centurion.

"Centurion Graves didn't make it. Adjunct Leeson is senior—he's in charge of my unit."

"Aw, dammit," Leeson said, coming up behind me. "You're right."

All the while this conversation went on, the Victrix guys behind Olsen kept looking at us like they smelled dog shit. They weren't even helping with our wounded. This pissed me off.

"Sir," I said to the Centurion. "There are over a thousand heavy troopers out there, encircling our position. They have giants at their backs. You have the rank, so you are in command of this fort. What are your orders?"

Olsen looked hard-eyed, but she also looked worried.

"Man this breach, Varus. You led them to us, the least you can do is stop them here."

"We'll do it!" Leeson shouted. "Toro, get your team to carry our wounded down into the mud pit over there. That used to be a bunker—dig it out. The able-bodied need to take up firing positions on the wall. McGill, you and Harris put your platoon in the breach itself."

"Thanks for the opportunity to serve with distinction, sir," I told him. "Really."

He clapped me on the shoulder as he moved past me downslope. He walked into the middle of the fort to help with repairs.

"No need to thank me, McGill! You've earned this duty a thousand times over."

-44-

The fort was a wreck. It'd been smashed and overrun not a day earlier. We'd expected a full-on rush by the enemy to our broken walls, but that wasn't what we got. Not right off, at least.

Instead, they kept steady fire on our position, but they only encircled us and didn't advance. The Victrix Centurion chewed her nails over this and kept pacing the battlements and cursing.

"What the hell are they doing out there?" Olsen demanded.

I knew she wasn't talking to me specifically, but I took it upon myself to provide her with a logical answer.

"Sir," I told her, "I've fought plenty of squids in my day. My bet is they want more reinforcements before they crush us."

She shook her head. "It's bad tactics. We're shoring up these broken walls, patching up our wounded, setting mines and drones. Why wait?"

"Well, I'm no squid, but I'd say they don't want to take further losses. That bunch out there looks pretty beaten up. They won through the line just hours ago, and now we've slipped in behind them. Maybe they're playing it safe."

"No," she said, "that's not it. They have *millions* to lose. They're waiting for something else."

She walked off before I could say any more.

Harris approached me after that, grinning.

"You're not getting any tail from Olsen, McGill," he said. "You might as well forget about that."

"That wasn't my intention, Vet," I told him. "But if it was, let me assure you, I could do it."

He chuckled and seemed bemused. He also didn't argue, which led me to believe he might have accepted my boast at face-value.

We enjoyed nearly an hour of desperate fort-fixing before the other shoe finally dropped. At that point, a team of enemy weaponeers finally arrived, dragging heavy guns behind them. They were small, rounded-headed machines shaped like barrels. They floated on gravity-repelling units. I knew from the look of them they were star-falls—or something like that. Something built to operate where normal artillery on this battlefield was hindered.

"That's how they broke these forts in the first place," Leeson said when I showed him the guns being set up about a thousand meters off.

"We need to take them out," I said.

"I'll configure Toro's rifle platoon by changing them over to sniper weapons. You hold here in the breach. I'll warn that Victrix queen, too."

Later, I saw him talking to Centurion Olsen, who immediately strode to my position and crawled up in the mud to the lip of our walls to have a look for herself.

"McGill," she said, "are those weapons going to drop salvos right on our heads?"

"Yes sir, that's my honest assessment."

She nodded, her helmet optics cranking back to normal. She flipped onto her back in the mud and appeared to be thinking hard.

"That's why they held off on attacking us," she said. "Why lose troops? They can kill us all now without losses."

I decided to exercise unusual restraint. I didn't mention that I'd suggested just such a thing an hour ago, and she'd scoffed at it. That kind of talk had never made a superior officer happy, in my vast experience of such moments.

"That's about the size of it," I agreed. "Looks like they did the same thing to this fort earlier—same tactics."

She looked at me, and some of the sneer was now gone, I could tell.

"This isn't good," she said. "I don't know what to do."

"Let me ask you, is there any chance that Victrix is sending more reinforcements to shore-up these walls?"

She shook her head. "Zero. What about Varus?"

"Same here. Looks like both legions figured it was the other guy's problem to hold the center."

"I wish Graves was here," she said. "I know his reputation... What do you think we should do?"

"We only have two options. We have to attack or surrender. Just sitting here waiting for the end makes no sense."

"Attack? They outnumber us at least five to one."

"Yep. At least that. But you know, they only seem to have one squid ordering them around. At least, that's all I've seen."

She looked at me thoughtfully. "What will those genetic freaks do without a commander?"

"Even one kill can upset this enemy, sir," I said. "And by upset, I mean like water on an anthill. They won't know what to do without a squid to tell them, but I'm sure their reaction will be violent."

"That's why you wanted to kill their officer when you first saw him, right?"

"You heard about that?"

"I did—from Leeson. He thinks Graves should have approved it, but that he was hell-bent on reaching this position."

"He's always been a man to take his orders seriously."

"I am too—but I know you can't always achieve success the way the brass wants you to."

I smiled. I was beginning to like the way Olsen's mind worked. It was too bad she wasn't going to be around much longer—none of us were.

"Can you kill that squid officer for me, McGill?" she asked suddenly.

My mouth worked for a second, then I closed it. I rubbed a mixture of sweat and rainwater from my face.

"Well... I could give it shot."

"Okay. Do whatever you need to. Just kill him."

Now, that was the kind of order I *never* heard from one of my superiors in Varus. Maybe, I thought, that was because Varus officers didn't like to give such open-ended directives.

But I knew better. It was because Varus officers knew me too damned well to let me out of my cage without a leash.

Slowly, a smile that had begun lurking on my face transformed into a grin. An inkling of an idea had grown up and turned into a scheme.

"You got it, Centurion," I assured her. "Just give me a couple of minutes."

She watched me curiously as I stood up and walked away from her toward the bottom of the pit the fort encircled.

I walked kind of quickly, so she couldn't change her mind or ask me what the frig I was going to do. I had big plans, and I didn't want her to get cold feet before I could try them.

-45-

The first thing I did was go to Kivi. She was in the wounded bunker in the center of the pit.

There was mud everywhere—and other stuff that was worse than mud.

"Are you here to kill me?" she asked.

"Nope, no such luck."

She put her head back in the mud again. "I'm ready for this to be over. Everything hurts and stinks. If they're going to kill us, I want it to be now."

"That's enough defeatist talk from you, Specialist," I said.

She frowned at me, and cocked her head, catching on. "You've got a plan, don't you McGill?"

"I always have a plan."

"And it's a crazy one—right?"

"What other kind is there?"

She gave me a huffing laugh and groaned as she pulled herself up into a sitting position.

"I'm in. What do you need?"

"Some of that tech wizardry of yours. Plug me into the enemy command channel."

She shrugged. "Won't do you any good. They're encrypted, just like we are."

I shook my head. "This isn't some kind of spying effort. I want to talk to them in the clear."

She stared at me for a second. "That's not allowed under our rules of engagement."

"I've been given the authority to do so," I said firmly. "From the highest source available."

"Who?" she snorted. "Leeson?"

"Higher than that," I said. "What's the matter? I thought you said you were in."

She sucked in a breath and let it go. "Sure, why not? I already followed you in an attack against Central and got myself nearly permed. Why not do it again?"

"That's the kind of can-do attitude I like to hear, Specialist!"

She mumbled and cursed while she worked her equipment. Kivi wasn't a naturally gifted tech, like Natasha, but she was pretty good at doing her job. Within a few minutes, she'd tapped into the enemy com-links and gotten me onto their radio network.

What I heard in my helmet sounded like a bunch of static, but I didn't care. I spoke up like I owned the place.

"This is the commander of Earth forces, New York Sector," I boomed into the transmitter. "I want to talk to the squid in command of this unit—uh—the Cephalopod Overlord, that is."

There wasn't any response for about a minute while I loudly and with great exaggeration of my status repeated my message in various forms.

At last, I got a response.

"This is Overseer Dribble," said a voice.

The name made me smile. A half-dozen snappy jokes came to mind, but I managed to avoid saying anything insulting. All the squids seemed to have names that had something to do with one property of water or another. Maybe "Dribble" was a really cool name on their world.

"Overseer," I said, "I wish to discuss surrender terms."

"What is this? Who are you?"

"I'm Earth Officer James McGill. Maybe you've heard of me."

The fact was, I'd become somewhat famous among squids. They believed I was some kind of important leader on Earth. That wasn't true, of course, but they couldn't imagine how else I'd managed to make so many crucial choices whenever Earth and I met up with their forces. In their world, small fry didn't buck the system and do things on their own.

"The McGill?" Dribble asked. "Can you verify your reality?"

The translation was obviously imperfect, but I went with it anyway.

"I *am* the McGill," I said. "The same man who's killed a thousand cephalopods if I've killed a hundred."

"What is the nature of your offer?"

"Servitude," I said. "What else?"

"Personal servitude? To me?"

"Yep. I'll put on an apron and clean your squid-box for you, if you like."

"Your statements are jumbled and almost meaningless. I believe you are offering to submit to me personally. Is this correct?"

"It is. But in return, I want your forces to withdraw from this position."

"Impossible! Unlike you, McGill, I do not operate with unbridled freedom. I have orders from my own Overlord. I cannot change them."

That was pretty much what I'd thought, but I figured I might as well go for broke.

"Okay," I said, "then how about this: you allow my troops to withdraw from this fortress, and I'll surrender to you personally and serve your will."

The squid made an odd, snuffling sound. The effect was kind of creepy, like he was turned on or something. I got the distinct feeling I'd made him shiver with greed.

Cephalopod culture wasn't like ours, not exactly. They were a race of slavers. Everyone was a slave to the next squid up the line. They gained rank by having cool slaves. With me as his slave, I knew this squid felt sure he'd be promoted. Hell, he was probably mentally fitting me for a gold collar right about now, planning who he'd parade me in front of to show me off.

"All right," he said in a lusty voice, "I accept your conditions. But, you must exit your fortress and march out here alone to my position. I'll collar you, and only then will I allow your troops to withdraw."

Kivi looked at me with a mixture of shock and horror. She was, of course, listening in to our little chat.

"Don't do it, James!" she hissed at me. "Better to die on your feet right here."

I grinned. Despite her misgivings, this was exactly what I'd planned on all along.

"I accept, Overseer Dribble. Give me your coordinates so that I can come to you and surrender."

His transmissions, up until this point, were untraceable as we'd tapped into a network of surrounding forces instead of a single individual. The network was naturally protected and his location hidden.

I snapped my fingers at Kivi, who looked down and began to work her tapper.

Lord Dribble hesitated, but only for a second or two. Then he gave me the coordinates.

Now, you have to understand that underneath it all, I'm a man of my word. When I make a deal with human, bug or squid, I aim to keep it. So it was important in my mind that I march up to the breach where Harris and his troops were hunkered down.

Holding up a white flag, I stepped outside the fort into the open. The hail of gunfire had stopped, but the rain still fell in endless depressing sheets from above.

"I see you!" Dribble said excitedly. "You have the stature, the voice patterns match—I can't believe my good fortune."

"That's right," I said, "you are one lucky squid."

Right at the end, I thought I could see him as well. He must have climbed up to a high point as he'd done before when I'd first spotted him.

That's when Kivi's buzzers all dashed in at once to nail him. They didn't have much of a charge when they were set to self-destruct, but when twenty of them did it at the same time, it made a pretty big splash of fire.

Burbling sounds came out of my helmet speakers.

"Is that you, Dribbles?" I said. "Sorry, but I can't quite make out what you're saying."

"You... lied."

"Not at all, sir!" I boomed back at him in an offended tone. "The deal was that I would surrender to you, and I'm in the act of doing so right now. I negotiated for *my* troops safety—not yours!"

Old Dribble might have said something else, but it was lost in the sound of the rain. He was with us no more.

"Squids and squid-slaves, hear me," I said on the open channel. "Since my master is no longer alive, I'm declaring myself free again. Any objections?"

There were no other squids around to complain, but there were plenty of genetic freaks that he'd left behind.

All the while I'd been standing around with my little white flag in the open, they'd been staring at me, holding their fire as they'd been ordered. But in my opinion, from what I could see through the rain, they weren't in a friendly mood.

As they began to grasp what had happened, they came to a chaotic but unanimous decision.

They rose up, roaring with incoherent rage, and they charged our walls.

-46-

This was the secondary effect of my plan that I'd hoped for, but I hadn't been certain I would accomplish it. When deprived of their leadership, these altered-human slave-troops were somewhat unpredictable. I'd seen them go mad in other, less effective ways before.

Maybe they had the impression that I'd played their officer unfairly. But I will always, now and forever forward, disagree with that assertion. To my mind, my conscience was as clean and clear as cut glass. The squid overseer had made a deal in greedy haste, that's all, and his mistake had cost him his life.

But the details of our former arrangement no longer mattered much. The enemy troops were attacking with the clear intent of wiping us out.

To me, it was *they* who were breaking the deal. We'd been guaranteed safe passage out of our predicament, not a howling mob-attack.

The biggest benefit of the situation was the fact they were so angry they weren't using their star-fall cannons to destroy us the easy way. Their emotions had gotten away from them and no one on their side was running the show.

Usually, it was best not to fight while angry.

"Incoming!" I shouted and dived back into the breach.

Muskets cracked and explosive pellets showered my armor with shrapnel. Fortunately, I was wearing a breastplate and a body-sock of tough material underneath. The shrapnel felt like someone was hitting me in the ass with hammers, but it didn't penetrate my protective layers.

Growling and pumping my legs in the mud, I was reduced to crawling before I made it to cover. Harris himself hauled me to my feet and shoved me behind the walls.

"McGill," he said, "I've watched you piss people off for years—but this time, you've gone and outdone yourself."

Looking out through the breach, I could see what he meant. The heavy troopers were charging us from every direction, slogging through the mud despite a constant shower of plasma bolts from legionnaires on top of the walls.

Behind the heavy troopers loomed the giants. They were hulking silhouettes in the rain. Their shields splattered in white flashes with every plasma bolt that hit home.

Cutting through the sounds of the rain and the gunfire, there was a roar to be heard—the cry voiced by a thousand large throats. Their cries were both human and inhuman at the same time.

The overall noise-level was deep and unnatural. Not since the days of gigantic apes, which had gone extinct after the last ice age, had such battle cries been heard on planet Earth.

We killed hundreds before they reached the walls, but we couldn't hope to stop them all at a safe distance. Heavy troopers sprang up and grabbed the rim of the crumbling wall with hands that looked like they had five thick thumbs each. They hauled themselves up, and despite the fact most were shot to death on the rim, they kept on coming.

A pack of them reached the breach all at once. They were intent on breaking through. Point-blank fire from both sides staggered and shocked the combatants.

The human legionnaires were cornered and desperate, but the enemy was insane. The battle was bloody, and lightning began to play in the skies overhead as it heated up.

We held the breach even when it became choked with squirming, dying fighters. Every time a trooper managed to claw his way past the bodies and grab onto the throat of a legionnaire, we shot him a hundred times or more until he sagged down, another lifeless hulk. The fallen formed uneven bricks, and they were slowly walling off the breach as they piled deep.

Up on the rim of the wall, things didn't go quite as well. There were mostly Victrix troops up there, and they were stretched too thin. Grabbed and hurled down from the top of the battlements, Olsen's soldiers were being killed too frequently.

"McGill!" Leeson shouted at me. "Take a team and clear the top of the walls in a sweep. I'll help with the breach now."

Leeson had pretty much put himself into the reserves by staying with our wounded in the central bunker. He left his shell at last, but only after seeing how the battle was turning. Behind him, a grim-faced group of injured soldiers hobbled painfully toward my position. Kivi was among them.

"All right," I said, "Harris, Sargon, Carlos, Montgomery and Bissel, you guys come with me."

They weren't happy, but they didn't argue. They marched at my sides. On my order, we shot down heavy troopers who'd managed to scale the walls and fight their way past the defenders.

Before we'd gone half-way around, though, the nature of the battle shifted. The giants had arrived.

As effective as heavy troopers were, the giants were five times more lethal. It wasn't just about their height, it was about their weight, vitality and shielding.

They didn't have to run and jump or scramble over our walls. They only had to scale them as a man might vault or climb over a fence.

The Victrix troops defending the wall top were rolled down into the central pit, often struck dead. Using their energy projectors like clubs, the giants smashed Victrix people down and stood like avenging demons all around the rim of the fort.

Then, as one, they roared in triumph and beamed the central bunker. It was melted to slag, then something inside exploded. The injured, who'd been too weak to fight, perished in searing flames.

"Big bastards," I said. "Let's take one out—we've done it before."

My four-man team was right behind me. Advancing on the nearest of the giants, we got his attention with a volley of fire. The guy that really made his shield flicker was Sargon. From the erratic, orange flashes pulsing over the target, I thought the giant was about to go down.

But he turned and ran in our direction instead. He lifted his projector cannon at point-blank range.

"Charge!" I roared, and I began running toward him.

A blinding gush of lavender-white power coursed past me, but I didn't stop.

We tackled him as fast and hard as we could, but we were like a tribe of pygmies grappling an elephant's legs. He didn't fall, he didn't even stagger.

His big weapon pumped up and down, whistling like a falling tree. He hit Sargon first, maybe because Sargon's belcher had actually affected his shielding.

Like a broken doll, Sargon's lifeless body whirled away into the darkness past the walls. The rain and the night swallowed him. He never made a sound, but I was certain he was struck dead.

"Combat knives!" I shouted. "Hamstring him!"

Bullets and beams couldn't penetrate a shield, but a knife and a gauntlet could. We clung to those ankles and sawed at them. Blood gushed, and finally, Harris cut through. With a confused roar, the monster fell and rolled down into the pit. He'd grabbed Harris with a fist as big as a Christmas ham and took him along for the ride.

I watched, panting, as Harris got a few more licks in with his knife before the giant's arms bulged and Harris' head popped clean off. It was the freakiest thing I'd seen in years.

During the fight, however, the giant's shielding had gone out. We beamed him to smoking meat and headed toward the next monster, who was standing tall and roaring at a circle of Victrix people.

One of them was Centurion Olsen herself. Her eyes were wild with fear and anger. Her unit had been all but wiped out.

We came in to join them, rushing low under the giant's guard. Once the Victrix pukes knew what we were up to, they came in to help. Only two more died before the giant was brought down.

"You're insane," Olsen told me.

"Some say so," I told her with a shrug, "but I think I just get really, really mad during a fight."

She blinked away rain and her finger came up to waggle at me.

"You brought this on my unit! You enraged all these aliens! You destroyed my command!"

"What?" I asked. "That's crazy-talk. I saved us from the star-falls."

"You weren't supposed to enrage all of them at once! You weren't supposed to go out there and parlay with the enemy without permission!"

"Now, hold on a second," I said, "I had permission. It's recorded in my tapper, in fact, with your voiceprint clearly identified. I was just following orders—Your orders."

Her eyes filled with hate and disbelief. It was an odd mixture, but one I'd seen before.

"You knew this was going to happen, didn't you?" she demanded. "It was a foolish mistake to trust a lunatic of your caliber. McGill, after this is over, you'll never—"

I would have liked to have heard the rest, but I never got the opportunity. At that precise moment one of the giants who still had a working beam projector aimed it in our direction and blasted Centurion Olsen into two equally blackened halves.

"Damn, that was close!" I said. "Let's keep moving, people. We have plenty more fighting to do."

We made it to the next giant and took him down, but that was when the breach Leeson had been defending finally gave way.

Leeson himself contacted me. "It's all you now, McGill. Toro, Graves, Olsen—you're the last officer here."

I tried to question him, but he didn't answer, and his name went red.

After that, it was a grim fight to the finish. A few hundred surviving heavy troopers and two giants hunted down and killed my rebel team. Right at the end, Carlos revealed something to me. It was a plasma grenade.

He showed it to me and I gave him the nod. Together, we raced into the arms of a giant. Unbelieving of his good luck, he lifted us up into the night sky, one in each hand.

The squeezing strength in those fingers was superhuman. Carlos wasn't wearing a breastplate, so his ribcage crushed with a crackling sound.

The plasma grenade fell from his lifeless fingers. It fell into the mud at the giant's feet and glimmered there, active and gathering energy.

Despite my agony, I had time to smile before it went off.

-47-

When I was revived and returned to my accursed life, I fully expected to be thrown back onto the battlefield. That was the normal lot of any legionnaire killed in action: to be promptly reequipped and sent out to fight again. Before I could even think clearly, I was envisioning more combat with giants, squids, and the heavy troopers invading the New York mud.

But that wasn't how it happened.

I knew something was wrong right off, while I was still flat on my back on the delivery table. The room was too quiet. There was no distant crump and thud of heavy weapons. No sirens, no radios blatting out bursts of static. Nothing but the quiet gurgle of alien machinery.

"How are his stats?"

"They're good enough."

"Okay, get him out of here."

My eyes burned. I tried to look around, but all I could make out was the ceiling. It was a textured alabaster. It was made of puff-crete, of course, but done the old-fashioned way. When they'd first begun building large structures with the stuff, they'd done so in the style of older buildings. They'd kept the look of textured ceilings and lighting fixtures from a century back.

I'd seen those types of ceilings before, and I knew I was in Central.

"Why...?" I croaked aloud.

"What's that, Adjunct?" asked an irritable male bio. They always seemed to be annoyed about something when they were delivering a new man back to life.

"Why am I back at Central?"

"Because you died with the rest of them. I'm not sure why they asked me to revive you so soon. It's been mostly high-ranking people all day."

My eyes worked well enough to focus on the bio specialist's face. He was young but haggard looking. I could tell right off he'd pulled a long, long shift.

"How many days? How long was I gone?"

"Three days," he said, glancing at his tapper. "The records say you were lost three days ago."

"What happened up in New York Sector?"

The bio shook his head. "I haven't got time to explain. I'm recharging for another revive. No breaks. No sleep—no nothing. Get off my table and get your explanations from the guys upstairs, will you?"

I didn't get mad. He'd obviously been working to the point of exhaustion. I could respect that. I got up, dressed, and staggered out into the passageways.

Along the way to the elevator, I looked down into the city streets outside through rain-streaked windows. The streets were mostly black. Some buildings were lit here and there, but only sparsely. Could this be a security blackout? Or worse, a power outage?

There were troops down there in the streets. Lines of them were setting up defensive positions in the grid-work of ground traffic. That was a bad sign—a very bad sign. They were preparing to fight in the streets around the building.

By the time I made it up to Varus headquarters, I was pretty worried. The news on my tapper had told me a grim tale.

We'd lost the battle in the north. We'd lost *everything*. Legion Varus had been a wipe. Victrix too. After the hog lines broke between the more experienced legions, our gambit to seal the hole had failed. I'd died days ago, so I'd missed some of the fun.

An all-out assault had begun on our positions in my absence. They'd poured literally millions of troops into the breaches. Strangely, they didn't seem to care about their losses anymore. Encircling the hold-out legions, they crushed them by sheer weight.

Reaching my quarters and my locker, I found the place empty. Could I really be the only one in my unit who'd been revived? If there was anyone else, they weren't around.

Dressing thoughtfully, I heard a voice behind me as I pulled my boots on.

"McGill?" asked an unpleasant voice. "It's about time you showed up."

I turned in surprise and faced Primus Winslade. "Winslade? They haven't managed to perm you yet, huh?"

His eyes narrowed. Such talk was acceptable between officers who were giving one another a hard time, but there were a couple of ranks and a lot of bad blood between us, so he knew I meant it.

"Funny," he said like he was spitting out the word. "Very funny. We're to report to upstairs immediately."

We headed back to the elevators. I'd been planning to stick around my unit's quarters, but that clearly wasn't what the higher-ups had in mind.

Primus Winslade marched primly in front of me, and it was hard not to daydream about fragging the little bastard.

In the elevator, he punched up a very high floor number and that lifted my eyebrows.

"Why are we going up to the top?" I asked. "Isn't that a little extreme?"

"What would be extreme is if you could keep silent for two minutes."

I studied him while he focused on the elevator digits, which spun rapidly.

"You know what's up, don't you?" I asked him. "You came down here to get me personally. Who sent you?"

"Your commander did," he said. "Your *rightful* commander."

His words left me with a confused frown. I could count any number of rightful commanders in my chain to the top. Any of them could have been the one to demand my presence, but I didn't know why they'd bother.

As we approached a pair of golden doors, I began to replay all my most recent crimes in my head. Which one had brought me to the attention of the brass on Gold Level this time?

It could have been any of several things. The first that occurred to me was a fresh inquiry into my role in the initial attack on Central. That would explain why Winslade was coming along and his attitude. Sure, the attack was old news, but the military rarely forgot a sin.

There had also been several irregularities during the teleportation missions. When I thought about it, nothing much had gone right with that effort from the start.

Then, of course, there was the latest interaction with the squids. I doubted that would come back to bite me in the ass so soon, but you never knew.

When we finally got past several of the guards and checkpoints, we made our way into Drusus' office. There, I was in for quite a shock.

Drusus wasn't alone. Graves was there too, and both Drusus and Graves were standing at attention over by the window.

Sitting ramrod straight behind the desk was one of the last people I'd ever expected to meet again: Equestrian Nagata.

My mouth sagged, and I glanced at Winslade. He gave me a tiny smirk which indicated he'd been in on this all along.

"There you are, McGill," Nagata said. "Good. We can now proceed. I need you as a witness."

"Hold on!" I boomed. "I thought you'd been permed, sir!"

Nagata flapped a hand at me. I thought it was an odd gesture, one I couldn't recall seeing him perform before.

"Quiet," he said. "Someone obviously found a backup of my memory and DNA." He turned to Drusus. "As I was saying... in my absence you took over Central's defensive operations. Is this correct?"

"Yes."

"Wasn't there anyone else more suitable to assume command?" Nagata demanded.

"If you mean someone more experienced in battle with the cephalopods—no, there wasn't."

"I'm talking about someone of superior rank. I find it absurd that a mere tribune from an independent legion was chosen to lead Hegemony to her destruction. In fact, I find the situation highly suspicious."

"I was given the rank of Imperator, sir," Drusus pointed out.

Nagata nodded with an unpleasant expression. "Yes... your motivations in this matter are very clear."

My eyes swung to Drusus, who was looking a bit worried. Had there been some funny business going on that I hadn't been involved in? I began to wonder if Drusus had tried to go off-script.

Officers had talked to me in the past about my unsanctioned actions, at times even admiring them. But I'd always cautioned them against trying to mimic my behavior. Some men have a knack for that sort of thing and some don't. Drusus had always impressed me as a straight-arrow. If he had tried to pull something, I wasn't surprised that it'd turned into a disaster.

Nagata spoke in a doom-laden voice. "You took command. You didn't attempt to get a superior officer for the job. Now, our defensive army has been decimated. There's nothing between Central and two million invading troops."

"I thought it was three million," I said loudly.

He glanced at me. "They didn't kill our army without losses. They seem, in fact, to be careless about their losses now."

I shut up. I hadn't meant to speak out in the first place, but it had just happened.

Still, I was impressed. Even I was able to do the math. A million invaders face-down in the mud? We'd bloodied them pretty good.

Unfortunately, it hadn't been good enough because they were still on the march.

"Well?" Nagata demanded. "What do you have to say for yourself, Tribune?"

He was still refusing to acknowledge Drusus' new rank, and that made everyone uncomfortable.

Everyone turned their attention to Drusus, and he hesitated. "The top brass here at Central were all dead at that time—including you, I might add, Equestrian. I was told they'd all been permed. As the most senior officer on site with the appropriate experience, I assumed command."

Nagata's eyes were stern.

"Amazing," he said. "Such wild hubris. You never asked for an emergency replacement from the ruling council, did you? Just a promotion?"

"An emergency replacement? No, sir."

Nagata got up from his desk. He put his hands behind his back and began to pace around the office.

"So, instead of calling for another officer to fly in from Geneva or Shanghai, you took the reins of power for yourself—*without* authorization."

"It was a temporary situation," Drusus said firmly. "I relayed my decision to the council. And for the record, I think I did rather well, considering."

"Do you? Dare you go so far as to call that slaughter in the north a success?"

"We didn't win, no. But we took more than our weight in enemy troops with us. Remember, we were outnumbered four to one."

"Tribune," Nagata boomed. "Consider yourself demoted. Your actions here amount to an ill-conceived power-grab. We've been invaded by an alien power. The enemy is on the march. Their ground-mobile shields are preventing us from bombarding them, and we have no significant ground forces between Central and this growing menace. Does that sound like a job well done to you, Graves?" he asked suddenly, turning to face the centurion.

Graves looked worried as well.

"I'm sorry sir," he said. "I'm not fit to judge."

Nagata drew his sidearm. It had a long, thin barrel. He pointed the wicked-looking gun at the ceiling.

"Yes!" he shouted. "There we have it—the wisdom of a man who knows his place. A man who has a rank he is content with. A man who doesn't dare to ape his betters and lose the home world as a direct result."

303

"Hold on," Drusus said in alarm. "Are you trying to blame this entire invasion on me?"

Nagata stared at him through slitted eyes.

"No," he said at last. "That would be going too far. You didn't bring the enemy to our doorstep. What you *did* do was seize power in a moment of opportunity."

"Sir, the top brass was all permed as far as I—"

Again, Nagata's gun popped up. He shook it at him.

"Not so! There was another officer who should be alive and running things right now. I'm talking about Imperator Turov, of course."

We all stared at him, dumbstruck.

"But sir," I said, unable to keep quiet any longer. "She's a traitor."

He glanced at me unpleasantly. "So you say. So you've been told. Are you a traitor as well, McGill?"

"Uh... I don't think so, sir."

"No, no, of course not. You've only been doing what you think is best for Earth, isn't that right? No one has permed you for doing your best, have they?"

"I guess that's true, sir."

He nodded and glanced at his tapper. "Well, we'll sort this all out in a few moments. Imperator Turov will be here in—"

The door popped open before he could finish his sentence.

There, at the entrance, stood a snarling Turov. Her hair was still wet from her revival.

"I've been gone for weeks!" she exclaimed. "Why?"

"I believe it was Graves who shot you," Nagata said, waving his hand at the centurion.

Turov awarded me and Graves a snarling glance, but her eyes fixed on Drusus.

She stepped up to him, and they squared off. There'd never been any love lost between these two. In fact, they were as bad as Harris and I about bumping each other off.

"So," she said. "You prefer to stand silently while Graves, your faithful lapdog, barks for you. Is that it?"

"I did what I had to," Drusus said firmly. "I'd do it all again, if the decisions were mine to make today."

"Yes. Exactly as I thought. A mutineer to the last."

Drusus turned back to Nagata. "I fail to see why you revived her. Her accusations are absurd. She's the traitor—hell, she's the one who had you killed, Nagata. Almost permed."

Nagata nodded his head thoughtfully. "Yes, that's true. This is a difficult decision. I need a good commander, but I don't seem to have one."

They both looked astonished at his words. Clearly, both Turov and Drusus thought they were the logical candidate for command.

"Justice must be done!" Turov demanded.

This surprised me. In my mind, justice would have started off by leaving her dead.

"Hmm," Nagata said, pacing again. "Yes, justice... I've received word from the council. Extreme measures are now acceptable to them—*Any* extreme measure that I deem necessary. The enemy must not be allowed to take the capital."

"What kind of—" began Drusus, but Nagata waved for silence.

"First of all, I'll begin with the easiest choice. Graves, you're hereby sentenced to death. McGill, carry out the sentence immediately."

I was shocked. I reached for my pistol, but I didn't draw it. Graves had placed his hand over mine.

"Not necessary," he growled as he watched Nagata with a cold, unblinking stare.

Calmly, he drew his own weapon and, although the other officers winced, he put the muzzle to his head.

"Earth must not fall," he said and shot himself.

This just flat-out stunned me. I'd been planning to draw my pistol and threaten the officers with it. Shooting Graves—hell, he was only man in the room who definitely didn't deserve it.

His body toppled forward and lay still. We all gaped at it.

"That was bullshit!" I said loudly. "Sirs."

Nagata's gun was up again. "Shut up, McGill. Your fate has not yet been determined."

He carefully considered Drusus and Turov next.

"What am I to do with you two?" he asked. "Only one of you can command here at Central. Only one of you is fit to do so—but which one?"

"That would depend on your philosophy, sir," Drusus said. "Do you believe in surrender or a fight to the finish?"

Nagata sucked in a deep breath and nodded. "Well stated, Drusus. A month ago, the choice would have been easy. Back then, surrender was unthinkable. But since then, we've witnessed the strength of these aliens. More gateways have appeared in strategic locations on Earth—you didn't know? It's true. The invaders are still pouring onto Earth's soil. They have a planet full of soldiers behind them. Perhaps in the end they'll bring a billion troops to our home world."

Drusus' lips became a tight line. "I can see how this is going. Am I to be arrested?"

"Yes," Nagata said.

"Are you putting me in command or not?" Turov demanded suddenly.

Nagata looked at her in distaste.

"Yes," he said at last.

"Good," she said. "As my first action, I hereby order *Tribune* Drusus to report to the brig for processing."

He walked out, looking proud but resigned.

"This is crazy," I complained. "You're putting *her* in charge?"

"Silence, McGill!" she said. "I'll have you shot again if you don't stop talking."

"What the hell for?" I demanded. "Sir."

Nagata answered before she could. "Because you conspired to take Central."

I pointed at Turov. "But so did she!"

"That's not all," Nagata said. "You've performed countless criminal acts since this invasion began. You've even withheld vital intelligence from your superiors. In fact—I demand you hand over the Galactic Key right now."

We locked stares. I was stunned that he knew about the key. It explained why I was here in the first place, and that didn't make me happy.

His hand flexed, palm up.

Slowly, I drew the item he had demanded out of my pocket. Turov bit her lip and watched hungrily.

"You mean this seashell-thing?" I asked. "My mama found it for me on the beach."

"Hand it over, you fool. If you don't I'll have you executed as well."

After a few seconds of hesitation, I tossed it to him. He caught it and smiled.

"Excellent," he said, admiring it. "I've been waiting to hold this in my hand again for a long time."

Then, in his moment of distraction, I smoothly drew my sidearm. In the same motion, I shot him in the face.

It was rather neatly done, if I do say so myself.

-48-

"McGill!" Turov screeched. "Are you crazy?"

"Maybe," I said, walking over to the body and kneeling down.

She came up behind me and pried open Nagata's dying fingers. I knew what she wanted, and I let her have it.

"Why'd you do it?" she demanded.

"Why? With Nagata out of the picture, you're the one in charge here."

"That's not really Nagata, you idiot," she hissed at me. "That was Claver in disguise."

"Oh yeah," I said with a shrug, switching off the box at his belt. "I thought he was acting a little funny."

She looked at me suspiciously. "You knew it was Claver?"

"Sure did."

"Then why did you take so long to shoot him?" she asked. "Why wait until Graves was dead, and Drusus had marched himself to the brig like a boy scout?"

"Well..." I said. "I thought you and I might be able to come to some kind of an arrangement with the others out of the picture."

Her eyes narrowed like an angry cat. "What kind of deal are you fishing for, McGill?"

"I need your brass to get me out of my troubles—and to change an order I don't like."

She thought about that, looking me over.

"Of course," I went on, "I could just shoot you right now, but that would be hard to explain. If there's any more funny business between us, we'll both be permed in the end."

"You're nothing *but* funny business," she complained.

"Can't you even guess what the deal is?"

She sighed. "Tell me."

"You get to keep that special item you just put in your pocket," I said.

Reflexively, her hand went to her hip. She squeezed, gripping the lump she found there. "How can I trust you now?"

"We could seal it with a kiss," I suggested.

She scoffed at that idea.

"I get to keep the key," she said, "and you get to keep breathing. But stay out of my way."

"Uh-uh," I disagreed, shaking my head. "Not good enough. You're going to tell the lab people I'm back on the project. I'm going to explore the last teleport location."

"What good will that do?"

"Do you know where the last selection on the dial goes?"

"No, of course not. Only Claver knows how that works. The teleportation angle was all his: the suits, the tech—everything. That's what he brought to the cephalopods with a promise Earth would be subdued easily."

"With him left in charge as planetary governor in the end, no doubt."

Her eyes flicked downward, and she made a pouting gesture with her lips.

"Wait a second!" I said, catching on, "*you* were going to be the governor? That's why you were part of this coup? What was Claver getting out of it?"

"Highly lucrative shipping contracts."

I made a noise that was somewhere between a sigh and a hiss of rage. "You two never quit. You've been working on a scheme like this for years. You're never going to rule Earth, Galina, I'll tell you that right now."

She looked at me and gave me a tiny smile. "I'm leading Earth's defense forces at this moment, thanks to you, McGill."

I wanted to kill her, but I controlled myself.

"Reinstate all of us: Graves—my entire unit. I want the slate wiped clean of all investigations and allegations."

"Done. Now, report back to the labs. Have fun with your squid-suits. I'm done with all that."

I eyed her thoughtfully. "You're going to surrender to the squids, aren't you?"

She shrugged. "Not yet. The rest of Earth will never accept defeat until Central falls. It will be a few days—maybe a week."

Shaking my head, I couldn't believe the lack of concern I heard in her voice.

"Galina," I said, "how is it you want to be the slave of a cephalopod so badly? Don't you want to be free?"

"Freedom is an illusion. A recruit who dies at the word of his centurion—is he free?"

"Maybe, if he does it willingly as a volunteer," I argued.

"We've lived under the thumb of the Galactics for more than a century. Were we free all that time? No. There is no freedom. There's only survival and whatever you can grab today with your hands."

She made a grasping motion with her fingers for emphasis.

I stopped arguing with her, even though I wanted to keep going.

She let me go, and I thought about what she'd said as I rode the elevators down to the labs.

I wasn't interested in trading one alien master for the next. From what I'd seen, the squids were worse. They lived closer to Earth, for one thing, and they liked to mess with humans more. I could see them editing our species right here on our home world. Maybe that was their real goal: gaining a fresh breeding stock to replenish their genetically designed troops.

People were in a grim mood down at the labs when I got there. They were just suiting up Ferguson again for another experiment.

Ferguson looked like a hound dog left out in the rain. His face was so long, so forlorn and miserable, it was painful to look at.

"I'm sorry," Lisa told him, "I'm so sorry…"

She adjusted his suit and jiggled at the sleeves, as if fixing them.

"Get on with it!" Adjunct Toro called. "Let's fry this fish then go eat."

Ferguson was almost shaking. He looked like he'd filled his pants already and was considering doing it again.

"Hold on!" I said as I stepped into the lab. "Lisa, don't touch that switch."

She whirled and her face went through a quick series of emotions. She was relieved, pissed, and sad all at once.

I felt a pang, because I knew why she felt like that. She rushed to me and thumped a fist on my chest even as she hugged me.

"You took the key," she said, "you took it, and I couldn't find it. Tell me you still have it? They started up the tests again, and they keep dying."

I nodded and patted her absently. "I've got it, don't worry. Take me up there. I'm going to take Ferguson's place."

Ferguson perked up as I approached and asked him to relinquish his suit.

"It's been bad, McGill," he said. "Whatever magic we had before, it hasn't worked today. I've been fried four times in the last four tries. We can't even duplicate our earlier experiments."

"I'll take the next ride," I said.

"You sure? You just got out of the oven yourself, I hear."

"Yeah, I'm sure."

He shook my hand with both of his. "Thanks, man. I really owe you."

It was hard for me to accept his thanks when I knew that my carelessness had already cost him several trips through the guts of a revival machine. But I managed to keep a straight face. If my lips were too tight and bloodless, he'd probably chalked it up to fear rather than shame.

A few minutes later, I was suited up.

"I'll take a short hop, just to test the system," I said.

"We tried that," Toro said tiredly.

"I know. Just give me a chance. I'll put the old James McGill touch on things."

311

Toro rolled her eyes and walked away.

"Okay," Lisa said, adjusting my gear. She had to let the suit out in the armpits, as I was bigger there than Ferguson was. "Here's the plan. You just port to the number one position then pop right back. This is a system integrity test. Nothing fancy required."

"Uh... okay."

She looked at me sharply. Unfortunately, she was starting to get used to me, and she knew when I was full of shit.

"You're not..." she said. "What are you planning? Don't mess around, James, this is too important."

"I know," I said, "it's just about all that's left. That's why we have to take our chances with a big play. You know what Mark Twain used to say?"

"What?" she asked.

"That necessity was the mother of taking chances."

She looked at me and laughed. It was a bittersweet sound.

"Do whatever you want," she said. "You're going to anyway."

She really *was* getting to know me. I gave her a smile then scooped her up for a kiss before she could race away.

It was about then that a scuffle began out in the hallway. Everyone looked, wondering what was going on.

Everyone except for me, that is. I knew it was Turov. I knew her voice, and I knew why she was coming down here as pissed as a long-tailed cat in a room full of rocking chairs.

She stepped into the room and lifted the key I'd given her. She smashed it on the floor.

"A seashell?" she demanded. "You gave me an honest-to-God seashell?"

Except for Lisa and me, no one else knew what the hell was happening. But the pack of MPs at Galina's back clued them in. The bystanders backed away from her, from me, and melted toward the exits.

The hog MPs lifted their rifles and aimed them at me.

I smiled a big, Georgia smile at them. "You boys going to shoot me? Go ahead, I dare you."

Turov jumped between us.

"No!" she shouted. "Hold your fire. James, get out of that monkey suit and give me my property."

"I can't," I said, "not quite yet."

With those words, I made a little spinning motion with my fingers in Lisa's direction. She had big eyes, but she knew I had the key, and she knew it looked like a seashell. She also knew that Turov had been declared a traitor not days ago.

Lisa cranked up the generator, and it began to hum.

"Dammit!" Turov screeched, running toward me, grabbing at my hand. "Give me that key! Get away from that—"

I clicked the selector to the first position. We jumped together, melting and reforming several hundred floors down.

Galina fell against me, breathing hard. "What was that? What did you do?"

"I took you downstairs," I said, "away from your goons."

A few confused-looking people stared at us. They were there to accept arrivals, but they hadn't expected me to come in with an Imperator in my arms.

"McGill," she said, breathing hard, "that was so strange. I was torn apart and reassembled, wasn't I?"

"That's about the size of it." I replied.

"What's it like to travel to the stars?" she asked me, her eyes half-closed in fear.

"Very strange. It's like you die, but instead of going to heaven or hell, you just drift for a while until you get where you're going."

She shuddered. "Give me the key."

"I can't. I can't fly without it."

"Damn you! We made a deal!"

"I know, and I *will* give it back. I have to borrow it for one last trip."

She looked wild and desperate. "You might not come back. I'll lose it forever."

"That's possible," I admitted. "But I've done this several times before. Your property will be in good hands."

She made another grab for it then, but she couldn't pry my fingers off of the smooth object in my palm.

"Imperator," I said gently, "I'm going to charge up, and I'm going to fly. When I get back, I promise I'll give you the key again."

"I'll have you shot."

"Won't matter. You'll just be risking the thing you're trying to protect."

Her eyes were wild with worry, exasperation and hate.

"Why did Claver bring you back into this?" she demanded. "He should have left you dead!"

"I've been wondering about that too," I said calmly as I walked over and attached my suit to a power outlet with an adapter the techs had worked out over recent weeks. "Maybe we're still playing his game, even now. Maybe he—"

I felt a tug at my hip. She'd taken my pistol from my belt. She aimed the gun at the suit's power-pack determinedly.

"Aw now, come on," I said. "Listen, Galina, that's not a good idea. We need this suit, don't damage it."

"I won't if you cooperate," she said.

She looked up at me defiantly, and I could see she was dead-set on not letting me teleport out with the key. My first thought was to do it anyway, fast and mean, before she could fire. That might work, or it might get us both turned into charred ash.

"What's the big deal?" I demanded in frustration. "Just let me go."

"No, you're not taking my key away! I'm going with you."

-49-

Now, you have to understand that Imperator Galina Turov was probably the last human on Earth I wanted to take along on a commando mission, but I didn't have much choice. She had the gun.

She aimed the pistol at the power intake on my suit.

"I'll blow it off," she said, indicating the power box, "so help me."

"Then I'll destroy the key."

"Just take me with you."

"Why?"

That made her pause for a second. She bared her teeth, and her fingers were white where they gripped the gun.

"Because, I know where the last position on the dial goes. You'll probably be killed out of hand if I don't go with you."

This surprised me in several ways at once. "You know where—?"

"That's what I said!"

"Are you going to tell me, or—?"

"Will you believe anything I say at this point?"

I thought about that, and shook my head. "Probably not."

I considered killing her. I could do it real fast if I had to. But after a moment's reflection, I passed on the idea. If she really wanted to teleport into the blue with me, well, she could damned-well come along and enjoy the ride.

Galina watched me closely as I considered my options.

"Your mission is hopeless," she said, "but I know you. Without seeing reality with your own stupid eyes, you'll never let go of this fantasy you have of saving Earth. I can't stop you from porting out—but I can make sure you come back and give me my property. Now do you understand?"

"Not entirely," I admitted, "but I'm willing to take you along if you want. Hop in."

She looked at me blankly. "What?"

"You've got to get inside this squid-suit with me. It'll be a squeeze, but there's an extra set of arm and leg holes I'm not even using. If you just—"

"Are you insane?"

"It's a funny thing, but people ask me that all the time."

She glowered at me doubtfully.

"Why would I get into that suit?" she asked. "Why can't I travel with you as we did when we came down here from upstairs?"

I shook my head. I'd done that before. I explained how a squid hitch-hiker had turned into fried calamari on just such a trip not long ago.

She shuddered.

"Okay," she said, "and thanks for telling me."

Only then did I realize that I could have let her hug my leg or something and then burn her to death in the interstellar void. But that wouldn't have sat right with me.

We found helmets and attached them to our uniforms. Like all legion uniforms, they were airtight and could function in vacuum in a pinch. That would give us some protection and a small air supply for the trip.

"Just get in," I said, helping her into the jump suit. I pulled it over our bodies and our uniforms together.

People stared at us in growing concern. There were twitters, and Turov ordered them all to report upstairs. They cleared out in a hurry.

When we were all charged up, she looked at me seriously.

"James McGill," she said, "if I find out that this entire thing about sharing the suit was proposed to get your body into contact with mine for a cheap thrill, I'm going to have you castrated."

"Got it," I said, giving her a smirk. "It's just a fringe benefit. Now, buckle up. This is going to be quite the ride."

I touched the shell to the control unit and twisted the dial. We jumped into the void.

The trip was bizarre. I knew Galina was there, despite the fact I couldn't really hear or see her. There was just a sense of pressure, of a presence that wasn't my own. I was left with the impression that our molecules were being mixed together and interwoven during the trip. That thought was more than a little disturbing.

When we arrived, I looked around with my rifle upraised. We weren't outside—not exactly. I got the feeling of a vast, enclosed space. The building—if it was a building—was *huge*. If I had to take a guess, I'd say it was the size of a football stadium at least. It was so big, it had a haze of misty air that hung around us like a cool fog.

Looking up, I saw the ceiling was cone-shaped and had a spiraling organic texture to it.

My tapper beeped then and displayed a green symbol, suggesting the atmosphere was safe. I didn't open my helmet anyway, just to be sure.

She was held up against me, and her body felt warm and tight. This version of James McGill had yet to be laid, and I found her closeness quite distracting.

Then Galina began retching, and the spell was broken.

"That trip made me sick," she said.

She popped open her faceplate, and I could feel her muscles tightening up. I heard that awful gulping, hitching, gagging sound.

"Hey, hey," I said, turning her away and aiming her toward the ground. "Don't puke in my suit!"

While she threw up, I plucked my pistol from her fingers. She didn't seem to even notice.

"It's not your suit," she managed to gasp out a minute later. "Let me out of here."

She started to wriggle, but I wrapped a hand around her and pinned her.

"James!" she complained.

"Shhh! Look!"

317

I pointed toward a looming shape that wasn't all that far off. It was a massive growth of gnarled fibers and veins. Because of the hanging mists, I couldn't see the beginning or the end of it.

"This atmosphere is thick," I said. "It's hampering our vision."

"What the hell *is* that?" she whispered, staring at the shape that looked like an alien root.

"I don't know," I admitted, "but I think it's alive. Stop fighting me. We might have to port out of here in a hurry."

She looked up at me over her shoulder. "You're rubbing against me."

"Sometimes you like that," I said, tossing down a smile.

Her face soured further. "Not today. Let me out."

"What if I find a power outlet? What if I have to port out on you?"

She thought about that. "Then you can tell them to revive me from the memory banks in the data core. We can't walk around like this. We'll be slow and ridiculous."

Figuring she was right, I let her squeeze out of my suit. She stood stretching and panting. It was only then that she noticed she'd been disarmed. She reached for the pistol on my belt again, but I caught her wrist and brushed her away.

"You're not pulling that one again," I told her.

"I'm your superior officer," she said. "I should be the one who's armed."

Shaking my head, I stepped past her and took a really good look around. The floor was like sand, but it was very fine and gray. It was almost ashy.

"What do you make of this material?" I asked her.

"How should I know? I'm not a tech. Sample it and take it home to the nerds at Central."

Following her suggestion, I scooped up a tiny amount into a sample bag and moved uphill.

I was suddenly struck by an overpowering odor.

"What's that stink?" I asked.

"There's a breeze in here, and it shifted," she said. "Something is rotting. Something *big* is rotting."

I had to agree with her. It smelled like all the whales on Earth had washed up on the same shore and died at once.

"Well," I said, "for all we know this is what a squid city smells like. Think about it, we're inside a large structure with heavy humidity and overpowering sea-odors. That sounds like heaven if you're a squid."

She began to explore diffidently. I noticed she didn't move too far from my side. Imperator Turov was no chicken, but she wasn't a martial artist either. She'd won her way to the top of the heap through careful calculation rather than by shooting the bad guys.

"Let's go downhill," she said, "I want to see something."

I followed her with misgivings. After about a hundred steps, we found water. It was as brackish and as black as a squid's ink.

"You think they live in there?" I asked her.

"Either that, or they use it for a toilet. Let's go back uphill."

We moved away from the gnarly tentacle thing, but it didn't matter. It seemed to follow us. After a few minutes, we both realized we were surrounded by its mass.

When we got closer, I recognized it.

"I know what this thing is!" I said in surprise.

"Shhh!"

"It's a root. A Wur root. This whole interior space is some kind of fetid den. Maybe the biggest nexus brain-plant of all time is down here."

"Yes..." she said. "I think you're right."

"But where are we?" I asked. "You said you knew where this teleport setting went—where is this?"

"It's not what I expected, but Claver said it would take us to the cephalopod home planet. They call it their Throne World."

"Ah. That makes sense. But it seems like a strange place to land. Why'd you want to come along if you knew we were headed here?"

She shrugged. "I thought perhaps I could talk to the cephalopods. It never hurts to meet your new leaders in person."

319

"Oh… so Claver has been doing all the deals, has he? You thought maybe you could get a better arrangement for yourself if you talked to them personally?"

She made a dismissive gesture.

"It doesn't matter now," she said, holding out her palm. "We've seen enough. There's no one here. Hand over the key."

"What?"

"I've kept up my part of the bargain. We're porting back to Earth."

I looked at her in amazement. "But we're so close to figuring things out."

"No, we're not. We don't know a damned thing! We're messing around in some kind of alien chamber on or near an alien capital. There have to be guards of some kind. Someone has to know we're here by now."

"Look," I said, "there has to be a reason why all these points are presets on the teleport dial. Going back to Earth won't do anyone any good. We're going to lose to the squids at Central within days."

She stared at me from under hooded eyes. "Don't you think I know that? What have I been trying to tell you all along?"

Ignoring her outstretched palm, I headed directly for the tentacle-like root.

"McGill, damn you!" she hissed, following in my wake. "Why don't you ever listen? I'm ordering you to stop and take us out of here."

"That's exactly what I'm doing, sir," I said. "But we have to have power to recharge, remember? Have you seen any sources yet?"

She growled in frustration and followed me.

Naturally, I hadn't been looking for power outlets. If we did find one, well, that would be luck. But I almost didn't care right now. If we died here on this nameless world, at least I'd tried to do something besides surrender.

We reached the root, and we found it formed an effective wall we couldn't pass. We marched along it, heading uphill to the highest point we could reach. From there, it spread out in two directions, both heading downhill.

"We're trapped," Turov said, "between this tangled growth and the water. What are we going to do? There's no power here."

"There has to be something. Keep looking."

We followed the root the other way until I could hear and smell the water again. That's what finally gave me an idea that might explain everything.

"Hey Galina," I said.

"Don't call me that."

"Listen, the squids are aquatic, right? Why would they put a teleport landing spot on an empty beach?"

"I don't know, you fool."

"Because this beach isn't important. The beach isn't where we've got to look."

She followed my eyes. I was gazing out into the brackish, stinking water.

"Oh no," she said. "I'm not going in there."

"We've got faceplates and pressure suits. It's no worse than going into space. In fact, it's a lot safer than that."

She complained, but in the end, she followed me into the water. It wasn't like wading into the ocean, not exactly. It was thicker than that and more still. The only waves were lapping, rippling ones like you might find on a quiet lake at midnight. I figured that maybe this world didn't have a moon to stir things up like Earth did.

The inky water was cold, nasty and almost like swimming in black snot. If I had to compare it to something I'd experienced, I would say it reminded me of training in the mud pits back on *Corvus*, my legion's old transport ship.

Damn, I missed that ship.

-50-

What we found under the water was freaky. First of all, it was dark as hell. We had to turn our suit lights on but kept them at minimal level—like high beams in the fog, we were blind otherwise. Floating everywhere in the liquid were clear globules. They were round in shape and full of some kind of jelly. Holding one up to Turov's headlamp, I saw each of the globes had a dark core you could make out inside. We pushed these strange objects aside, groping ever deeper into the murk.

Turov had attached a line to my suit, which she tugged on irritatingly. She also used it to communicate privately on a closed circuit. It wouldn't do to broadcast radio packets on our suit's normal com channel in the middle of a hostile alien camp.

"McGill—this black pond is full of *eggs!*" she said with a mixture of disgust and fascination. "I can see things squirming inside these globular sacs."

"Yeah," I said, "I noticed that."

"Why didn't you say something before we sank ourselves three meters deep into this mess?"

"Are you any happier now that you know the truth?"

"No," she admitted, "but we have to get out of here. If these are cephalopod-eggs, there must be guardians. We must find a power source and teleport home."

For once, we were in agreement. This location didn't seem to be helpful at all. An egg hatchery? All we could hope to do here was piss off the watchers of the nursery.

"You know what I don't get?" Galina said as we shuffled along the bottom, pressing our way deeper still. We had to be four meters down now. "I don't understand why the cephalopods would have that root-thing growing over their hatchery. That seems like Wur technology."

"True, but I can tell you why. The Wur rule the squids. It's probably part of their agreement. The squid officer I met on Death World told me all about it. The Wur have enslaved the squids, just as the squids enslave others. For all we know, this is how they did it."

"By growing some kind of dome over their hatchery?"

"Sure, why not?"

We saved our breath for plowing through the eggs for a while. I would have been worried we were going to lose our way if I hadn't had a depth meter and compass built into my tapper. I could only tell we weren't going any farther down now, and we were moving in a more or less straight direction.

At last, the wet ashy sand under my feet began to slope upward. The gloom lessened as we made our way to shallow slime, so I killed the lights. With great care, we pushed our helmeted heads out of the muck to take a look.

Through the thick streaks of jelly running off our faceplates, we saw something that resembled civilization. I was relieved. Sure, it wasn't a human-looking type of civilization, but it was better than another empty beach.

There were small buildings here that looked kind of like clam-shells. They were quite large, about five meters across and two high. They were crusty with growths. Fluids leaked out and ran toward the lapping waves. I walked to the nearest of these shells and tried to pry it open.

"What the hell are you doing now?" Galina whispered behind me. "Can't you leave that alone?"

"See these cables at the base of this clam-shell thing? That has to be made of polymers, maybe with a metal core. I'll look for an outlet."

Nervously, she stood in my shadow studying the beach area while I grunted and strained.

At last, the shell's lid broke suction and opened with a dramatic slurp. Inside, I found something I just hadn't been

323

expecting. It was a mama-squid. She was *huge*, at least as big as any four male squids I'd ever seen. She was all tucked in there like a tick in a dog's ear.

Before I could do much of anything, a tentacle snaked out and wrapped itself around my midsection. I knew right off I was in trouble. I'd once seen a squid queen pop Carlos' eyeballs right out just by squeezing him.

My right arm and my rifle were pinned to my side. Whether that was by accident or by design, I wasn't sure, but I *was* sure that I was being hoisted up effortlessly into the air by an angry she-squid.

"Take my gun!" I shouted, fumbling out my pistol with my free hand and dropping it.

Turov darted in and snatched up the gun. She fired it immediately, singeing the tentacle, but that only seemed to make it squeeze me harder. I could feel a few ribs starting to give way already.

"Do something!" I demanded with a wheeze. "My breastplate won't hold!"

Galina was a naturally tricky woman when she was in a tight spot. She ran up, reached into the clam-shell thingy and grabbed a slippery egg. Inside, a tiny baby squid wriggled.

She put the pistol to the egg she still held on to, meaningfully holding it up so the mama-squid could see it. Some of the queen's eyes now tracked me while others tracked Galina. Straining to crane my neck around enough to see Galina, I noted another tentacle snaking up behind her.

"Look out," I gasped. "Behind you."

Galina wasn't the motherly sort. She fired her pistol into the mass of eggs, burning a hole through a half-dozen of them. Then she put her pistol back to the one in her hands.

The squid queen made an angry sound. It was somewhere between a hiss and a fart, but she'd gotten the message. Her tentacles retreated from Galina.

"Okay," I said, "she's easing up on my ribs. Use your tapper. We've all got their language stored in our software now. Turn on the translator."

Turov did so, and we heard a tirade of bizarre curses.

"—egg-stealer! Beast-of-the-sands! Disgusting dry-thing!"

"Shut up," Galina said. "We're humans, and we're here to negotiate."

"Negotiate? You offend us with that word."

It was about when she used the word "us" that I noticed something: other clam-shells had yawned open all around us. Each held a queen and her brood. Apparently, these eggs started off in the protective embrace of their mothers, but were eventually taken down into the central pool to incubate until hatching.

"Don't you want to save your young?" Turov asked.

"We will. You will be expunged. We've already alerted the guardians."

I didn't like the sound of that. "Hey," I called to Galina, "tell her to put me down."

Turov did so. Soon I was standing on the sand and rubbing my sore ribs. It felt good just to be able to take a full breath again. I thanked my lucky stars I was an officer these days. I'd been issued a tough breastplate that came with the rank. With only light armor, I'd have been dead within seconds.

"Here are our terms," Turov said. "We demand that you call off your attack on Earth, and that you throw off the yoke of Wur and declare neutrality with us!"

Bubbling air erupted once more from the moist folds of the creature. I knew this one from experience. The squid-queen was laughing.

"You are almost amusing, despite your evil. Can you possibly believe threatening one of my offspring will motivate me to do anything? My offspring have proudly died by the thousands in battle."

Galina cocked her head.

"Why do you serve the Wur, then?" she asked. "If you don't care about your children, why not destroy the dome that sits oppressively over us right now?"

"I hope you survive what's coming," the queen said malevolently. "I must see you boiled in ink. I will donate from my own fluids to aid with the ceremony. You should feel honored that I hate you this much, egg-stealer."

Galina's mouth opened again, but I could tell from the look on her face she wasn't going to say anything helpful.

325

"Hold on, Imperator," I said. "Let me have a shot."

Reluctantly, Galina shut up. That wasn't in her nature, so I really appreciated her newfound sense of cooperation.

"Lady-squid," I said, addressing the queen, "we don't have to threaten one another. We can help each other. We're sorry about your offspring, but we were attacked and reacted the way predators always do when they're injured."

The queen squirmed, regarding me. "What is this?" she said. "Which of you is in charge?"

"I am," Turov said.

"Then why is your slave offending my auditory organs by speaking to me? Is this a fresh variety of insult?"

"No, no, hold on," I said, holding up my hands.

The squid looked alarmed, rearing up a bit and throwing her own tentacles high. I realized that lifting limbs might be construed as a prelude to an attack by some species, so I put my hands back down at my sides again. The squid then relaxed a little.

"I'm Imperator Turov's surrogate, her spokesperson."

"Ah, a slave with a special purpose. I comprehend."

"Let me explain the nature of our offer," I said, "we hate the Wur. You hate the Wur. We would like to break their hold over your kind. We could help you cast them off and make you free again."

"That isn't logical," she said, "and therefore, it must be a trick of some kind."

"Uh... why?"

"All beings seek mastery. All species of intellect wish to dominate, consume or eradicate their competitors. Therefore, you cannot possibly want to help us."

"But it's in our best interest to help you," I argued. "We're a smaller power than the Cephalopod Kingdom. We're also smaller than the Wur. If we can free you from the Wur, we both gain."

"At last I see your thinking. You are clever for such a tiny food-creature. You wish to embroil two of your betters in a conflict. With luck, one or both will be destroyed."

"Well, hold on—" I began, but the squid-queen wasn't listening.

"My initial assumption was therefore correct," she continued. "Your goal is our destruction, but you wish to accomplish this in a clever way. Even so, your offer is tempting, but impossible."

"Why impossible?" Galina demanded. "We'd both gain."

A tentacle tip rose, and it pointed toward the walls of the chamber. Down these walls came dark shapes.

It took me a second to recognize them. They were spiders like the one's I'd met up with on Death World. They crept rapidly down the arched walls and spread out stealthily on the sands.

When it comes to quick action, I'm the man you want to have at your side. Instead of shooting at the spiders or the squids, I grabbed the teleport suit from where it was bundled at my waist and began to shake it out. By the time I had an arm and a leg in the suit. I dropped to one knee and began tugging at the power-lead that snaked into the clam-shell.

"Tell them to stop!" Galina shouted, aiming her gun at the queen.

The queen eyed her with several orbs at once. "You are a cretin. You do not understand us. I'm not in charge here. I rule nothing. My masters have sent their servants."

"You mean the spiders? The spiders are in charge? Maybe I should talk to them."

Again, the queen made a farting sound. "Be my guest."

My suit was charging by now, but I had to hold the cord up and keep the lead shoved into my power-pack to force the connection. It wasn't quite fitting right despite the fact it was supposed to work as a universal connector.

"Come on, hurry," I said, waving to Galina. "We can't fight a hundred spiders."

Galina climbed into the teleport suit awkwardly while I held it open with one hand.

"Interesting," said the queen. "You mate in your final moments. This must be some kind of feral instinct of lower-ordered species. It won't do any good. If you do produce offspring, I will simply torment the creatures to death."

Galina snarled and tossed the egg she held in her hands into the air. The queen reached up and snatched it down again.

Those eyes were filled with an even greater malevolence when she'd recovered her egg and turned them back down to regard us.

Fortunately, the suit was charged enough to make the jump.

"Faceplates!" I shouted.

Galina reached up and slammed both of ours down. I took out the Galactic Key, reaching right across her field of vision with it, to touch the dial on the teleport suit. Her hand slipped out to grab at it, but in that moment I twisted the dial to take us home.

The next instant we were flying through a nameless void, blind and torn apart into our constituent molecules.

I had to wonder if she was still trying to take the key from me in that endless expanse of darkness.

-51-

We reached Central minutes later, but it felt like an eternity had passed.

The second we got there with the slimy fluid on our suit dripping off in steamy glops, Galina began to struggle with me.

She was doing two things at once, in my estimation. She was trying to wriggle out of our shared suit and take the key from my hand.

Normally, when I have an attractive young lady wrestling with me in close quarters, I'm a happy camper. But today, I was annoyed. I had my fingers wrapped tightly around the key, and I wasn't letting go of it for anything.

"McGill, you promised!"

"Hold on," I said, "we've got company."

She turned her head to follow my gaze. The room was chock-full of people. It looked like Graves had brought down the entire teleportation tech team. Lisa was there, and she looked disgusted. Graves look amused but a little annoyed, too.

"Perhaps we should leave and let you two have the room to yourselves," he commented.

"Centurion Graves, I want you to arrest this man!" Turov said.

"Hmm," he said. "I'm not sure how that will play, Imperator. You're still under investigation."

"What? Nagata gave me authority. He—"

Graves was shaking his head. "No, he didn't. We found him dead on the floor in his office, and after checking over the body, guess what we found? That wasn't Nagata at all. It was Claver doing his illusion trick."

Turov shut up at last. Her hands had been wrapped around my wrist in a hopeless struggle to take the key out of my grip, but now she let go. She climbed out of the teleport suit and turned to face Graves fully.

"What are you saying, Centurion? Is this more of Drusus' rebellious scheming?"

"Hardly—not unless you think *he* helped Claver take over," Graves replied. "I have to hand it to McGill, here. I don't know how you spotted him, but you shot him down before he could do any permanent damage to our defense efforts."

Turov climbed out of my suit and stood in the open. People looked at the black jelly-like material that still dribbled off her in alarm.

"So this is how it's going to be?" she asked. "You're creating another crisis of leadership. Do you accept my rank and my authority or not, Graves? Have you received any orders to depose me?"

"That's not the point. Your reinstatement wasn't sanctioned by an actual officer."

"Where is Drusus then?" she demanded. "Why isn't he here?"

"Because he was shot in your absence. He's dead in his cell. Investigators are going over the scene now."

"Really?" Turov asked. "How tragic. What about the other high-ranking Hegemony officers?"

Graves shook his head. "The ones on this continent died here at Central. There are plenty who died in the field fighting the enemy's advance, but they were lower ranked than you—tribunes only. Mostly Varus people have been revived since then. Drusus thought we could defend Central better than a pack of hog bureaucrats."

Turov laughed bitterly. "Of course. Let me translate: he didn't want any challenge to his authority. Well, without any other superior officers at hand, Primus Winslade is your current commander. Where is he?"

Graves lifted his chin and looked at her coldly. "I had him arrested. He's my prime suspect in the murder of Drusus."

"What! I never thought I'd see this day! How could you take up arms against your commanders, Graves? You were always the reliable one."

"There's a difference between reliability and playing the fool."

Turov looked around the assembled group. They were obviously hostile but conflicted. Would they really back a mere Centurion against a high-ranking officer? It was a confusing situation.

"I see," she said, "you must make your decision then. I've done nothing that I didn't think was in the best interests of Earth, whether you agree with my choices or not. Either accept me as your rightful commander, or execute me now."

She stood with her head thrown back. I had to admit, she did have guts when it came right down to it.

Graves looked uncomfortable with his position. I could tell he'd never wanted to have to make such a call.

What he did next surprised me. He turned to face me and asked me a question.

"McGill, you've been hanging around Imperator Turov for a long time. What's your opinion on this? What have you been doing—aiding in Earth's defense or trying to subvert the chain of command here at Central?"

"Uh..." I said, trying to think.

To be honest, I thought it was a little of both. But that kind of answer wouldn't make anyone happy. Whatever I said, I had to make it firm and final.

When I started to speak at last, I went with my heart.

"An army without a leader is in a terrible spot," I said. "We're dying out there on the battlefield. In my opinion, we only have a day or two left before we lose this war. And how are we spending our final moments? Huddling in Central like a bunker, waiting for the enemy to crush us."

I had everyone's attention now. They were all looking at me, listening. I'd half expected some scoffing, but I didn't get any. They knew the truth of my words.

"We're all on the same side," I said. "We're just not in agreement as to how to go about things. Turov, I think,

331

honestly thought we couldn't win this battle. She sought to negotiate the best possible end to the conflict at hand."

She nodded. She was approving of my words—but I could tell she was also worried about what I'd say next.

I tried not to think about the weight of the situation. I tried to keep my mind clear. These people needed to be brought together, and sometimes a little old-fashioned horse-sense could do that.

"Listen," I said, "let's drop the investigations and accusations. If we live longer than a week, we can delve into all of that later. We need Turov and Drusus both—"

Graves shook his head. "We can't get Drusus back. At least, we haven't found a backup yet. He was deleted as well as shot. The intention was to perm him."

"Winslade…" I said, gritting my teeth. Then, I took a deep breath. "Okay. It has to be Turov then. It's either that or we pull out some hog who will probably do nothing effective anyway. What do you say, Graves? We can't trust her fully, but we must have a leader."

Galina looked a little shocked. I think she'd figured she was as good as dead. Slowly, a smile crept over her face despite the fact she was trying to contain her joy.

"Very well, then!" Turov said in a commanding tone. "Let's retire to—"

"Hold on," Graves said. "I want to know where you two have been. Your latest adventure was unsanctioned."

Tapping at my arm, I flashed the video over to Graves. He looked it over, fast-forwarding the part where we were swimming through squid-eggs for half an hour.

"Interesting," he said, "these teleport waypoints don't make any sense to me, but in another way, they do. How can this help us, McGill? What if we sent in a team to wipe out those squid queens? Could we cripple them?"

"No," I said firmly, "I don't think so. What we have to do is get the Wur to capitulate to us, or take away the hold they have over the squids."

"How the hell are we going to do that?"

"Well sir," I said, "I have a plan that might do the trick."

Everyone looked at me with a strange new light in their eyes. They needed hope, and I'd just given it to them.

As soon as I'd said those words, however, I regretted them. They were a lie. I had no idea what to do next.

But a man like me knows the first rule of being a liar. The insurmountable, overriding truth about all lies: Once you'd aired them, you were stuck with them. You had to back them up and never, never admit you were full of grade-A bullshit.

"Okay," Graves said, to everyone's relief. "Turov is in charge again. On paper, that won't be a problem. But let me warn you, Imperator. I'm watching you. We all are. Any attempts to surrender to the enemy before this war is finished will be viewed as treason. Every allegation against you will be remembered in that moment."

Galina licked her red lips and gave him a tight smile. Then she inclined her head to me and to the crowd.

"Excellent," she said. "Now that this unfortunate misunderstanding is behind us, we'll move forward with our defensive efforts. I will be taking over Nagata's office and his quarters—Drusus' spider-hole is unsuitable."

She went on like that for a time, ordering people around. They hopped up and hustled. I could tell they weren't overjoyed to be listening to her, but they needed a leader and they needed orders. Now, at least, they had them both.

When she was finished handing out tasks to pretty much everyone in the room, she turned to me and cocked her head. She studied me for a while before coming to some kind of internal decision.

"McGill," she said, "we have matters to discuss in private. Come to my new quarters. Immediately."

I really wanted a shower, but I'd received orders like everyone else. My eyes, which had been lingering on Lisa as she pouted near the lab equipment, slid over to Turov. Shrugging, I walked after her.

I was certain she wanted the key. I wasn't sure if I was going to give it to her yet or not, but I was the one who'd put this situation into motion, so I had to play it out.

Underneath, I was thinking about the plan I'd told everyone I had. Inspiration hadn't struck me yet, but I figured I would bide my time.

-52-

When I got to Turov's new quarters and walked inside, she turned to face me.

She gave me that up-down appraisal again. I felt like a bug on a plate. The woman was clever, after all. Could she see through me?

"James McGill...." she said slowly. "You're my greatest obstacle and my greatest asset. How can you be both at the same time?"

"I've heard that one before," I admitted, "and I've never had a good answer."

She shook her head, bemused.

"We have to get cleaned up," she said. "We're disgusting."

On that point, we were in complete agreement. She walked to the bathroom which adjoined Nagata's—now Turov's—spacious living quarters. Without ceremony she removed her garments and tossed them into a chute to be recycled.

A moment later, I heard water running. Looking around, I found a chair but decided not to sit on it. My teleportation suit had been left at the lab, but my uniform was still a sticky mess of squid-stuff. I didn't want to wreck old man Nagata's furniture, if only to honor the poor guy's memory.

The walls were covered with depictions of famous battles from centuries past. I was studying an image of tanks rolling over the yellow wheat fields of Kharkov when I heard the Imperator's voice again.

"James? Come in here, will you?"

Surprised, I walked cautiously into the bathroom. She was in the shower, but the glass was all steamed-up.

"Uh... what seems to be the problem, sir?"

"My back needs scrubbing. Can you help me with that?"

Now, a man such as myself has a very hard time saying "no" to such invitations. Sure, I knew Galina was a manipulative monster after all, and I'd recently become involved with Lisa. But... there she was—exquisitely youthful and lovely. I knew from recent experience that she was good in bed.

Sighing, I shed my clothes and climbed into the shower. I was washing her back with a cloth within minutes, then her front. It wasn't long after that before things progressed dramatically to their foregone conclusion.

When we were finished, I lay on the bed beside her, still as wet and naked as a jaybird in a rainstorm.

"Why did that happen?" I asked her seriously.

"You waited until now to ask my motives?"

"Well... I never look a gift-horse in the mouth."

"As you say, it was a gift, James. You deserved it. You could have tried to get Graves to execute me today. Instead, you saw the light. More importantly, you convinced Graves to follow me again. That's a trick I know wasn't easy."

"Hmm," I said thoughtfully. I hadn't seen today's actions from her point of view. I'd only been trying to save my planet—not Turov. But,... what the hell? A man had to seize life's benefits now and then.

"Now," she said, in a soothing tone, "don't you think it's time you returned my property?"

"Your what? Oh... you mean the key?"

"Yes James, that's right," she said with an air of infinite patience.

"Well yeah, it's almost time for that. But I need it for one more teleportation trip first."

She sat up instantly. Her demeanor changed in a flash. I don't think I'd ever seen a woman go from loving, cooing and playful to spiteful, alley-cat-pissed so fast in my entire life.

"You bastard!" she said, slapping me hard.

I was so surprised that I didn't even manage to catch her wrist before the slap landed. It stung there, and I blinked at her in shock.

"Look," I said, "I'm going to give it back. Don't you even want to know why I need it?"

"No, I don't need any details. I'm sure you plan to head off into yet another deadly environment. You won't be happy until you lose my property."

"Why do you care so much about the key, anyway?" I asked. "Soon, it won't even work if you get your way. You'll surrender to the squids when they take Central. Then we'll be under their rule and all this Galactic junk-tech the key opens will be a thing of the past."

She laughed at me, but with a nasty edge to the laugh. "Idiots: Winslade, you—sometimes even Claver. He thinks he's some kind of genius, but he dies all the time when his schemes backfire. Why do I surround myself with idiots?"

"Well, I have a theory on that point—"

Wham! She'd slapped me again. This time, I caught her hand before she could pull it back for a third one. I was beginning to get a little pissed off, myself. She'd caught me off-guard twice in a row. Somehow, her delicate, nude body being so close to mine had taken the edge off my reaction time.

"Come on, girl," I complained, "stop doing that."

Reluctantly, I let go of her, but every time she moved, I flinched.

"You don't see the future clearly, not like I do, McGill," she said after she'd calmed down some. "There are still many examples of critical Galactic tech everywhere on Earth. Even after we end trading with the Core Systems, we'll still trade with local worlds. Their tech security is handed down by the Galactics and is therefore breakable with the key. The key will be useful for many years to come."

I nodded, seeing her point. "Okay then, I've listened to you. How about you hear me out?"

She curled her lip, but she let me talk.

"Okay, it's like this," I began, "you remember the second place I jumped to, the island with the green sea and sky?"

"I saw the vids."

"You know anything about that world?"

"Not really," she said. "Claver said it was one of the first of the cephalopod worlds infected by the Wur."

"Ah... that fits."

"Fits what?" she demanded, crossing her arms over her bare breasts.

For some reason, that made her realize she was still naked and still within my reach. As she was angry with me, she slid out of bed and into fresh clothes. I was sorry to see her fine shapely figure vanish under a uniform again.

"The second time I went to that planet," I said, "I took a team. We found a Wur inside the building there, and a Nexus brain-plant in a cavern underneath."

"Yes, yes," she said, "I told you I saw the vids and examined the reports since my revival. You were gone for days after the battle in New York, I'll have you know."

"Right. Well anyway, there was a lot of equipment in that building. I talked to the brain-plant and before we killed it, I learned it was in communication with others of its kind. Clearly, it was able to talk to them somehow. I think there's more to that place than meets the eye."

"What good is such knowledge now?" Galina demanded. "You blew that opportunity. You can't sue for peace with the Wur at this point. Only utter capitulation will be considered."

"Yeah... but I'm not looking for the Wur or an opportunity to surrender. I'm looking for Claver. He's the only one who really knows what the hell is going on. He's the only one I've seen who has real control over these suits. He's been teleporting wherever he wants to."

"You'll never find him there," she said, snorting at me.

I cocked my head and took a few steps toward her, bringing myself within arm's reach.

"You know how to find him, don't you?" I asked. "He even had a preset on the dials that went directly to your library—but then, you knew that already, didn't you?"

Her mouth opened in alarm. Slowly turning aside, she put her hands behind her in reaction, leaning back on Nagata's desk.

338

"You teleported to my house?" she asked, raising her eyebrows. "I didn't see that discovery in the recent reports. Did someone delete that detail?"

I smiled. "Maybe they did. It wasn't me, but anyway, Graves knows you're involved with Claver. Maybe that's why he doesn't trust you at all. He only trusts me. Now, what do you think will happen if I turn up dead in your new quarters?"

She glared at me for a moment. I reached for her arm, which had discreetly dug in the desk behind her. She had a needler in that hand, one of the small ones that are shaped like a man's palm.

Shaking it out of her grasp, I watched it clatter on the floor. I sighed. "You make love to me then you want to kill me?"

"You bring out the best in women."

"Yeah…" I said. "Hey, about that, don't tell Lisa about this visit, okay? Or anyone else?"

She looked like she could kill me with her eyes. "I wouldn't dream of it. I don't brag about my sexual conquests the way you do."

"Okay, good. You feel like telling me how to find Claver?"

"Not really."

I shrugged. "All right. I'll just have to go teleporting around randomly until I figure it out."

She made a growling sound in her throat which made me smile. I knew I had her.

After making me swear never to tell anyone how I'd figured it out, she told me how to catch that wily old goat named Claver.

-53-

Catching Claver took a little brainstorming from each of us.

"You mean he's been operating on Earth for years?" I asked Turov. "All this time, using teleportation suits and the like, to keep one jump ahead of the law?"

"Quite literally, yes," she said. "Claver's real talent is for making deals. But he's not as good at elaborate schemes. They always seem to unravel."

"Deals like buying contraband tech from deeper in the Galactic Empire and using it out here on the frontier? You mean that kind of deal, right?"

"Exactly. If you think about all his appearances over the years, they've begun to seem unlikely, haven't they?"

"They've *always* seemed that way. Too many coincidences to chalk up to luck."

"Right. The logic is simple. He's had to have a way to get around. Something better than that small smuggling ship of his."

I nodded slowly. Looking back over all the times the rat had surprised me, it was a wonder I hadn't thought of something like this before.

"So, how do we catch him?" I asked her.

"Ah-ha, now you've hit upon the crux of the problem. I don't know how. He has the power to set these suits to destinations of his choosing, that much I understand. He's not limited to preset landing spots. But where will he land next? You tell me."

340

After thinking about it for a minute, I frowned at Galina.

"That's all you've got?" I demanded. "A hint? I thought you said you knew where he was going to end up next."

"No I didn't. Scroll back through your tapper's audio recordings if you don't believe me."

I waved her off, trying to think. She was right about finding Claver. He was critical. No one else knew the things he knew—but how?

"I recall that when he set a trap for me, an ambush," I said, "he was waiting in your library. Another interesting detail was that when I first met up with him, he was here in this very office, looking for something."

My eyes scanned the office and landed on the bookshelf. Hadn't Claver been standing there when I'd found him?

"The key to catching Claver is figuring out where he'll appear next," I said. "All I have to do is stake out a spot and wait. The tricky part is knowing where that will be ahead of time. I recall he was interested in these books…"

Turov looked alarmed for an instant, but she quickly recovered, letting her face go slack again.

"Any suggestions?" I asked her.

"No, I'm afraid not. But wherever you're doing this stake out, it won't be in here."

She clearly didn't like the fact I was thinking of this office as being part of the puzzle. Come to think of it—why had she made such a big fuss about getting Nagata's office for her own use? I'd figured at first that she'd been living some kind of revenge strategy. I could see how setting up camp here on her dead rival's territory gave her a thrill. But now, I was wondering if there was more to it than that.

"I'll have to think about this," I said, "I'll go talk to the techs about where more of these teleport destinations might be, and if they can be detected."

"You do that," she said, looking relieved. "Make sure you report any further findings back to me."

"Will do."

I went for a last kiss goodbye, but she ducked me. At least it wasn't another slap.

Walking down the passages, I stared outside for a time. The neighboring buildings were filling up with troops. Every rooftop was being fortified. I didn't have much faith in the untested hog soldiers, but at least they were giving it their best shot. They'd die defending Central in a few short days.

Already, the invading troops had surrounded the city and were tightening up the noose around us. The horizon showed continuous bursts of light, indicating the fighting that was going on sporadically in the surrounding countryside.

"Two days," a voice said from behind me. "That's all I'd give them."

I turned in surprise. It was none other than my skinny-armed commander, Primus Winslade.

"I thought maybe you were dead," I told him. "Good to see you up and about again, sir."

"No thanks to you and Graves," he said. "I was kept on ice for too long. How did you fare in the battle for New York Sector?"

"That wasn't a battle, it was a slaughter."

He nodded, stepping to the window and staring down at the streets below.

"You ever wonder why doomed men work harder than anyone else does, despite the fact it's hopeless?"

"Nope."

He snorted in amusement. "It's because they're self-deluded. They don't know that they're doomed—or they won't allow themselves to know it. They fight on, right until the end, when they finally accept the truth and perish."

"That's why you're up here chatting with me? Because you've already accepted your fast-approaching death?"

"Not at all," he said, "I came to talk to Turov, and you happened to be walking out of her office. For some reason, I'm not surprised."

"Hey," I asked as he turned to go, "you know what Claver is looking for? What causes him to lurk around libraries and books?"

He made a mistake then. He flinched. That told me all I needed to know.

342

I was on him like a stack of bricks one second later. He squawked indignantly.

"Get off me you oaf! What's the meaning of this? I'll have you up on charges!"

"I don't think so," I said. "The rules have changed. This is the end. Hegemony is going down. All Earth is going down. You stand around looking out windows and sounding like it's happening to someone else. To me, that means you've got an angle."

"McGill, you're assaulting a superior officer. That's a grave error."

I shook my head. "See this?" I said, pulling out the Galactic Key. "I can erase you with this, Winslade. Turov has considered perming you before, but we didn't do it. Perhaps now is the time."

"What? Why?"

"Because you're withholding vital information. You're a traitor, no matter what you told the hogs and Drusus. You're the smallest man in this rebellion, and I'm making my play against you first."

Winslade looked very worried. He'd never been a physically brave man. Snotty and arrogant, yes, but not brave.

"I'll see you in prison for this," he told me.

"No you won't. Graves is one step from arresting you and Turov both. The rank and file will follow him, regardless of your ranks. Sometimes things go like that when the chips are down for an army. The most popular officer takes over."

He looked worried, knowing the truth of my words.

"What do you want to know so badly?" he asked, changing his tune.

"You heard me before, dammit. What's Claver looking for?"

He glared at me like an angry snake. We'd killed one another a few times in the past, Winslade and I, and that sort of bad blood never clears up completely.

"Scramble your tapper," he said.

"What?"

He rolled his eyes, and reached into his uniform pocket. I grabbed his hand, expecting that he was pulling out a needler.

But he didn't. Instead, he had a tiny brick-shaped jammer in his palm. He turned it on, and I knew we'd just transformed into blobs of static for our body-cams and the pin-sized security cameras in the walls.

Letting him stand straight again, but not letting him get out of my reach, I gestured for him to get on with the story.

He smoothed his ruffled feathers and put his nose in the air.

"If you must know, he's looking for another artifact. He's spoken of it often—I'm almost surprised that he never told you about it. I suspect he didn't trust you with the information. Wise, I think now. It would be like trusting a child with a blowtorch."

"What kind of artifact?" I demanded. "What might be in Nagata's office or Turov's library?"

"A book, of course, what else?"

I thought about that then nodded. The story fit. I still had no idea what kind of book we were talking about. After a litany of threats, I didn't think Winslade knew, either.

"Okay," I said, "no one will ever get from me where I got this tidbit of information."

"Unacceptable," Winslade said sharply. "I want to hear your cover story."

"Cover story? I don't know right now. I tend to make those up on the spur of the moment."

He twisted up his mouth and shook his head in disgust. "It's a wonder you get away with anything. Blame Turov. That's your best option."

I considered it and immediately rejected the idea. Turov was a better ally than Winslade could ever be. Why rat her out?

"Good idea," I said with a bright smile. Lies are always told best when you smile. "I'll do that."

"All right then. We'll part ways—but don't try this kind of physical nonsense with me again, McGill. I decided to help you on this occasion for the good of our world, but next time, I won't tolerate such gross insubordination."

"Right Primus. My apologies, sir."

We separated, and I let him save face by not laughing behind his back. I'd already made an enemy out of him—all over again. There was no point humiliating the guy further. That might just make him hell-bent on revenge.

It just so happened that Central had an old-fashioned public library. There was pretty much no need for physical books these days, but some people still liked them as decorations, the way some folks like to hang swords and spears on their walls.

The library was big and musty. There were no windows, so the place seemed dark to me. I wandered around the chambers while an elderly man watched me sourly. It seemed like he had me pegged as an obvious book-thief.

That gave me an idea.

"Hello sir," I said, approaching the librarian. "I'm investigating a rash of thefts on this floor. Have you had any—"

"It's about time they sent someone!" the librarian said, jumping to his feet. "But why send a member of Varus? Is it because you people are all too familiar with the art of stealing?"

I blinked twice before I forced a smile.

"That must be it," I said. "I'm here to investigate your reported losses. Have you got an inventory report?"

"What? Am I hearing rightly? Is it possible you've lost *everything* I've sent in?"

"Afraid so."

He growled and began digging in his desk. "Here it is. I always make a hard copy. Always."

I'd expected a computer scroll, but I could read print on paper if I had to. I looked it over carefully. The paper rattled in my hands. I almost tore the sheet as I was unaccustomed to handling anything so delicate.

Three titles were listed: *Flowers for Algernon, Les Fleurs de Mal* and *Planet of Flowers*.

"Huh," I said, unimpressed by any of them. I looked them over for a moment while the librarian's eyes darted from me to the list and back again several times with growing impatience.

"Sounds like they're all about flowers," I said at last.

He snatched the list from me and made a sound like an angry cat.

"*None* of them are about flowers," he said. "What kind of a fool have they burdened me with?"

"An officer who's trying to help. If you haven't noticed, there's a war going on outside, sir. This place is likely to be burned to the ground in a few days."

Pinching his lips together so tightly they turned white, I watched him pace around. "It's the pressure. It's getting to me. There was a man—a ghost. He took the books. I saw him do it. He even gave me the finger before he left."

He turned to face me.

"You don't believe me, do you?" he demanded. "That's why I left him out of the reports."

I began to grin slowly.

"I do believe you, sir," I said. "What's more, I really, *really* want to catch your book-thief."

-54-

The librarian and I set up a sting. It was based on two things—books about flowers, and the fact that Claver would suspect my involvement the moment he saw me here.

My part was the easy one. I sat in a comfy chair and fell asleep. The librarian suggested it, and I for one thought he was a genius for coming up with the idea.

While I napped, he piled up every book in the place that had some kind of reference to a flower in it. Then he closed up shop and left.

I ate half a sandwich and answered complaints on my tapper for about an hour. Then, I tried to read a few of the books. Several were Shakespeare, because apparently plenty of his stories had characters named after flowers in them.

It was Viola from *Twelfth Night* that did me in. I was snoring before I knew it.

A prodding in the belly woke me up with a snort. It was Claver, and he had a pistol in my face.

My instincts saved me. Some people, when they're startled and faced with death, will confess, beg, rage or whatnot. Not me. My first move is almost always to play dumb.

"Claver? What are you doing here?" I asked fuzzily.

"McGill..." he said, taking a bite of the sandwich I'd left unfinished on a stack of books. "This isn't your usual haunt. And I know that the librarian isn't the sort to attract your attention."

"Well…" I said, sitting up and rolling a crick out of my neck. "I like to read at night. It makes me fall asleep."

He chuckled briefly. "That part I believe, but such reading! Shakespeare? Tolkien? Classics of a dozen sorts. Why so *many* books, if all you want to do is fall asleep? Wouldn't any single title do the job?"

I shifted uncomfortably in my chair. The muzzle of his weapon traced my every motion. It seemed to be tracking my nose.

"I don't know," I said. "I guess I was just looking for something good."

Claver shook his head. "Such a pathetic effort. I've always heard that you were the best liar on planet Earth. You're disappointing me."

"Now hold on," I said, "I never said I was the best. Hell, you're a much better liar than I am."

"Thank you. But let's get back to the matter at hand. You're here, in my home-away-from-home, reading books about flowers. Let's put aside your opening fabrication and call it an embarrassing failure. Why are you reading these books?"

I shrugged. "Orders, I guess."

"Ah! Now we're getting somewhere! Someone sent you here, didn't they? This idea didn't come to you on your own."

"Maybe not," I lied.

In my vast experience, the best lies involved elements someone else pushed you to admit. When a man suggested a lie and had to badger you into confessing it was the truth, he never disbelieved it afterward.

"Good, good," Claver continued. "Give me a name, please."

"I've been ordered not to."

He looked angry for a second, but that passed.

"Even if I threaten to shoot you?" he asked.

"Won't do much good. I'll just come back tomorrow."

"Really?" Claver asked, and he lifted an object into my sight. It was the Galactic Key.

Startled, my hand went to my pocket. Claver's gun made me freeze again.

"You left it on the table in plain sight," he said, tsking. "Don't you even remember?"

"Oh, yeah," I said.

"You know," he said, "you're not the only one who knows how to perm a man with one of these. In fact, if I remember correctly, I taught you how to do it."

I sat silently, watching his gun and his demeanor. He was tense, but he was trying not to show it.

"It was Winslade," I said. "He sent me down here. He wanted to know what you were looking for in these libraries."

Claver nodded sagely.

"A good play," he said. "Plausible, and almost believable. But I don't buy it. Turov did this. She's the one you've always favored. She's led you astray. You really have to stop letting your dick rule your mind, boy."

I squirmed. Claver was tricky and smart. As he was fond of pointing out, I couldn't keep up with him in the brains department. My only hope was to be even trickier than he was. That was going to be a tall order.

"All right," I said, "you got what you wanted—a name. Now, let's shake hands and go back to bed."

He chuckled. "No, I don't think so. You've done as I've asked, yes, but I can't have you helping my rivals. I can't allow this sort of thing to go unpunished."

"What? You're going to shoot me anyway?"

"Afraid so. You see—"

He never got out another word. My hand, which was still in my pocket, had already uncapped an anti-personnel grenade that I had in there. When Claver had indicated he was going to shoot me regardless, I'd depressed the detonator button and let her rip.

We were both blown to kingdom-come. All that was left behind was a pile of shredded books with blood on every page.

-55-

Thinking outside the box. That's what I excelled at in these situations—even blowing up the box if necessary.

When I was revived, I came off the gurney snarling and clawing at my eyes. I knew I had to get to Claver before anyone else did.

"Don't let him escape!" I shouted at the vague, blurry forms that surrounded me.

"Did we get a bad grow here?" asked a familiar, gravelly voice.

"I don't think so…"

"Adjunct McGill," Graves shouted at me. "Stand down! That's an order."

It took me a second or two to realize what was going on. I turned toward Graves, breathing hard. He had a pistol in his hand and steel in his eyes, but I didn't care.

"Centurion," I said, "we have to find Claver. We have to find out where he's being revived."

"What did you do up there in the library?" he demanded.

"Well, right at the end I died."

"I *know* that. What else happened?"

"Claver," I rasped. "Claver happened. He was practically in my lap. Check the rosters. If he's being revived, it has to be under guard."

Graves stared at me for a few more seconds then grumbled under his breath and lowered his weapon.

"I must be out of my mind to trust you again, McGill," he complained.

He stepped to the nearest computer. The bio specialist manning it made indignant noises, but he ignored her.

"Well I'll be damned," Graves said. "Looks like Claver was slated for revival twenty minutes ago—he's in the oven now." He wheeled on the bio specialist. "Who authorized this revival? The signature field is blank."

"I don't know, sir," she said, flustered. "I'm not in charge of the queue. Alterations have to go through—"

"Turov," Graves said, cutting her off. "Turov or Winslade. Come on, McGill, walk it off."

I tried to obey. I pressed myself into clothing, but my shirt ended backwards and inside out. By the time I'd figured that out, we were in the hallway.

"I was told you'd committed suicide in the library," he said. "Normally, my policy is to leave suicides in their tombs for a week or more as punishment. But I had to find out what you were really doing. The person you were with—you're claiming that was Claver?"

"Yeah."

"Hmm... There were body parts for two, but all scorched and shredded. Everyone had assumed you'd met up with a woman and things had gone badly—as they so often do when you're involved."

"Things *are* bad, sir, if I'm right in my assumptions. Real bad."

Then I filled him in on some of the basics. I asked that we go back to the scene of the crime first, because I wanted to find my key—it was tough Imperial-made monomolecular material and should have survived the explosion.

But Graves was adamant that we be there when Claver was born again instead. We rushed to the correct revival room and pushed our way past the bio people who squawked about regulations.

There he was, sitting, up the minute we got there. He appeared to be in much the same mood that I'd been in when I'd come alive again.

"That was dirty pool, McGill," he said when he saw me. "You've never been one to fight fair."

"Neither have you, Claver," I said.

"You're under arrest," Graves told him.

Claver chuckled. "You'd better check my status on your tappers before you try that."

Frowning, Graves did check his tapper. His eyebrows rose. "This is unusual."

"See? I told you."

Graves turned toward me. "We've been ordered to recycle this man immediately."

"What?" Claver exclaimed, looking from one of us to the next. "By whose authority?"

"Imperator Turov's," Graves said. He turned toward the nearest bio. "What's the procedure?"

"He's not a bad grow—"

"I know that. What do you do in special circumstances?"

"We have a sedative…"

"Now hold on just one frigging minute!" Claver shouted. "You can't be serious. You're telling me you have authorization to execute me? What about my rights?"

"Recycles have been litigated. They're not technically the same thing as an execution. Anyone who's been alive less than an hour can be recycled without a court order."

"You're bluffing."

Graves looked at him with pitiless eyes I knew all too well. "I don't bluff."

Claver thought about that for a moment.

"No," he said at last. "I don't suppose that you do."

"Are we going to do this the hard way or the easy way?" Graves asked him.

Claver's eyes were wide now, and they were darting all around the revival chamber looking for a way out. They landed on me.

"McGill, I have information you might find useful. Step in and help out a buddy, will you?"

"What's the matter, Claver?" I asked. "Did you forget to set up an alternative body somewhere?"

"What do you want? What do you need?"

I snorted and crossed my arms. "Nothing from the likes of you. I've got the teleport suits, that's tech enough."

"No! No it's not. You don't know half the secrets of those suits. I could help you gain full control over them."

"That would turn you into an upstanding citizen," I said, "wouldn't it, Centurion?"

Graves still had a hand on his sidearm. "I don't know. I've got orders."

"From that witch Turov?" Claver asked. "She'd as soon perm all of us and spit on our graves."

"That may be," Graves said, "but I have my orders."

"Wait! McGill, I'll show you how to program the teleport suits. You'll be able to jump anywhere, and you won't need the key to bypass the security system anymore."

"What's this about a key?" Graves demanded suddenly, looking at me.

Shaking my head and throwing my hands up in the air, I did my best to look clueless.

"I don't know, sir," I said. "Maybe he *is* a bad grow. I'm thinking we should get to work on that recycle right away."

"All right, hold on," Claver said quickly. "You two clearly don't have the key. If you have one it really helps to operate these suits safely, but we can do without."

Graves looked at Claver, then at me, frowning. He knew he was missing something. I kept my face completely blank, and that seemed to fix it. Graves turned back to Claver.

"You've got less than an hour to show McGill something useful. After that, you're going into the chute, dead or alive."

He walked away, and after the bio people cleaned Claver up and put him in irons, I was given his leash.

It wasn't a situation I was happy about. Claver wasn't a nice pet to lead around. He was more like a snake than a hound dog.

The second we were out of earshot of the bio people, Claver lifted his manacles up to me and shook them suggestively.

"What?" I asked him.

"Take them off!"

"I don't even have the keys."

He rolled his eyes. "You've got the Galactic Key, don't you, you big dummy?"

Grabbing up his chains and giving them a tug that sent him staggering, I let him know who was boss. "Come on, we've got work to do."

Our first stop was the library. I was given an earful there.

The librarian was in rare form. He scolded me like I was some kind of vicious vandal. I was accused of every library crime I'd ever imagined—and a few I hadn't.

"How dare you come back to this shrine of learning? Are you here to gloat? That's it, isn't it?"

"Uh... no sir. I'm here to look for an object of my property that was inadvertently—"

"You can check the lost and found box," he hissed. "Oh, but wait, that was burned to ash! I'm so sorry for your loss."

"Well, if you don't mind, I'd like to take a look around all the same."

Snarling and spitting, he let me pass. Claver followed irritably.

"McGill," Claver said, "if you tell me what you're looking for, I'll tell you what I've been looking for in this library and all the others."

For the first time in the last hour, he had my full attention.

"All right," I said, "I'm looking for the Galactic Key."

"Ah, of course. You didn't have time after your revival to retrieve it. What do I get if I find it for you?"

"Nothing," I said, digging around among the charred books. "But you can tell me what you were looking for anyway, like you promised."

"Very well. I've been searching for an old text. I very much hope you didn't destroy it."

"Something to do with flowers?" I asked him.

He stared at me unhappily. "Have I been so transparent?"

"I'm afraid so."

"Yes... it's a book about flowers."

"Okay... but why do you need something like that? Are you feeling sad?"

He laughed. "There's supposed to be a book about the Mogwa—an old book that explains how they operate as a culture. Its title has some sort of floral reference. The book is supposed to get some things wrong, but—"

Before he was finished talking, I cut him off and pointed at him. "Wait a second." I hopped out of the debris field and went into the nearest bathroom. I made my way to the last stall in the corner and found something I forgot I'd left in there.

I returned to find Claver kicking through pieces of library.

"You mean something like this one?" I grinned. "*The Eaters of Lotus?*"

Claver waved a hand in my face.

"No," he said, "don't be so pleased with yourself. I've read all about that Greek nonsense. It's *too* old. How could the ancients know anything useful about the Mogwa, even if they did meet them by some chance so long ago?"

"This isn't about ancient Greeks. It's by Weinbaum, written in the 1930s."

Frowning, he snatched the book from my hands. "Why were you reading this?"

I shrugged. "I was looking at flower-related titles, same as you. I happen to like science fiction. Still, this book put me to sleep. Most of them do. Luckily, I left it in the restroom."

He paged through it in concern. "What's it about?"

"Well, I didn't get to the end, but I know it's not actually about flowers. It's about a strange alien race that's plant-like and very smart."

He was breathing hard now, skimming the pages. "So short... could this be an account derived from a real experience? Many of those early UFO reports were false, but others were later documented as sightings of Galactic investigators. This *might* be what I'm looking for. I'm astounded."

"Why's that? Because it took you so long to find it?"

He stared at me suspiciously. "This situation goes beyond the bounds of coincidence, McGill. Once again, I'm being forced to suspect your entire self-presentation as a dunce is fabricated."

"I'm not sure if you're insulting me or complimenting me, but either way I'd accept a hearty thank-you instead."

Claver sucked in a breath and let it out again. "Thanks, James McGill. You've done me a service. Now, I must be on my way."

It was only then that I noticed two things. For one, his hands weren't manacled anymore. He'd been paging freely through the book, but I'd been too distracted by the search to realize it.

Secondly, he had my Galactic Key in his hand.

-56-

Among other things, the Galactic Key gave the user a get-out-of-jail-free card. Quality hardware like our manacles was alien-made. It had always seemed odd to me that so many locking devices and the like were patented products in the Empire. You had to import them from another star system if you wanted anything good of that kind.

And it wasn't just locks, either. Database encryption algorithms, transmission security systems, surveillance cameras—they were all alien-made.

Once I'd learned about the keys, it all made a kind of sense. In order to freely bypass all our security, the Galactics had to restrict the lesser species. We'd been forced to buy and use locks they could break at every level. Lowly types like Earthlings, out on the frontier, had been dupes from day one.

I reached out and grabbed onto his shirt with one hand and plucked the key from his hands with the other. The manacles, forgotten, clattered on the scorched floor of the library.

"You're not going anywhere," I told him. "We had a bargain."

"So we did," he said. "To reprogram the suits, all you have to do is go to the first teleportation set-point on the dial. There, you'll find a laboratory. The Wur there can assist you."

"Hmm," I said, holding onto him. "That's not going to work. I've been there. The Wur and the nexus brain-plant in the cellar are both dead."

"What? You destroyed the scientific genius that cracked the algorithm on these suits? What a waste!"

"How else can we do it?"

He shrugged. "You've made it vastly more difficult. Your techs will have to figure it out for you. The equipment is all there in that building—a good place to start. Now, if you don't mind, I must be on my way."

"I *do* mind. How long do you think it would take to figure out how to program these suits?"

"A month? A year? How do I know? I'm not a tech. I deal with techs, but I don't do the work myself."

I eyed him while thinking unpleasant thoughts for a moment. He knew we didn't have a month or a year. Central would fall within days. He obviously had a buyer for this book about lotus-people or whatever, and he wanted to be off to collect a finder's fee.

That led me to another logical conclusion: If he had a business deal to perform, it could hardly be on Earth. He needed a teleport suit to go wherever he wanted. There had to be one stashed somewhere as he hadn't been wearing one while accosting me in the library the night before.

My eyes roved the singed books and charred furniture. It probably wasn't far off.

"Let's get your suit out," I said. "I'll help you get into it."

"That's hardly necessary."

"I insist."

Marching him at gunpoint, he led me to where he'd stashed it. A locker off the main corridor was full of janitorial supplies, but one pair of coveralls dwarfed the others.

He began to put the suit on, but I yanked it away from him and got into it myself.

"This is theft!" he complained. "You can't port out without me!"

"You should have thought about that before you put a gun in my face last night."

His beady eyes were scheming. I could see the wheels turning in his head.

"Hold on," he said. "I could help you reprogram that suit."

"I thought only a dead brain-plant could do that."

358

"I might have been mistaken. You stay here. Give me the suit so I can retrieve the appropriate programming equipment."

It was my turn to laugh. "Right, like I'm going to trust you to return after you jump out on me."

"We're at an impasse, then," he said. "May I point out that you don't even know where you're going?"

I looked at him then at the suit. It was the same size as the rest. It had been built to hold a large, multi-limbed, male squid.

"There are a lot of extra arm-holes in here," I commented. "If you wouldn't mind squeezing for a few seconds..."

Claver was alarmed. "Unnecessary! I've got another one..."

I followed him to a janitor's closet. There, up high on a shelf, was a bundle. He got it down and soon we were both suited-up.

A few minutes later, after Claver worked on the dial with a circular disk I'd never seen before, we jumped through space to Green world. There, we hiked up the shore to the Wur laboratory. I hurried after him, worried he would escape me somehow.

"This is it," he said, tsking over the state of the workshop. "The body of that Wur stinks. Couldn't you even be bothered to bury it?"

"No," I said. "Now, show me how to use this programming equipment."

He began giving me a technical lesson which soon left me in the dust. I recorded all of it with my tapper. I figured Kivi or Lisa could figure it out later on.

At last, he clapped his hands together and plugged in his suit for a recharge.

"Where do you think you're going?" I asked him, frowning.

"Off on my business trip, of course. You've got an extra suit, and you can keep it. We'll meet again, I'm sure, my friend, but—"

My pistol was up and my laser dot shined on the sweaty patch of skin between his eyes.

"I don't think so," I said. "No charging that suit, no nothing. We're going to test this system of yours right now."

He sputtered and complained, but I herded him away from the charging port. Then I made him take off his suit. Several details about his entire act simply hadn't added up. He was too familiar with this place, for one thing.

"Okay," I said, "I've heard lots of bullshit in my day, much of it coming from my own lungs, but you've always taken the cake, Claver. I don't buy any of this. Let's talk plainly."

"I'm sure I don't know what you're talking about—more importantly, we're wasting time."

"Hmm," I said, "about that. Why would you be in such an all-fired hurry? Could it be that you need to make your transaction before Central falls?"

"Not a worry," he said with a false smile. "I'm sure you'll save Earth with the secrets I've provided you today. It would be considerate of you to make sure you mention my name when you triumph, McGill. It's the right thing to do."

I snorted.

"Let's talk plainly," I repeated. "You're the master of the house here on Green World, aren't you? Now that the plants are dead, there's nobody on this planet other than us."

His eyes darted around, but then he nodded at last. Maybe he couldn't come up with a lie that he liked.

"Yes," he said. "That's right. There's no one else here."

I nodded, thinking it over. "We thought we were investigating squid hotspots, places that they'd preset their suits to go. But this is *your* place. These are *your* settings."

"I licensed the technology to them for a very reasonable fee."

"But," I said, smiling, "you never gave them the knowledge they needed to change their destinations. You only provided preprogrammed suits, set up out here at your little lab."

Claver shrugged. "Business is all about maintaining a competitive advantage. If your customers can do it by themselves, why would they pay you?"

"Fair enough by me," I said. "I don't care if you gouge the squids. Now, what do you think you know about my plans?"

He twisted his mouth into a sneer.

"Such things are obvious to a thinker like myself," he said. "I'm a man who sees the world as it really is."

"Okay, then tell me what I'm going to do."

"First, you'll head back to Central. You will demonstrate your claims with my suit. After that, you'll pop back to Throne World and attempt to capture the cephalopod queens. It's likely you'll also irritate an attractive woman along the way with your ham-handed sexual advances."

His brisk description alarmed me. Mostly, because he was pretty much dead-on.

"I see," I said after a pause. "Your guesses are shrewd ones."

He looked smug while I figured out what to do next.

"So," I said, "it follows that the planet with the hatchery is their Throne World. Is that right?"

"Of course. That's the home world of the cephalopod race. All of their young are born there. You would think they could inhabit a world like this one happily, but they're like salmon. They prefer their home waters."

"The trouble is, Claver, I'm a slow man when it comes to learning new skills. You'll have to demonstrate how to reprogram these suits."

"Demonstrate? How?"

"Reprogram this dial. Have it take us to Central—but not to the basement this time. Have it take us to the rooftop landing zone."

He frowned. "Us? I'm not going with you. I thought I've made that abundantly clear."

"Oh, but you are."

He crossed his arms and glared at me. "I won't do it. I won't be bullied in this fashion any longer. I've been more than generous with you, McGill, and—hey, what are you doing?"

I'd stood up during his little tirade and grabbed his teleport suit. Throwing it over my shoulder, I made as if to jump out.

"Leave that here!" he warned.

"What's the matter? Don't have another one stashed around here? Well, don't worry. I'll bring yours right back."

Reaching up, I began charging the suit and touched the Galactic Key to the dial.

Claver began to breathe hard. He looked very agitated.

"All right," he said as I slowly moved my hand toward the dial again.

"All right what?" I asked.

"I'll go with you. Don't touch anything. As it's set now, it will teleport you into the core of the nearest star."

Unsurprised, I let my hands drop. He worked on both our suits for a while, and I watched to make sure he reprogrammed them both exactly the same way.

It took careful work, but I soon had a set of presets on the dial of that suit that I wanted. I made a vid of every detail of the process.

Even so, each time I jumped I felt a lump of worry in my throat. That first one was a long trip through the void. I didn't know if I was experiencing my last moments or not. I'd watched him do the setup closely enough that I *thought* I was going to a valid destination, but it was hard to be a hundred percent sure.

In the end, Claver either decided to play it safe or he couldn't come up with a good way to screw me. Each of the destinations I asked for was proven accurate by testing. I did this by jumping away with both suits then returning. He knew that if I didn't come back, he'd be stuck out there.

After I'd tested them all, I returned and tossed his teleport suit on the sand between us.

He looked at it thoughtfully.

"Why did you want some of those settings?" he asked. "I don't understand."

"That's fine with me," I told him. "Now, piss off."

He shrugged, grabbed up the suit, and charged it. He gave me a nod as he reached for the dial.

"You played me fairly," he said. "I won't forget that."

I gave him a nod in return, and the world shimmered. He was gone an instant later.

Then I jumped to Central. It took some serious convincing, but I managed to convince Graves and Turov I'd gained full control of the teleport suits.

They weren't approving of my methods, but they couldn't argue with the results.

-57-

Less than twenty-four hours later, I stood at the head of a commando team again.

We were all in teleport suits and ready to go. Graves watched every move I made carefully, his suspicious thoughts plain to see on his face.

Drusus had been revived, but he'd been chastened. Maybe Turov had threatened him with being permed if he didn't cooperate with her leadership.

Whatever the case, as he watched me suit up he seemed more agitated than Graves was.

"This is entirely unsanctioned!" he kept saying.

That fact wasn't bothering me, but I was used to either disobeying orders or just plain making them up as I went along. Drusus still believed his corrupt chain of command was worth listening to. In my eyes, that was a weakness, but I still liked the man.

"We'll be back before anyone knows what happened," I said. "Harris, you're next. Pick up the package and jump."

Harris gave me a venomous glance.

"I couldn't help but notice you're not taking the point this time, Adjunct," he said.

I made a speeding-up gesture with my hands, and he picked up a large package sourly. Lisa touched his dial and he vanished.

Ferguson stepped up to the plate next. Within seconds, he was gone too.

There were only three people with suits left. Lisa and I were two of them.

"Are you sure we're not killing them all?" she asked me nervously. "I haven't been touching the key to any of these suits, James."

"I know. Don't worry."

Claver had shown me how to disable the fail-safe on the suits. They were built to recognize their owners using biometric identifiers, exactly like the way a smart-gun worked. We'd been bypassing that security system with the key up until now, but Claver had shown me how to switch it off entirely.

We almost made it out of Central before things went bad—almost.

Turov appeared at the lab entrance. She had a squad of hog MPs at her back. She wasn't wearing her happy-face today, either.

"You're all under arrest!" she shouted. "Everyone put down their weapons, right now!"

All around me, Varus troops reluctantly obeyed her.

"Get away from that charging unit," Turov demanded, walking toward Lisa.

Her direction of attention away from me was the opening I'd been looking for. I hadn't put down my weapon, I'd only let it fall to my side.

As quick as a gun-slinger, I whipped my carbine back up and fired from the hip. I was glad I'd been taught by Sargon—he was the best.

She'd made her mistake when she'd stepped away from her circle of guards, giving me a clear shot. I took her down with a single opening burst.

Everyone was in shock, naturally. I took that moment to drop my gun for real and throw up my hands.

The stunned guards circled their fallen officer then aimed their weapons in my direction.

"That's not Turov!" I said firmly. "It's Claver again. I'm surprised you guys could get sucked in so easily twice in a row."

Frowning uncertainly, they knelt to look over the body. I made a get-going gesture toward Lisa.

She bit her lip. She looked like she had to pee—and she probably did.

"It *is* Turov!" shouted one of the officers.

"No it isn't!" I insisted. "Check that box at her hip. It's a power supply. Unplug it, and—"

My suit hummed against my back. It was a tiny vibration, one I knew well by now. It was charged up and ready to go.

With a practiced movement, I twisted the dial and jumped out.

At least two of the guards fired. One shot down Lisa. I could see her slowly knocked off her feet, blood and burning hair flying. I watched her freeze that way in midair as the second guard fired at me.

I could see the plasma bolts, as if through a haze of smoke. Three hot streaks traced through the air in my direction—and then I was gone.

The following trip through space was the longest damned one I ever took. I didn't know if I would arrive hale and whole, or blasted apart and burning.

In the end, the final results were somewhat surprising. When I was coming into focus, so to speak, I found myself in the midst of my team at the LZ. But the weird thing was I could *tell* it was taking a split-second longer than usual for me to arrive.

Could the suit be malfunctioning? Damaged by gunfire? Or could it be trying to sort out the blasted molecules of my body, figuring what shape I should be reconstructed into?

I didn't know which it was, but before I could freak out too much about it, the shimmering ended. I was standing on the beaches of Green World.

My hands went to my belly, and I felt around. Harris walked up to me, frowning fiercely. He put a finger up to my gut and poked a hole he found there.

"You've damaged this suit, Adjunct," he said. "How'd you manage that?"

"I'm not sure," I lied.

"Well," he said, smiling, "I bet they dock your pay for a year when we get home."

I was so happy to be alive, I smiled back at him. "Maybe they will at that, Vet. Where's your package?"

He pointed up the beach. An oblong object shaped like a football rested in the sands.

I chewed him out until he hustled back to it and scooped it up again.

"These things are your babies," I told them. "Nobody puts one down. Sargon, where's yours?"

"Right here, Adjunct," he said, patting a burden he'd slung around his belly.

"Damned right it is. Harris, are you slacking?"

He glared at me. "No, sir."

"Good. Let's move out."

He kicked people in the butt after that, all the way up the beach. I didn't interfere. It was like my officers had always told me: in Legion Varus, shit always flowed downhill.

Inside Claver's strange-looking workshop, I had the team drag out the ripening Wur body and leave it near the waves. Kivi was my only tech, and I put her straight to work.

"Where's Lisa?" she asked me.

I shrugged. "There was a malfunction back at Central. You're on your own today, Kivi."

She narrowed her eyes. The problem with Kivi was that she knew me too damned well. She saw the hole in my jump-suit and put her finger there too, as Harris had done.

"She's not coming after us, is she?"

"Nope."

She shook her head. "McGill, I don't know if I can do this without her. I'm not the best programmer. Lisa was a pro."

"She *is* a pro," I corrected, "but she's not here right now. You're going to do just fine."

Looking glum, she headed over to the programming equipment. There, she spent about an hour tinkering.

"I don't think so," she said at last. "I can't do it. I can't change the settings."

For the first time, I began to feel worried. Lisa had learned everything from my vids that she could, and after experimentation she'd managed to jump people from spot to spot around Central flawlessly.

But the trouble was, the programming effort wasn't an easy one. It took a lot of calculus with limits, derivatives and whatnot. The best she could explain it to me was that it wasn't about typing in a simple list of x, y, z coordinates. You had to take a lot of other factors into account, such as the gravitational effects of the local stars—both at the start and end points—time in-flight, etc. Setting up a destination, particularly one that was light years distant, required a whole bunch of math I didn't have a clue about.

"Hmm," I said, "who could do better?"

"Better than me? Better than Lisa?"

"Yeah."

She thought about it. She shrugged. "I don't know. I wish Natasha were here. She could—"

My hand touched her shoulder. She looked at me.

"You really want Natasha back?" I asked.

Her eyes widened. "Of course! You sound like you have a plan, McGill. You know where she is?"

I hesitated before I answered her. I *did* know where Natasha was—both versions of her.

Years ago, there was an accident out around Dust World. Natasha was revived as part of the legion, but the real Natasha—the original—hadn't actually died like we thought. She was revived without confirming her death first. It's a Galactic-level crime to duplicate anyone before they actually die. So her friends, me among them, had kept quiet about it since finding out that the original was still around.

The upshot of the situation was that there *was* another Natasha. The same fine mind, the best tech in the legion. That other version was the legit original. She'd been living back on Dust World all this time, stuck out there in hiding since the duplication.

It also happened that I'd had Claver preset one of the destinations on my suit's dial to Dust World. I'd done that for personal reasons—I'd always wanted to meet my daughter, Etta. I'd figured that before Earth fell, I'd try to make the trip.

Today, it looked like I might get to do so ahead of schedule.

-58-

The trip out to Dust World was a strange one.

I'd been worried before while flying between the stars, but I'd never been so thoughtful and nervous about it. To see Etta for the first time—I had no idea how that was going to feel. How was she going to react to me? Was my child going to accept me as her daddy? I'd missed so much of her early life. How could I ever make it up in one visit?

And on top of that, there was the whole Natasha thing—that was going to be downright weird. What was freaking me out was that this would be the *real* Natasha, the one I'd left behind on a desert planet for nearly a decade. Just thinking about it was stirring up thoughts that had long been dormant.

I'm not an overly emotional guy, don't get me wrong. But when faced with questions about my reality, even *my* armored mind can be affected.

We'd gotten so used to our alien revival technology. Had we lost track of who and what we are? Were we all just three dimensional printouts of human beings? Or were we really human in the traditional sense, something that went above and beyond mere collections of cells and chemicals?

Usually, when I died and came back, I'd managed to ignore such questions. But when faced with the reality that there had been *two* Natashas, both alive and well for years, it was difficult to pretend any of us was special. If there had been twin versions of her, there could be copies of any of us—and if there were two, why not a thousand?

I couldn't answer these questions, so I put them away neatly somewhere in the back of my brain for a later time. A time I sincerely hoped would never come.

My arrival was as neat and clean as it could be. I suddenly found myself standing in the middle of a wavering region of space on a large, flat rock.

That was nothing unusual on Dust World. Most of the planet consisted of large, flat rocks blasted smooth by sandstorms.

No one was there to greet me, so I put away the suit and marched downhill toward the central pool of black water that the valley encircled. I was in an oasis of sorts. It was really a deep canyon in the planet's crust. Such rare places were the only inhabited regions on the planet. These canyons allowed water to collect and life to flourish at the bottom.

A thousand meters above me was the rim of the canyon. Above that, there was nothing but a circle of empty blue sky. Since we were fairly close to what passed for a polar zone on this world, the sunlight never touched the bottom of the valley directly, even when the star had risen to its zenith. If it had, it would've scorched everything down here. Dust World was too close to her sun. All animal life in the valleys would perish and every plant would shrivel up and die if exposed directly to those hot rays above us.

Heading toward the shoreline, I reached habitation sooner than I expected. It did my heart good to see humans out in the open, no longer fearing the slavers who came down from the skies to harvest them. Instead of huddling behind the walls of the canyon in caves, they'd set up a village. There was wood smoke, the sounds of playing children and even the barking of a few dogs.

"A star-man!" shouted the first kid who saw me.

He was dirty-faced and half-dressed. He had a small hunting crossbow in his hand. He pointed a finger at me like he'd accused me of some kind of unholy sin.

"A *star-man!*" he repeated, more loudly than before.

An adult soon showed up as I walked closer. I forced a smile to stay frozen on my face. The man held a weapon, a black blade that dripped with deadly nanites.

Seeing that, I halted. I understood that Dust Worlders were a socially divergent group. They'd been cut off from the rest of humanity for about a century. As a result, they had their own ways of doing things out here in this star system.

Black blades weren't to be trifled with. Trained nanites could eat their way through flesh, polymers and anything else softer than steel. One touch from that black blade, and I'd be a goner.

I could, of course, shoot the man. But that wasn't why I'd come all the way out here. Halting, I held up a welcoming, empty hand.

"I'm from Legion Varus," I told the farmer and his son. "I've come to talk to Natasha. Do you know who she is?"

The two stared at me suspiciously.

"There's no Natasha here," the father said. "You must leave now."

This was a problem I hadn't anticipated, but maybe I should have. Natasha had told Della and everyone else that her existence among the people of Dust World had to be kept secret. If the Galactics ever found out, they'd have her promptly killed for illegal duplication.

Earth maintained the same law locally, despite the fact the Galactics weren't often in our neighborhood these days to enforce their will. No one on Earth had so much as seen a Galactic in over three years, but that didn't mean their influence wasn't felt by all of us. Besides, the restriction on self-duplication seemed like a good rule to have. The law had never been repealed or altered in any way.

"Listen," I said, "I know Della, and I know her father the Investigator. I'm James McGill from Legion Varus."

The man stepped sideways a few paces. He kept his blade pointed at me. I noticed he hadn't ordered his kid to stand down either. Dust Worlders didn't coddle their children. They let them run free over the landscape. If they got hurt, well, they figured that would just make them stronger and better prepared for a harsh life as an adult.

"Della is not here," the farmer said, "but the Investigator might speak to you. Come this way."

The man turned and nodded to his child. Both of them lowered their weapons and stepped apart. I walked between them, keeping a wary eye on the farmer and his weapon.

Now, at this point, I have to explain that it had been a long time since I'd been to Dust World. I'd kind of forgotten how suspicious they were of strangers.

For the last decade, colonists from Earth had been coming out here to settle. Almost all of them had gone to the other habitable planet in the system, a cooler world covered with oceans. Still, I kind of assumed these people had become more or less civilized over the years.

But apparently the people who'd been left behind on the hotter of the two planets weren't the most trusting sort. They were so used to living in such a deadly environment—a desert full of weird plants and animals—that they'd never let their guard down.

In short, I should have expected what happened next, but I didn't. I was completely taken in.

The kid shot me in the ass.

I swear, I never saw that coming. One minute, the little bastard was walking along behind me with his small hand-crossbow aiming at the ground. The next, I felt a jolt of pain.

I turned, and both of them crouched at the ready, teeth bared and eyes gleaming.

"I told you I was Varus," I said in exasperation, "why would you shoot me?"

"You aren't the first to come here speaking lies," the farmer said. "We see your suit. We see your face. Now, we see your blood on the stones at your feet and foresee your death."

The pain was spreading steadily. That meant it was a nanite-tipped bolt, just as I'd suspected. I was a dead man.

"Tell Natasha," I said, "tell her that James McGill wants to meet his daughter, Etta."

I could have done a lot of things at that point. I could have shot them in my dying moments. I could have raged or used my tapper to transmit a desperate report.

But I didn't. Instead, I fell to the ground gasping. I rolled over onto my side and stared up at the distant, perfectly blue circle of sky.

"I've died here before," I said to them as they paced around warily. "I died on this world fighting the cephalopods. You should all be taken by a slaver ship for being such poor hosts."

"That's an evil thing to say!" spat the man, showing me his teeth.

"Be sure, be safe," I said to him.

He nodded sagely in agreement. "Be sure, be safe. Good advice!"

Then, probably with the intention of being both sure and safe, he shoved his black blade into my heart and finished me off.

* * *

When I awoke, there was only one thought on my mind. How many days had passed? Had Earth perished in the meantime?

It was a grim thought. Blinded, I clawed at hands that clasped my newly grown wrists.

"Let go," I said. "Where am I?"

"James? Is it really you?"

I knew that voice, and I stopped struggling. "Natasha?"

She sobbed then. "I'm so sorry. The people here are harsh and very protective. I'm so sorry."

"Natasha, listen to me. How long was I dead?"

"I don't know... maybe twenty hours. The farmer didn't report the killing until nightfall."

I could see her now. I stared at her fine face.

She'd aged. She was a beautiful, older version of the Natasha I remembered. She was Natasha still—but not exactly *my* Natasha. Not the one I'd spent the last several years serving with in the legion.

"Listen to me," I said, and I quickly told her what was happening back on Earth.

She was surprised by the news. The colonists out here on Dust World had heard about our growing conflict with the squids, but apparently, the news we'd been invaded and were about to lose Central hadn't yet reached them.

Looking around, I was surprised to see the revival machine nearby. Of course, there had to be one, but how had it come to be here?

"Why do you have a revival machine?" I asked her. "Did you Dust Worlders buy it?"

She laughed. "No, we could never afford something like this. We found it, left behind for dead by your legion. I nursed it back to health and put it into service for the good of the colony."

That made some sense. The colonists were masters at repairing old equipment and developing their own. I'd been impressed the first time I came here by just how much they'd done with so little.

They were also secretive as a people. Due to their history of betrayal and abuse by other powers, they'd always held their secrets tightly.

But there was something else in her words that didn't add up to me. She'd said "we" could never afford such a machine, and that it had been left behind by "your" legion. That told me she now considered herself to be one of the colonists. She wasn't part of Legion Varus anymore—at least, not in her mind.

"You've gone native," I told her, "but I can't blame you for that."

She glanced at me sharply. "These people may not be a forgiving lot, but they took me in. They allowed me to work and live among them. That's more than Varus was willing to do at the time."

I nodded and put my clothes on with clumsy fingers. There was a hole in the back of my suit I could put two fingers through.

"Did the farmer give you my dying message?" I asked her.

She was messing with her equipment, but she stiffened.

"About Etta? Yes, the boy told me."

"Well?" I asked her. "I don't have much time."

She turned around and looked at me squarely.

"I'm sorry about what you've been through, and I know you've every right to take her—but you can't have her. She's mine now."

373

-59-

There was clearly a misunderstanding going on. I frowned at Natasha, trying to puzzle it out.

"I'm not going to take her from you," I said, "I just want to meet her."

She looked at me with eyes narrowed in suspicion.

"You want me to believe you came all the way out here to see your daughter, and you don't have any intention of kidnapping her?"

"No, that wouldn't be right. It wouldn't be the best thing for her, either. Just let me meet her."

"I can't take the chance. You can teleport. In an instant, you'd be thirty lights away. I raised her, James. It's not fair!"

"That's crazy talk. You know me. You know I'd never do anything like that."

"It would be so easy for you. All you'd have to do is put your arms around her and vanish. No one on this planet cares for her—they don't care for any of their children. I'm not like that. I can't—"

"Listen," I said. "I'm still trying to get my mind straight after the revive, but it's not Etta I want to take home from Dust World. I came here for you."

That stopped her. She stared at me like I might bite her.

"I can't go home. I'd be executed."

"No, you won't. Your other self died recently. I didn't report it because I realized it was a chance for you to come home. There was no revive—you are the one and only Natasha."

She put her hands on a stone table and leaned on it, thinking hard.

"I can't believe this," she said. "You've managed to make me sick to my stomach with worry again. Do you know that you've always had that effect on me? It's been so long, I almost didn't remember."

I took a deep breath and moved to comfort her, but she dodged away.

"You never tried to come out to see me. You didn't call. You didn't even tap out a text. You knew I was out here trapped in this desert for years, living a harsh life among hostile people."

"Yeah," I admitted, "I've been kind of busy fighting wars among the stars. I also knew you couldn't come home while the second version of you was running around. If the Galactics had found out about the illegal duplication, we might all have been permed."

She sighed. "I've followed your exploits and those of Varus. You've covered a lot of lightyears and done permanent damage to many worlds."

Shrugging, I didn't argue. I couldn't, because she was right about that part.

"Look," I told her, "Earth needs you now, Natasha. I need you—even Etta needs you. Without your help, I think we're all going to be permed or enslaved."

I told her the full story then. About the squids invading Earth and surrounding Central. Soon they would win, and Dust World would be enslaved or destroyed immediately afterward.

Then I told her about the teleport reprogramming systems, and how I needed her to help me with them.

She bit her lower lip. "Did I tell you I'm feeling sick again? Like the old days?"

"You mentioned that."

"Let's say I went along with your crazy plan," she said. "How am I going to protect Etta?"

"Can she take care of herself for a few days?" I asked. "I would take her back to Earth, but she might not survive for long there if things go badly. I wouldn't want to introduce her to her home world only to have it fall to the squids the next day."

Natasha looked at me with longing. I knew then that she wanted to go home. She'd been exiled for so long she'd probably come to accept she'd never see Earth again. Given the chance now, however…

"I'll talk to the Investigator," she said. "He's displayed some degree of interest in his granddaughter off and on. Maybe he'll help with her."

"Can't I just see Etta now?" I asked.

"No," she said, putting up a hand to stop me, "I still don't trust you. This could all be a big pile of crap. I know you, James. Remember that."

"Yeah… okay."

I waited while she went to make arrangements. It was a chance to rest, so I took it. The nap did me good. I was snoring by the time anyone came back to the place.

"Well," said a sonorous male voice from my past, "if it isn't our star man. Why are you here, James McGill? Are you out for an evening stroll?"

The Investigator was just as I remembered him, except a lot older. He was tall and thin with muscles that stood out under his skin like cables. He had long, white hair that hung down past his armpits in an unruly mass.

"Hello sir," I said, "I came to take Natasha back home with me. Etta too, if you'll let me."

"Both of them? That's ambitious. I'd thought you might have been satisfied with my daughter, Della."

That made me blink. Could the Investigator be upset that his daughter had joined Varus and left Dust World behind? Maybe she'd done it to get away from him. He'd always been a strange one, even for a Dust Worlder.

"Della is an excellent soldier, sir," I said. "But Natasha has talents we need now."

"Yes…" he said, glancing back at someone who had appeared in the doorway behind him.

It was Natasha herself. She held back and stayed quiet outside.

376

"This is the way with Earthers," the Investigator went on, "in my experience. You come and take what you need, leaving behind only our wind and our sand."

"We're all in this together," I told him. "If Earth falls, Dust World will be next."

He gazed at me earnestly. "You've struck upon the very reason that you're breathing again. I approved the revival precisely so I could learn how badly the home world has behaved. It would seem that you've resisted the cephalopods until they've finally decided to rain death down upon you."

"Will you help us?" I demanded. "Will you help both our worlds?"

He looked thoughtfully at me, then Natasha.

"I will allow it," he said at last, nodding to Natasha. "Etta will be cared for. Go home and see what can be done for Earth."

Natasha, looking scared and maybe a little bit sick, came into the room and blinked at me nervously.

I couldn't blame her. She was in for quite a ride.

* * *

The long teleport trip across the cosmos was full of worry and memories. To have Natasha—the original one—up against me in the same suit was something I'd never thought I'd experience.

My biggest regrets concerned Etta, however. I'd gotten Natasha to come home, but no one had trusted me enough to allow me to so much as meet my own daughter. If I'd had more time, I would have argued more—but I knew that I didn't. Delaying could mean the difference between life and death for all of us.

When we arrived on Green World, Natasha looked around in wonderment.

"This isn't Earth!" she exclaimed. "Is this some kind of trick? Or a malfunction?"

377

"Neither," I said, "you're technically still part of Legion Varus. I'm still on active duty, and so are you. We're here to perform a mission."

I climbed out of the suit, and she did the same, numbly. I folded it up and stashed it while she examined the warm waves and the pebble-strewn beach.

She followed me up the shore to the only scrap of high land in sight. On top was the strange, organically-shaped building. We went inside, and I let her look over the equipment.

I'd been here twice before. Some of the items had been removed to Central for study, but the main console was embedded into the building itself. The walls appeared to have grown right over the console like melting wax.

"This is very strange," she said, "some of this is Imperial tech, but most of it I've never seen before."

Natasha was intrigued. I dared to smile behind her back. She'd always been a sucker for technological gizmos.

Soon, she had worked out what it was for, that it attached to the teleport suits.

"But, what's the purpose?" she asked me. "If you can charge the units from any power source with a compatible plug, what's this do?"

"According to Claver, it's a programming system. It allows the user to set the control options on these suits."

"I see..." she said. "I guess such a system must exist."

"They're set for destinations now, but I can't change them. Squids supposedly have finer muscle control and understanding of these units and can go places by merely twiddling the dials precisely. We clumsy humans must use the presets."

She frowned at me. "Who's Claver?"

I'd forgotten how long she'd been out of touch. So many years... I'd met Claver on Tech World, after Natasha had been left behind on Dust World.

I showed her the vids of Claver programming the suits. She marveled at the process and all the small references to things she knew nothing about.

"I've been out of the loop for a long time," she said.

378

"I'm sorry we left you out there," I said. "We thought it was for the best. Our other Natasha—we liked her too. How could we have chosen?"

She looked at me thoughtfully. "Did the other Natasha die at some point? Didn't you consider your options then—about maybe retrieving me from Dust World, I mean?"

"Well... no," I admitted. "I didn't have any easy way to get here, and your existence was a secret. Only Della and I knew. We didn't have any power over the officers. If we'd told them to get you back instead of performing a local revive, it would have been proof of an Imperial crime."

"Right," she said, sighing. "I held out hope for years, but I knew it wasn't likely you'd come back for me. How could you risk it? The Hegemony brass would have moved to perm me out of caution—and maybe you too. Otherwise the Galactics could rightly charge them with aiding a criminal in a high crime."

"Can you do anything with this programming system?" I asked her.

"I think so. In fact, I think it's going to be easy."

"Why's that?" I asked.

She smiled, holding up a data chip. "Because, this console has landing spots preprogrammed for every world in the Cephalopod Kingdom already worked out. All I have to do is load the set we want into the suit. The hard part would have been figuring out the location algorithms for spots without presets—but the squids must have worked that out years ago. You just have to tell me where you want to go."

Staring at her, a slow smile grew on my face.

"Easy..." I said, echoing her words.

I had plans—big plans.

And this time, just maybe, they were going to work out.

-60-

Feeling like winners, we went back to Central a few hours later. We had the suit reprogrammed. I had Natasha in the suit with me, and I could rightfully claim I'd rescued her.

Not from the squids, of course, but from Dust World. She'd promised to pretend I'd brought her back from a squid planet. With luck, no one would be the wiser.

My good mood evaporated about three seconds after we got home. Central was in emergency lock-down.

We'd popped back into the underground landing zone, but no one was there. Not Graves, Lisa—no one.

But the yellow flashers told the tale. The computer was talking, and emergency arrows were lighting up the floor.

"We have a breach at floor one hundred sixty-two," the computer said calmly. "All emergency personnel are to report to floor one hundred-ten for triage setup. All combat personnel are to report to the ground floor for defensive deployment..."

The computer went on like that, and our tappers were spitting out data as well.

"What's going on?" Natasha asked, wriggling out of the teleport suit.

"I don't know, but it looks like the cephalopod armies are in the city."

It occurred to me, as we raced through deserted corridors, that we'd been gone for at least thirty hours. I'd been completely out of touch all that time.

"My tapper is working fully again," Natasha said, marveling. "I disconnected it on Dust World from the local net, not wanting anyone to know who I was. But now, here it is, synching up like nothing ever went wrong."

To me, *plenty* had gone wrong, but I didn't want to ruin her moment. I half-dragged her down the corridors to the elevators while she looked at her tapper in fascination.

"It's backing me up," she said excitedly. "It's a long refresh for the data core. Ten years' worth! It's barely one percent done."

The elevators were out of order, so we rushed to the stairs. We didn't even make it that far before my tapper lit up.

"McGill?" Graves asked, his face appearing to me on live chat. "Have you got her?"

"Yes sir, I do."

"Did you figure anything out?"

"We're now able to program the teleport suits," I said, my voice tinged with pride.

"What took you so damned long? It better not have been romance."

"Negative, sir. She doesn't even like me much anymore."

"Good. Listen, we're taking heavy shelling. The building is badly damaged on the upper floors, but with heavy puff-crete construction and nano-fiber—"

"Sir," I said, "these red arrows are guiding me to the defensive effort on the ground floor. Should I follow them?"

"What? Hell, no. You're to come down here to floor minus five hundred. Report as fast as you can and bring Natasha."

Taking the steps downward two at a time, I felt the building shake now and then. Even though we were far underground the echoing reports of shells landing on the roof still reached us.

It occurred to me that the enemy had a grossly unfair advantage. They could shell us, but we couldn't shell them back. Only short-range fire at low altitude could strike past the dampening fields. They'd managed to suppress our defense and drive us steadily back into the city.

When we'd gone down about thirty flights of stairs, I decided to try the elevator again. I managed to find one that worked. We rushed inside, and I pecked at the console. Soon we were moving, and I breathed easier.

Natasha had managed to patch into the local news streams by this time. She looked at me with big eyes and showed me what they were playing.

The city around us was on fire. Camera drones transmitted the vid feed in night-vision mode. We could see brilliant bursts of greenish-white as the city became engulfed in flames and billowing smoke.

"They're tearing us apart," she said, "we can't hold out long."

"Don't worry about it," I told her. "We're not going to be here much longer."

She looked at me quizzically. "But... hey, this elevator is going up, not down!"

"So it is," I said, "don't worry about it."

She looked at me in fear. "James, there are shells and squids up there. Why are we going up instead of down like Graves ordered you to? He's not going to like that."

"Hmm, you're right," I said. "He's going to figure it out pretty quickly, too. Have you got a jammer on you?"

She looked at me for a frozen second. "You know I always have a jammer on me."

"Turn it on. I don't want them to trace us."

"James..."

"Come on, Natasha," I said, "do you really think Graves has a plan that will save us?"

"No, not really."

"Trust me then."

She sighed and turned on her jammer. We were instantly untraceable.

Instead of getting out of the elevator far underground, we got off at floor one hundred. Things were a lot more exciting up here.

A section of the building was missing. The hallway just went along, perfectly smooth and natural-looking, until it ended in a ragged finish. Beyond it was open air and the sounds of a city under siege.

Wind and the smell of smoke filled the corridor, but I walked out and gestured for her to follow.

Natasha was hesitant, slow. I could tell years out of active duty had made her go soft. At least her technical skills were still good.

"It should be here somewhere," I said, "at the end of the hall. Look for a security door. It might be buried in debris."

"James, the end of the hall is a three hundred meter drop into the streets."

"Right… I didn't mean all the way to the end."

We pressed ahead, and we heard the sky rumble outside. The star-falls were being lobbed onto us. They smashed into the building and neighboring structures. They were so big and dramatic the explosions almost looked like they were in slow-motion.

A flare of orange flame, followed by a ball of black smoke, rolled up over the end of the hallway. Natasha fell to her belly and covered her head.

I reached down as gently as I could and hauled her up.

"You go on, James," she said, "I can't help you here. It's been so long since I've done anything like this. I'm just not battle-ready yet."

There was a moment of indecision, but then I nodded. "Go back down. Go to floor minus-five hundred. Help them as best you can."

"Good luck, James," she said, giving me a kiss on the cheek.

Putting gloved fingers to my cheek, I touched the spot then turned away.

When I reached the right door, I had to use the Galactic Key to hack the lock. The sign over the door said, "Weapons Storage, No Admittance."

Opening the door and bypassing the security systems, I slipped inside.

When I got in there, I went to the storage lockers. Most of them were empty, and I cursed inside my helmet, which I'd shut to keep out the smoke.

"Adjunct James McGill?" a pissed-off voice said in my ear.

It was Graves. I realized then that I was no longer within range of Natasha's jammer. She'd been carrying it, and it had served to block all communications and tracking—but not anymore.

"Uh... just a second sir, I'm busy."

"McGill, you were given a direct order. This is gross insubordination."

"I'm sorry sir," I said, "Natasha had an idea. It was a good idea, so I thought—"

"Do not attempt to slur that woman's good name," Graves said. "McGill, are you coming down here to minus-five hundred or not?"

"I sure am, sir," I said. "I'll be there with bells on any time now."

Graves fell silent, but he didn't disconnect. I knew he was thinking.

"You're in the weapons storage unit. How the hell did you get in there? That's top-secret, and it's locked down."

While this conversation went on, I was searching every damned locker in the place. I'd found all sorts of weird-looking alien devices, but not the one I was looking for.

"McGill, damn your dark heart to hell," Graves said. "I'm going to have you drawn and quartered if you don't get your ass down here right now!"

"My I ask why I'm so important?"

"You have that teleport suit, don't you? I know what presets you managed to program into it. I've been in contact with Natasha."

I closed my eyes and gritted my teeth. She'd turned off the jammer and reported in.

That was my big problem with Natasha. She was smart as a whip, cute, and she'd always loved me. But she was way too much of a rule-follower. That deficiency in her personality had always been a problem in our relationship.

"I see," I said. "Well, sir, whatever plans you have you can use Natasha to help. She can reprogram those suits to go wherever you want."

"That's not our problem, and you know it."

384

Right about then, I finally jimmied open a locker that had the item I'd been seeking. Inside was a big steel canister. It looked to be about the size of a watermelon.

I'd found what I wanted at last. Grinning, I pulled it out of the locker. Checking to make sure it was functional, I tucked it under my arm and staggered out of the lab. Another star-fall had just landed, scorching the walls outside and opening new wounds in Central's thick skin. The thunder from its detonation was unimaginably loud and deep.

"McGill?" Graves demanded. "Are you still with us, McGill?"

Climbing over wreckage, I kept quiet. Maybe he'd figure I bought it in that last strike.

There was no such luck. Graves knew me better than my own mama did by now.

"My displays show you're still moving, McGill. Talk to me."

"I'm making my way back down to you now, sir," I said. "Just give me a minute."

"McGill, don't you pull any cowboy shit on me today. This war is way, way beyond your competency zone. Do you understand me?"

"I sure do, Centurion. Don't you worry about a thing. By the way, what do you need me for so badly? What's the nature of my mission?"

"You're to teleport to the squid home world. You'll present our surrender. According to Claver, they have FTL communications with their army here on Earth. They'll stop the attack immediately."

Claver? I couldn't believe what I was hearing. Somehow, that worm was acting as a go-between again.

Stopping my efforts and breathing hard, I looked down the hallway. Beyond the crumbling termination point of the corridor, the city was laid out. I could see pretty far from up here. All the way to the horizon it was fire, smoke and destruction. We'd been well and truly beaten.

Looking down in a moment of malaise, I saw what I needed—an outlet. It was part of the building's auto-cleaning system. Stooping, I levered open the cover and plugged in my suit.

Sitting down and waiting for it to charge up, I contacted Graves one last time.

"When is this diplomatic mission leaving?" I asked him.

"Maybe ten minutes," he said. "We've got twelve people here, all in teleport suits. Turov is among them. Natasha is here now, and she's reprogramming their presets. Are you going to lead this historic effort to save our world or not?"

"I'm afraid I'm not going to make it down in time," I told him. "My apologies."

"McGill...? Don't screw with me! McGill...?"

I didn't have the heart to tell him that I'd already made my decision.

The next star-fall salvo was arcing beautifully down from the heavens outside. Instead of waiting for it to land, I teleported out.

-61-

When I appeared on Throne World, they seemed to be ready for me. A delegation of squid queens and their armed consorts approached from every angle.

"You are the Claver?" asked the nearest of the males. He was an overlord. I could see that from his insignia.

"No," I said.

"Why are you here? Do you serve the Claver? Are you bearing Earth's surrender?"

"I don't serve the Claver," I said, "but I've got a message from Earth for all of you squids."

"Excellent. Give us the message."

"Come a little closer. Don't be shy now, gather around."

They shuffled their tentacles uneasily.

"You are not behaving with appropriate decorum," the overlord complained. "Fall to your knees, slaveling."

"Are you guys recording this?" I asked.

"Our entire planet is watching. This moment is one we've long awaited."

"Good," I said, then I fell to my knees and placed an oblong metal ovoid object on the sand. I gave it a pat and reached up to my teleport dial.

"What is this?" the overlord asked.

"It's a gift. An answer. A treaty of sorts."

"We need no treaties. We demand supplication, nothing more."

"That's just fine. You squids can demand away. Talk to this device. It will transmit your thoughts and speech back to Earth."

"How is that possible? Do you have FTL deep-link technology? I thought that was reserved for Galactics."

"You thought wrong, squid."

"I don't care for your tone, slaveling," the Overlord told me sternly. "Punishment will be long and difficult for you when this process is finished."

"That I believe," I said, and I touched the second preset on my teleport suit's dial.

The squids weren't happy about that. They flapped their appendages and no doubt cussed me out, but I couldn't hear them.

The suit had just enough juice left in it for a very short hop. I made it to an open area outside their capital city. Natasha had found the coordinates in the squid data core on Green World.

This place was up high among some rocky peaks. For obvious reasons it was uninhabited by squids. They didn't like rocky heights much.

Looking to the west—or what would be called west on Earth—I saw their city laid out at my feet. It was huge. I was pretty sure no human city had ever been that large.

How many squids lived there? I couldn't be sure. Maybe a billion?

The explosion came two minutes after I'd ported out. It was a grand sight. The heavens lit up, and even through my suit I was given a lethal dose of radiation.

It wasn't enough to kill me instantly, but it was enough to mean I was nothing more than a dead man walking.

An anti-matter explosion is something to behold. If you ever get the chance to see one up close, I recommend it. Mind you, nuclear bombs, both fission and fusion types, are impressive—but they just don't compare. Don't get me wrong, but there's something about gigatons that leaves a man breathless and filled with a unique sense of awe.

The light should have blinded me, but our faceplate technology was pretty good. It blocked enough of the initial glare to keep it from burning my eyes out of my skull straight away.

The shockwave rushed outward in every direction. You could see it consuming their city, building by building.

At that point I figured I'd bought the farm, but the end didn't come quite yet. Something stopped the shockwave from getting out of the city and reaching me. It took me a second to see the outline of a mighty dome over the city itself.

That impressed me. These squids really *were* ready for war. They'd decided to put a force-dome over their entire capital. What a fine feat of engineering that must have been.

The mushroom cloud puffed up next, pushing higher and higher. Suddenly, it stopped rising into the atmosphere and spread out instead. That had to be the dome. The explosion inside the dome reverberated and crisscrossed back and forth on itself. Damn, I'd seen some destruction before in my time, but this beat all that to Hell-and-back six times!

There was a grin on my face. I lifted my hands and slammed my gauntlets together, clapping.

The chaos lasted for a few more seconds before the dome gave out. Then the released energies and gasses, along with a billion tons of molten matter, flew in every direction.

One chunk of something jagged arced up and came down right at me. I had a chance to see it clearly for a split-second before I was struck as dead as a mackerel on a trawler's deck.

* * *

When I came back to life, I was utterly incredulous. I'd always figured from the minute I went out to Throne World that I was perming myself. I'd kind of figured I might have permed Earth in the bargain, too.

"Where am I?" I asked the bio.

"You're home, McGill," Graves said.

Another surprise—Graves, here at my bedside?

"You guys going to torture me to death a dozen times for disobeying orders?"

389

Graves chuckled. "We should. Honestly, we really should. But that's not my call. What do you say, Imperator Drusus?"

"Adjunct James McGill," Drusus said slowly. His tone was that of a man who's carried a heavy burden for a long time. "We should have rejected you the first day you reported to the Mustering Hall over ten years ago. Your psych eval said it all back then.

That made me laugh, which promptly turned into a coughing fit. The lungs always seemed to grow back with too much phlegm in them.

"I get that, sir," I said. "Couldn't have blamed you for it then—or now."

Rolling into a sitting position, I looked around the room. The first thing I noticed was the lack of bombardment.

"The star-falls are quiet," I said. "Are we still in Central?"

"Yes. We're still there. The war is on hold."

"Uh... could someone fill me in on what happened, sirs?"

"This isn't the time to play dumb, McGill," Graves said. "We know what you did. We know you took a jump-suit and set off a bomb on Throne World. The squids captured all that on video. They also monitored all your suit's transmissions and transmitted your mental engrams back to us. We were able to revive you from that data."

"Ah..." I said. "That's why I can remember what happened."

"Right," Drusus said, "but we're still sketchy on what you thought you were doing—besides getting Earth permed."

"It's mighty fine of you to revive me to ask," I said. "It goes like this, sirs. I've been doing some hard thinking. I finally decided I wanted to hurt the squids, to hurt them real bad, before bowing out of my existence."

"That's pretty much what we figured—but your plans went no further than that?"

I looked from one of them to the next. Something was up. I wasn't sure what it was, but I thought I should play along. A schemer like myself never passes up opportunities to make a play.

"It was a hard choice," I lied, "to be sure. Most men, it's my contention, wouldn't have risked the annihilation of the species on an uncertain plan. But even though I wasn't sure how things would turn out, I figured it was better to die the way we humans were meant to: on our two feet with a knife sticking out of our opponent's belly."

They looked at one another, frowning. My answer clearly wasn't what they were looking for. Accordingly, I cleared my throat and went on in a stronger voice.

"But that wasn't all of it. I thought the squids would only stop hitting us after their greatest city, and a load of their queens, were wiped out."

Suddenly, they looked at me with hungry eyes.

"Is that right?" Drusus asked. "Why?"

"Well, that's obvious. You've just about told me yourselves. The squids have sued for peace, haven't they?"

"This was *your* plan? No one else was directly involved. Correct?"

"Sure was."

They both looked relieved. They smiled and Drusus clapped his hands together once, loudly.

"That's it," he said. "We've got a full confession. The squids will have to accept it. Stop the broadcast."

I frowned at each of them in turn. "I don't get it. Didn't the squids surrender?"

"No, they didn't," Graves told me, "your actions made things much more difficult. In order to surrender and save our planet, we must comply with a new list of their demands. They want three things: All our antimatter bombs, all our teleport suits—and the man who single-handedly killed countless numbers of their civilians."

"You're talking about me, right?"

"That's right," Graves said. "They've demanded we give them a scapegoat, and you've just confessed your sins, James McGill. It's time to prepare yourself for some unholy torment."

"Seems like you made quite an impression on them, Adjunct," Drusus commented.

"Yeah... I tend to do that."

-62-

I've been shackled in irons before, but this time, no one was taking any chances.

My ankles were about twenty centimeters apart, connected by jangling links. My wrists were manacled in front of me, and my elbows were connected to a bar across my back. They even put a collar around my neck. Someone said they thought the squids might like it better that way. I had no doubt they were correct in that assumption.

Shuffling along like a lame robot from a century back, I was escorted to the teleportation lab one more time.

We passed a lot of familiar faces along the way. Most of them dropped their eyes, either too ashamed or too upset to meet my gaze.

There were two exceptions. One was Natasha, who looked at me openly and appeared to be ready to burst into tears. That made me feel bad. I'd brought her back home just in time to get myself offed as a traitor. That was a fine way to treat the girl I'd left behind a decade or so ago.

The other exception was Carlos. He grinned at me and gave me a thumbs-up. That uplifted my spirits. If anyone here could fathom what I'd done, it was his crazy ass.

"McGill," he said as I passed him, "man, all I have to say is that when you fuck up, you go big."

"Thanks Carlos. See you in Hell."

"Keep my chair warm!"

Then he was gone, and I was prodded forward into the lab itself.

Turov was there. She stared at me with blazing eyes.

"May I have a word with the prisoner?" she asked.

Drusus and Graves looked at one another.

"I don't see the point," Drusus said.

Turov showed her teeth. "I still outrank you, Drusus. I have seniority."

"The jury is out on that, Imperator. You're under investigation. The Ruling Council might revoke your rank any day. In the meantime, I'm in charge of Earth's defense, and you're out of line."

She licked her lips with a quick motion. Her eyes darted from side to side. I could tell she was thinking hard.

"He has some of my property," she said.

Drusus snorted. "He was just revived. He came back with nothing on him, just like any of us."

"Give me one minute," she said. "I'll stop resisting your right to command if you give me one minute."

Drusus and she locked gazes. I could see there was no love lost between these two.

"All right," he said at last. "We've got an hour before the ultimatum expires."

Graves grumbled, but he let Turov move closer to me and whisper in my ear. The other officers stepped away, shaking their heads and cracking a few jokes. No doubt they thought she was making a fool of herself.

"James," she said, "where is it?"

"Where's what?"

"The key, damn you! Where's my key?"

"Oh, that... I imagine it blew up back on Throne World."

She looked at me in hate, but she shook her pretty head.

"No," she said, "I know that's not true. They sent us all your files as proof of what you did, remember? The key wasn't on your person."

"How's that possible?" I asked. "I would have needed the key—"

"Stop with the bullshit, we only have seconds left. I talked to Natasha, and I know you reprogrammed the suit to go where

393

you wanted to go. I know you didn't need the key anymore because she broke the security somehow. The key wasn't on Throne World, and even you wouldn't destroy such a powerful tool for nothing. Where did you leave it?"

I saw a great opportunity, and I took it. I smiled at her.

"You'll never find it, Galina. I'm about to be permed, and I'll be damned if I'll help you out one last time. You'll just have to do your rank-climbing without it."

She hissed at me. "No, fool! That isn't what I want. There won't be any rank-climbing, don't you see? The squids don't want to enslave us now, not after you—"

"Time's up," Graves said, coming close and grabbing onto me. He hauled me away toward a fresh teleport suit.

Lisa stood by, looking ashamed and sorrowful. She had the suit peeled open and ready for me to climb in.

Looking back at Turov, I could see she was highly agitated.

"James, I beg you!" she cried out.

That made me think. Of all the things she'd ever done, she'd never begged me for anything.

My mind tried to follow what she'd been saying. She needed the key, but not for her usual shenanigans. She needed it because of the squids?

What else had she indicated? That the squids wouldn't enslave us?

That could only mean one thing. There were only two ways out for a species under the tentacle-tip of the Cephalopod Kingdom. One was as a slave. The other was as an historical footnote.

Extermination? Extinction? Could that be what they really wanted for us now?

The more I thought about it, the more it made sense. We'd pissed them off—*really* pissed them off. Well... I had, anyway...

They'd demanded we turn over all our bombs and all our teleport suits, plus my sorry carcass as a trophy.

Why would they ask for those things? To pull our teeth? To make sure we couldn't hurt them again?

"Sirs," I said as the jump-suit closed around me. "Maybe we should rethink this."

"No, I don't think so, McGill," Graves said. "Sorry about your fate. I hope they make it short, but I wouldn't count on it. You have to admit, you did earn it."

I struggled to reach the dial on my suit as they powered it up, but I couldn't do it. I was still all chained-up.

Lisa kissed my cheek. Her own face was tear-streaked.

"I forgive you," she said. "Whatever you did out there, I—"

"Turov!" I shouted across the room.

Galina's head snapped around to look at me. Lisa looked hurt, but I didn't have time to massage her feelings now.

"Lisa has it! Ask her!"

Turov's eyes blazed again, but instead of a fierce glare, she wore a grim smile.

Lisa looked alarmed. She looked from me, to Turov, and back again.

"Just give it up, Lisa," I told her. "It will go easier for you that way."

She opened her mouth to reply, but then, she wavered.

Everyone wavered. Graves had reached out and twisted the dial on my chest.

I was teleporting back to Throne World.

* * *

I never did find out what the squids did to me out there on Throne World. That's probably for the best. I wake up with nightmares often enough as it is.

When I was eventually brought back to life again, I was even more surprised than I had been the last time.

"What the hell...?" I asked blearily. "Haven't you folks had enough of old McGill?"

"Some would say we have," Turov said, "but I'm in charge now."

Blinking, I looked around. Everything looked different. This was Central—at least, I thought it was.

The ceiling was no longer fake plaster. Instead, it had that perfectly smooth cloth-like texture to it. A common enough look for a quick puff-crete patch-job.

"Where are we?" I asked.

"Central," she replied. "Good old Central."

"Imperator?" I asked Turov. "How come the ceiling looks different? How long has it been?"

"Since we remodeled? About six months. Maybe longer."

"What!?" I demanded, trying to get to my feet.

Turov put a gentle hand on my chest.

"Don't worry, James," she said soothingly. "You're alive again, and that's all that matters. You know, I missed you. I didn't think I would—but I did. Strange, isn't it? It's like missing a favorite pair of boots even though they always hurt your feet."

"You have to tell me what happened," I said, sucking in deep breaths and coughing. "I can't believe I've been dead six months."

"Actually, it was more like a year... or so."

"A frigging *year*? Are you kidding me? Why'd you bring me back at all?"

"It's complicated. After the Cephalopod Kingdom surrendered—"

"Hold on! What do you mean they surrendered?"

"It was the second bomb that did the trick," she said. "We had eleven teleport suits left, you see, but only one functioning bomb. I sent that gift to them with a volunteer in one of the suits."

"A volunteer? Who?"

"His name was Ferguson, I believe. A dedicated member of Hegemony. One of our best."

"Poor bastard..." I said thoughtfully. "So, you air-mailed another bomb to the squids *after* you agreed to surrender?"

I started grinning. I couldn't help it. After all, the squids had already tortured one version of James McGill to death by this point of her story.

She shrugged and pursed her lips.

"Their surrender was a technicality," she said. "I never personally agreed to the terms. The Ruling Council negotiated the whole thing without my approval. History will call it an unfortunate miscommunication."

"But... okay, whatever. How did you pull it off?"

"Natasha knew how to program the suit for another target. With the key I was able to get from that tech you liked so much—"

"Lisa, right... I have to look her up."

Her mouth twitched, but she didn't say anything about that.

"Anyway," she continued, "it wasn't difficult for us to get the bomb. Even easier, probably, because I knew which lockers contained working weapons."

"Right," I said, thinking hard. "So, you lit up another of their cities, and you threatened to keep doing it."

"Yes. That part was a bluff because we were out of small antimatter weapons, but they didn't know that. All they knew was they were losing billions of citizens."

"I can see how they would sue for peace, but how could you possibly get them to surrender?"

She gave me a calculating smile. "I hit the Wur enclave the second time. The highest concentration of those vicious plants on Throne World. Once their masters were gone, we threatened to exterminate all their queens. They had to surrender or face genocide."

"Wow, I'm floored. You're one ruthless bitch, Galina. I really mean that."

"Thank you, James," she said.

"Two more questions," I said as I clawed my way into a fresh uniform. "Why are you the only one here? Did you do this revive by yourself?"

"Yes, I did."

"Hmm..." I said thoughtfully. "Then you must have brought me back for a reason. What do you want from me?"

"There have been... problems. New problems which fit your special talents."

"*My* talents?" I laughed. "All I'm good for is tearing things up."

"Exactly," she said. "We'll talk tomorrow. Go get cleaned up and rest."

"I rested long enough in the grave," I said, "I'm going out to find a steak and a beer."

-63-

The events that had come to pass during my long rest in the void were a mixed bag. Sure, we'd defeated the squids. Further, they'd sworn allegiance to us the only way they knew how—by becoming our slaves, our subjects.

The situation seemed kind of weird to me, but in squid psychology, there were only two possible stations any group or individual could hold with regard to any other. You were either the master or the slave. I guess the third state was death, but usually no one opted for that.

It was strange because I'd figured I'd pretty much consigned my species to total destruction after bombing the squids. Instead, my rash move had been imitated and ratcheted up a notch by Turov. She'd always been an opportunist and a fast-learner.

From the point of view of Earth's citizens, all this was old news now. Earth was rich but still licking her wounds. Much of the New York Sector had been devastated. The squids had been ordered to supply us with money, labor and equipment to help clean it up, but the capital was still full of blackened hulks where great buildings had once stood.

Millions of our people had been permed during the war. Nagata was among them, as his data was never recovered. I thought of others we'd lost, too, such as Primus Rossi and Veteran Weber. Everyone had lost someone they knew.

Many of the others in the hog brass had suffered the same fate. I was suspicious of Galina Turov in that regard, but as they were talking about promoting her again to the three-star rank of Equestrian, I decided to keep quiet—besides I was on her good side right now.

After I'd cleaned up and left Central to have a look around the city, I found myself feeling oddly out of place. Everything looked both the same and different all at once. There was plenty of visible damage from the war, but some things had been repaired. These details served to remind me just how long I'd been dead. It *looked* like I'd been gone for years.

Contacting Graves and a few others, I learned Legion Varus had long since been demobilized. We were without assignment for now, and that meant I could head home to Georgia Sector if I wanted to. I considered going down there, but I knew Turov wanted to talk to me in the morning.

Sucking in a beer at a local bar, I took a deep breath and called my folks.

"Hey... Dad? Guess who!"

What followed was a very weird conversation. He cried and carried on for quite a while at first. I tried not to let it get to me, but it did a little.

They'd thought I was dead and gone, permed by Central or the squids. No one had ever told them what had happened, other than that I'd been lost in defense of planet Earth. My actions had been deemed highly classified, and they hadn't even pretended to deliver my remains home. The casket was empty, and the funeral had been brief.

"I'm sorry, Dad," I said. "I guess the hogs lost my file for a long time. They *are* bureaucrats, after all, and there was a war on. But listen, I'm back! Soon, I'll come home to see you all. Maybe we can go out to Dust World together like we planned. I've got about a year's back pay coming, and... what—?"

"She's already out there, James," he said. "Your mother saved everything we had and left with a one-way ticket. I'm supposed to sell the house and follow her next month."

I felt a little sick. Things really *had* changed. Somehow, as a military man, it had always been good to have a steady place to go back to. Home had been a place I could rely on. Now, that was falling apart.

"When did she go?" I asked him.

"A few months ago. She's already met Etta. After you fell in battle, meeting Etta was all she could think of."

"I understand, Dad. I'm sorry, I really am."

"It's all right. Come home when you can. We'll talk about what we should do next."

The channel closed, and I sat in shock. Looking up friends in the local area, I got Carlos to come join me.

We didn't leave the bar until they kicked us out, and when I woke up at his place in the morning, I didn't remember how I'd gotten there.

"Hey tiger," Carlos said, slapping at me. "Time to go shake your butt for Turov. You should demand a conjugal visit for all the shit she's put you through."

Groaning, I rolled off his couch and staggered to the shower. An hour later, I was in Turov's office. She looked prim and serious.

"James McGill," she said, "I'm reactivating you."

"What? Hold on. I only just got revived after a year's sleep. I don't feel like dying again quite yet."

"There will be benefits," she said. "First of all, I'm promoting you to Centurion—Graves is a Primus now, did he tell you that?"

"Uh... no sir. At least if he did, I didn't listen."

"Of course not... Are you listening to me now, Centurion?"

I wasn't. I was gazing outside the window. The city was alive again. Damaged, but alive. I tried to feel the part of the hero, but somehow I didn't. Maybe the price had been too great. My mom had skipped off the planet. My life had skipped a year. I barely knew who I was.

"Centurion?" she repeated.

"Yes, sir?"

"Listen to me... we have problems—new, unforeseen problems."

"Like what? We beat the squids fair and square. They're kissing our butts. Hell, technically, Earth controls three hundred worlds now."

She pointed a finger at me and nodded.

"You've hit upon the source of the conflict. You were researching the political situation last night, weren't you?"

"Uh…" I thought about the bar and Carlos' nasty couch. I shook my head. "I can, in all honestly, assure you I don't know what our political situation is, sir."

"What do you remember about Galactic Law?"

"Just what they taught us in school."

"That's good enough," she said. "What do the Galactics think about provincial powers colonizing or conquering new worlds?"

"It's not allowed. We were almost burned when they found out about Dust World. Oh…"

She nodded. "Now you understand. The Mogwa are upset. They've decided things have gotten out of hand here on the fringe of the fringe. They've released Battle Fleet 921 from service among the Core Worlds."

"You mean the fleet is finally coming home?"

"That's right."

"Have the civil wars in the middle of the galaxy finally ended?"

She got up from her desk and struck a languid pose at the window. She was still occupying Nagata's office, and I could tell she took a perverse pleasure in that fact.

"We don't know," she admitted. "All we know is that more than twenty thousand worlds were scorched to ash in the center of our galaxy."

"Twenty thousand worlds? Holy… that's crazy!"

She nodded quietly. "It makes our dramatic strides forward as a civilization seem ridiculous, doesn't it?"

"Yeah, I guess it does. Well sir, what do you want from me?"

She looked at me. "I need a jump-troop commander. I need the very best."

"What for?"

"That's none of your concern right now. If you don't accept the mission, you won't get the promotion, and you won't ever learn of our plans. What do you say?"

I thought that over. "How about one more thing?"

She rolled her eyes then finally asked, "What?"

When I told her what I wanted, I thought she was going to have what my grandma would have called a conniption.

She argued and waved her arms around a lot, but in the end, she grudgingly agreed.

-64-

The next day, I jumped out to Dust World.

That was what I'd wanted from Turov, access to a jump-suit for personal use. That was a tall order, despite the fact that Earth had hundreds of them now. We'd confiscated them from the squids as part of our terms of surrender.

When I arrived on Dust World, it was as hot and unpleasant as I'd ever seen it. There was a sandstorm blasting by just a few kilometers up on the surface, high above the shadowy hole in the ground where Della's people lived.

I kept my faceplate closed, and all the other folks I met up with had their heads wrapped in cloth. They wore goggles so crusty with dust I couldn't make out their eyes.

After talking to a few of the locals, I managed to get to the Investigator this time without being shot in the back. That was no mean feat on Dust World, where Earth's laws were considered only suggestions for polite conduct.

The Investigator was a year older, but he looked a bit less curmudgeonly than he had the last time I'd seen him.

"James McGill," he said, eyeing me in surprise. "You do show up at the oddest times. How could you know that I was thinking of you this very morning?"

"Uh... I don't think I did know that, sir."

"An honest statement from the most dishonest of men. That, in itself, is a sort of revelation."

These seemingly random statements were the norm from the Investigator. He wasn't what I'd call a regular guy. He was a thinker, a philosopher and a scientist. His greatest flaw was he tended to overthink things. He saw secrets and patterns where there most likely weren't any.

"Let me think," he said, "first of all, I get a message over the deep-link from Central about the Battle Fleet returning to our humble Province 921. Suddenly, Earth is interested in the Empire again. And do you know what I thought of?"

"Me, sir? For some reason?"

"Yes. You were the man who first told me of the Galactics. Years ago, you educated me briefly on the topic. You were quite detailed. Since then, I've spoken with countless officials from your planet, but they've never managed to shed light on the true nature of the political situation in the Galaxy as well as you did."

"Well, sir, that might be because they're all circumspect. Most people talk about the Empire and the Galactics who run it with the reverence people used to reserve for the Almighty himself."

He nodded his head slowly. "Yes. That must be it. You, however, hold the Empire in relative contempt, don't you?"

"I don't know about that. I think it's more that I hold just about all authority figures in some kind of contempt."

He laughed then. It was a rare sound I could hardly recall ever having heard before. He ended the laugh with a brief coughing fit, after which he spat on the floor and sighed deeply.

"These dust storms," he said, "we've been plagued by them since the very beginning. Did you know that I once held out fantasies of leaving this world? After we were reunited with Earth, I thought I'd get the chance."

"Well, why not just do it?" I asked him. "You must have the means now."

"Yes," he said, "but I'm your opposite. I'm too fixed in my ways. Too full of responsibility. Dark days are ahead—and I'm not just talking about the angle of our local stars."

"Hmm, okay. On another topic, Mr. Investigator, I was wondering if I could—"

"See Natasha?" he asked.

"No, Etta," I said, "your granddaughter. My daughter."

He nodded. "Of course you can. You don't need my permission for that. You have the right as the father."

"Yes, well... Natasha seemed upset by the idea last time I tried to see Etta. She thought I would abduct her and take her back to Earth."

The man seemed bemused.

"Why would anyone want to do that?" he asked. "The girl doesn't listen, and she's much too stubborn. I find her to be the most irritating child I've ever met."

"Oh..." I said, figuring that I probably knew why that might be. "Well sir, if you could direct me out to her place of residence, I'd like to see her now—how old is she, by the way?"

"She's in her ninth standard year of life."

"Really? That's a shocker."

"Let time slip by, did you?"

"I guess that I did, sir..."

Following the Investigator's directions, I traveled the stark valley floor. The rocks were loose under my boots. The drifting sands from the dark skies above quickly erased my footsteps.

I found the place at last, high up in the region known as the Jambles. I saw a hut with a fabric dome. The hut was lit by a yellow glow from inside. There was a figure standing just outside. She was wrapped up to keep out the blowing dust. I eyed her carefully as I approached.

As I got closer, I could see the figure was holding a weapon.

"Natasha?" I called out to her.

The figure shifted uncertainly on her feet and then dashed away into the rocks. I walked forward warily. Dust Worlders were ornery people. My back tingled, expecting a stab of pain to come any minute.

When I got to the dome, the flap was pulled aside.

"Come in, James," Natasha said.

My eyes widened, and I looked around behind me. I didn't see anything of the girl who'd been standing right there earlier.

"She's shy, James," Natasha said. "Surely you can understand that?"

"*That* was Etta?" I asked. "She was as tall as you are—and mean-looking."

Natasha smirked. "She's your daughter after all—and Della's daughter too. What kind of child were you expecting?"

"I don't know... Maybe one that wasn't half-wild."

I walked inside, and my mother jumped up to embrace me. We hugged, and she cried. When she had the crying under control, she slapped me for being dead for so long and scaring her. Then she cried all over again and hugged me some more.

When all this was finally done with, I took a seat and drank some weak tea with the two of them. There was a tiny fire in the center of the dome, and a pot bubbled above it.

"Seems like you've changed your mind about me," I told Natasha. "Last time I was out here, you treated me like some kind of bandit."

"I'm sorry about that. I guess meeting your mother in person made me believe in your good intentions. No one would send their own mother out to Dust World if they didn't sincerely care about Etta."

"Um... yeah. Speaking of the girl, isn't it kind of dark and dusty out there?"

"That doesn't bother her. She's a native. She's as comfortable on a dry stone as a spine-rat in the summertime."

"Right... Can you call her in so I can meet her properly?"

The two women exchanged tight glances.

"She'll come in when she wants to," Natasha said. "Have another mug of tea."

I stood up, becoming annoyed. They called after me, but I walked outside and stood tall.

"Etta!" I shouted, seeing nothing but blowing sands. "This is your father. I've come out here to this godforsaken planet twice now, and I still haven't properly laid eyes on you. Now, come out from wherever you're hiding and—"

I felt a poke in the butt. It wasn't a pleasant, playful poke either—it was more of a hard jab in the ass, to be honest.

Whirling around, I stared down at a wild-child.

She was dirty. Her face and skin were crusty with sand, but her blonde locks stuck out here and there.

Then there were her eyes. They were blue, and they glinted with light reflected from the fire inside the dome.

"Your armor held," Etta told me. "I wasn't sure if it would."

With a sudden move, I snatched the crossbow out of her hand. Sure enough, the bolt she'd poked me with had a black head. The nanites would've eaten into my flesh and killed me, if they'd penetrated.

She looked surprised at my action, and she showed me her teeth in a snarl.

"I've killed for less!" she shouted.

"So have I, girl!"

We stared each other down for several long seconds. Then, without any warning, she rushed in close and threw her arms around me. She squeezed my belly in a desperate hug.

To tell the truth, my balls were crawling in fear during those brief moments, but I controlled my natural urge to protect my soft parts.

Looking past her, I saw Natasha peering out from under the tent flap. She looked worried, but she smiled when she saw the girl hug me.

"She's very affectionate when you get to know her," she said.

Awkwardly, I patted Etta's unruly hair. "She sure is!"

When we finally got Etta to settle down inside the tent with the rest of us, we talked and ate food tainted with grit.

During a private moment, when the other two were occupied, my mom sidled up to me and gripped my bicep tightly.

"James," she whispered, "you have to get me out of this hellhole. This was a big mistake!"

I chuckled. "I told you, mama. I told you."

* * *

When I finally got back to Earth, I took all of them with me: Natasha, Etta and my mom. It took several jumps, but I managed it.

407

Leaving all three of them in Waycross, I jumped up to Central next. I barely made it in time for my meeting with Turov.

After turning in the jump-suit and making my way to her office, I was shocked to find someone else there waiting with the Imperator.

"Claver?" I demanded. "You should be as dead as a doornail by all rights!"

"I think the same of you, McGill."

"Let's be civil," Turov said, propping her butt against her big desk in-between us.

"Why am I here?" I demanded.

"I told you, Centurion," she said.

As she spoke, she picked up a tiny box from her desk and handed it to me.

"The Mogwa are upset," she continued. "They're sending their battle fleet out to our province again."

"What the hell am I supposed to do about that?"

The box she'd handed to me held my attention. I knew what had to be inside it. I opened it despite my misgivings.

There they were... Two emblems, a pair of twin silver bars for each side of my collar. They were nano-adhesive rank insignias. All I had to do was take them out of the box and touch them to my uniform. They'd stick there, and I'd have reached a rank I'd never thought I'd attain.

"Are you in?" Turov asked.

"In for what?" I demanded. "You never did tell me."

"No, I didn't. You have to commit before you're briefed."

They both looked at me expectantly, smugly.

I knew their game. They'd obviously cooked up some kind of elaborate scheme. Something that would get me into trouble with Legion Varus, Central and the Almighty himself. The centurion rank pins were supposed to buy me, to make me their servant.

Heaving a sigh, I shook my head. I closed the box and tossed it back onto her desk.

"Sorry," I said, "I'm not in. Find someone else to do your dirty work."

Claver leaned forward, suddenly glowering. "You're making a big mistake, boy. I know you're not in the habit of listening to your betters, but this time—"

"No," I said. "That's my final answer."

He leaned back and glanced up at Turov.

"Told you," he said.

Turov looked pissed-off, but she wasn't furious. She nodded and aimed her finger at the door behind me.

"Am I dismissed, sir?" I asked her.

"Get out."

Turning around smartly, I marched out of her office.

Behind me, neither of them said a word until I was gone, but I didn't care.

I felt free at last. It was time to go home, get to know Etta better and catch up with Natasha. I'd let the stars take care of themselves for now.

The End

More Books by B. V. Larson:

UNDYING MERCENARIES
Steel World
Dust World
Tech World
Machine World
Death World
Home World

STAR FORCE SERIES
Swarm
Extinction
Rebellion
Conquest
Battle Station
Empire
Annihilation
Storm Assault
The Dead Sun
Outcast
Exile
Demon Star

Visit BVLarson.com for more information.

Made in the USA
Middletown, DE
08 September 2019